THE WHITETHORN
OF THE DANCING

This story takes place in 1988-1989. Ireland's 1987 Status of Children Act, which came into operation in 1988, provided that children born outside of marriage were no longer considered illegitimate. DNA testing in paternity cases was not available at that time.

THE WHITETHORN OF THE DANCING

Tom McCaughren

SOMERVILLE PRESS

Somerville Press Ltd,
Dromore,
Bantry,
Co. Cork,
Ireland P75 NY22

First published 2022

Designed by Jane Stark.
Typeset in Adobe Garamond Pro
seamistgraphics@gmail.com

ISBN: 978-1-8382544-2-1

Printed and bound in Spain
by GraphyCems, Villatuerta, Navarra.

For Fran

FOREWORD

Shortly before a friend of ours died of cancer, she came to Dublin for treatment in St. Luke's Hospital, Rathgar. Over dinner she told us a fascinating story about an extraordinary event that occurred on the morning of her parents' wedding day, an event that prevented them getting married. She asked me to write a book about it, and this is that book. It is not about her, but is written around the story she told us about how she came to be born out of wedlock.

Part 1

New York – New Jersey

Summer 1988

ONE

The young nun pulled down a small battered suitcase from the top shelf of her wardrobe, opened it on the bed, and took out a silvery pistol. The pistol had a mother-of-pearl handgrip and an inscription on its flat surface just above the trigger. As it rested neatly in the palm of her hand she read the inscription, *For Services Rendered*, and smiled wryly, for she had a good idea what it meant.

The gun had been lying on the few clothes she had been wearing on the day she had first entered the convent. After smoothing the top garment with her hand to remove its imprint, she dropped it into her dark blue handbag and put the suitcase back in the wardrobe.

A quick look at the clock on her bedside locker. It was time to go. As she hurried along the darkened corridors, she met no one, a small mercy for which she gave thanks and, a few moments later she stepped outside.

In the shadows of a run-down apartment block and an empty warehouse – both of which always seemed to combine to blot out the sun – she quietly closed the door of her convent and made her way out though the narrow passageway that ran alongside the adjoining church. Several down-and-outs, who were hanging around the outside gate, raised their grubby hands in a gesture of respect, for it was the nuns who fed and clothed all who came there, irrespective of colour or creed.

In the scale of life represented by the high-rise skyline of New York, those who availed of the convent's generosity were of no importance. Nor were the small church and convent. They had been overtaken by time and the shifting pattern of big business and now nestled among the derelict buildings like dolls' houses, deserted by progress and forgotten by all except the poor.

The nun walked a block or more until she came to a busy street where she hailed a passing cab and asked the driver to take her downtown to the Staten Island ferry. As they wended their way between the skyscrapers that formed the more opulent streets of Manhattan, the driver complained loudly now and then about someone else's driving but said nothing that required a response from her, and she was glad, for she was preoccupied with her own thoughts.

She watched people rushing here and there and listened to the cacophony of sound that was part and parcel of everyday life in New York – the hooting of horns as drivers of cars and trucks vied with each other for short-term advantage, the wailing of sirens as police cars, ambulances and fire engines made swathes through the traffic. And now and then a siren that was louder than all the rest, whooping like a monkey in a zoo, waiting to be fed.

What was it all for she wondered? All this rushing around? The hurry to get from A to B, and then the hurry to get back. The traffic jams, the horns, the sirens. Perhaps, she thought, it would have been better if she had used the subway. However, Mother Celine had always warned her never to travel on the subway alone, even though it was cheaper. She felt the hardness of the metal in her handbag and gave a wry smile. Not that she was in any danger. After all, she had the little pistol to protect her. She had threatened someone with it once, but that was a long time ago and she wanted to forget it.

Focusing again on the reason for her visit to Staten Island and the quest that lay ahead of her, she lapsed into deep thought. She was only vaguely aware of passing under the bridges that spanned the East River to link Manhattan with Brooklyn and only realised they were approaching the ferry terminal when the driver drawled, 'Battery Park, Sister.'

From the terminal's departure area upstairs, groups of tourists were going outside to look for the ferry and get a glimpse of the Statue of Liberty or Ellis Island. But the nun had seen these things before. She noted the time when the next ferry was due to sail and scanned the long wooden benches for a place to sit. Here and there, curled up and shunned by everyone else, one or two unfortunates whom life had left behind. Asleep, she thought, or in a self-induced stupor. It was difficult to say. Other people, larger than life, eating burgers from serviettes and licking long, ketchup-coloured fingernails. A few, listening to headphones, strumming their fingers to the rhythm of silent music, lost in a world of their own. And, as always, clusters of tourists, chatting excitedly in foreign languages as they consulted maps.

The nun picked a spot and sat down to wait. The ferry boats, she knew, were used by commuters from all walks of life – people for whom driving across the Verrazano Bridge each day was not an option – and by visitors from all over the world, curious to see the woodlands and wetlands of Staten Island that were part of New York City.

The pigeons that roosted in the recesses of the ferry terminal had come to appreciate this daily traffic and as the passengers waited patiently on the long rows of benches, the birds walked up and down in front of them to see who was eating what.

Forgetting her troubles for a moment, the nun smiled. A few crumbs from the burgers, a more generous morsel from a tourist, and some of the birds returned to their roosting places, only to swoop back down a moment later looking for more. A bit like the poor devils who came to the convent, she thought. A bite to eat, a place to sleep. They sought no more from life and sometimes received a lot less. She remembered the first time she had gone to the convent, homeless herself, hungry and greatly distressed. Yes, she thought, a bite to eat and a place to sleep were so important to someone who had neither.

As the ferry drew away from its docking sheath of long wooden piles, tourists gathered at the stern to admire and photograph the island of skyscrapers they were leaving behind, an island dominated by the twin towers of the World Trade Centre. A short time later they switched their attention to the Statue of Liberty and Ellis Island. But, like the cormorant that winged its way across the water in the same direction as the ferry, the young nun's thoughts were still firmly focused on Staten Island. It had been many years since she had made this journey before and there was a memory of poverty and pain, an emptiness in her soul that time had not been able to erase.

It was only when a boy spoke to her that she realised he was there. Looking up, she saw that he was a black boy. While she had been immersed in her own thoughts, he had been eyeing her up and down, his big eyes taking in her short blue and white head-dress, white blouse, navy cardigan, navy skirt and dark blue handbag.

'You're a nun,' he said.

She smiled. Considering what she was wearing, this was stating the obvious. But then, he was only about seven years old. Almost absent-mindedly she fingered the silver crucifix that hung around her neck, and told him, 'Yes, I am.'

'What's your name?'

'Sister Mary.' If she was waiting for the boy to say anything else, he didn't. Instead, he slid off the seat and went running along the deck to rejoin his mother who was trying to cope with several other children.

Hearing the engines slowing down, the nun looked ahead to see the ferry port looming up, the encounter with the boy already forgotten and a short time later boarded a bus. She seated herself beside the window and as the bus gathered speed, watched the remnants of a once bustling shoreline flashing by – wooden posts that might have supported a quay, the ribs of a boat, half-submerged and for all the world like the skeletal cage of a dead body, other maritime debris the purpose of which she couldn't even guess.

The bus headed inland. Car parts. Workshops. Wheels and tyres. Indecipherable graffiti. Tree-lined roads. Copper beeches. Schools. Timber-clad houses. Cherry trees. Azalea bushes. Pink. Magenta. Pink. People getting on. People getting off. The chatter of African-American voices from the back of the bus. She closed her eyes and felt the warmth of the sun on her face. And then she was there.

As the bus drew away, she walked alongside a marshy area where masses of reeds swayed in the summer breeze. Across waste ground she turned onto a street of run-down houses. Felt tiles torn and flapping on the roofs, wooden tiles on upper walls weathered and worn, slipping away never to be replaced. All the houses had seen better days, and so, she knew, had the people who lived in them.

Finding the house she was looking for, her knock on the door was answered by a man she knew to be Don Diego. Grossly overweight from eating junk food, drinking beer and watching television, he wiped a sip of a Budweiser from his moustache, saying, 'Well, if it isn't Marguerite.'

'Don't call me Marguerite – I'm Sister Mary.'

'Ah, Sister Mary is it?' he repeated. He had a can of beer in his other hand and, with an exaggerate sweep of his arm, added, 'Come in, Sister Mary.'

With some hesitation and not a little apprehension, she went in ahead of him.

The room stank from the squalor in which Don Diego was living, but he seemed unaware of it. And while he was of Latin-American origin, there was, paradoxically, the slightest suggestion of an Irish brogue in his voice.

Leaning back against the kitchen work top, he took another sip of beer, saying, 'Well, Sister Mary, what brings you to see the likes of me?' Without waiting for an answer, he added in mock solemnity, 'No. No. Don't tell me. You want to know how the poor people of Staten Island are managing to survive.'

'Please. I just called to see if I could do anything for you. Maybe talk a little.'

'Talk?' She could smell the beer on his breath and there was a dark look of disdain on his face. 'Listen lady, talk's cheap. It doesn't cost anything. And it sure as hell doesn't put bread on the table.'

'I don't have any money. Just the fare to get back.'

'Here, let me see,' he said, reaching for her handbag.

She stepped back, afraid now of what he might do. At the same time, she remembered the purpose of her visit and opened her handbag to get the gun.

Seeing the fear in her face, he smiled broadly and, leaving the can of beer aside, opened his arms wide, saying, 'No need to be afraid. Come here.' Before she could get the gun, his huge arms were around her, squeezing her.

'Stop it, you're hurting me,' she cried, and struggled frantically to free herself.

But if the hug had started out as some kind of embrace, it quickly turned to something else. Don Diego was now aware of the shapely body that was struggling beneath her modest mode of dress. And, drunk as he was, it aroused feelings in his own shapeless form – feelings he had not experienced for some considerable time. He tried to press his lips to hers, and the fear that had gripped Sister Mary suddenly turned to panic. Turning her head away from him she shouted, 'Let me go. Let me go.'

'Don't worry, Sister,' he smiled, 'I'm not going to hurt you.'

'Please don't,' she pleaded, but her pleas fell on deaf ears. Putting his hand over her mouth, he dragged her into the adjoining room. Her arms were pinioned to her sides but her kicking made him stumble. For a moment she found herself free and lashed out at him with her handbag. Clumsy as he was, he managed to regain his balance and, swearing under his breath, grabbed the bag. She tried to hold on to it, but he tore it from her and slammed it down on the bedside locker. As he did so, she tried to get past him, but he caught her again and threw her on to the bed. Next thing she knew, he was astride her and with both hands was ripping open her blouse.

Desperately she struggled to get out from under him, crying, 'Please don't. Please don't.'

His response, however, was to draw out and hit her across the face with the back of his hand.

He was between her legs now, and as he started groping her, he muttered, 'First time I've had sex with a Bride of Christ.'

Don Diego was heavy and all her efforts to push him off had no effect. Then as she stretched out her arms, she felt her right hand touching her handbag on the bedside locker. With her fingers she prised the bag open a little farther and found the pistol. It was cold and heavy. Bringing it up with all the force she could muster, she hit him on the side of the face with it.

'Fuck you,' he grunted, grabbing her hand.

She could see there was blood on his face and she held on tightly to the gun, hoping she could strike him again.

Surprised at her strength, he forced the gun down from his face. As he did so, she found the trigger and pulled. There was a muffled explosion and she heard him take a deep intake of breath. For a terrifying moment, time seemed to stand still. He stared down at her in disbelief, but didn't move. His hand was still clasped tightly around her hand and the gun, as if it was locked in some sort of convulsive reaction to the shot. Then she felt him come to life again.

'You bitch!' he shouted. 'You've shot me.'

Fearing that he might turn the gun on her, she squeezed the trigger again. This time he collapsed on top of her with a loud moan. She managed to push him over and he fell on to the floor, coming to rest on his back. Scrambling out of the bed, she looked down at him. He was still moaning, but wasn't moving. She could see there were bullet holes and powder burns in the front of his shirt but no blood. She knelt down and opened the shirt slightly, looking for the wounds. To her surprise, she found none. Yet it was plain to see the life was ebbing out of him.

He had stopped moaning now and she put her fingers to his wrist, then to the side of his neck, checking for any sign of a pulse. She failed to find one and knew he was dead. For a moment she wondered if she should telephone the police. But then, she thought, they might not believe her. They might not believe that anyone would attack a nun, especially her father. And if they didn't believe it was self-defence? The reality of her situation now dawned on her. If they didn't believe it was self-defence, they would charge her with murder.

She pulled the sides of her torn blouse together and discovered that her crucifix was missing. Gingerly she walked around the body looking for it. There was no sign of it, nor was there any sign of it on the bed or on the floor around it. She was still trembling from the shock of what had happened, so much so that she could hardly button her cardigan. She retrieved her handbag from the bedside locker and was heading for the front door when she remembered the gun. Her fingerprints would be on it, she thought, and she wondered what she should do? Acting on impulse, she went back into the bedroom. The gun was lying not far from the body so she lifted it with the corner of a sheet, wiped it and dropped it into her handbag. Then she hung the handbag on her wrist, finished buttoning her cardigan and headed for the door.

A moment later, she was back out on the street. On a bare patch of ground nearby, children were playing with a ball, but they paid no attention as she hurried past. She could feel the warmth of the sun on her face now and put up her hand to shade her eyes, only to be reminded by the pain that her right eye was probably bruised. As she walked on she became aware that there were other people around, so she continued to hold her hand to her face as if to shade her eyes, and kept going.

How she found her way into the woods of Staten Island, she herself didn't know. Perhaps it was the instinct of self-preservation that made her leave the streets and the roads and seek the cover of the trees. Her mind was in turmoil, her body trembling with fear. Leaning against the deeply furrowed trunk of a large tulip tree, she tried to steady herself. She was shaking, sobbing uncontrollably, and, even though the evening was still warm, she was cold.

Unaware now of her surroundings, unaware even of anyone outside her own being, she wept until she could weep no more. As the strength drained from her slight frame, she collapsed between the protruding roots of the tulip tree and there she curled up, drawing her cardigan tightly around herself and staring unseeing into the gathering gloom.

Somewhere above her she thought she heard the call of a whip-poor-will. Or was it just her imagination, an echo from her past? She didn't know. Nor did she react by looking up to see if the bird was really there. Trauma was setting in with the darkness, paralysing her mind and taking her into a darkness blacker than anything nightfall could bring.

TWO

The arrival of a police patrol car, its lights flashing, siren wailing, alerted all and sundry to the fact that something terrible had happened at Don Diego's house. A short time later, the policemen strung a tape around the house and garden to preserve the scene, and curious neighbours who had gathered in little groups on the sidewalk learned that he was dead.

Detective Antonio Florentine took a pen from his pocket, hunkered down and pushed the sides of Diego's shirt to one side, then another. 'Jeez, Sully. That's a strange one. Looks as if he's been shot. Holes in the shirt where the slugs went through, but no holes in the body.'

Detective Sullivan leaned over so that he could have a closer look. There were powder burns around holes in the shirt and he remarked, 'Looks as if he has been shot at close range.'

'I know. But where? No entry wounds that I can see. And no blood.'

Sullivan borrowed the pen and parted the shirt so that he could see for himself. 'You're right. What do you make of it?'

Before Florentine could reply, a uniformed officer came in to inform them that an investigator from the Medical Examiner's Office had arrived and they were pleased to see that it was Sam Mortimer.

They had established a good working relationship with Mortimer on previous cases. A tall, thin man with horn-rimmed glasses, he had a slight stoop and his clothes hung rather loosely on his body. This, together with his thinning hair made him look older than he probably was. 'Well, Toni,' he said, adjusting his glasses, 'what have we got this time?'

'A strange one, Mort. Looks as if he's been shot to death, but we can't see any entry wounds on the body.'

Mortimer looked at the body from every angle before touching it.

'What do you reckon?' Sullivan asked.

'I remember working on another case.' Mortimer paused as he opened the shirt. 'The victim was found on the sidewalk. Dead as a dodo. A bullet hole in the front of his shirt. But no hole in the chest. Just like this guy. What did you say his name was?'

'Diego. Don Diego.'

'Well, just like Don Diego here, it was obvious he had been shot. But where? Then I opened his belt. I'll never forget it.' He leaned down, pulled up the shirt and carefully unbuckled Diego's belt. 'When I did so,' he added, quickly stepping back, 'the blood spurted up like a fountain.'

Even as he spoke, a fountain of blood erupted from Diego's abdomen, forcing the two detectives to jump back out of the way.

'Jeez, Mort.' Florentine protested. 'You should have warned me. I almost got it all over my clothes.' He dusted off imaginary specks of blood. 'How did that happen?'

Mortimer opened his bag and began his preliminary examination. 'Well, this guy they found on the sidewalk. The way I figured it, he had been mugged. In the struggle his assailant probably caught him by the head, pulled it down and shot him. The slug went through his shirt, up here, but because he was bent over, it missed his chest and lodged in his abdomen. When his assailant released him, I reckoned, he straightened up and fell back. The pressure of his belt against the entry wound inhibited the flow of blood. Maybe a build-up of gas in the intestines and, when I unbuckled it – whoosh! Just like Diego here.'

'So you reckoned he was robbed?' Sullivan asked.

'I'm not saying that. Look at the place. It's a dump. No one in his right mind would want to rob somebody who lives in a place like this. A tourist getting off the ferry – right. But not someone who's living on beer and junk food, like this guy. No, all I'm saying is that the trajectory of the slugs would indicate that he was shot when he was bending over. Why he was bending over, I don't know. That's for you guys to find out.'

The two detectives withdrew to the next room to let him get on with his work.

'Who found the body?' asked Florentine.

Sullivan consulted his notebook. 'An old guy who lives next door. Name of Durane.'

'Right. We better talk to him.' Florentine turned to one of the uniformed officers. 'Let me know when Mort has finished.'

When the two detectives persuaded Mr. Durane to open the door, they found that he was not only old, but frail and frightened. 'Nobody knows who the killer is.' he whispered. 'Or where he's going to strike next.' He took them into a sitting room that was sparsely furnished, but clean. 'It could have been me, you know. I mean, who's to say he didn't knock on my door, or try to get in some other way?'

'Don't worry,' Florentine assured him. 'Whoever killed Don Diego, he sure as hell ain't coming back. The neighbourhood is crawling with cops. So calm down and tell us what happened.'

'Don Diego Româo,' the old man corrected him.

'What's that?'

'Don Diego Româo. That was his stage name. He used to be an actor, you know.'

'Oh, yeah, yeah.' Florentine eased himself down onto the threadbare couch. 'Now tell me, Mr. Durane, how did you come to find his body?'

The old man sat into a sagging armchair at the window and looked out through net curtains that had once been white but now were grey with dust, neglect and the passage of time. 'I just called in to share a beer with him. He likes company when he's drinking, you understand. But the door was open. Well, it wasn't exactly open, but it wasn't properly closed. I knocked but there was no reply. So I pushed it open and went on in. And there he was, lying on the floor of the bedroom.'

They queried him about the approximate time he had found the body and asked him if he had heard a shot, but he shook his head. 'No, nothing like that. I mean, I heard the children playing baseball over there on the vacant lot. And I heard the dogs barking.'

'Dogs? What dogs?' asked Sullivan, who was jotting down everything he was saying.

'I don't know what dogs. Pet dogs, stray dogs. They're always barking. And the children are always shouting. But it was no different from any other day.' As the old man looked out through the faded net curtains again he remembered seeing a nun walking past, but didn't think it was important and didn't say anything about her.

'Tell us about Mr. Diego,' urged Florentine.

'Don Diego Româo. Well, let me see. He was always a bit vague about his origins. But once, when he had a few beers – a few more, maybe, than he should have – he told me about the time his forebears came to this country. He didn't say where exactly they came from, mind you, but I suspect it was somewhere in South America. He said they looked at the map and, seeing San Diego in California, decided that Diego was a more fitting name than the one they had.'

Sullivan looked up. 'Well I'll be damned.'

However, Florentine just nodded. He could understand that. After all, his family had taken their name from the city of Florence, or so he had been told. When that was, or why it was done, he didn't know. Originally it had been Florentino, but over the years in America the last letter had gone the way of the O in O'Sullivan. 'You said he used to be an actor.'

'That's right. As a young man he was very handsome. He used to show me photographs of himself. He reminded me of some of the leading men in the old black and white movies. You know, sleek black hair, thin moustache. And he was a great guy for the woman. Well, that's according to himself. He used to take great pride in telling me about his romantic exploits, all his conquests, and how his pals used to call him Don Juan. He added Româo to his name in the hope that it would help him become a big star. He reckoned it sounded like Romeo and that it would get him a lot farther than Diego. However, I gather his acting wasn't up to much. He got a few bit parts and then, finito, that was it. I suppose good-looking guys are two a penny in the movie business and if you can't cut the mustard, you're out.'

'What did he do then?' Florentine prompted.

'After that, he went into real estate. According to himself, he used his charms on the wives of prospective clients, and he did very well. Married an Irishwoman, bought a big house out on Long Island, and reared a family.'

'An Irishwoman?' asked Sullivan. 'You don't happen to know her name, do you? Or where she is?'

The old man scratched the grey stubble on his chin. 'Nora. Yeah, that was her name. They split up. I think it was his drinking.'

'Did they have any children?'

'He said he had three, including twins, but I've never seen them around here.'

'He didn't happen to say what their names were?'

'Well, he said the boy's name was Felipe. His twin sister's name was… let me think. It was Vitoria. And the older girl, I think he said it was Marguerite.'

'They must be grown up now,' Florentine said.

'Reckon so. Probably in their twenties.'

'Do you know of any reason why anyone would want to kill him?' Sullivan asked.

'Nope. But then some people don't need a reason these days, do they?'

A uniformed officer knocked at the door to inform them that Mortimer had finished his preliminary examination and, as they returned to the house, they met him on the sidewalk.

'How long do you reckon he's been dead?' asked Florentine.

'Not long. Three, maybe four hours.'

'How many shots?'

'Two, maybe three. We won't know for sure until we do the autopsy.'

The forensic team had begun their work now and one of them came out of the house saying, 'Look what I found.'

'A crucifix,' said Sullivan.

The forensic man nodded. 'The chain's been broken.'

Florentine turned it over to examine the hallmark on the back. 'Silver. Where did you find it?'

'On the kitchen floor, near a few empty beer cans.'

'Well done.' Handing it to his partner, Florentine said, 'What do you reckon? Is it his?'

'Looks a bit fine for a man's.'

'So, tell me, who else would wear a crucifix?'

'A Catholic? An Irishwoman? The wife maybe?'

'Could be.' Florentine looked around. Only now did he notice that it was beginning to get dark. 'Tell you what, Sully. Get a team together. First thing tomorrow, we canvass the area. Somebody must have seen something, and we want to know what it was.'

'Okay, we'll start with the neighbours, but how far do we go after that?'

'You stop when you get the information we need.' Florentine smiled. 'I tell you what. Just pretend it's St. Patrick's Day and you're looking for an Irish pub. You'll find it.'

Florentine liked the Irish for most of the year, but not on St. Patrick's Day. The Irish mafia, he called them. They came out of the woodwork on St. Patrick's Day. Took over the whole friggin' place and the job of policing New York fell to officers like himself. Oh, how he hated them on Patrick's Day. Started off praying and ended up drinking. Whooping it up for the whole day while the rest of them had to work. But then, what the hell. Every dog had his day. And Sully was a fine detective. A third generation policeman and absolutely dependable. Absolutely, that was, except on St. Patrick's Day.

'Off you go now, Sully,' he added. 'Get that team together. And give them the usual questionnaires.'

Sullivan turned to go.

'And stay off the booze tonight.'

Sullivan said he would, but Florentine knew he wouldn't. The Irish were all the same.

THREE

Birds were calling to one another somewhere high in the trees. Slowly, Sister Mary sat up and opened her eyes. Her right eye smarted and filled with water and she could hardly see out of it, but with the other she saw a canopy of branches above her. For a moment she wondered where she was. Suddenly it all came flooding back to her. The Staten Island ferry. The bus ride. The knock on the door. The step across the threshold. The attempted rape. The gun! It was all like a bad dream.

Frantically she opened her handbag. There it was. The small silvery pistol she had brought with her from the convent. It hadn't been a dream. She had killed Don Diego. Dazed, she wondered almost absent-mindedly why she still had the gun. Then she remembered and she was glad. With any luck, the police would think he had been killed in a drunken brawl. What was it the papers said? A moment of anger, a life in prison.

The thought of a life in prison sent a shiver down her body and she realised she must get rid of the gun, but where? She could just throw it into the bushes, but then someone might find it. Closing her handbag, she pulled her cardigan tightly around her shoulders, shivered and wondered what to do. Above her, she could see two cardinal birds sporting themselves among the branches of the tulip tree, flashes of crimson in a tree that sprouted yellow flowers in spring. Painfully, she pushed herself to her feet. Her whole body was aching and so was her heart. She was also cold from the night spent in the open and for a while she limped around until the circulation came back into her legs.

Eventually she straightened up and told herself that she must pull herself together. She brushed down her clothes with her hands and took a mirror from her handbag. It was a very small mirror which she carried, not for purposes of vanity, but to make sure her head-dress was on correctly. Her right eye was paining her and, when she looked in the mirror, she cringed. The eye, or what she could see of it, was badly bloodshot and the swelling around it was black and blue.

Making her way through the trees, she came to a pond dotted with loosestrife and other wildflowers. The sun was in her eyes now, so she stopped and rooted in her bag for her sunglasses. In doing so she realised once again that she must get rid of the gun. She looked around and, seeing no one in the vicinity, threw it out into the water. A blue heron that had been standing on a rock watching for fish, took off and she glanced around again to make sure she hadn't been seen. Her eye was smarting again, so she slid the sunglasses gently on to her face and looked in the mirror. The bruising was barely visible behind the dark glass and she blessed herself, saying, 'Thank God for that.'

A woodland path ran alongside the pond and she set off in search of the nearest road. However one path led to another and after a while it seemed as if she was in a maze. Some of the paths petered out and led to nowhere; others branched off to the left and right and there was no knowing which one to take. None seemed to lead to a road, but she kept going and eventually found herself in a marshy area where reeds were swaying in the breeze. It was then she realised that she had come full circle. Beyond the reeds was a piece of waste ground and on crossing it saw to her great relief the stop where she had got off the bus.

It was still early in the day but people were already waiting for the bus that would take them to the ferry. Thankfully, they didn't pay any attention to her when she slipped in behind them. Nor did any of them talk to her on the bus and for that she was grateful. Nevertheless, she propped her elbow on the bottom of the window frame, held her hand to her head and hoped none of them would see that she had a black eye. However, she needn't have worried. They were too busy talking to one another, or looking ahead, thinking perhaps of their work or wondering what the day would bring and soon she was part of a torrent of people streaming into the ferry terminal.

News of the murder hadn't hit the headlines yet, at least not as far as she could see and no one else seemed to notice the presence of extra policemen at the terminal. But then, why should the innocent notice things like that? She only saw them because she knew she was the one they were looking for. Fortunately, the policemen didn't know who they were looking for when they scanned the sea of faces, and she boarded the ferry unhindered.

As the ferry gain speed, she took out her rosary beads and prayed. She prayed for forgiveness for what she had done and she thanked God for the fact that she had made good her escape from the island. But now Manhattan was looming up. How could she face the other nuns after what had happened? How could she face Mother Celine?

Almost before she knew it, the ferry had slowed down and was preparing to dock at the Manhattan terminal. Everyone was looking ahead, waiting patiently for the safety gate to be pulled aside, but she held back for a moment and opened her handbag to drop her rosary beads into it. As she did so, she felt a hand on her elbow and, turning around, found herself looking up at the face of a tall young policeman. Her heart sank. Was this how it was going to end? she asked herself. And, like people who see their lives flashing before them as they drown, many thoughts and fears crossed her mind.

'You've dropped something, ma'am,' he said.

'P..p..pardon?' was all she could manage to say.

'Sorry. I didn't mean to startle you, ma'am. But I think you've dropped something.'

Looking down, she saw her rosary beads lying at her feet. Hardly able to believe her good fortune, she bent down to pick them up. But he was there before her and, with a smile, dropped them into her open bag.

'Thank you officer,' she said. 'Thank you very much.'

The policeman tipped his cap in a gesture of respect. 'Pleasure ma'am.'

By this time the safety gate had been pulled aside and the passengers were streaming out. Hardly able to keep her composure, she followed. Now and then she bumped into people who were boarding by coming in against the exit sign. But she was unaware of them, aware only of the need to get out, to seek safety among the multitudes of Manhattan.

For a while she stood on the sidewalk as the traffic lights on the busy streets changed, telling people when to walk and when not to. Some hailed cabs and disappeared into the teeming traffic. Others hurried across to the far side when the lights told them they could do so, leaving her behind. However, it wasn't a change of lights she was waiting for. Still traumatised by what had happened to her, her mind seemed paralysed and she had to force herself to think. What should she do? Take the subway back to the convent, or hail a cab?

Undecided, she was still looking across the street. Suddenly she became aware of a stone statue looking back at her, arms outstretched in the manner in which Christ was often portrayed. It was not a statue of Christ, she could see, but the hands were open, reaching out to all who passed, telling them that they were welcome to come in. The statue was in an arched recess above the door of a redbrick church. Beside the church was another redbrick building, its colonnaded front curving with the street. Both were hemmed in by skyscrapers which seemed to have sprouted up like giant beanstalks, dwarfing them and leaving them small by comparison.

Strange, she thought, that she had never taken note of the church before. But now it held out the possibility of shelter, perhaps even sanctuary.

With a quick look around to make sure she wasn't being followed, she hurried over the crossing, the white stripes of which were worn thin by the incessant traffic. A sign that hung out over the sidewalk beyond informed her that she was at the shrine of Elizabeth Ann Seton, 'first American-born saint'. Almost as if she was in a dream, she peered over her sunglasses to read a bronze wall plaque, which recorded that the Setons had lived in a house on the site from 1801 to 1803.

'Mrs. Seton, wife, mother, educator,' she read, 'and foundress of the Sisters of Charity was canonized, September 14, 1975. This tablet erected in loving memory by New York State, Catholic Daughters of America, January 4, 1977.'

She could feel her bruised eye watering again from the strain of reading and lifted her sunglasses with one hand so that she could wipe the water away with the other. In the porch at the top of the steps another sign told her that she was entering the Church of Our Lady of the Rosary. Unclear as to which was the shrine and which was the church, or if they were one and the same, she hurried inside and sat down in the first pew.

How long she sat there she did not know. She held her hands tightly together as if in prayer, but it was to keep her hands from trembling that she did so, not to pray. Somehow she couldn't pray, not yet. Her body was wracked with pain, her mind no less so. She felt dazed, betrayed, bewildered. A mixture of emotions that hurt so much she wanted to die. And it was so dark.

After a while she realised that she was still wearing her sunglasses and that they were making the interior of the church seem darker than it really was. Yet she was afraid that if she took them off someone would see the bruising on her eye. She could hear voices behind her and, to the right, foreign voices and a voice with a hint of an Irish accent. Probably one of the priests showing a group of visitors around, she thought.

Sliding forward on to her knees she slipped her glasses off and put them into her handbag. Then she leaned over so that her elbows were on the pew in front and her head was resting on her hands.

With her face thus hidden from anyone who might pass by, she looked towards the altar. She was, she could see, in a beautiful church. It seemed to be oval in shape with a balcony on each side curving in towards three stained-glass windows. Her bruised eye was watering again and she gently soaked the water up with her fingers. To the right of the altar, in an alcove, was a statue of Mary and the Child Jesus. At least, she thought it was them. She could hardly see out of her right eye now.

Then, as she tried to focus on the statue, she relived for the umpteenth time the horrible thing that had happened to her, and she felt defiled and ashamed. Ashamed to have taken the name of Mary, the Virgin Mary, to whom she looked up and prayed to every day of her life. Ashamed to be called a Bride of Christ. Somehow, she felt she had betrayed Christ and was no longer worthy of Him, so she pulled the silver ring from the third finger of her right hand and dropped it into her handbag.

As she did so, she felt a hand clasping her shoulder. Startled, she looked up expecting to see the young policeman who had approached her on the ferry. To her relief, she saw that it was one of the priests.

'I'm sorry, Sister,' he whispered. 'I didn't mean to startle you.'

An elderly man with thinning grey hair and a kindly face, he was standing to the left of her. Instinctively, she had kept her right hand over her bruised eye and was hoping he hadn't noticed it.

'I was just wondering if I could be of any help to you. Are you in some sort of trouble?'

When she nodded, he slipped in beside her. 'What kind of trouble?'

She sat back, her right hand still covering her bruised eye, and began to cry. 'Terrible trouble.'

'Come inside where we can talk in private.' Taking her gently by the arm, he steered her along the back of the church and into a small office. Another priest brought her a cup of coffee, but left it to the older man to talk to her.

'You've a black eye,' he observed. 'What happened?'

As she held the cup with both hands and drank the coffee it gave her a few moments to think and she wondered how to reply.

'You're in quite a state,' said the older man as the young priest withdrew. 'Were you mugged?'

Putting down the cup, she wiped the water from her black eye with her hand, sniffed to clear it from her nose and nodded.

'I thought as much.' He asked her a few more questions and when she didn't respond, he added, 'Okay. Stay here and I'll get you help.'

Left alone, she took out her beads and began to say a decade of the Rosary. At the same time she began to rock in her chair. Who was the priest going to bring? she wondered. A doctor? A policeman? And what would she tell them? That her father had tried to rape her? That she had shot him dead? But why hadn't she gone to the police on Staten Island? And, if it was self-defence, why had she taken the gun? Why had she thrown it into the pond? There were so many things she couldn't explain. So many things they wouldn't understand. So many things she couldn't bring herself to talk about. Not to strangers.

She waited for another moment to see if the priest would reappear and, when he didn't, she rushed out into the street. She was almost blinded by the sun so she put on her sunglasses. Her good eye adjusted to the light, but her bruised eye smarted and began to water again. However, she kept going until she reached Battery Park. There she paused to look back, then hurried along beneath the trees, past park benches where tourists were resting and young lovers were kissing, and disappeared down the steps of the nearest subway.

When, a short time later, she arrived at the gate of her convent, it was almost as if she had never been away. The down-and-outs, who depended on the convent for survival were still there, sitting, lying, or just lounging around as they waited for their next handout. They saluted her in the usual gesture of respect but she hurried past. She was afraid the police might be on her heels and had to stop herself from running down the passage to get to the side door. With another look back to make sure she wasn't being followed, she opened the door and slipped inside.

As she made her way through the convent, she was afraid some of the other nuns might see her and ask her what had happened. Fortunately, there was no one else around and with a sigh of relief closed the door of her bedroom behind her. Throwing her handbag on to the bed, she bent close to the mirror and examined her injured eye. The skin around it was puffed up and black and painful to the touch, while the eye itself, or what she could see of it, was inflamed, irritable and very red. Even as she looked at it she was taking off her torn clothes and a moment later was in the shower. There she tried to wash away the pain caused by the sexual intrusion of his groping hands. However, Don Diego had violated not only her body but, it seemed to her, her vow of chastity, and wash as she would it seemed to make no difference.

Having towelled, she again looked at her eye in the mirror. It was very sore and she douched it with handfuls of cold water in an effort to get the swelling down. The water made the irritation worse but did little for the swelling, so she decided to leave it alone.

In her anxiety to get into the shower, she had dropped her clothes on the floor and walked out of them. The only other clothes she had were in the small brown suitcase on the top shelf of her wardrobe. They were the ones she had been wearing when she had first entered the convent and they had lain there untouched ever since. Untouched, that is, until she had taken out the pistol that had lain on top of them and smoothed them to remove its imprint. In spite of that, the imprint was still on the top garment, so she took it out and shook it vigorously as if shaking off an unpleasant memory.

Some of the clothes, she found, were small and ill-fitting as her figure had changed over the years, but she didn't care. When she had put them on she towelled her short, boyish hair again and took out her raincoat. Even though the coat had been folded neatly, it was creased, but she put it on too and closed the belt.

The only things remaining in the case now were a few dollars which she had managed to save over the years and two pieces of memorabilia – a blue plastic music box in the shape of a heart and a grubby rag doll, things that had given her great comfort as a child. There was nothing to comfort her now, except the money which she knew she would need in the outside world. She retrieved the purse from her handbag and after checking to see how much she had altogether, tucked the purse into her raincoat pocket. Apart from the purse, these few belongings and the name of Marguerite were all she had brought to the convent and were all she would take with her.

Then her eyes fell on the torn clothes she had left on the floor and she wondered whether to take them with her or leave them. Better take them, she thought, so she dropped them into the case and closed it.

She looked around the room to check if she had forgotten anything, but there was nothing left. Putting on her sunglasses she picked up the case and walked out, closing the door behind her. As far as she was concerned, Sister Mary had ceased to exist.

When, a short time later, a young woman with short hair walked towards the side gate, some of the down-and-outs whistled. But they didn't know her, and she was glad. Forcing a smile, she closed the gate behind her, adjusted her sunglasses and walked briskly away.

FOUR

The death of Don Diego merited no more than a paragraph in the *New York Times*. The short report noted that he had once been an actor, although few readers would have recalled ever seeing him on the silver screen. More would have remembered him as a successful real estate agent, and quite a few women now desperately trying to preserve their fading beauty, would have read the notice with a wistful look in their eye.

'Do you remember that nice man who sold us our first house?' said one woman as she and her husband read parts of the paper over breakfast in their Manhattan apartment.

'What man?' asked her husband absent-mindedly.

Drawing deeply through her gold cigarette-holder, the woman raised her plucked eyebrows and smiled, happy in the knowledge that her husband had never discovered her indiscretion with Don Diego and knowing now that he never would.

'The man who sold us the house in Long Island.'

'Yeah, what about him?'

'It says here he's been murdered. Shot to death in a house in Staten Island.'

'What was he doing in Staten Island?'

'I don't know. It says investigating officers are trying to contact his estranged wife.'

Her husband turned the page as he studied their stocks and shares and she could see that the death of Don Diego was already old news to a man for whom a rise or fall of a percentage point was of much greater interest.

The report in the *New York Times*, however, served its purpose. Within 24 hours, Nora Diego contacted Detective Florentine and she was able to tell him more about the rise and fall of her estranged husband. As she spoke to him, she painted a picture, not of a failed actor, but of a successful real estate agent who rose to the pinnacle of his profession in a wealthy area of Long Island. They were happy years, she recalled. Years when they were comfortable and wanted for nothing.

Sure, Don Diego had other women. But he always came back to her and, like the good Irish Catholic she was, she turned a blind eye for the sake of the children. Then, slowly but surely, he developed a drink problem and things began to fall apart. Gradually his business declined and went to the wall and they moved to Staten Island. As his problems got worse, so also did his behaviour and eventually she had to kick him out.

When Florentine showed her the silver crucifix, she shook her head, saying, 'It's not mine. I've never seen it before.' She shrugged and, with a smile of resignation, added, 'But then, as I told you, I wasn't the only woman in his life.'

While Florentine and Sullivan now had a pretty good idea of Don Diego's background, they still hadn't established a motive for the killing. Nor had their search of the house and garden turned up the murder weapon. However, they knew what they were looking for as the forensic people had recovered two empty casings from a .25 handgun. According to the autopsy report, which had now come to hand, both bullets had entered Diego's abdomen. One hit the pelvic bones, and both the bullet and bones splintered, rupturing several of his vital organs. The other severed the main artery to the right leg causing massive internal bleeding, and lodged in the femur.

Florentine nodded. Probably a junk gun. Bought over the counter for a few dollars, like countless others that contributed so much to the crime rate. Low calibre, poor manufacture, but able to kill, especially at close quarters. And kill they did. Usually in a Saturday night binge or a drugstore burglary. 'Any sign of it yet, Sully?' he asked.

Sullivan shook his head. 'We're still searching the woods and the divers are checking the lakes in case he threw it in there.' But...', he gestured with his open hands, 'no luck so far.'

'And your canvass of the area?'

'Nothing to report yet.' Sullivan pushed back his hat and wiped the sweat from his brow. 'But we're widening it out.'

By this stage, Sullivan's team had called at all the doors in the immediate neighbourhood. Armed with questionnaires, they had inquired if any residents had seen anything suspicious on the day of his death, especially any unsavoury characters hanging around; where they themselves were at the relevant time, and so forth.

The police had ticked off one question after another and, when all their questions had been answered, they had gone away happy. The residents were also happy. They were assured by the fact that the police were doing such a thorough job and glad to be able to report that they had not seen any suspicious characters hanging around. Like Mr. Durane, some did remember a nun calling to inquire about Mr. Diego, but they didn't see the relevance of that. It was suspicious characters the police wanted to know about, not nuns who were trying to help the elderly and the poor.

While Don Diego had, in the words of his estranged wife, reached the pinnacle of his career as a real estate agent, it was in a poor piece of real estate that he was buried. The place to which his mortal remains were brought was used as a cemetery simply because it was good for nothing else. Not much higher than the marshy ground around it, most of its tombstones were covered with lichen, their lettering obliterated, their dead long forgotten.

It was raining as the hearse drove through the trees and parked just inside the gate. The undertakers wheeled the coffin along a narrow pathway and placed it beside a freshly opened grave. There were only a few mourners at the graveside. Nora was there with her twins, Felipe and Vitoria, and their spouses. There were also one or two relatives from Don's side, people Nora hadn't seen for years and didn't want to see again. Marguerite was there too, but the person who identified the mourners for a reporter hadn't seen her since she was a teenager and didn't recognise her.

As the local newspaper would also report, police officers investigating the shooting mingled with the mourners. But then, they always said that. In truth there were only two officers present – Detectives Florentine and Sullivan – and, out of respect for the family, they stood well back among the trees.

Beneath an umbrella, a priest waited at the graveside for everyone to gather round. The rain was getting heavier now and other umbrellas went up. Finding Marguerite at her shoulder, Nora turned and hissed, 'What are you doing here?'

Marguerite sniffed to hold back the tears and pulled her sodden headscarf forward, saying, 'I wanted to see him buried.'

'If you were so fond of him, why did you leave?'

Marguerite's tears were mixing with the rain, but she could still feel the salt on her lips. 'You left me no option.'

'Well, you can save your tears. He doesn't need them now, and neither do I.'

Marguerite's brother and sister listened in silence to the exchange of words, then turned to look at the grave as the priest began his funeral oration.

Marguerite walked back along the narrow pathway and sat down on a wet wooden bench at the foot of the boundary wall. She was sobbing, not because Don Diego was dead but because of what he had done to her.

A woman who had been standing some way back from the main group of mourners, followed and stopped in front of her saying, 'I don't wish to intrude. But are you related to Don?'

The woman spoke with a distinctly Irish accent and, looking up Marguerite saw that she was elderly and thin to the point of being frail. She was wearing a small black pillbox hat, a long black coat and black shoes, although whether she was wearing black because she was attending the funeral, or because it was her normal mode of dress, was difficult to tell. There was also a strong odour of cigarette smoke from her clothes that betrayed the fact that she was a heavy smoker before she gave a long rumbling cough.

'Yes, I'm his daughter, Marguerite.'

The woman nodded. 'I thought that's who you might be.'

'But… I don't think I know you.'

As the woman sat down beside her, she added, 'No but I knew you when you were little. And I knew Don.'

Marguerite lifted her head slightly and raised her eyes saying, 'Oh, I should have known.'

The woman gave a long choking cough and when it subsided, she added, 'No. Not like that. I knew him because I was your nurse.'

'I never knew I had a nurse.'

'Not that kind of nurse. I was the nurse who brought you here.'

Puzzled, Marguerite turned her head and lowered a handkerchief that was soaked in rain and tears. 'Brought me here? I don't understand.'

'Oh.' The woman sat back, visibly shocked. 'Sorry. I didn't realise your parents hadn't told you.' She got up to go. 'I can see now I've made a mistake. This is not the time or the place.'

Marguerite got up and followed her. 'The time and place for what?'

Even though they were a good distance away, some of those at the graveside heard Marguerite's raised voice and glanced around.

The woman paused. 'Look, when I read about Don Diego's murder I came here to tell you something that's been on my mind for a long time. But, as I say, this is obviously not the time or the place.'

As the woman continued along the path, Marguerite hurried after her and caught her by the arm. 'Hold on. What did you mean when you said my parents had obviously never told me?'

'I was the nurse who brought you here for adoption.' The woman lowered her voice. 'I thought you knew you were adopted, otherwise I wouldn't have intruded.'

Stunned by what the woman had said Marguerite stood back and looked at her. For a moment she was speechless. Then, as the woman's words sank in, she had the urge to march over to her mother and ask her if it was true. But, as the woman had said, this was hardly the time or the place.

As if reading her mind, the woman took a packet of cigarettes from her purse and wrote something on the inside of the flap. 'Here,' she said tearing it off. 'You can contact me at this address.'

The priest was now extolling the virtues of Don Diego, probably because he had been paid to do so, not because he had known him. At the same time, some of those who were related to Diego nodded. They would tell one another how good a man he had been and how he would be greatly missed. None of them would say a bad word against him, even though they had known him to be vain and worthless.

However, Marguerite wasn't listening to what the priest was saying. It was the words of the woman in black that she was hearing. She was still trying to comprehend what the woman had said. If it was true and she was adopted, why had her parents not told her? On the other hand, why would the woman say it if it wasn't true? She looked around but could see no sign of her.

'Unto God's gracious mercy and protection we commit you,' the priest was saying. 'The Lord bless you and keep you. The Lord make His face shine upon you and be gracious unto you. The Lord lift up His countenance upon you and give you peace. Now and forever more. Amen.'

Someone threw a Mass card in on top of the coffin but no one waited to say a silent prayer.

Still thinking about what the woman had said, Marguerite watched the others make their way between the headstones to return to their cars. She caught up with them at the gate and, raising herself on her toes, saw the delay was being caused by two men who were stopping and talking to each of them. As she drew closer, she also saw, to her dismay, that they were flashing police badges.

So as not to attract attention, she examined the writing on one of the headstones nearby, then turned and walked back along the wall to the bench where she had been approached by the woman in black. Glancing back, she saw that the policemen were talking to the last of the mourners and, thankfully, were showing no interest in her. Instead of sitting down, she moved slowly forward towards Don's grave and stood watching the gravediggers filling it in. As they did so, dark memories of her childhood came flooding back into her mind, only to be superseded by images of her last fearful encounter with Don and she was glad he was dead, glad that it had all come to an end. But then, she thought, it hadn't really come to an end. She looked around and was startled to find the two policemen approaching her.

'Detective Florentine,' said one of them, showing her his badge. 'And this is Detective Sullivan. We're investigating the murder of Mr. Diego.'

Terrified that they were about to arrest her, she opened her mouth to speak but no words came out.

'And you are?'

'Marguerite – his daughter.'

Florentine nodded. 'We just need to know where we can contact you – in case we need to talk to you.'

Marguerite gave them the address of a deli where she had managed to get work, and when Sullivan had jotted it down in his notebook, they left.

With a sigh of relief, Marguerite watched them go. She hung back in case they might change their minds and come back to ask her some questions, but when she reached the gate she saw no sign of them. Even then she decided to stall a while longer, just to be on the safe side. She also wanted to see what she had come to see – Don Diego buried.

As she watched the gravediggers filling in his grave she knew that none of his relatives would ever return to it to pray for his soul. Nor would she. But when the gravediggers had completed their work and gone to another part of the cemetery she saw two large rats rush across to the grave and burrow down into the soft soil. Even though she hated her father, the thought of what the rats were doing turned her stomach. She also knew that they would continue to visit his grave long after he had been forgotten by his fellow men.

Brief though it was, the encounter with the two policemen had unnerved Marguerite. She thought she would never get back to her apartment, and when she did it was with a sense of relief that she closed the door behind her. She heard voices outside and peering out the window saw boys playing basket ball on a makeshift court across the street. She hadn't given the two officers the address of the apartment which she shared with two girls from the deli. However, she realised it was only a matter of time before they came knocking on her door.

She sat down at the table beside the window and wondered what to do. Paramount in her mind was the need to get away. At the same time she couldn't help thinking about the woman in black and what she had told her. If it was true that she had been adopted, why had her parents never told her? And what else had the woman come to the funeral to tell her? Something, she said, that had been on her mind for a long time. She felt a great need to know, but the need to get away was greater.

The question was where could she go? She wondered if she should just keep moving and lose herself among the populace of New York, or hop on a bus and go to another State. Maybe even work her way up to Canada. Perhaps it was a fanciful idea, but the thought of going to Canada appealed to her most. However, if she decided to go there she would need a passport. To get one, she had been told, she would need a birth certificate, but as she had spent most of her adult life in the convent she was quite ignorant of life on the outside and had no idea how she might get one. In any event, she had just started work in the deli and couldn't go very far without money.

All things considered and disagreeable as it was, Marguerite came to the conclusion that the only person who could help her was her mother. Their relationship had never been good, nor had it healed with the passage of time as her mother's curt rebuff at the graveside had shown. Perhaps she resented the fact that Don had shown her so much affection when she was a child. Maybe that was why she never listened to her complaints about him. Whatever the reason, her mother never really had much time for her, and when the twins were born things had gone from bad to worse. Don cosied up to her of course, but his consolation was for another purpose and soon the situation became intolerable. Her mother knew what he was doing, but her complaints fell on deaf ears. She had run away twice and twice she had been brought back. The third time she made sure no one would find her. Thirteen and homeless on the streets of New York was a tough call. But then the nuns took her in and she lived under their protection, feeding the poor and praying to God to forgive the sinners of the world. It was in the spirit of forgiveness that she eventually tried to effect a reconciliation with her parents. However, a visit to the family home in Staten Island had been a wasted journey. According to neighbours her mother had taken up with another man and was seldom at home. Don had long since been thrown out but one of the neighbours knew where he lived. He had changed his place of abode, she had found, but not his ways. Now he was dead and she was on the run.

Marguerite jumped when the door opened, but it was only one of the girls she shared the apartment with. She had been lucky to get a job in the deli a few streets away and the other two were glad of someone else to share the rent. It was a shabby apartment to say the least, but convenient and just affordable. When the other girl came in she made up her mind. No point in waiting for the police to call. She would go back to Staten Island, confront her mother – if she could find her – and maybe get the documents she needed.

She was tempted to take the ferry back, but decided not to risk it. She feared the police might now be on the lookout for the nun who had called to some of the houses asking the occupants if they knew where Don Diego lived. And the young policeman she had met on the ferry might just remember her. So she decided to go by bus, just as soon as she got paid.

The house where Marguerite had spent her childhood was on the other side of Staten Island, well away from where Don had spent his last days. As she approached it on foot, it occurred to her that the police might be there, perhaps to interview her mother. There was no sign of them but it was with a feeling of trepidation that she stopped on the opposite side of the road and looked up at it. Wooden in structure, it backed on to the woods – the same woods, she recalled, where Don used to take her. It was for target practice, he would tell Nora, practice with his little silvery pistol. But she knew full well what he was up to. She had to. Who in their right mind would think a young girl needed to be shown how to fire a gun?

The house, Marguerite found, had been broken into, which wasn't surprising since Nora was seldom there. Vandals had gained entry by breaking the glass in a rear window. It was now boarded up, but she had no problem forcing open the little side window by which she had left many years before. Contents of cupboards and drawers were strewn all over the place and it quickly became apparent that the house had been ransacked. It was the same in the garage attached to the house. The cover of Don's old roller-top desk which had never opened very easily had been torn off and numerous brown envelopes and letters were scattered across the floor. She picked up some of the letters and smiled. The thieves must have been greatly disappointed to discover they were demands for unpaid bills. Most had been sent to his original house on Long Island and re-directed by the new occupants. A few more envelopes remained in the desk, abandoned by the robbers when they had found nothing but bills.

In the hope of finding a birth certificate, she opened a few of them only to find more bills. Then she came across two containing acknowledgements for payments of $250 each. They pre-dated the demands for unpaid bills by some years and had become faded with time. However, she was able to read them. Attached to one was a short letter saying, *Dear Mr. Diego, Thank you for your latest donation. Mother Benignius asks me to convey her appreciation and assure you that it will be put to good use. I hope the baby is well and that you are happy with our little 'transaction'. Signed N. Gaynor.*

Marguerite read the letter again. It had a Dublin, Ireland address and was dated 1957. That was the year she had been born. And if, as she now knew, she was adopted, it must have referred to her. But what did it mean, 'our little transaction'?

In the absence of her mother, Marguerite realised that the only person who might know what the letter meant was the woman in black. As the nurse who had brought her here, she might also be able to tell her where she could get a birth certificate.

FIVE

Detective Florentine sat back in his car and looked at the report form on the clip board in front of him. The DD5, as it was known, was the bane of his life. Indeed, it was the bane of every detective's life when he was in charge of a case. It had to be filled in every week, outlining for the information of his superiors the progress that had been made. The problem was that, as far as the Diego investigation was concerned, there was very little progress to report. And Florentine knew that if there was nothing to report, Lieutenant Jacobs wouldn't be happy. He would want to know what the problem was.

Leaving aside the DD5, Florentine looked again at the questionnaire they had used and wondered. As an officer of some considerable experience, he was aware that if a policeman asked the right question, he stood a good chance of getting the right answer. Conversely, if he asked the wrong question, he stood a good chance of getting the wrong answer. Even the way he asked was important. Ask nicely and some old dear might give him a vital piece of evidence. Ask in a threatening or overbearing manner, and he got nothing.

The canvass of the area had drawn a blank. No one had seen any suspicious characters hanging around. In fact, no one had seen anything suspicious at all. And that, as far as Florentine was concerned, was just not possible. A killer could not come and go without being seen. He wasn't invisible. If the residents hadn't seen him, then maybe someone else had.

'You know, Sully,' he said. 'I'm beginning to think that maybe we didn't go about this thing the right way.'

Sullivan, who was in the process of finishing off a burger, asked, 'How do you mean?'

'The canvass. Maybe we didn't ask the right questions.'

'But they were standard.'

'I know, I know. But I think we're going to have to do it again.'

Sullivan wiped his lips and put the remains of the burger in a paper bag for disposal later. 'You mean you want us to do it all again?'

Florentine sighed. 'I'm sorry, Sully, but there's no other way.'

'The boys will love that.'

'Well, it can't be helped. The people in this neighbourhood must have seen something. Maybe if we changed tack. Instead of asking them if they saw anybody suspicious hanging around, just ask them if they saw anything suspicious. Better still, just ask them if they saw anything at all that day.'

'You mean, anything unusual?'

'Yeah. Anything unusual. Anything they can remember. Maybe something they didn't think was important. It just might be important to us.'

'Okay, but I wouldn't say the team will be over the moon when they hear this.'

'So, what about it? They might as well be occupied doing that as anything else. And Sully.'

'Yeah?'

'Tell them to ask nicely. You know, the way you would ask your own mother. Some of these people are old. They may even be afraid of cops. So, gently does it. Right?'

When his partner had gone, Florentine went back to his office and rang his wife to tell her he wouldn't be home for lunch. Not that Maria was expecting him, but it was nice to talk to her, even if it was to say he wouldn't be home. Then he opened the file on Don Diego and went through it again.

The profile that had emerged from their inquiries was of a man whose violent tendencies had gone up as his career had gone down. While there were many plush houses on Staten Island, he had been forced to move to an area that was distinctly downmarket. Good looking and a philanderer in his earlier days, he had become a slob whose sole interest was drink. He had also earned himself several convictions for assault.

According to Nora Diego, he had also become violent towards her and the children during bouts of drinking. The twins had left when they were old enough and, eventually, Nora said, she too had had enough and followed them. The eldest girl, Marguerite had already left. Apparently she had run away twice, but had been bought back. The third time, she had been old enough to look after herself and hadn't been seen again until Nora pointed her out to them at the funeral.

So why had Don Diego been killed? Had someone he assaulted returned to take revenge? This was a real possibility and one that would have to be checked out. Or had he borrowed money from a loan shark and failed to repay it? That too was possible, considering his circumstances.

Florentine picked up the silver crucifix and looked at it again. Somehow he felt it was the key to what had happened to Don Diego. But where did it fit? Who did it belong to? And how did it come to be lying on the kitchen floor? Nora had confirmed that it did not belong to her. And yet it suggested the involvement of a woman. Had Diego made a move on someone else's wife? Perhaps even been caught in the act by an outraged husband? No, he was no longer the handsome Romeo of his early days. And yet, old habits died hard.

Whatever the motive, Florentine was acutely aware that the investigation was not progressing as well was it should have been. The forensic examination of the house had not produced any more clues. Searches for the murder weapon were continuing, but there was still no sign of it. The questionnaire, he was sure, would have produced something, but it hadn't and he was badly in need of a lead. He closed the file and put away the crucifix with its broken chain. Perhaps, he thought, the team might come up with something in their second canvass of the neighbourhood. If not, he was in deep trouble.

The address given by the woman in black was in the Woodside area of Queens. As Marguerite made her way to it she couldn't help wondering about the things the woman had said to her in the cemetery. If she was the nurse who had brought her to New York, how was it that she was living in New York herself? And what was it she wanted to tell her? Something, she said, that had been on her mind for a long time. But what? For the life of her, Marguerite couldn't imagine what it might be.

By the time the bus arrived in Woodside it was raining heavily. Her inquiries indicated that she had still some distance to walk, but she was determined to press on. The address the woman had given her turned out to be an apartment in an area that had seen better days. So too had the apartment as she found when she climbed the steps and rang the bell.

The woman who answered was wearing a full-length apron and without the black outfit she had worn at the funeral, looked quite different. Her husband was sitting in an armchair, a glass of whiskey in one hand, puffing away with the other, and not surprisingly the apartment reeked of cigarette smoke. He too had a choking smoker's cough and as a non-smoker, Marguerite couldn't help wondering why people inflicted so much hardship on themselves. The woman offered her a chair, but she declined, saying, 'What was it you wanted to tell me?'

'You're drenched,' the woman said. 'Here, take off your coat and I'll get you a towel.'

When Marguerite had towelled her hair, the woman took her into the kitchen saying, 'We can talk here. But first you'll have a coffee to warm you up.'

She also made a coffee for herself, and as they sat facing one another across the kitchen table, Marguerite clasped hers with both hands to warm them and wondered what she was going to hear.

The woman drew deeply on a cigarette. 'I'm sorry,' she said. 'I didn't introduce myself.' She put her hand up to her mouth to try and control a deep chesty cough, and Marguerite could see that like her husband she was a heavy smoker. 'My name's Nancy Gaynor.'

Marguerite was still clasping the coffee mug and didn't shake hands. Instead she was saying to herself, 'So this is the N. Gaynor who wrote the note about *our little transaction*. She wanted to ask her what she had meant by that, but decided it could wait. First she wanted to hear what the woman had to say.

'Would you please tell me what this is all about?'

Mrs. Gaynor put a hand up to her mouth to stifle another cough and seemed to have difficulty in putting whatever she wanted to say into words.

'Tell her,' shouted her husband from the other room. 'Isn't that why you went to the funeral?'

Mrs. Gaynor nodded and gave another slight cough as if to clear her throat. 'As I told you at the cemetery, I was the nurse who brought you here. Don and Nora had visited Ireland at least twice. They had no children of their own, so they decided to adopt a child from the convent where I was a nurse.'

'If you were a nurse back in Ireland how come you're living here?'

'I brought several babies out here for adoption. Not all to New York, of course. But I really loved New York. So we saved up and after a while emigrated. We both lived and worked in various places but finally settled down here in Woodside. There's a great Irish community here and we felt at home.'

'My parents never told me I was adopted,' said Marguerite. 'How do I know this isn't some kind of scam?

'It's no scam,' the woman assured her. 'I know you're mourning the death of Don Diego, but he wasn't your real father.'

'I don't know why you're telling me this, but I don't believe you.'

'Well then, let me think… When you were a baby you had a music box. It was blue, in the shape of a heart. You probably had it for a few years, so you might remember it.' When there was no response, the woman continued, 'I can even tell you the tune it played. *O Dear, what can the matter be*? Am I right?'

Marguerite nodded and lowered her head. 'I still have it.'

'Well, maybe now you'll believe me.'

Marguerite's mind was in turmoil. In spite of what the woman had said about the music box, she still wondered if this was some kind of scam.

'If what you say is true, what do you hope to get out of it?' she asked.

'Well, I'd happily settle for peace of mind.'

Marguerite looked at the woman, wondering who she really was and what she meant. She had thought a lot about their first meeting in the graveyard, and it was far from peace of mind that she herself had got. She had gone over and over it so many times, for if it was true that she was adopted it would explain a lot. Her mother's attitude, for example. The way she had turned against her when the twins arrived. Her father's attitude too. Yes, it would do a lot to explain her father's attitude and a very unhappy childhood in general.

Mrs. Gaynor expelled a long plume of blue smoke. 'Don and Nora were living in Long Island at the time. I came over with you on a liner.'

'When exactly was that?'

'1957. Which means you're thirty-one now – right?'

Marguerite nodded. 'So I was someone else's baby?'

'I'm afraid so.'

'But how could anyone give their baby away?'

'Well, in Ireland in the fifties, babies were given away for adoption almost every day.'

Marguerite put her head in her hands, saying, 'I still find it hard to believe.' She looked up. 'I mean, you turn up out of the blue and tell me I was adopted – something my parents never told me. Why tell me now? And at my father's funeral of all places?'

Mrs. Gaynor gave another choking cough and when it had subsided she said, 'As you can probably gather, I'm not a well woman and certain things have been on mind lately – things I think you should know about. Unfortunately I didn't know where to contact you until I saw Don's death notice in the paper.'

'What things?' asked Marguerite. 'You mean there's more?'

Mrs. Gaynor nodded. 'As I say, in Ireland in the fifties babies were given away for adoption almost every day. But in your case, it was different.'

As Marguerite listened, she began to comprehend for the first time the deeper implications of what she had been told. If she had been adopted it meant that her childhood should not have been the nightmare it was, her life should not have turned out the way it did, and the shooting of Don

46

Diego should never have occurred.

Struggling to make sense of it all, she gladly accepted another mug of coffee saying, 'I don't understand. You said that in Ireland back then babies were given away almost every day for adoption. How was it different in my case?'

Mrs. Gaynor lit another cigarette. 'Well,' she said, drawing the smoke deeply into her lungs, 'it may seem strange today, but in the part of Ireland where your mother grew up – that's your real mother I'm talking about – there was no such thing as contraception.'

'How come?'

Mrs. Gaynor shrugged. 'Contraception was against the teaching of the Catholic Church, so the sale of contraceptives was banned. Anyway, I doubt if people like your mother would have used them – not in rural Ireland. They were too religious.'

'What were they supposed to do then?'

'They were supposed to wait, or should I say, they were expected to wait until they were married before having sex. And so, if a young woman made a mistake – if she got pregnant before she was married – it brought great shame on her family. It was all right if the young man responsible agreed to marry her. Then a marriage would be quickly arranged and their secret would be safe.'

'But that meant they had to get married whether they loved one another or not?'

Mrs. Gaynor nodded. 'The important thing was that the pregnancy should be covered up. They were called shotgun marriages. And usually they worked out quite well.' She shrugged. 'I suppose they had no option. There was no such thing as divorce either.'

Mrs. Gaynor sipped her coffee. 'There was also no such thing as abortion available to a young woman who found herself in that position. And if, as often happened, the man refused to marry her, she would have to leave home rather than bring shame on her parents.'

'So what did she do?'

'Well, it was the Catholic Church who opposed contraception in the first instance, so the nuns ran homes for unmarried mothers. Mother and baby homes they were called. The girls would pretend they had gone to Dublin or to England to work, while in reality they were working in the homes and giving birth to their babies. Shortly afterwards the babies were given up for adoption, the girls returned home and no one was any the wiser.'

'But how could they give away their own babies? It must have been a very difficult thing to do.'

'It *was* difficult, very difficult. Even for girls who were pregnant for the second or third time. I was working in a home in Dublin and I was bringing out a baby belonging to a young woman called Bridie Flynn for adoption.'

Marguerite now realised that if what Mrs. Gaynor was saying was true, the baby she was talking about was her. That would mean Bridie Flynn would have been her real mother.

'Bridie was from Dublin,' Mrs. Gaynor continued, 'and she had been in the home at least once before, if not more…'

'What was my name? I mean, her baby's name?'

'Brigid Mary. But sometimes we would get a girl who would refuse to give her baby away, and a girl like that was travelling with me. Her name was Catherine. She had arranged to come out to New Jersey, baby-sit for her aunt and bring her baby with her. Poor Catherine. She was from Tipperary. She only made one mistake and she paid dearly for it.'

'And what did she call her baby?'

'Katie. They travelled with me and Bridie's baby on the liner.'

'So I'm Brigid Mary?'

'Well…' When Mrs. Gaynor didn't answer her husband shouted from the next room again, 'Tell her. Get it off your chest once and for all.'

'No, actually. You see, that's the problem. I think you may be Katie.'

Marguerite's mouth dropped open. 'But how? I… I… don't understand.'

Mrs. Gaynor gazed into her coffee cup and shook her head. 'It's difficult to know where to begin.'

Marguerite was looking at her intently now, wondering what she was going to hear next.

'You see, the main concern of the Catholic Church was that the adoptive parents should be Catholics. The Diegos also had the added advantage that Mrs. Diego was of Irish extraction. Anyway, I was taking little Brigid Mary out to them and Catherine was bringing Katie out to raise her as her own. Everything was arranged and we set sail from Cobh in County Cork on the liner *Atlantia*. Nothing, it seemed, could go wrong. But it did go wrong. Horribly wrong.'

She stubbed out her cigarette. 'We weren't long under way when Catherine became ill. The ship's doctor said it was some kind of virus and that, with the sea air, it would soon clear up. But it didn't. In the meantime, I was left to look after both babies.'

'But if I'm Katie, how come I was the one that ended up with the Diegos, not Brigid Mary?'

Mrs. Gaynor lit another cigarette and took a long pull to calm her nerves. 'That's what I want to talk to you about. But not now.' She got up and opened the drawer of a cupboard behind her saying, 'First I want you to read this.' She took a notepad from the drawer and sitting down again, slid it across the table.

'What is it?'

'When Catherine became ill she decided to write it all down. She said that if anything happened to her, she wanted her daughter to read it some day so that she would know everything that had occurred. If I'm right, and you are Katie, then it's for you.'

'So she didn't survive the journey?'

Mrs. Gaynor shook her head. 'No. I'm sorry.'

Marguerite's eyes misted over and she sniffed to clear them. The notepad, she saw, was headed RMS *Atlantia*. It was filled with small, neat handwriting and began, *My Dearest Katie…*

'She filled several notepads like that. I can't lay my hands on the others at the moment, but, don't worry, I'll find them. Some of her letters too. Then maybe we can meet again.'

'When?'

'How about this day week? That should give me enough time.'

'Where?'

'No use dragging you all the way out here again. And I always enjoy a day in Manhattan. Do you know Pete's Tavern? John and I used to go there when we were younger. It's at the corner of East 18th Street and Irving Place. Near Gramercy Park.'

Marguerite was already putting on her raincoat. She stuffed the notebook into her pocket, saying, 'No, but I'll find it.'

SIX

Detective Sullivan didn't think the second canvass of the area had been much more revealing than the first. However, Florentine was well pleased. This time a number of residents reported that a nun had called at their door on the day of the murder. Furthermore, she had inquired if they knew where Don Diego was living. On its own, this might not be very important. But… He opened his hand to look at the silver crucifix once more.

'What do you think?' asked Sullivan.

'I think it might be hers.'

'How come?'

Florentine looked at the broken chain. 'I don't know. Unless she walked in on something.'

'You mean, she may have witnessed the murder? Maybe even tangled with the killer herself?'

'Could be.' Florentine put the crucifix away. 'I tell you what. Put the word out that we're looking for a nun as a possible witness. But say nothing about the crucifix. We'll keep that up under wraps for the time being.'

Florentine reached for a DD5. Now, at last, he had something to report. A lead that might take them to the killer. But first they had to find out how the nun came to be in the neighbourhood, how she left, and where she went. Then, with a bit of luck, they might find out who she was and what she was doing there.

Marguerite sat down at the table in her dingy apartment. Outside, neon lights flashed on and off in a world to which she felt she no longer belonged. If what Mrs. Gaynor had told her was true, Don Diego was not her father and Nora was not her mother. She hadn't even been born in America, but was the illegitimate daughter of some Irish girl, born in a home for unmarried mothers in Dublin. But who was she? And who was her real mother, this woman called Catherine?

Eager to find the answers to these questions, she switched on the reading lamp and unrolled the notepad from the RMS *Atlantia*. For a while it had seemed she would never have the privacy to read what was in it. The others who worked with her in the delicatessen would, she feared, be looking over her shoulder to see what she was reading and that was something she was anxious to avoid. But now, at long last, they were at work and she had the apartment to herself.

She looked again at the neat, closely penned text which, according to Mrs. Gaynor, her birth mother had written for her. It was dated, 14th July, 1957, and read,

My Dearest Katie, I am writing this on the liner Atlantia as I voyage to America. I want you to read it some day – some day when you are old enough. Where you will be then or where I will be, God alone knows, as I must confess I do not feel at all well and am beginning to fear I may not survive this voyage. But whether I do or not, I want you to read what I am writing. I made one mistake. One silly mistake and I am paying dearly for it. Not as dearly, perhaps, as some others I have met. Nevertheless, it has changed my life forever and I don't want you to make the same mistake. I also want you to know who I was and who you are.

It is now two days since we sailed from Cobh in Co. Cork, yet the music of the band as we set sail is still ringing in my ears. Somehow I feel so guilty – not guilty about having you, I must add. I am so so proud of you; you look lovely and I will always cherish you. But I feel so guilty about having deceived my parents. As we drew away from the quayside, the band was playing 'The Holy Ground', and some of the passengers were singing it, knowing in their hearts and souls, I suspect, that they might never see it again.

And still I live in hope to see the Holy Ground once more –

Fine girl you are!

That's how the song goes, and it has always been the custom to sing the last line with great gusto. *Fine girl you are!* But it was far from a fine girl I felt. There I was, waving farewell to the family I loved, the mother and father who had reared me and loved me, the brothers and sister I had played with and fought with… and all the time I was deceiving them. Somehow they looked so small and forlorn on the quayside. They were crying because they were losing me. I was crying for them too – and for someone else I was losing – but above all, at that moment I was also crying for what I had done to them. But what else could I have done? When I discovered I was pregnant, I couldn't tell my parents. It would have broken their hearts. And of course, it wasn't something I could tell my brothers, or my sister, Susan. She's only twelve. So I told them I was going to Dublin to work, when in reality I was going to a mother-and-baby home to have my baby.

When I was leaving for America and I visited them for the last time, they gave me such a wonderful send-off. They even got Peadar MacIlfadda to come with his accordion and play for us. Peadar is the best accordion player in the county, if not the whole country. They say his name comes from the Gaelic and means Peadar of the Long Elbow. But whether that's true or a makey-up name the locals gave him, I don't know. All I know is that once he straps on his accordion and his long elbows start to pump it, the result is magical. Friends and neighbours came from far and wide and they danced and sang until the small hours of the morning. Mostly songs of emigrant ships and emigrants, and, of course, hopes of coming back to be reunited with loved ones. And then, when they had all wished me well and taken their leave, my mother called me into her bedroom and gave me a silver locket her mother had once given to her. I can still see my father standing in the doorway. He looked distinctly uncomfortable in his best cap and suit, but he was smiling. A sad smile if there can be such a thing. But you know what I mean. A loving smile, and he told me, 'Just a little something to remember us by.' His words brought tears to my eyes and I hugged them both and cried. They cried too, and then we all knelt beneath the picture of the Sacred Heart in the kitchen, elbows on the chairs – the way we always used to do – and recited a decade of the Rosary.

The red light that burns dimly at the bottom of the Sacred Heart picture is the only one that is never extinguished in our house. But later, in Cobh, when *we were saying our good-byes, Susan told me that before my mother went to bed, she lit a small oil lamp and placed it in the window. That saddened me too, for I knew it would burn in the window until I returned, just as my absence would burn in their hearts.*

And so it was with a heavy heart that I bade them all farewell at Cobh. I had long planned to go to New Jersey and help look after Aunt Lily's children. Ed and herself have eight, and when I told them I was pregnant, they said to come on out, that one more wouldn't make any difference. I had to make them swear not to tell my parents, of course. Funny how I could tell them, but not my own parents. The nuns in the home where you were born made all the arrangements. Nurse Gaynor, who is bringing another baby out to America for adoption, took both of you on board long before we arrived at Cobh. And so my parents were none the wiser. But why, you may ask could I not tell them? And how did I come to be pregnant in the first place?

Well, to understand these things, you need to know where I came from and why I did the things I did. The home I am leaving behind is in Tipperary. It's a lovely county where the hawthorn blossoms fall like snow in spring and the rowanberries burn like fire in autumn. It's a county where people fought hard for Ireland's independence from Britain and where they feel strongly about the fact that Britain still governs our six north-easterly counties. They are also strong, hard-working people who get up with the dawn in the Golden Vale and bring their milk to the creamery by ass and cart.

When they're not working they like to drink and sing. They sing about their rebellions and their patriots, about people who had to emigrate through lack of work, and about the loves they have won and lost. They also sing about their mountains and their glens, beautiful glens like the Glen of Aherlow. One mountain in particular has given them their county song – Slievenamon. They sing it on many occasions, and it's a popular party piece when, as I say, they get together for a few drinks.

For all that, they're a very religious people. Catholics would never miss Mass on Sunday, nor would Protestants miss a church service. (Not that I know many Protestants, mind you, but the few I do know seem to be very religious in their own sort of way.) In some places Catholics also celebrate the feast

54

days of saints with what they call patterns. Those are very special days and if there's a holy well they will walk around it saying the Rosary, Hail Marys and Our Fathers for healing and other causes. You may find some of these customs strange, but they are all part of our Catholic culture, a Gaelic culture that has also given us some strange, almost unpronounceable, name-places.

If, as I hope, you will visit Ireland some day, you will find, on the road from Dublin to Cork, a place called Skeheenarinky. To the stranger this may seem a very strange, name indeed, but it comes from the Gaelic, Sceichin a Rince and, I'm told, means the little whitethorn bush of the dancing. Isn't that beautiful? Perhaps it comes from the days when people believed that fairies danced around the whitethorn by moonlight. Who knows? But to this day the whitethorn bushes are considered sacred. No farmer will cut one down and no council will move one, not even for a new road!

I mention Skeheenarinky, not because I come from there but because I spent many happy times beneath a whitethorn up in the mountains with the one I loved, the one I still love. It was our own whitethorn of the dancing, you might say.

It was beyond the Galty Mountains that we met. They are to the south of where we lived, rising above the Glen of Aherlow. I often wondered what lay on the other side of them and, at the age of seventeen I got the opportunity to find out. Work was scarce at home and when Uncle John and Aunt Mags wrote from Mitchelstown to say someone was looking for a young girl to work in one of the big houses, I couldn't wait to leave.

And so it was on the other side of the Galtys – in County Cork to be precise – that I met Shaunie. He was the love of my life. The one I used to walk with through the fields and along the narrow by-roads we call boreens. The one who pulled me up with his fine strong arms at a mountain lake on warm sunny days. The one who chased me around our own whitethorn of the dancing. The one who caught me there and kissed me and promised to love me forever.

So, if this woman Gaynor was right, Marguerite thought, the name of her real father was Shaunie. What a peculiar name. She had come to the end of the notepad and, as she put it carefully away, she wondered what the others would reveal.

SEVEN

The sign above the front door of Pete's Tavern tells visitors that it opened in 1864 and is the oldest original bar in New York City. Marguerite crossed over to Irving Place and after pausing for a moment to read the sign, entered the tavern between people who were seated at tables on the sidewalk. Even though it was not quite lunchtime, the bar was busy and some of the booths opposite were occupied. In the second booth she found Mrs. Gaynor, still dressed in black and sipping a glass of red wine.

As Marguerite slipped into the seat opposite her, Mrs. Gaynor smiled, saying, 'Glad you could come. I take it you had no difficulty finding it?'

Marguerite shook her head and reached for the menu.

'They've a very nice restaurant in at the back, but I prefer to eat out here when I'm having a snack.' Mrs. Gaynor leaned across to look sideways at the menu, adding, 'The mozzarella and tomato salad is lovely. And they're noted for their fried calamari.'

'I'll have the calamari.'

'And I'll have the mozzarella. You'll have a glass of wine?'

Marguerite shook her head and told a waiter, 'Just water.'

As they waited for their food to arrive, Mrs. Gaynor looked around. 'It's lovely, isn't it? They get lots of famous people in here, you know. And it was in this booth that O. Henry wrote *The Gift of the Magi* in 1905. Did you know that?'

'I never heard of him.'

'I didn't either,' Mrs. Gaynor confessed. 'Until I read it up there.'

Marguerite could see that a number of newspaper cuttings on the wall beside them recorded the event, and pushed up to have a closer look. 'O. Henry,' she read to herself, 'was the author's pen name. Real name William Sydney Porter from Greensboro, North Carolina.' She sat back down as the waiter arrived with the food. 'The magi,' she said to him, 'weren't they the three wise men?'

'The very same ma'am. The old guys who brought gifts to Jesus when he was a baby in the manger.'

'And *The Gift of the Magi*? Is that a holy book?'

The waiter smiled. 'Not at all. It's a while since I read it, but from what I recall it's about a couple who gave one another presents they didn't need.'

When the waiter had gone Mrs. Gaynor said, 'I see in the newspapers the police are looking for a nun. They say she may be an important witness. Have they been in touch with you yet?'

'Not yet.' Marguerite took a ring of calamari and dipped it in a bowl of marinara. 'But they have my address. I gave it to them at the funeral.'

'I wonder who killed Don Diego and why?'

'Whatever the reason, it was good riddance.'

'As bad as that?'

Marguerite nodded. 'As bad as that.'

There was another uncomfortable silence, which they filled by concentrating on their food.

'If what you say is true, how come I was given to the Diegos instead of the other baby?'

Mrs. Gaynor stopped eating, a forkful of tomato salad suspended midway between the plate and her mouth. 'It was a…' She put the fork back on the plate. 'It was an unfortunate mix-up.'

'Unfortunate is right.'

'Anyway, I'll tell you about that later, after you've read what your mother – your birth mother – wrote for you. I'd like you to get to know her first.'

'She seems to have been very nice, and I would like to know more about her. But are you sure she was my birth mother? I mean, the last time we met you said you *thought* I was her daughter; you didn't seem to be a hundred per cent certain.'

'Well, let's put it this way. The more I thought about it over the years, the more convinced I became that I was right. And I've brought the other notepads with me so you can read about her yourself.'

'But you knew her. You knew what she was like. Tell me so that I can imagine her when I read them. And tell me about the home where I was born. Tell me everything. I want to know.'

Mrs. Gaynor hesitated. Then, reaching into her handbag again, she said, 'I can do better than that. I can show you what she was like.' Taking out a tattered envelope, she emptied a silver, oval-shaped locket on to the table.

Marguerite examined the locket closely. She could see that the decorative scrolls on the front had almost been worn off with age. 'Is this what I think it is?'

'It was Catherine's. She wanted you to have it.'

'Yes, she wrote about it in her notes. She said her parents gave it to her before she left. And what's this inscription on the back? It's in a foreign language.'

Mrs. Gaynor put on a pair of reading glasses and peered at the faded inscription. 'It's in Irish. It says… Let me see now. It's so long since I spoke the language. It's an old Irish proverb… Good wishes for someone who is leaving home.'

'But what does it say?'

'Well, it begins by saying,

May the road rise to meet you…

May the wind be always at your back'…

She tried to translate the next few lines, but confessed, 'I can't remember it all, but I know it ends by saying…

And until we meet again…

May God hold you in the hollow of His hand…'

'That's beautiful,' said Marguerite, taking the locket back. 'Can I keep it?'

It was the first time Mrs. Gaynor had seen her smile and she smiled back, saying, 'Of course you can. After all, it *is* yours. Why don't you open it?'

'Can I?' Marguerite prised the locket open and found that it contained a tiny photograph of a man and woman. 'Who are they?'

Mrs. Gaynor shook her head. 'I don't really know, but at a guess I'd say they're your mother's parents. And see what's behind it.'

Using her fingernail, Marguerite picked out the photograph and found one of a younger woman underneath. Looking up, she asked, 'Is that…?'

Mrs. Gaynor nodded. 'That's Catherine. That's your mother.'

'She's lovely. What colour was her hair?'

'Auburn. Just like yours, only a bit longer. She wore it down to her shoulders, and turned in at the bottom. That was the fashion in Ireland at the time. It suited her that length, for she was tall and slim – well, you know what I mean – when she got her figure back.'

As Marguerite examined the photograph, Mrs. Gaynor added, 'There's another one behind that.'

Seeing that it was a photograph of a young man, Marguerite exclaimed, 'Then this must be… This must be Shaunie. She wrote about him in her notes.'

'Could be. I mean, who else would she keep in there?'

'So he's my real father then?'

'Well, only Catherine would have known that for sure, but I'd say it's a fair bet that he is. I think you're very like him.'

'Really?'

'Sometimes I can see your mother in your eyes. But then, when I look at that photograph, I think you're like him. And you can see why your mother fell for him. He's very handsome, isn't he?'

Marguerite nodded, and Mrs. Gaynor could see there was a satisfaction in the way she did so, a satisfaction born of the knowledge that she now knew who her real parents were and approved of them.

'So tell me about her,' said Marguerite. 'Tell me everything you can about her. What she was like, I mean, as a person, what the home was like, everything she did when she was there. Who her friends were – everything.'

'Well, it was a long time ago, and yet, it seems as if it was only yesterday. I remember taking Catherine and yourself over to the American Embassy to get your papers sorted out. And I remember the girls in the home playing Elvis Presley songs. Elvis was all the rage at the time. Rock 'n' roll, all that kind of thing. Sometimes I think the girls never played anything else but Elvis.'

Mrs. Gaynor lit a cigarette and, when she had recovered from her first convulsion of coughing, continued: 'Anyway, I suppose you could say we got two types of girls in the home. Well, maybe three, if you take into account the ones who were the victims of rape. But by and large there were two types. There were a few girls who just liked having a good time and who were always getting pregnant. Their children would be adopted and off they would go again. But the majority were the girls like your mother – the ones who had just made one mistake and would never be back again. Sometimes their babies would be adopted, sometimes they would keep them. Your mother was never in any doubt about what she wanted to do. She was determined to keep you.'

The waiter came back and Mrs. Gaynor ordered another glass of red wine. 'The home must have been quite a culture shock for your mother. I gather she came from a family that was fairly religious. You know, mass on Sundays, maybe even during the week as well, the Rosary at night, Sacred Heart lamp – all that sort of thing. Of course, the girls in the home had to attend mass in the convent chapel every Sunday too but, apart from that, it was a very different home to the one Catherine was used to.'

'In what way?'

'Well, for a start, the language of some of those ladies was anything but ladylike – especially our regular customers. It was always f... this and f... that. Sister Aloysius tried to get them to stop using the f... word, for it sounded terrible. But she was wasting her time. And they never seemed to talk about anything else but sex. You would think they would have learned their lesson after their pregnancy, but no, some of them never seemed to learn.'

'Did my mother use bad language?'

Mrs. Gaynor shook her glass slightly so that the wine swirled around inside. 'Of course not. I told you. Catherine wasn't like that. Mother Benignius had a saying that only the good girls got pregnant, and in a way it was true.'

'What did she mean by that?'

'Well, I suppose she meant that the good girls didn't know any better. They didn't know how to avoid it – and they only got pregnant once. The ones who kept coming back to us knew well how to avoid it, but I suppose they just didn't care.'

'Did they ever talk about the fathers?'

'No – at least, not to us.' Mrs. Gaynor smiled. 'When it came to filling in the birth certs some of our regular customers claimed that Willie D was the father.'

'Willie D? Who was he?'

'He was a soccer star of the fifties. I can't remember his second name. Jones or James, I'm not sure. Apparently he was a great man for dribbling the ball down the field, so he was known as Willie the Dribbler, or Willie D.'

'But surely he couldn't have been the father, could he?'

'Not at all. But that's what they said. Needless to say they weren't going to tell *us* who the real father was. In some cases they probably didn't even know themselves. So I suppose the name Willie the Dribbler appealed to their coarse sense of humour, if you know what I mean.'

Seeing that Marguerite didn't know what she meant, she explained. 'In Ireland the word willie is slang for the thing that makes you pregnant.'

Marguerite looked at her for a moment, then realising what she meant, said, ' Oh yeah. Of course. Very funny!' At the same time she was thinking what a weird world Catherine had found herself in and asked, 'How did she – how did my mother get on with the others?'

Mrs.Gaynor lit another cigarette. 'Well, some of the ones who had been in the home before would try and take the mick out of people like Catherine, especially if they were from the country.'

'The mick? I don't understand.'

'Oh, sorry. In Ireland, taking the mick out of someone means making fun of them, or making little of them, you know, teasing them. The dubs, that's the girls from Dublin, would call the ones from rural areas culchies or rednecks. That put them outside their own circle, made them feel isolated. But Catherine was lucky. She had a great friend in Bridie Flynn. Remember, I told you about her and her baby, Brigid Mary? Well, as I told you the last time, Bridie had been in the home before – two or three times, if my memory serves me right. She was a small, dumpy little thing with short black hair. And her language was dreadful. But she took Catherine under her wing, you know, befriended her and looked after her. In fact, she was fiercely protective of anyone who became her friend and she made sure no one teased Catherine or took advantage of her.'

'That was nice.'

'I remember Catherine showing me the new outfit she'd bought for the voyage. She said Bridie had gone in to Dublin with her and helped her to choose it. Afterwards she took her up to the top of Nelson's Pillar and showed her the sights. You could see the whole of Dublin from the top of it, it was so high'

'As high as the Empire State Building?'

Mrs. Gaynor smiled. 'Ah no. It was probably very small in comparison, but we thought it was high. Bridie also persuaded her to go to a dance in Clerys one night, but I don't think she was in the mood for dances.'

'How come?'

'Well, I remember she came back early on her own. I reckon she had her mind set on going to America and didn't want to let anything change that – you know, like meeting a new boyfriend. Bridie, of course, would have been looking forward to a bit of action, but not Catherine.'

Mrs. Gaynor reached over and put her hand on the back of Marguerite's hand in a gesture of friendship. 'You see, what I'm trying to tell you is that your mother was an innocent abroad compared with some of the others. She was a lovely person. A bit like Father Michael, I suppose. Poor Father Michael. He was an innocent abroad too. Young, good-looking. Imagine putting a young priest like him into the home as chaplain. Sure it was like throwing him to the lions. They nearly ate him.'

'Why, what happened to him?'

Mrs. Gaynor stubbed out her cigarette in the ashtray and lit another. 'Well, he was hardly in the door when some of them started making eyes at him. You know, flirting with him any opportunity they got. I suppose one thing led to another, for I heard afterwards that Mary O'Reilly – she was one of our regular customers – had put on some kind of bet that she could seduce him. Or maybe it was a dare, I don't know. But imagine: a priest, in there to try and look after their spiritual welfare and they wanted to seduce him!'

Marguerite took another sip of wine. 'And did they? I mean, did she?'

Mrs. Gaynor blew out a long stream of blue smoke. 'Of course she did! I'll never forget it. Mother Benigius nearly blew her top. And Sister Aloysius wasn't much better…' She coughed again and when the coughing had subsided she said, 'Anyway, enough about that.' Taking several more notepads from her handbag, she added,

'You'll find out all you want to know about her in these.'

EIGHT

In some precincts what were known as 'skull' sessions were held every week, usually on Fridays to review important cases and during one of these sessions Florentine briefed several officers who had been asked to help them with their enquiries. He outlined the circumstances in which Don Diego had been found, gave the gist of the forensic and pathological examinations and showed the areas where searches for the murder weapon were still being carried out. He also listed the results of enquiries he and his partner had already made in their efforts to track down the killer.

Two people Diego was known to have assaulted had been traced and were being checked out, while the whereabouts of two others were unknown. He owed money to various people but, according to the lenders, they were only small sums. Whether or not more was involved and whether welching on them might have amounted to a motive for murder, still had to be determined. As for his love life, he had been cited once as co-respondent in a divorce case, but that had been a long time before and was no longer considered relevant. Whether or not he had since incurred the wrath of another jealous husband would require more work and, it was generally agreed, would be difficult to establish.

'I still think the nun is our best lead,' said Florentine, dangling the silver crucifix from his right forefinger. 'We've established that she was in the neighbourhood on the day of the murder, knocking on doors and asking people where Diego lived. This crucifix was found on the kitchen floor, and if it's hers, it places her at the scene of the crime. Even if it's not, it's likely that she did call at Diego's house and it's possible that she may have seen the killer.'

'Maybe,' said Sullivan, 'she found the door open, walked in and witnessed the shooting. Who knows, maybe the killer even tried to kill her too and the crucifix was torn off in the struggle?'

'You say in your report,' said Lieutenant Jacobs, 'you've now established that she got a bus as far as the ferry. That would indicate that she may have come from Manhattan.'

Florentine nodded. 'That sighting was the day after the murder. We're trying to discover where she spent the night.'

'And, of course,' Jacobs added, 'you'll have to find out if anyone saw her on the ferry.' He got up to indicate that the session was at an end. 'Right then, all these things will have to be followed up and that's going to take a lot of leg work. Let me know how you get on.'

Florentine had also asked for the deployment of uniformed officers on the ferries to see if they could get a lead on the nun. For a while it seemed that the move was a waste of valuable manpower, but then came the break he was looking for.

Many of those who commuted on the ferries each day just stared vacantly ahead during the 20-minute crossing, minding their own business and not really noticing what other people were doing. One black woman who was asked by a uniformed officer if she had seen a nun on the ferry on the date in question, said it was all she could do to keep an eye on her children.

As the officer talked to the woman one of those children, a young boy, tugged at the leg of his trousers. He brushed the boy away and continued to question the woman.

'Why don't you ask him if he seen anything?' said the woman at last. 'I sure as hell ain't.'

Exasperated by the lack of co-operation he was getting, the officer went up to the food counter and ordered a hot dog. As he waited, he felt a tug on the leg of his trousers again and looked down to see the same boy standing beside him. 'Now listen, son,' he said, 'go over there and sit with your mother.'

'I seen a nun,' said the boy, standing his ground.

'Your hot dog, officer,' said the man behind the counter.

The officer put his hand up saying, 'Just a minute. Just a minute,' and bent down to the look into the face of the boy. 'What did you say?'

'I seen a nun.'

The officer took the hot dog, gave it to the boy and guided him gently across the deck to an empty bench. There he sat him down in front of him and, leaning forward, asked him intently, 'Now, when did you see this nun?'

'We were on the way back to Staten Island. Say, can I have more mustard?'

'Right, right. But don't you move. You hear?'

The boy was still there when the officer returned, but by this time his mother and the other children had come over to join him.

'They like hot dogs too,' said the woman.

The officer sighed. 'All right. I'll be right back. And I suppose they all want plenty of mustard?'

'You got it. And I like plenty of ketchup.'

The officer raised his eyebrows as if to say, 'I should have known.' Standing with his back to the counter while his order was being made, he wondered for a moment if he was being taken for a ride. But no, he assured himself, the boy didn't seem to be making it up.

'Now,' he said, when they were all munching their hot dogs, 'tell me again, son. You say you saw a nun?'

'I told you,' said the woman. 'You should have asked him in the first place.'

'Please ma'am. Let the boy speak.' Turning to the boy again, he said, 'Now this nun, was she young or old?'

The boy wiped a dollop of mustard from the side of his mouth with the back of his hand and said, 'She was old.'

'Maybe she was, but then again, maybe she wasn't,' the woman cautioned. 'You see, he thinks anyone older than himself is old.'

Unable to quarrel with the logic of that, the officer nodded. 'Right,' he told the boy. 'Describe her to me.'

'Well, I was sitting here and she was sitting there, just like you are. She was wearing this blue and white thing on her head and she had blue socks and everything.'

'He means tights,' said the mother.

'And she had a cross around her neck,' said the boy, 'with God on it. I asked her if she was a nun and she said she was.'

'Good for you. You're very observant. This may be important.'

'Will I get a reward?'

The officer smiled. 'How about another hot dog?'

'Let the boy finish,' said the mother.

'But he has finished. That's why I asked him if wanted another hot dog?'

'I don't mean that. The woman shifted her considerable weight with some irritation. 'I mean, let him finish telling you about the nun.'

'You mean there's more?'

The boy nodded.

'What?'

'I asked her what her name was?'

'You did?'

The boy nodded again. 'She said she was Sister Mary.'

Marguerite was immersed in the notepads when a colleague returning from work informed her that someone called Florentine had phoned the deli looking for her. Her heart sank, and fearing that they might have given him the address of the apartment, she picked up the notepads and left. Out on the street she checked to see if there was any sign of the police, and when she saw none, hurried over to a nearby park. There she sought out a secluded bench beneath the trees and wondered what to do.

After much thought, Marguerite realised that unless she got another job and another place to live, there was nothing she could do, except keep out of Florentine's way. From the shade of the trees she watched people come and go, in case Florentine or other policemen might have tracked her down. However, it soon became clear that that she hadn't been followed. Nevertheless, the sound of an occasional police car racing along the street, siren blaring made her jumpy. But then, she told herself, the police were always doing that and after a while she convinced herself that for the moment at least, she was safe. So she unrolled the notepads again and checked that they were in chronological order. But before continuing to read them she reflected on what she now knew about her adoption.

From what Mrs. Gaynor had told her, and from what she had already read, she had gained a good insight into what life had been like for her birth mother in the home in Dublin. Mrs. Gaynor had told her everything she could remember, up to the time they had returned from the American Embassy. However, she hadn't told her about the mix-up that had resulted in her being handed over to the Diego family instead of the other baby.

Mrs. Gaynor had suggested they meet in a week's time at Battery Park where the ferries took tourists out to see the Statue of Liberty and Ellis Island. Why she had chosen Battery Park as a meeting place Marguerite didn't know, but another trip down town would be worth it if she could get to the bottom of the affair. Furthermore, Mrs. Gaynor had promised to bring her more of Catherine's personal possessions. She was curious to know how Mrs. Gaynor had come to have these. However, all she would say was that they were letters and things that she had promised to pass on to her.

Marguerite fingered the silver locket which she was now wearing around her neck, and thought of the heart-shaped music box which her birth mother had played to her when she was a baby. Having leafed through the latest notes and picked out a few points here and there, she now knew why the box was blue instead of pink. It had come from Catherine's aunt in New Jersey. Not brand new but probably a welcome present for someone who had found herself in such a predicament – like the baby clothes her aunt had also sent. Anxious not to miss anything, she went back over the notes and read them line by line.

When Aunt Lily and Uncle Ed went to America, Catherine wrote, *they never forgot the rest of us back home in Tipperary. They knew times were hard – after all, that was why they went away – and the parcels of clothes we got from America are among my happiest memories. Their arrival was always occasions of great excitement and they wouldn't be opened until everyone was present. To prevent a scramble, my mother would do the honours, peeling back the layers of paper carefully in case she might damage anything. As we watched, my brothers* and I would be bursting with anticipation, waiting to see what the parcel contained and if there was anything in it for us. Inevitably, of course, two of us would lay claim to the same thing and a row would break out. However, a stern word from Dad and a threat from Mother not to give us anything at all, soon sorted that out.

When I was in the home in Dublin, the other girls were just as excited as I was if Aunt Lily sent me a parcel of baby clothes. Their eyes nearly popped out of their heads and there were ooh's and ah's as I rooted in the box and held each item up for them to see. And it was no wonder, for there were beautiful pink dresses embroidered with hearts, frilly knickers with floral designs, woollen jackets with teddy-bear mittens attached to the sleeves, bootees with tassels of red, white and blue and, would you believe it, earmuffs. 'Well, that's good one,' I remember Bridie Flynn saying, 'muffs to keep the baby's ears warm. It would take the Yanks to think of a thing like that.' But then, as Sister Aloysius remarked, the Americans have their own way of doing things. Sister Aloysius, by the way, was very good to me, but the other girls didn't like her. They said she was always spying on them and I won't tell you what they called her behind her back!

Everyone was amazed to hear that Lily and Ed had eight children, but it explained why they were able to send so many clothes. And they didn't look like cast-offs. In fact, they looked as if they were brand new. When I chose the clothes I wanted for you, I gave some to Bridie for her child and what was left over I gave to Sister Aloysius to distribute as she saw fit. Then Bridie found something among the wrapping paper that we had overlooked. It was a blue heart-shaped music box with a blue ribbon on top and a cord underneath. It must have belonged to one of Lily's boys. But, pink or blue, it didn't matter. When Bridie pulled the string, it played 'Oh dear, what can the matter be?' It was lovely and I often played it to get you to sleep. However, I must confess that the first time Bridie sang the words of it, I felt as if they were plucking at the strings of my own heart. 'O dear, what can the matter be, Johnny's so long at the fair.' I know it's just a nursery rhyme, but somehow the words reminded me of my own dear Shaunie and what happened to us.

Here, it seemed to Marguerite, Catherine had taken a break for there was a gap and a couple of smudges on the paper.

Anyway, it was great for getting you to sleep – that and a little lullaby called
The Monkey Song. It was a silly little song, but if the music box didn't get you
to sleep, it seemed to do the trick. How did it go now?

I will-a-lish I lill-a-lived in mull-a-lunkey la-la-land
The la-la-land where I-la-li was boll-a-lorn
A mull-a-lunkey kill-a-lissed me oll-a-lon the chill-a-leek
And will-a-laved good bal-a-lye to all-a-all…

It just means…

I wish I lived in monkey land
The land where I was born
A monkey kissed me on the cheek
And waved good bye to all…

As I say, a bit silly, but I would sing it to you and sometimes Bridie would
sing it to her baby. When we were sorting out the clothes, I told Bridie about
the great fun my friend Eileen and I used to have with some of the things that
came from America, especially the long clothes and the high heels. Of course,
I couldn't wait to grow up, and when I was 13 or 14, Lily sent me this lovely
flared dress. Flared dresses were all the rage and I was always trying to stiffen
the underskirt with starch until one day my uncle who works in the Sugar
Company in Thurles, told me sugar was the best thing to use. He was always
bringing us sugar and we had loads of it. Anyway, I used sugar instead of starch
and it was great. I had the stiffest dress in town. Of course, I thought I was
the bee's knees. Then one day, I washed it and hung it out on the line to dry. It
must have been very stormy, for the next thing I knew, the dress was in shreds.
I thought at first that somebody had torn it, but my mother told me it was the
sugar. It must have rotted it! Well, it wasn't funny at the time, but Bridie and I
had a good laugh when I told her about it. She said I was a right eejit.'

New Jersey was only across the Hudson River from Manhattan and
Marguerite wondered if Lily and Ed still lived there. Catherine hadn't
recorded their address in her notes, but perhaps it might be in the letters
that Mrs. Gaynor had promised to give her.

As she continued to pore over the notes, Marguerite thought that
Tipperary sounded like a nice place. The whitethorn of the dancing! How

romantic. Perhaps, some day, if things worked out, she might go to Ireland. She might climb that mountain and find the whitethorn of the dancing. For a moment she could see herself holding on to the trunk of the whitethorn with one hand and swinging around it, just as her mother had done.

Flicking back and forth from one page to anther, she chuckled to herself. Imagine, stiffening a dress with sugar! What a daft thing to do. She smiled. Somehow she got the impression that her mother had a lot of fun when she was young. But what of Shaunie? Why had the nursery rhyme on the music box reminded her of him? Why had the words plucked at her heartstrings the way she said they had done?

Shaunie, Marguerite now knew, was her real father, yet he was the one person in her past that she knew least about. What was he like? she wondered. Tall and certainly handsome if the photograph in the locket was anything to go by. He would probably be about fifty now if he was still alive, but she had no way of knowing if he was alive or dead.

Then there was Catherine's friend, Bridie. She seemed to have been a great character in spite of the fact that she had been in the home more than once. The notes confirmed what Mrs. Gaynor had said: that Bridie had been urging Catherine to 'let her hair down', go to a dance and enjoy herself. Catherine didn't say whether she enjoyed the dance or not, but she did say she enjoyed the view from the top of Nelson's Pillar.

If you ever go to Dublin, she wrote, and I hope some day you will, make a point of going to the Pillar. It's in the centre of O'Connell Street, just opposite the GPO. You will have to climb a hundred and sixty-six steps to get to the top, but it's worth it. You can see the whole city from the top. And it only costs sixpence!

As Marguerite continued to read her mother's notes, she found herself back once more in the Ireland of the fifties. And she wondered once again how she had come to be given away instead of Bridie's baby.

NINE

The newspapers had more or less ignored the Diego murder, simply because it didn't seem to have the makings of a good story. These, as all cub reporters are told, are sex, snobbery and religion, and for a while it seemed that the Diego killing didn't have them. But now things were beginning to change. With the emergence of a nun as a possible witness, the newspapers were becoming interested. Suddenly all the ingredients were there. Don Diego, a former leading man, even if he was, in truth, a bit-piece actor, but by all accounts a very handsome one and a womaniser. That provided the sex. A prosperous real estate agent from a wealthy area of Long Island falling on hard times. That provided the snobbery. And now the NYPD looking for a witness – a nun. That provided the religion.

As a result, the headlines were asking, 'Who is Sister Mary?' They weren't front page headlines, nor were they yet double column. Nevertheless, they had begun to ask the question. So had Detective Florentine. He put his feet up on his desk and studied the display board for the umpteenth time. Below a photograph of Don Diego was the outline of his killer, blank except for a question mark where the face should be. Beside that, the outline of a nun, blank except for the name 'Sister Mary?' Next to that the outline of another person, blank except for words 'loan shark?', and beside that, another outline, blank except for the words 'jealous husband?'

Below the row of blanks was a row of photographs: Diego's wife, Nora, their eldest daughter, Marguerite, and their twins, Felipe and Vitoria.

Getting to his feet, Florentine attached another photograph to the display board to begin a third line. It was a photograph of the boy who had talked to the nun on the ferry. The uniformed officer who had found the boy had done well. The sighting confirmed that the nun had come from Manhattan. It also gave them her name. But where in Manhattan had she come from? That was the question.

'I take it the guys in Manhattan didn't come up with anything?' said Sullivan, when they discussed the matter a short time later.

Florentine shook his head. 'They say it's like looking for a needle in a haystack. Anyway, I suppose they've more important things to be doing than looking for a nun who may or may not have seen a murder on Staten Island.'

'So where do we go from here?'

'Well, Sully, I don't know about you, but I'm going home. With a bit of luck I might be able to spend the weekend with my wife and children. I suppose you're meeting the old man in the Ferryman's?'

'Yeah. But not tonight. I said I'd drive over to his place. Maybe run a few things past him.'

'Once a cop always a cop?'

'Yeah, he likes to hear how thing are going. It helps to keep his mind active. But you needn't worry, he knows how to keep his mouth shut.'

'Oh, I've no worry on that score, Sully. Give him my regards.'

'I will. Thanks.'

'Ciao.'

'Ciao. And tell Maria I was asking for her.'

While Detective Florentine was looking forward to a weekend with his family, Marguerite was looking forward to her next meeting with Mrs. Gaynor at Battery Park. However, it was a meeting Mrs. Gaynor was not looking forward to. When the plane trees were in leaf and the cherry trees in bloom, the park presented an oasis of peace, but she was far from being at peace. She had arrived early and was sitting on a bench trying to read a newspaper to pass the time. She read a report about the Diego murder but found she couldn't concentrate on anything else and put the paper down beside her. A grey squirrel raced down one of the trees and darted out from beneath a hedge to see if a tourist might have left a morsel of food, but if she saw it, it didn't register. All she could think of was what she was going to say to Marguerite. Her conscience had been at her for a long time now, and she knew the time had come when she would have to face up to what she had done.

A shadow fell across her and she looked up to see that Marguerite had arrived. There was plenty of room on the bench, but she moved up a bit anyway, thus inviting her to sit down beside her. 'Did you hear the news?' she said. 'They've identified the nun.' When Marguerite shook her head she continued, 'It's in today's paper. Apparently she spoke to some boy on the ferry. Told him her name was Sister Mary. Here, see for yourself.' As she waited for Marguerite to read the report, she added, 'I wonder if she walked in on the murder?'

Marguerite shrugged. 'If she did, she was lucky she got out.'

'Did you read the other notepads I gave you?'

Marguerite nodded. 'It told me a lot about her – I mean, my mother. She seems to have been very nice.'

'She was.'

'But I still don't know much about my father – Shaunie.'

'Why don't you go to Ireland yourself some day and find out?'

'The thought has occurred to me all right. Tipperary sounds a lovely place.'

'According to Catherine, Shaunie's people had a big farm in Co. Cork. Maybe there's an inheritance waiting for you there.'

'Not if Shaunie is still alive – and I hope he is.'

'Of course. But if you do end up as Lady of the Manor, don't forget who put you there. I wouldn't mind going back to Ireland myself.'

Marguerite managed a faint smile. 'Me? Lady of the Manor?'

'Well, it may not be so far-fetched as you think.' Mrs. Gaynor took another notepad from her handbag. 'Maybe this will help you make up your mind. It's the last one.'

'But I still don't know what happened. You know, how I came to be mixed up with Bridie's baby.'

Mrs. Gaynor got up. 'Let's take a trip out to the Statue of Liberty. We can talk on the ferry.'

They strolled over to Castle Clinton, the brown sandstone fort that housed the ticket office and as Mrs. Gaynor queued for the tickets, Marguerite read a plaque recording the history of the fort and other information posted for the benefit of tourists. While the sky was overcast, it was quite hot and she reckoned it would probably have been hotter but for the breeze coming in from the sea. Yet Mrs. Gaynor, she had noticed, was still wearing the long black coat and black pill-box hat she had been wearing at the cemetery. It was almost as though she was always dressed for a funeral.

The thought made her shiver, so she got up and went out to the seafront where tourists were already beginning to queue for the ferries. The smell of grilling burgers filled the air and, while some people waited for these, others pored over the souvenir stalls, looking for miniatures of the Statue of Liberty, the Empire State Building and anything else that would bring back happy memories of their visit.

When Mrs. Gaynor rejoined her, the sound of Caribbean music came to their ears as some enterprising young men with steel drums conjured up rhythmic images of their homeland in the hope of getting the first queue to part with a few cents.

'The queue for the other ferry's shorter,' said Mrs. Gaynor. 'Let's try it.'

There, a man with an accordion was entertaining those waiting to go on board. When he recognised some of the accents as Irish and saw their smiling faces, he struck up a few bars of 'When Irish Eyes Are Smiling'. This brought loud cheers – and some loose change – from the Irish group, who were in high spirits and felt they couldn't say no.

Lapsing into one of her Irish phrases, Mrs. Gaynor remarked, 'Fair dues to him,' and followed Marguerite on to the ferry.

They made their way up to the top deck and, as the accordion player wooed the last of the passengers to go on board, Marguerite couldn't help thinking of that other accordion player, the one with the strange name of Peadar McIlfadda who had played at the going-away party for her mother in Tipperary. How quaint. And how sad. A going-away party or was it a wake?

While most of the other passengers had eyes only for the panoramic view of Manhattan, with its Twin Towers rising high above its other skyscrapers, Mrs. Gaynor turned her back on them and led Marguerite up towards the bow. There, they found plenty of space to lean on the safety rail, look out to sea and talk.

'Ellis Island,' said Mrs. Gaynor, pointing to their right.

'I know. I've seen it before.'

'Of course.' Mrs. Gaynor lit a cigarette and, even though the wind seemed to whip the smoke away from her, she breathed deeply until she was convulsed by one of her deep congested coughs. 'It's funny,' she said, when she got her breath back, 'but I still think of you as Irish after all these years.'

They were closer to Ellis Island now and could see that the large red brick building on it was dominated by four oriental-looking towers.

'We were told at school that it was used to process immigrants,' said Marguerite. 'Did I – I mean, did we – come through it when I was a baby?'

Mrs. Gaynor was still leaning on the rail, cigarette in hand, her handbag hanging on the crook of the other arm. Without taking her eyes off the island, she shook her head, saying, 'No. It was closed in 1954, and no harm. It was the poor that were processed through there – millions of them. Our boat went right up into New York – 41st Street, as far as I remember. It was so high it must have been two storeys above the wharf.'

'You still haven't told me what happened. I mean, the mix-up.'

'All in good time. First I want you to have a look at some of the other things I brought you.' Mrs. Gaynor rummaged in her bag again and produced a bundle of letters. 'These were your mother's too. You can look at them when we get off.'

Marguerite wrapped the letters in the notepad that Mrs. Gaynor had given her earlier and squeezed them into a pocket of her raincoat. 'Tell me about the music box,' she said.

'What more can I tell you?'

'The nursery rhyme it plays. Catherine said the first time Bridie sang the words, it upset her.'

'*O dear, what can the matter be? Johnny's so long at the fair.* I don't see why that should upset her. Unless there was anything in the rest of it. Can you remember it?'

Marguerite nodded. 'Of course I can. I've known it off by heart since I was a child...'

'*He promised to buy me a basket of posies,*
A garland of lilies, a garland of roses,
A little straw hat to set off the blue ribbons
That tie up my bonny brown hair.'

'I still don't see why that should upset her,' said Mrs. Gaynor.

'Maybe it was a broken promise. She said it reminded her of Shaunie and what had happened to them. Did she never mention it?'

'No. But then, it's not the sort of thing she would discuss with me. All I know is, she hung the music box on the top end of your cot and played it to get you to sleep. Bridie often played it for her child too. The two cots were beside one another.'

'Catherine says they also sang a lullaby called "The Monkey Song". Do you remember it?'

Mrs. Gaynor nodded. 'Of course I do...'

'What does it mean?"

'It's hard to say. As far as the nurses were concerned it was a lullaby. But when the mothers sang it, I often thought it might meant something else.'

'Like what?'

'Well, the bit where they sang, "I wished I lived in monkey land, the land where I was born", I thought maybe they were thinking of home. And the next bit, "a monkey kissed me on the cheek and said goodbye to all", maybe they were referring to the fella who kissed them goodbye and left them to deal with the pregnancy on their own. Then again, maybe they were thinking they would soon have to kiss their babies good bye. Who knows?'

'And how did it go? I mean, if you were to sing it.'

'You want me to sing it?' Mrs. Gaynor gave a deep rattling cough and when she had recovered from it, added, 'In my condition?'

'If you would. Just a little bit – to get the tune of it.'

Mrs. Gaynor looked around to make sure no one else would hear, then coughing again, this time to hide her embarrassment more than to clear her throat, she leaned close to Marguerite's ear and sang as best she could...

'I *wish I lived in monkey land,*
The land where I was born,
A monkey kissed me on the cheek
And waved goodbye to all.'

Having got the tune of it, Marguerite was singing it quietly to herself when, a short time later, the ferry came to a stop at the Statue of Liberty.

It looked as if it was going to rain now, and the passengers who had come on the previous ferry were already queuing on the pier for the return journey. The new arrivals, however, had eyes only for the statue towering above them. 'Three hundred and five feet to the tip of the torch,' someone said. 'Three hundred and five feet one inch,' said another who had read his guidebook more carefully. And while most of them climbed the steps to explore the inner workings of the famous statue, Marguerite searched around for a quiet bench where she could sift through the letters without being disturbed.

Realising that Marguerite needed some time to herself, Mrs. Gaynor went for a stroll among the trees. Occasionally she stopped to light a cigarette or look at the New Jersey coastline. Then she looked at the hunched-up figure on the park bench and wondered how she was going to answer her one remaining question: how she had ended up with adoptive parents in Long Island instead of with her relations in New Jersey.

Marguerite untied the pink ribbon with which the letters were bound. The outside envelopes were yellowed and dog-eared and had taken on a semi-circular shape from being bound so tightly. They had all been sent to Catherine at addresses in Dublin, not the convent home where she had given birth to her baby. Unfurling the letters, Marguerite noted that most were from her parents in Tipperary. One in childish writing was from her sister Susan and one was from her friend, Eileen. The rest were from her Aunt Lily and Uncle Ed in New Jersey. Marguerite looked up. She was just beside New Jersey now – in fact she was looking straight across at it – and she wondered again if Lily and Ed were still living there.

The breeze had turned chilly now and there was also a touch of drizzle in the air. Marguerite put on her headscarf and returned to the pier. A short time later she saw the ferry approaching and while she watched it slow down and dock, her mind was on the precious bundle of letters, and her mother's last notepad, in her raincoat pocket. She kept her hand on them to make sure she didn't lose them, and longed for the moment when she could sit down again and read them.

Mrs. Gaynor joined her and, when the new arrivals had disembarked, they followed the queue until they were on board. Most passengers, they found, were crowding on to the lower decks where they wouldn't get wet, so there was very little space and less privacy.

'Come on,' said Mrs. Gaynor. 'Let's go up on top. If you don't mind getting wet, neither do I.'

Marguerite followed her up to the top deck. All the wooden bench seats were empty but wet, so they leaned on the rails and talked. The only other passengers to come on top were a young couple who were also standing at the rails not far away. They had donned light plastic coats and were undeterred by the drizzle or the slight swell that now seemed to have developed beneath them.

'I don't understand,' said Marguerite.

Mrs. Gaynor closed the lower part of her long black coat to keep her legs dry. 'Understand what?'

'How there could have been such a mix-up?'

In spite of the rain, Mrs. Gaynor lit another cigarette. Once again the smoke provoked a low rattling cough in her lungs and, when it subsided, she said, 'Well, it's difficult to explain. As I told you before, we weren't long into the voyage when Catherine got sick. Some sort of virus they said. We didn't think much of it at first, but somehow I think she had a feeling about it, for she began to write things in those notepads for you.'

Throwing away the half-smoked cigarette, she lit another one before continuing. 'Then she developed a temperature. At that stage I was in my cabin with Bridie's baby and she was next door with her baby. She was burning up and was afraid that, whatever infection she had, her baby might get it too. So she asked me if I would take her baby into my cabin, which I did. She also showed me a cardboard box of letters and things and made me promise that if anything happened to her, I would give them to her baby.'

'Soon after that her condition got worse and the doctor decided to move her to the sick bay.' Mrs. Gaynor bit her lip. 'That's when the problem occurred. You see, the truth is, I got the babies mixed up.'

'But...'

'I know, I know. How could I? But you were both so alike. You were the same age, had the same fair hair, the same blue eyes. One day, after feeding and changing the two of you, I suddenly realised I wasn't sure which one was Katie and which one was Brigid Mary. Sometimes, whatever smile one would give, I thought I knew, but I couldn't be sure.'

Almost as if she was looking at her life going past her, Mrs. Gaynor was gazing down at the growing swell that was now rolling past the side of the ferry, and it seemed to Marguerite that she had suddenly become very old.

'I didn't see Catherine again. She didn't want me to come and see her in the sick bay in case I would take the infection back to the children. Not that it mattered. One of them got it anyway and was taken up to the sick bay too. I thought it was Brigid Mary, but I couldn't be sure. The doctor still couldn't figure out what the virus was, so when the baby got sick he put the sick bay off limits to visitors in case it would spread.'

Mrs. Gaynor's body was wracked with another spasm of coughing and, when she had finally cleared her throat, she said, 'It never really occurred to me that they wouldn't get better and I just couldn't believe it when the doctor came to me to tell me they had both died. I'll never forget his words. "I'm afraid," he said, "I've lost them." "What do you mean, you've lost them?" I said. I must have sounded very stupid, being a nurse and all, but I just couldn't comprehend what he was saying. "Catherine and her baby have both passed away," he said. "I couldn't save them. I'm sorry."'

Once again Mrs. Gaynor discarded her half-smoked cigarette and, for the first time since Marguerite had met her, she continued to talk without smoking. 'That was the moment I have regretted ever since. The moment when I should have spoken up and said, "Hold on a minute. I don't think that was her baby. I think it was Brigid Mary. I think this is Catherine's baby here in the cabin with me." But I didn't, and it has haunted me ever since. Suddenly I was faced with an impossible decision: do I give the baby to a couple who already have eight children of their own, or give her to a couple who have none? It was a bit like O. Henry's 'Gift of the Magi', I suppose. If I was right, and the baby I was left with was Katie, I would be giving the couple in New Jersey a gift they didn't need. At the same time I knew I would be depriving the Diegos of a gift they so dearly wanted.'

Marguerite was staring at her, an expression of incredulity on her face. 'So you kept quiet and said nothing?'

'Somehow I let the moment pass and… I said nothing.' Mrs. Gaynor turned to her, the look on her face pleading forgiveness. 'I know I've done you a terrible wrong. And I'm sorry.'

'You've no idea of the wrong you've done me,' Marguerite sobbed. 'No idea at all.'

'I've regretted it every day since,' Mrs. Gaynor went on. 'Every day and every night. When I returned to Ireland, I couldn't sleep thinking about it. So I persuaded John to come with me to New York to live. I wanted to be near you. To keep an eye on you, make sure you were all right. But when your parents – your adoptive parents – left Long Island, I lost touch with them. Then I read in the papers that Don Diego had been killed and I decided I must contact you, tell you everything. Give you your mother's things.' She laid her hand gently on Marguerite's shoulder, adding, 'Ask you to forgive me.'

'How can I forgive you?' cried Marguerite. 'You've ruined my life. You've ruined everything.'

Hearing her, the young couple glanced at them then moved farther away, and with his elbow leaning on the rail, the man turned his back on them as if to block out unwelcome voices.

Mrs. Gaynor gave a deep sigh. 'Well, at least I've told you. I've put the record straight.' She reached into her coat pocket and handed Marguerite another sheaf of papers. 'I know it's all been very upsetting for you, so I've written it all down – everything I told you. You'll also find some of Brigid Mary's papers there. Yours were sent on to Catherine's people in New Jersey.'

The clouds had closed in now, the rain obscured everything and Marguerite felt as f she was looking into her own future, a future where everything was closing in on her and she had nowhere to go. She sat down on the end of the nearest bench and buried her face in her hands. As she continued to sob, she railed against Mrs. Gaynor in the darkness of her mind. How dare she do such a thing to her! How dare she do such a thing to anybody! She must have known which baby was which. But she just went on and did it. Their 'little transaction', she had told Don. And then to suggest that the possibility of an inheritance might make it all right.

Moments later there was a loud splash and the young man rushed back along the rail, pointing at the water and shouting, 'Someone's overboard!'

Marguerite was also looking down over the rail now. 'She's thrown herself in,' she cried. 'She's thrown herself in.'

A short distance from the ferry they saw a sodden patch of black floating on the surface of the water. A small black pillbox hat bobbed up and down nearby. Grabbing the nearest lifebuoy, the man tossed it into the water, but no hands grasped it and it drifted away in the swell. The black coat floated after it and disappeared from their view as it sank beneath the rain-dimpled water.

Other passengers began to line the rails, some pointing at the small black hat that was still floating just beneath the surface. Then it also disappeared and there was nothing. No sign of life, no sign even of death.

Soon foghorns were sounding across the water, a life raft was launched and the ferry turned in a vain effort to rescue the missing passenger. Another ferry that had been on the way out to Ellis Island also joined in the search.

Within a surprisingly short time various rescue craft arrived to take over the search – coastguards from Governor's Island, someone said, a fireboat from Pier A, the police marine division. Then, some time later

– reluctantly, it seemed to Marguerite – the ferry that had joined them continued on its way and her ferry returned to Battery Park.

As the passengers disembarked, they were asked if any of them knew who the missing passenger might have been. And just as Mrs. Gaynor had once failed to speak up, so too did Marguerite. Feeling wet and miserable and deeply shocked by what had happened, she hurried over to the subway, and still clutching the precious bundle in her raincoat pocket, returned to her apartment.

TEN

Dan O'Sullivan bent over and used his secateurs to clip an azalea bush that clearly didn't need clipping. His garden had all the appearances of belonging to someone who had little else to do but look after it. When he straightened up to glance at the tree-lined street once more, it was obvious even to passers-by that, despite his age, he was a man of fine stature. Indeed, those who knew him were aware that before he became slightly stooped he stood at six foot four with a physique that was a match for any thug foolish enough to take him on.

After Ireland – or part of it – had gained its independence from Britain, the fledgling government had set up its own police force, calling it An Garda Síochána, the guardians of the peace. Dan's father, a Corkman, had been one of the first to join it, and he followed in his father's footsteps, pounding the beat in Dublin, and rising to the rank of Detective Sergeant.

When his father, a widower for many years, died and he himself was still young enough, he pulled up stakes and took his wife and family to New York. There he pounded the beat for the NYPD, before taking a desk job. Following the death of his wife he retired, and now amused himself in the garden, occasionally doing a bit of work for the Patrolmen's Benevolent Society and, once a year, looking after members of the gardaí who were invited over for St. Patrick's Day.

His occasional glance towards the street was to see if there was any sign of his youngest son, Thaddeus. While other members of his family took up well-paid jobs in civilian life and moved away from New York, Thaddeus, to his delight, became the third generation to join the police. Fair-haired, freckled and six-foot three, Thaddeus reminded him of himself when he was a younger man. Now he had been promoted to Detective Third Grade and was working on a murder case.

As Detective Sullivan drove towards his father's house, he might have noticed that Staten Island – or at least the part where his father lived – was looking well in its summer foliage. Shingle houses with copper beeches flashed by, bungalows with azalea bushes clipped low to give a greater spread of pink, purple and magenta. However, he was too engrossed in his own thoughts to pay much attention to them. The colours uppermost in his mind were blue and white – the blue and white of a nun's headdress. Who was this nun, he kept wondering, the one who called herself Sister Mary? And where had she gone?

As he turned his car into the street leading to his father's house, he was vaguely aware of the sun and shadows flitting across his face as he passed the trees, but the joys of summer were far from his mind.

'Ah, Thaddeus.' Dan's arms were open and his smile almost as wide when the car drew up. 'Good to see you.'

'You too.' They embraced and while the young detective sat down on a bench seat and waited for a beer, he reckoned that his father was the only person in the whole of New York who called him Thaddeus. When he was growing up in New York people would say, 'Thaddeus? Where did you get a name like that?' And, 'What's with the O in O'Sullivan?' Thaddeus, his father would tell them, was a fine Irish name. Mac, meant son of; O grandson of. 'But isn't everyone the son or grandson of someone?' they would say. And so they ignored his first name, shortened the second to Sullivan and nicknamed him Sully. It was a name that stuck and was used by everyone – everyone that is, except his father.

'Well, Thaddeus?' Dan handed him a beer and sat down beside him. 'How's this case of yours going?'

'What case would that be, Dad?'

'This Diego case.'

'Sure it's not my case, it's Toni's.'

'Aren't you his partner? Now stop your messing and tell me all about it.'

'I'm only kidding. Yeah, it's a strange one. You probably read in the paper that we're looking for a nun as a possible witness.'

Dan nodded, sipped his beer and waited to hear more.

'What's not generally known is that we discovered a silver crucifix in the house where the body was found.'

'Hers?'

'We think so. Toni reckons she may have walked in on the killing. The chain was broken, which would indicate that she may have struggled with the attacker.'

'Any thoughts on who the attacker might have been?'

'We're following a few lines all right. We think Diego may have welched on a loan or made a pass at some guy's wife. Always fancied himself with the women. What do you think?'

'Well, Thaddeus, it's not for me to tell you how to conduct your investigation.'

'No, really, I'd appreciate it.'

'Well, I remember, when I was a detective back in Ireland, I read a book once by a man who used to be a senior officer in Scotland Yard. When somebody was found dead at home, he said the first thing they checked was to see if it was a gas meter job.'

'What did he mean by that?'

'What he meant was that if the gas meter in a house had been robbed, it was more than likely that it had been done by someone in the house who was short of cash. And mind you, there was a lot in what he said. Whenever a woman was killed in her own home, the first person we looked at was her husband. And very often it was him.'

'And what if the victim was the husband?'

'Well, if there was no break-in, you'd still have to look at the family first. See if there had been some sort of a row.'

'But that was in Ireland. This is America.'

'Listen, Thaddeus, take it from me: human nature is the same the world over.'

'So you think we should be looking more closely at the family?'

'All I'm saying is you should check them out first. But – and it's an important but – don't approach it with tunnel vision. There are always exceptions, even in cases where you might think it was family, so you mustn't close your eyes to other possibilities.'

As they sipped their beer, Dan continued, 'What puzzles me about the Diego killing is how the nun got away. I mean, if it was a hit, for whatever reason – a bad debt, a move on someone else's wife – the killer would have been a man and I doubt if she would have got away from a man. Not a guy who was all fired up after putting a slug in Diego. He would have known all too well that she could finger him and there was no way he would have let her out of there.'

'So you think the killer could have been a woman?'

'I don't know. But as I said before, anything's possible. At least it's worth checking out.'

'The problem is, we can't get a line on this nun.'

'What do you know about her?'

'Very little, apart from the fact that she came over on the ferry and told a curious little black boy her name was Sister Mary.'

'What age was she? I mean, was she young or old?'

'Ah, that's the question. We don't know.'

'What do you mean, you don't know?'

'Well, the boy says she was old but, as the mother points out, he thinks anyone older than himself is old.'

'And what about the other people who saw her? The neighbours?'

'Well, there we have the opposite problem. Most of the neighbours are elderly. Mr. Durane – he's the old guy who found the body – just saw the back of her head as she walked past his window. Others won't open their doors to strangers and saw her only through the peephole or as far as the safety chain would allow the door to open.'

'And what was their impression?'

'They all thought she was young, but then again, when you're in your seventies or eighties, you might think fifty is young, even sixty!'

'Yeah, I know the feeling. But leaving that aside, do you think she was a real nun, or someone in disguise?'

'You mean, was she the killer posing as a nun?'

Dan shrugged as if to say again that anything was possible and sipped his beer.

'From what the boy said, she sounded genuine enough. We reckon she's holed up somewhere in Manhattan. The question is, where?'

When they finished their beer, they walked to the car.

'Sometimes,' said Dan, 'you can get too close to a case. When that happens, you can't see the wood for the trees. You have to stand back, take a good look at it. It's the same in Manhattan. Maybe the guys over there are too wrapped up in their own work to be of any help to you. My advice would be to stand back. Have a look at it and see what you can see.'

Before they parted, they embraced again and Dan smiled, saying, 'Slán.'

'Slán,' said his son, responding with the Gaelic for goodbye rather than the Italian 'ciao', so favoured by his partner. 'And thanks for the advice.'

'You're welcome. See you in the Ferryman's on Friday, if you're not too busy.'

'Yeah, if I can.'

Instead of going to his apartment, Detective Sullivan drove back across the island to St. George, grabbed a burger and a bottle of Coke and boarded the ferry for Manhattan. A large group of schoolgirls in blue pleated skirts and blue cardigans marched on before him and crammed the seats along one side, talking excitedly about things they had seen and done on their day trip to the island.

Sullivan seated himself at a window on the opposite side and, as the ferry gathered speed, he looked out across the bay. Tugs, their sides lined with rubber tyres, chugged across the water while others nudged the bow of a huge cargo ship to turn it around. Passengers who made the same journey each day also looked out across the bay, or simply stared ahead. For them the crossing was part of their daily grind, something to be endured and best passed by a self-imposed silence; for the schoolgirls it was a voyage of discovery and excitement, and their chattering seemed to pervade the entire vessel.

All these things, like the chattering of the girls, Sullivan was aware of. He could understand why few of the passengers would have noticed the nun. They were too preoccupied with the worries of the day to notice anyone else and the nun would have gone unnoticed had it not been for a little boy – a little boy with no worries and a curiosity reserved for the young. Why, Sullivan wondered, had the nun taken the ferry to Staten Island? Why had she called on Don Diego? And if, as they believed, she had returned to Manhattan, where had she gone?

A short time later, the ferry shuddered as it touched the long wooden piles that formed the berth at Manhattan, and he watched it slide between them like a sword returning to its sheath. The schoolgirls raced ahead to see who would be off the ferry first and he joined the mass of other passengers who followed. A few moments later he was back out in the sunshine, retracing the steps of Sister Mary down towards the busy street. He stopped and looked around. Would she have taken the subway or a cab? he wondered. And where would she have gone?

Taking his father's advice, he stood back and looked up at the forest of skyscrapers. Then his eyes fell on the red brick church that was sandwiched in between them. I wonder? he said to himself and hurried down to the street. There he stopped and looked at the church again. Would she have gone in there? After all, she was a nun. And if she had tangled with the killer she would have been in trouble – deep trouble. Perhaps she had seen the church as a place of refuge, a place to get in off the street, maybe even a place where she could get help.

Hoping he was right, he waited for the traffic lights to change and crossed over. High above the door of the church he could see a statue with its arms outstretched, and below it, to one side, the papal coat of arms. How often had he passed the church before and never even noticed it was there.

Above another door, a plaque at street level told him he was at the Chapel of Our Lady of the Rosary. Built into the wall beside it was a Celtic Cross, a familiar symbol from his boyhood days in Ireland. The Cross was above the door of the parish offices and, when he inquired inside for the priest, he was told that Father Pat was up in the church.

Father Pat, it transpired, was a busy young man who seemed to be dealing with visitors and a hundred and one other things at the same time. However, when Sullivan showed him his badge, he gave him his full attention.

'Now that you mention it,' the priest told him, 'there was a nun all right.'

'There was?'

'Yeah. Came in here in a dreadful state.'

'Did she say what had happened to her?'

'I think she said she was mugged. It was Father John who spoke to her. I just saw her when I brought her in a cup of coffee. Her right eye and the side of her face were very badly bruised.'

'What age was she?'

The priest threw open his hands. 'It's hard to say what with the bruising and all. Maybe late twenties, early thirties. Father John went to get her medical assistance but when he returned she'd gone.'

'Can I speak to Father John?'

The young priest shook his head. 'He's on his sabbatical.'

'You mean, for a year?'

'Something like that.'

'Do you know where?'

'Italy, the Vatican, Ireland – a sort of world tour.'

'Why didn't you come forward and tell us about this?'

'Why should we? We didn't know you were interested in her.'

'Don't you read the newspapers?'

Father Pat shook his head. 'Not really. Why?'

'We think her name is Sister Mary, and that she may have witnessed a murder.'

'Oh.'

'That's why we're trying to find her.'

'Well, we're trying to find her too. Apart from her injury, it's obvious that's she's in need of spiritual assistance. And now that we know her name, perhaps we can track her down.'

'You reckon?'

'Perhaps. I don't know. But we'll give it our best shot.'

90

'That would be a great help. It's very important that we talk to her.' Sullivan took a card from his wallet. 'If you do track her down, give me a call.'

Father Pat promised he would and, feeling very pleased with himself, Sullivan returned to Staten Island.

ELEVEN

It was another warm, sunny day and Marguerite was glad of the shade afforded by the trees whose branches reached over the park bench where she was scanning the morning's newspapers. Following her ill-fated meeting with Mrs. Gaynor on the Statue of Liberty ferry, she had searched the papers for any news of the drowning. However, a drowning was a common enough occurrence in New York harbour and, as far as she could see, the death of the Irish nurse had gone unreported. Now she was searching for any word of the body being washed up, but if it had, it obviously wasn't considered newsworthy either.

For two days after her final meeting with Mrs. Gaynor, she had to work in the deli and didn't have the privacy she needed in her apartment at night to go through the remainder of her mother's writings as carefully as she would have wished. In fact, it wasn't until the third day, when she was off, that she got the opportunity to read them. Even then, she was anxious to absent herself from the apartment as much as possible in case the police called, and once again the park seemed the best option.

The previous two days had been very difficult – almost too difficult to work – for her mind was tormented by what had happened to Nurse Gaynor and what she had told her. Among the papers Mrs. Gaynor had given her were Brigid Mary's travel documents, including the baby passport issued to her by the Department of External Affairs in Dublin and a copy of her birth certificate.

Of more interest to her, however, was Mrs. Gaynor's handwritten account of what had happened on the liner. How could anyone have done such a thing? she kept asking herself. Why couldn't Mrs. Gaynor have spoken up and said, 'No, this is Catherine's baby. This is Katie,' and taken her to her relatives in New Jersey? It wasn't as if they lived in California; they were just across the river. Not any farther away than Long Island. And yet there was a lifetime between the two. Her lifetime. And it had been wasted.

She wiped away a tear and was grateful no one was passing to see her cry. She looked at the youngsters playing basketball on the other side of the park. It was a hard, dusty outdoor court, but they didn't care; they were full of life, enjoying themselves to the full. Unlike the miserable childhood she'd had with the Diegos. She recalled no happiness whatsoever, no fun and games, no joy, only pain, the pain of being badly treated, the pain of not being wanted. Even today there was the same pain, the pain of not belonging, the pain of loneliness. And now the terrible pain of knowing that it had all been a dreadful mistake. No, not a mistake, a deliberate, cruel act that could so easily have been avoided.

Even after Mrs. Gaynor's untimely death, she could not bring herself to forgive her. She could still feel the woman's hand on her shoulder, still hear her pleading for forgiveness. But too much had happened. There had been too much pain, too much unhappiness. Things that even Nurse Gaynor didn't know about. Things nobody knew about – or wanted to know. And now her heart was like stone, hard and unforgiving. There was no one she could talk to, no one she could confide in, no one she could turn to for solace. Except her mother, her real mother. With each line of her mother's writing, she felt closer to her. She was, after all, writing to her – her daughter, Katie. And so it was to the final notepad that she now turned, the final notepad from the RMS *Atlantia* and the woman who had been such a loving mother for such a very short time.

As she had already observed, most of the letters had been written to Catherine by her parents and relatives in New Jersey when she was in Dublin. She would read them later. What she wanted to do now was to read more of what Catherine had written to her. Perhaps here she would find the answer to other questions that had begun to trouble her lately. What had happened to the great love Catherine and Shaunie felt for each other – the love by which she, little Katie, had been born? Why had they not got married? How had Catherine ended up in a home for unmarried mothers?

In the hope of finding the answers to these questions, she opened the notepad and once again felt the warmth of her mother's love with the opening words…

My Dearest Katie, This, I fear, may be the last letter I am able to write to you as I am feeling quite ill. I have asked Nurse Gaynor to take you into her cabin with little Brigid Mary because I am terrified that you might get whatever virus has afflicted me. I don't mind what happens to me as long as you are all right and, in penning these few notes, I hope you will one day learn more about me – and about your father. I have no doubt you will also be curious by now to know what happened, why we didn't get married, and I think you have a right to know.

As I told you in a previous notepad, it was on the other side of the Galty Mountains that I met Shaunie. Three counties – Tipperary, Limerick and Cork – meet at the Galtys and when I crossed over them I was in County Cork. Work was scarce in the area of Tipperary where we lived – indeed, it was scarce everywhere – and when Uncle John and Aunt Mags wrote to say someone was looking for a young girl to work in a big house, I jumped at the chance. That someone turned out to be Major de Brún, a retired British Army officer who had come to live in the old rectory. While I didn't know it then, the major was to play an important part in my romance with Shaunie.

The work in Major de Brún's house was long and hard, but I didn't mind. As I think I mentioned before, I had always planned on going to America and helping Aunt Lily and Uncle Ed look after the children, at least until I got on my feet. They even offered to pay my fare, but I wanted to put some money towards it myself, and now, at long last, I had a job that would enable me to do so. I had to be at the major's house before daybreak every day, including Sunday, as everything had to be ready by the time he got up. But I was young and strong and well able for it and it was all such a new and wonderful experience for me that I actually looked forward to it.

When I closed the door of Aunt Mag's cottage behind me in the mornings and headed for the rectory, I would look up at the Galty Mountains as if I was seeing them from the other side for the first time. Sometimes the mist that shrouded them during the night would be clearing and it seemed as if the peaks, like me, were after pushing themselves up with the first rays of the morning sun.

But what, you might ask, was a British officer doing living in republican Cork? Well, his real name was Major James Browne. I don't know if he had originally come from Ireland, but according to Mrs. Murphy – she was his housekeeper – he was very much into military history, and had written something condemning the way the Black and Tans had acted against the Irish during the War of Independence. He had also been very critical of the British role in the Indian Mutiny, although what that was about I do not know. Anyway, it seems he got into a lot of trouble over it with the British authorities. Mrs. Murphy said he resigned in protest, changed his name to Seamus de Brún, which is the Irish for James Browne and came to live at the old rectory which had been vacant for some time.

Going to work for a former British officer, even one who had condemned the activities of the Black and Tans, would have been frowned upon in such a staunchly republican area. But according to Uncle John, the major had been visited by two of the great heroes of the War of Independence, Dan Breen from Tipperary and General Tom Barry from west Cork, both of whom had fought the Black and Tans. After that, no one would dare harm him, and Uncle John assured me that it was quite safe for the likes of me to work for him.

Even though he had left the army, I found that Major de Brún ran his house on regimental lines. We all had to wear black with little white aprons and a little white cap. The silver had to be polished every day. He had to have his gin and tonic at a certain time of the morning, and the table had to be laid for his meals, even though he was the only one to be catered for. I was given a half day off every Friday as the major always went into Mitchelstown in the afternoon and I was told I wasn't needed. He had lost his left eye and left arm in some war or other and couldn't drive himself, so he had to get someone else to drive him. What he went into the town for I don't know, but I believe he usually ended up in the local hotel, where he would have a few more gins and tonic *and regale the locals with stories of the Indian mutiny and various other wars.*

Not everyone in the area has a car, of course. Many of the farmers take their containers of milk to the local creamery on a flat cart drawn by a horse or even an ass. Sometimes that is their only mode of transport and the first time I saw Shaunie, I had thumbed a lift on such a cart from a farmer who was going into Mitchelstown. There were no milk cans on it at that stage and I was sitting at the back with my legs dangling over the side, when the major's big blue Rover drew abreast. The driver sounded the horn and I saw this young man leaning across the major to give me a wave. I was flattered but I pretended to ignore him. As the car drew away, I saw the major putting his monocle up to his good eye and squinting out to see who his driver was honking at, and then they were gone.

I didn't know then who the young man at the wheel of the Rover was. However, the thought that he had noticed me stayed with me, for it pleased me a lot. In fact, I couldn't get it out of my mind and so, the next time I saw him, I decided to return the compliment – not directly, of course, but as we women often do, in a sort of roundabout way!

The major, in a gesture that greatly helped his acceptance in the community, had made one of his fields available for games of hurling and Gaelic football. And one day as I passed the field, who did I see standing near the boundary fence but the major's driver. He was togged out in his hurling gear and waiting for a game to start.

'Up Tipp!' I shouted and kept on walking.

'What do you mean, up Tipp?' he called back. 'Don't you know you're in Cork girl?

I must point out that whenever Cork and Tipperary supporters meet they're inclined to engage in a certain kind of banter, slagging one another about which is the better team.

'You can train all you like,' I replied, 'but you'll never beat Tipp.'

He immediately hopped over the fence and confronted me, saying, 'What do you mean we'll never beat Tipp.? Didn't Cork win three all-Ireland finals in a row and Tipp. weren't even there.'

'Didn't Tipp. win three in a row before that,' I said, 'and Cork weren't there.'

He had to smile at that and as he climbed back over the fence, he said, *'Shaunie's the name. And yours?'*

'Catherine,' I told him, and somehow I knew I would be seeing him again. *He was, I could see, a fine cut of a man. He had a head of wavy black hair, was well over six foot tall and had the build you would expect a good hurler to have. Later, when we began to walk out together, I learned that he was the eldest of a family of four boys and one girl. He lived and worked on his father's farm and was only obliging the major by driving him in and out of town.*

At this point, Catherine wrote that she was very tired and must take a rest. When she resumed her notes, she related how, one evening as Shaunie and herself walked up a narrow lane in the foothills of the mountains at the back of his home, she asked him why he spelt his name the way he did?

He told me that when his father was in America, the people there found the name Sean difficult to pronounce, so it became Shaun. Then, when he came along, his parents called him Shaunie, meaning, young Sean. That was when I told him I was going to America. Somehow it didn't seem important to us then. But as time passed, and our love for one another grew, that all changed.

Whenever we got the chance, usually in the long summer evenings, we would make our way up the lane towards a small lake that lay hidden in a valley between the mountains. Along the way, Shaunie would practice his hurling by tossing a small stone into the air and then, swinging the hurley with both hands, send the stone hurtling up into the mountain. Some day, he told me, he hoped to play for the county team. Then the argument about which county had the better team would resume, and if, as sometimes happened, the argument became a little hot and heavy, he would take me in his big strong arms and kiss me.

At the top of the lane there's a large boulder and we always stopped there to get our breath back, for it was a steep climb. As we rested, we would lie back against the boulder and listen to the stream that gurgled deep in the ravine beside us as it made its way down from the lake. We would marvel at the colours of the butterflies that flitted from flower to flower and watch the goldfinches feeding on the thistledown. Our hearts were as free and as happy as the finches and perhaps they knew this, for they never seemed to be afraid of us. It was almost as if, in our happiness, we were at one with nature and with the creatures that lived in it.

Before continuing we would stand and look back across the countryside which stretched away to the blue haze of the horizon. Then, as the wind caught my hair and flicked it around my face, Shaunie would brush it aside with his hand and tell me how beautiful I was. And we would kiss again before making our way across the heather to the lake.

Some might find it strange that I should be telling you such intimate things, but I want you to know how wonderful our love for one another was.

On the slopes near the lake was another large boulder that looked as if it had been hurled down the mountain at the dawn of creation and beside it was the whitethorn bush I was telling you about. Our whitethorn of the dancing. It was wedged so tightly against the boulder, it looked as if it had stopped it from rolling into the lake. But, of course, one was too old and the other too young. The whitethorn had simply grown up in the shelter of the boulder, and now both of them gave shelter to us.

However, shelter may be the wrong word because I only recall sunshine and happiness on the days we lay beneath the whitethorn. In early summer these small trees are covered in a mass of white blossoms, for all the world like snow. But when I looked closely at the blossoms on our whitethorn, I found they had a touch of pink and, when they fell, I thought they were more like, well, confetti…

How often did we sport ourselves around the whitethorn and its protective boulder, laughing like children and crying out in mock protest whenever we caught one another or tickled one another to the point of tears. And then, when we were exhausted, we just lay in each other's arms.

Shaunie's mother had died some years previously but his father made me very welcome. 'And how's the major?' he asked the first time I met him. 'Still talking about the Indian mutiny, I suppose?' Before I could reply, he went into a fit of coughing and only then did I realise that he was in poor health. 'It was the mines,' he told me when he got his breath back. 'I worked in the coal mines in Pennsylvania for years. It destroyed my lungs.'

Shaunie's brothers were always larking around and it was difficult to know whether they took my relationship with him seriously or not. Francie was the worst, and Mick and Pat seemed to take their lead from him. One minute he would be serious, the next he would be laughing. Then they would all start laughing and I couldn't tell whether they were laughing at one of his jokes or at me. Their sister, Maudie, however, was decidedly cool. Whether she thought someone who did the type of work I did wasn't good enough for her eldest brother, I don't know, but she never warmed to me.

Nevertheless, Shaunie and I continued to spend the summer evenings in each other's company. Sometimes we would go to a dance in Mitchelstown, travelling in style in his father's car. Whatever about his brothers, his father liked me, otherwise he wouldn't have allowed us to take the car. But he did and we would go to the dance in the Mayflower Ballroom.

Those were great nights, especially when Mick Delahunty and his Orchestra were playing. You will not have heard of Mick Delahunty, but he is a big name in the showband business in Ireland. The King of Glenn Miller music they call him and, to me and Shaunie and the multitude of others who crowded into the ballroom in Mitchelstown, he was the king. Immaculate in his black bow tie, black hair sleeked back, saxophone in hand, he would lead his orchestra through the whole range of Glenn Miller music. But 'Charmaine' was my song. 'Charmaine, my Charmaine.' When they played that, Shaunie and I danced a lot closer than the parish priest would have allowed. Everybody, I suspect, did the same. And then, all too soon, the evening was over.

Before I met Shaunie, I couldn't wait to go to America. Then I began to have mixed feelings about it. And, when Lily and Ed sent me a ticket, I was torn between wanting to go and wanting to stay. I knew Shaunie had his heart set on marrying me, but how could he? He had no money. Like his brothers, he just worked on the farm and got little more than his pocket money at the end of the week.

And so, as the time approached for my departure, we would lie under the whitethorn and talk about it. The blossoms had long since gone from the tree and there was a heaviness in our hearts. On the one hand, I could see a whole new world stretching out in front of me in America; on the other, a life of drudgery in the big house and no prospects of marriage. And so things drifted on until the fateful day came and we said goodbye.

I had to go to the shipping office to make final arrangements for the voyage, and it was with a heavy heart that I travelled to Cobh to do so. I remember getting off the train and walking along the promenade. I was so in love and so miserable. I just sat down on the first bench I came to and cried.

How long I sat there, I don't know. I remember hearing the carillon bells of the cathedral up behind me, but what they were playing, I don't know. The music seemed to go over my head and slip away across the sea. Just as my life was doing. The lovely life I was leaving behind. The love of my life. All I could do was cry and pray. Pray that he would come for me. Then I felt someone looking at me and, when I looked up, my heart leapt and I cried with joy, for it was Shaunie. My Shaunie. We hugged and kissed and he told me he was taking me home. We went into one of the cafés on the seafront and there we held hands and talked. He told me how his father had given him his blessing when he told him he wanted to marry me. His father also assured him that money would not be a problem as the farm would be his some day anyway. Even then, he feared he might not get to Cobh in time to stop me as his brothers took the carburettor out of his father's car. As I told you before, they never seemed to take anything seriously and probably thought it was all a great joke.

In desperation Shaunie went to Major de Brún who kindly offered him the use of the Rover. 'If you love her, my boy,' the major told him, 'don't let her go. Go after her and bring her back!' And that's what he did. However, we didn't return from Cobh immediately. Perhaps it was because we had come so close to losing one another, or because we had decided to get married, or perhaps it was both, I don't really know, but we booked into a guest house for the night and there we consummated our love.

I don't know whether or not my parents were happy with the news – I mean, they thought I was going to America – but when they got over their surprise, they were delighted and wished me every happiness. Whatever about Maudie and her brothers, Shaunie's father was delighted for us too. Unfortunately he died before the day came for us to be married, but we knew he would have wanted us to go ahead, and so, after the Month's Mind, we set another date.

By this time I had told Shaunie I was pregnant, and we knew there was no time to waste. My friend, Eileen, who is very good at dressmaking, made me a beautiful white wedding dress. All the arrangements were in place and we even had a rehearsal in the parish church not far from Shaunie's house. But for reasons I will never fully understand, the wedding never took place…

Here, Catherine's writing tailed off, as if she had become weak, or the memory of what had occurred was too much for her to bear. Frantically, Marguerite looked at the back of the page and at the next few pages to see if the narrative continued there, but it didn't. Deeply disappointed that she still hadn't learned why her mother's wedding didn't go ahead, and now more curious than ever to find out, she put the notepad away and took out the bundle of letters again. All the letters from Lily and Ed were from the same address in New Jersey and she wondered once more if they were still living there. She also wondered if they knew what had happened.

TWELVE

If Detective Sullivan was expecting his partner to give him a pat on the back for his initiative in finding out where Sister Mary had sought refuge after the killing of Don Diego, he was due for a disappointment.

'Sully,' Florentine said, 'what the hell do you think you're doing? Don't you know you should give them a bell before you start nosing around over there? Lieutenant Jacobs will have you by the balls if he finds out.'

'Sure, all I did was to go into the church and talk to the priest. What's the harm in that?'

'The harm is that if the guys in the local precinct hear you've been working their patch without telling them, they're going to be pretty pissed off. I mean, how would we like it if we heard that cops from Manhattan had been making inquiries on Staten Island and we knew nothing about it?'

'I suppose you're right.'

'Of course I'm right. But don't let it bother you too much. Come on.'

'Where are we going?'

'To Manhattan, of course – to take over from where you left off.'

'But you just said...'

'I know what I said. And try not to forget it. But the fact is you did very well. The only problem is you didn't go through the proper channels. Now I have and we'll see where we go from there.'

As they drove towards the Verrazano Bridge, Florentine asked, 'What made you think she might have gone into the church?'

'Just something my father said.'

'I thought as much. He's a wily old dog. I wouldn't mind having him on my team.'

Sullivan gave a wry smile. 'I don't think you'd like that.'

'Why not?'

'Well, he's not one for going through official channels, if you know what I mean.'

Florentine smiled and nodded. '*Touché.*'

It was another hot day and, as they approached the double-decked suspension bridge, Florentine said, 'Do you know the roadway over this bridge is twelve feet lower in summer than in winter?'

'Go on, pull the other one.'

'No, I'm serious. It's something to do with the contractions and expansions of the steel cables.'

'Now you're going to tell me Verrazano was an Italian.'

'Of course he was an Italian. Giovanni da Verrazano. Born in Florence – where my family come from.'

Sullivan cast his eyes up as his partner went on, 'He was the first European explorer to sail into New York Harbour – in 1524. That's why they named the bridge after him.'

'I thought Columbus was supposed to have discovered America.'

'So he did – in 1492. He was Italian too.' Florentine began humming to himself. With his gentle banter he was making up for some of the disadvantages he had suffered at the hands of the Irish on many a St. Patrick's Day.

'And, of course,' he went on, 'America was named after an Italian – another Florentine, Amerigo Vespucci. He came here after Columbus and wrote a book about it.'

They had left the bridge behind and were driving through Brooklyn towards the Battery Tunnel.

'You know,' said Sullivan, 'I'm beginning to think your education was sadly neglected.'

Florentine smiled. 'Go on. Give it to me.'

'Well, it's obvious you never heard of St. Brendan the Navigator?'

103

'Why? What about him?'

'What about him? Sure it's a well-known fact that he discovered America long before Columbus.'

'Come off it.'

'I'm serious. He was born in County Kerry in the fifth century.'

'This is another of those Kerry jokes – right?'

'It's no joke. I was told all about him when I was at school in Ireland. He was a great sailor and, after many voyages in and around Europe, he embarked on a seven-year voyage with sixty other monks in search of the Land of Promise.'

'Never heard of him.'

'Maybe not,' Sullivan went on, 'but scholars who have read the medieval manuscripts of the voyage believe he may have discovered America nine hundred years before Columbus.'

'Where are these manuscripts?'

'I don't know, but that doesn't mean they don't exist.'

'You can't swear that something exists if you haven't seen it.'

'Do you know, my father told me a story about an Irish lawyer who made the very same point.'

They entered the Battery Tunnel.

'Of course they don't call them lawyers over in Ireland,' Sullivan continued. 'They call them counsel, the same way as they do in England. Anyway, this woman – this 'oul' wan' as my father called her – was in the witness box, swearing to something she hadn't seen. "But Madam," said counsel, "you can't swear that something exists if you haven't seen it." "Oh I can your Honour," said the woman. "Give me an example then," said counsel, cock sure of himself. "Well," said the oul' wan, "I know that counsel has a hole in his butt. I haven't seen it, but I can swear it exists."'

Florentine laughed. 'Sully, you're an asshole. Did nobody ever tell you that?'

Sullivan laughed too and they were still laughing at the good of it when they got out of the car near the Chapel of Our Lady of the Rosary opposite the Staten Island ferry terminal.

'Seriously though,' said Florentine, as they crossed over to the church, 'we've got to find this nun – if she exists.'

'Why, do you think she might not?'

'I don't know. People swear they've seen her and that she does exists. But if she does, where is she?'

'Do you think maybe the nun's habit was some kind of disguise?' asked Sullivan.

'I don't know. Maybe this priest can tell us a bit more about her. What did you say his name was?'

'Father Pat.'

'Another Irishman. I might have known.'

Florentine went over the same ground with Father Pat as his partner had done, but the young priest was unable to shed any more light on the meeting with Sister Mary. 'Father John tried to find out more about the mugging,' was all he could recall, 'but she was in such a state she could hardly talk.'

As they headed for the local precinct, Sullivan asked, 'Do you think maybe she walked in on the murder and was attacked by the killer as he ran out?'

'I don't know. She's the only one can tell us what happened – but where the hell is she?'

'You said you were speaking to a local cop who might be able to help us.'

'Yeah. His name's Menton.'

Florentine stopped at the station's notice board which displayed photocopies of wanted felons and missing persons. Out of habit, he scanned each and every one of them and, as he did so, his eyes came to rest on one in particular, a picture of a missing woman. The details, which would normally have been at the bottom, had been shredded by the almost daily process of removing old photographs and stapling on new ones. However, the woman's face was intact and he studied it for a moment before going in.

Menton, they found, was an old-timer, a policeman who had put in many years as a detective but never got promotion. Perhaps, they thought, he never looked for it. He was obviously too old now to be running around after criminals and they reckoned he had been given a desk job to see him through to retirement.

'Coffee?' he asked.

They nodded and, when he brought the mugs over to his desk, he asked, 'Well, how're things over in Staten Island?'

'Busy enough.' Florentine sipped his coffee. 'Now tell me. The nun I spoke to you about on the phone?'

'Oh yeah. Sister Mary.' He reached into a drawer and took out a folder. 'You said you tracked her as far as the Church of Our Lady of the Rosary.'

Sullivan nodded. 'The church opposite the ferry terminal.'

'I don't suppose you found out which religious order she came from?' Florentine asked.

Menton leaned back on his desk, ran his hand back over his balding head and smiled. 'We've a saying over here. Miracles we can do; the impossible takes a little longer!'

Florentine smiled. 'Yeah, I know. We don't even have a photograph of her. In fact, we can't even tell you what she looks like.'

'Don't worry. We're working on it.' As they got up to go, Menton put the folder back in the drawer, adding, 'If we come up with anything, I'll let you know.'

Florentine thanked him and led the way out.

'I wouldn't say Sister Mary is at the top of their list of priorities,' said Sullivan.

They stopped at the notice board again and Florentine found himself looking at the same black and white photograph.

'Do you know her?' asked Sullivan.

'There's something familiar about her. But I can't just put my finger on it.' Florentine tore the picture off the board and, returning to the desk sergeant, asked for Menton again.

'She was a floater,' Menton told them. 'Fished her out near Pier A.' He reached into one of the drawers in his desk again and took out another file. 'Turns out she was on the Statue of Liberty ferry. Her husband thinks she must have decided to end it all. Not surprising, considering the autopsy report.'

'Terminal cancer,' said Florentine as he scanned the report.

Menton nodded. 'Somebody said she threw herself in. Tossed her a booee, but she didn't take it. Why, do you know her?'

'I've a feeling I've seen her before, but I can't for the life of me remember where. Here, what do you think, Sully?'

Sullivan studied the picture for a moment, but shook his head. 'She's kinda familiar all right, but...'

'Well, if you think of it,' said Menton, taking the picture back, 'give me a call.'

As they turned to go, Florentine put up his hand, saying, 'Hold it. I think I have it.' Taking the picture again, he said, more to Sullivan than Menton, 'Yeah, she was at Diego's funeral. Remember? She was the dame who was talking to his daughter, Marguerite.'

Sullivan took the picture and studied it again. 'You know, Toni, you could be right.'

Turning to Menton, Florentine asked, 'What's her name?'

Menton consulted his file again. 'Gaynor. Nancy Gaynor. Aged sixty-five. Married. Her husband John reported her missing a couple of weeks before she floated into Pier A.'

'Address?'

'Queen's as far as I remember. Yeah, here it is. Woodside.'

'I think maybe we should have a word with him, Sully.'

'Ok,' said Menton consulting his file again. 'There's a contact number here in Queens. You might want to give them a call.'

Florentine thanked him, adding, 'Want to come with us?'

Menton smiled. 'You must be kidding. Just keep me posted.'

Florentine thanked him again and promised he would.

As they wended their way up through the heavy traffic of Manhattan, Sullivan asked, 'Do you not miss all this?'

'You mean the traffic? Not on your life. But...' Florentine shrugged. 'There's nowhere like Manhattan. Sure I miss it.'

Leaving Manhattan behind, they crossed the East River into Queens and after checking with the local cops, followed their directions until they came to the Gaynor's apartment in Woodside.

'I thought I gave you guys all the information you needed when I identified the body,' said Mr. Gaynor.

'They were from the local precinct,' Florentine told him. 'We're from Staten Island.'

As the two detectives settled back into a settee, they observed that Mr.Gaynor was bald, except for a few strands on top and reckoned he was about seventy. His thin body was wracked with a deep rumbling cough and they weren't surprised when he picked up a packet of cigarettes and offered them one, an offer that only Florentine accepted. He also invited them to have a whiskey and, when they declined, he poured himself a glass and sat down in an armchair to hear what they had to say.

'Isn't that an Irish accent you have?' asked Sullivan.

Mr. Gaynor nodded. 'We came here from Dublin. And you? You said your name was Sullivan?'

'We came from Dublin too, but my family were originally from Cork.'

Seeing that Sullivan had gained his confidence, Florentine for once was grateful that his partner was Irish.

'We're not here about the death of your wife,' said Florentine. He drew deeply on the cigarette, adding, 'Well, we are and we aren't.'

'How do you mean?'

'We're pretty sure we saw your wife over on Staten Island – at a funeral.'

Mr. Gaynor took a sip of his whiskey and nodded. 'The funeral of Don Diego.'

'We thought it was her!' said Florentine. 'She was talking to Diego's daughter Marguerite.'

'That's right.'

'Do you want to tell us why?'

Mr. Gaynor looked at the floor, but his mind was elsewhere. 'Nancy was dying of cancer,' he said at last.

Florentine nodded. 'Yeah, we saw it on the autopsy report. I'm sorry.'

'No need to be. It was her own fault. She knew what she was doing.'

'How do you mean?' Sullivan asked.

'These.' Mr. Gaynor held up his cigarette. 'She had lung cancer. So have I.'

Florentine extinguished his cigarette. 'But what was she doing talking to Marguerite Diego?'

'She read in the paper that Diego had been shot, so she went to tell her something she thought she should know.'

'What was that?'

'That she was adopted.'

'How did she know she was adopted?'

'Because she was the one who brought her here. She was a nurse, you see. She was working in a home for unmarried mothers in Dublin. Of course, the Diegos weren't living in Staten Island then. They were in Long Island.'

'What was the point in telling her she was adopted?' Florentine asked. 'I mean, after all this time?'

Mr. Gaynor tapped the side of his head with his forefinger, saying, 'It was getting to her.'

'Was she seeing a shrink?' Sullivan asked.

'A psychiatrist? Not at all. She didn't believe in them.'

'Why not?' asked Florentine.

Mr. Gaynor lit another cigarette and they could see he was a chain smoker. 'Maybe it was because she had been a nurse,' he replied, inhaling deeply. 'But she would say that a psychiatrist was like a blind man in a dark room looking for a black cat that wasn't there.'

'Well that's a good one,' said Sullivan.

'Anyway, she didn't need a psychiatrist to tell her what was there.'

'Why, was there one?' Florentine asked. 'Was there a black cat there?'

'I suppose there's no point in denying it, now that she's dead.'

'Denying what?' asked Sullivan.

'Well, to tell you the truth, it was driving her crazy.'

Florentine leaned closer. 'What was?'

Mr. Gaynor poured himself another whiskey. 'It happened on the way over on the liner. She was bringing a baby out here to give to the Diego family.' He downed the whiskey in one go as if to fortify himself, and the detectives waited patiently to hear what he was going to say. 'But she got it mixed up with another baby. Or at least, she thought she did. You see, there was this other girl travelling with her. She had her own baby. She was coming out to join her aunt and uncle, but she died – caught some kind of virus. Then one of the babies died too. The problem was…' He coughed, almost as if what he was about to say was caught in his throat. 'Nancy wasn't sure which one was left. But she gave it to the Diegos anyway.'

Hardened as they were by their experience, the two detectives were stunned by what they had just heard.

'I know it was a terrible thing to do,' Mr. Gaynor went on. 'But the Diegos had no children, and the other girl was taking her baby out to a couple who had eight. So, tell me, what was she to do? Anyway, she did it. She gave the surviving baby to the Diegos. Then she spent the rest of her life regretting it. She worried that she had made a dreadful mistake. And the more she thought about it, the more convinced she became that she had given away the wrong one. That's why we came to live in New York. She wanted to be near the baby, maybe keep track of her; tell her some day. You know, clear her conscience. Then, when she read that Don Diego had been shot, she decided to go to the funeral and tell her.'

'And why do you think your wife took her own life?' asked Sullivan. 'Because of the cancer, or because of what she had done?'

Mr. Gaynor shook his head and lit another cigarette. 'I don't honestly know. After Diego was buried, she met Marguerite a couple of times. Gave her letters and things belonging to her real mother. The meeting on the Statue of Liberty ferry was to be the last.'

Florentine's eyes narrowed. 'You mean Marguerite was on the ferry with her?'

Mr. Gaynor nodded. 'She had some more things to give her.'

'Have you any more of these letters?' asked Florentine.

'I'm afraid not.'

'Well,' Sullivan said when they returned to their car. 'What do you make of that?'

Florentine lowered the window and put the red light on the roof. 'I think it's time we had a long talk with Marguerite. What's the address of that deli again?'

Realising that what they had just learned might have an important bearing on the case, they crossed back into Manhattan and, turning on their flashing light, made their way through the traffic to the deli where Marguerite worked. However, the manageress informed them that Marguerite had packed in her job and left.

'To tell you the truth,' said the woman, who was helping her staff serve a queue of customers, 'I wasn't sorry. Her mind just wasn't on the job.'

'And she didn't even tell us she was going,' said one of the girls who shared the apartment with her. 'One minute she was here. Next minute, she was gone.'

Back in the car, Florentine wondered what to do next. 'Maybe her mother knows where she went,' he said, more to himself than his partner.

'Did you not get the message?' asked Sullivan. 'Mrs. Diego rang the station to say she was going up-state for a few days for a break.'

'Did she say when she would be back?'

'No. Just that she was going.'

'I don't suppose she left an address or a telephone number where she could be contacted?'

'Not as far as I know.'

Florentine banged the steering wheel with his fist. 'What kind of fucking investigation is this? We ask everyone who is a potential witness to let us know if they are changing address or leaving town. And what happens? Mrs. Diego goes up-state somewhere and doesn't bother to tell us where's she's going. Marguerite packs in her job and God knows where's she's gone. And now this other woman – Nurse what's-her-name.'

'Gaynor.'

'She might have been an important witness – and she turns up at Pier A, dead as a dodo. And the one really important witness in the case – Sister Mary – she disappears without trace.'

'Maybe Mr. Gaynor might have another look for us and see if he can

111

find any more of those letters he was talking about. They might give us some idea why Marguerite has gone. Maybe even where.'

When they returned to Mr. Gaynor's apartment, they found him still sitting in the armchair, sipping whiskey and looking into space in the way people do when death robs them of a loved one.

'I told you,' he said, 'she took all the letters with her.'

Florentine gave him his card. 'As I said before Mr. Gaynor, we're sorry for your loss. If you do come across any more of those other letters, give us a call.'

THIRTEEN

'It's weird,' said Marguerite, running her fingers over the gold lettering on the black granite headstone. 'To think that I'm supposed to be buried here.'

The headstone recorded the deaths of Catherine and her infant daughter Katie on a transatlantic crossing in 1957.

'It wasn't possible to take them back to Ireland,' Lily said. 'So Catherine's parents agreed that they should be buried here in New Jersey.'

'The news of her death broke their hearts,' said Ed.

'Not to mention the fact that she had a baby,' Lily added. 'They had no idea.'

'We knew, of course,' said Ed. 'But Catherine made us promise not to tell anyone.'

'It was a difficult decision for us,' Lily continued. 'On the one hand, we wanted to help her. On the other, we had to deceive her parents. But what else could we do?'

'So we told her to come on out,' said Ed. 'Bring her baby with her and stay with us. We had eight, and one more wasn't going to make much difference.'

Marguerite put her arms around them. 'Thank you,' she sobbed. 'If only it had worked out the way you planned. You've no idea the difference it would have made.'

Ed was holding a large bunch of flowers that had been made up for them by a local florist and when Marguerite had placed it at the foot of the headstone, she stood back, saying, 'According to Mrs. Gaynor, it's little Brigid Mary who's lying down there. She was the one who was destined to become Marguerite, not me. I'm Catherine's daughter, and I'm very much alive.'

'I know, I know,' Lily cried, and they both hugged her.

Ed smiled through his tears, saying, 'And we're so happy to have you – even if it did take you thirty years to get here!'

He hugged her too and as she wiped away her tears she said, 'Thirty-one years. I'm thirty-one.'

Seeing her take rosary beads from her handbag, Lily whispered, 'I'm glad to see you've still got your faith.'

They dried their tears and recited a decade of the Rosary and after blessing themselves, walked back out to the car.

'So, what are we going to call you?' asked Ed. 'Marguerite or Katie?'

'Well, I've been Marguerite all my life and I suppose it would feel strange being called anything else at this stage. But I know who I am.'

'You're Catherine's daughter,' said Lily as she sat into the car, 'and that's all that matters.'

The arrival of the young woman at their house in New Jersey only a couple of weeks earlier had been a very dramatic moment for them all. When Ed opened the door to her she smiled at him as if she had known him all his life, saying, 'You'll find this very difficult to believe, but I'm Catherine's daughter.'

Shocked and puzzled by what the stranger had said, Ed called Lily, and when he asked the woman to repeat what she had said, Lily almost had a heart attack. Not knowing what to make of it, she patted her breast and despite her palpitations, managed to say, 'I don't know who you are, but you'd better come in.'

Both of them were now in their seventies. Ed's hair, which had been jet black when he had first arrived in America, was silvery grey, but he was an active man and had kept his figure fairly well. Lily was more inclined to sit around the house and was overweight, but she disguised the grey in her hair with a tint of blue and looked quite glamorous for her age.

The stranger declined a drink, but Ed made up highballs of whiskey and soda for Lily and himself to steady their nerves. Then they listened with great interest to everything the woman had to say. Having told them that her adoptive father, Don Diego, had been found shot to death, she related the strange events that had followed – her meetings with Mrs. Gaynor at the funeral, and Mrs. Gaynor's story about the mix-up.

'She even knew about my music box,' she recalled. 'That it was heart-shaped and played, "*Oh dear, what can the matter be…?*"'At this, Lily burst out crying. 'I know. It was blue. Somebody gave it to us for one of the boys, but we already had one, so we sent it to Catherine when she was in the home. Don't tell me you still have it.'

'Of course I do.'

'I could see right-away that she had Catherine's blue eyes,' Ed later told Lily. 'And the same colour hair.'

'Except her hair's short,' Lily added. 'Catherine always wore hers down to her shoulders, remember?'

Over the following few days they exchanged memories and memorabilia and any other bits and pieces of information they could think of. Lily and Ed were fascinated to find that Catherine had kept notes of what had happened and while they began to read those, Marguerite was delighted to be able to read the letters Catherine had sent in reply to theirs.

'And I recognise the locket you're wearing,' said Lily.

Marguerite smiled. 'Catherine said her parents gave it to her before she left. It's all in her notes.' She took it off so that they could have a closer look. 'Mrs. Gaynor said it was among her things.'

'It was my mother's,' Lily told her. 'She wore it for as long as I can remember. Then, shortly before she died, she gave it to my sister, Catherine's mother. You can see how smooth it is.'

'But you can still read what it says on the back,' said Marguerite.

Lily nodded, and Ed, who was looking over her shoulder, read, '*Go n-éirí an bóthar leat…* May the road rise to meet you. May the wind be always at your back.'

'And until we meet again,' continued Lily, 'May God hold you in the hollow of His hand.' She wiped away a tear. 'How many times did my mother tell us what it meant when we were children.' Opening the locket, she said, 'That's Catherine's mother and father.'

'There are two more photographs behind it. Here, let me show you.' Marguerite levered them out with her nail and gave them to her.'

'Catherine,' said Lily.

'And the other one? Is that Shaunie?'

'I don't know. Here, you have a look at it Ed.'

Ed put on his glasses and studied the tiny photograph. 'Must be.'

'We never met him,' said Lily.

'What happened?' asked Marguerite as she put photographs back in the locket. 'Why did they not get married? I mean, they were so much in love. I just can't understand it.'

'We never understood it either,' Lily told her. 'We went over for the wedding. Everything was arranged. We had all taken our places – his guests on one side of the church, hers on the other. But the time for the wedding came and went and there was no sign of Shaunie, or his brothers. Then his sister, Maudie, came in and announced that there would be no wedding. She said Shaunie had gone. We all wanted to know where he had gone, but she just said he had gone and that the wedding was off.'

'Poor Catherine,' said Ed. 'She was still being driven around and around, waiting for Shaunie to arrive and go in ahead of her.'

'We were all shocked at the news,' Lily continued, 'but you can imagine how Catherine felt. She was devastated.'

'So were her parents,' said Ed. 'They drove up to Shaunie's house with her to find out what was going on. I think the priest went with them. Or did he go up in his own car? – I'm not sure. But he was very annoyed too.'

'Did they find out anything more?'

Ed shook his head. 'Nothing. All they were told was that Shaunie had gone.'

Marguerite nodded. Now she understood why the nursery rhyme had upset Catherine the first time she had heard it. *Oh dear, what can the matter be? Johnny's so long at the fair.* It must have reminded her of the day she was to have been married and of her agonising wait, wondering why Shaunie was so long in coming to the church.

116

'So what did she do?'

'What could she do?' said Lily. 'She went back home to Tipperary, but she couldn't stay there, knowing she was pregnant. It would have been a terrible scandal. So she went to Dublin and a priest put her in touch with the home for unmarried mothers.'

'Where I was born. But did Shaunie never contact her? Did he never tell her why he didn't turn up?'

'Mags, my other sister – Catherine stayed with her down in Cork – she told me that Shaunie came looking for her but she told him she had gone and that she didn't want anything more to do with him. Then he had the gall to go up to her house in Tipperary. As you can imagine, her parents were very angry about what had happened, for they knew how much she had been hurt. When they told him Catherine didn't want to see him, he came back some days later with a letter for her. She had left home at that stage, so her mother just tore the letter up and gave it back to him.'

'We never heard of him again,' Ed said. 'Catherine got in touch with us from the home and told us about the baby. There was no way she could keep the baby – not in Ireland in those days – so we told her to come on out to us and bring her baby with her.'

'This photograph,' said Marguerite, tapping the locket with her finger. 'It's the only one I have of her and it's very small. You wouldn't happen to have a better one?'

'She's a lot younger in the ones we have,' said Lily, 'but there's the one in her passport. It was probably taken a short time before she left Dublin.' She gestured towards one of the cupboards, saying, 'Ed, would you see if you can find that box?'

Ed searched around in a few drawers before producing a rather tattered shoe box. The lid and its flaps were split with age and use and were tied to the box with string.

'After they released the bodies,' explained Lily, as she untied the string, 'the authorities sent us this. I suppose ours was the forwarding address. They said it contained her personal belongings, but we were surprised to find it only contained her passport and a few other things.'

'We were going to send them to her parents,' said Ed, 'but they were heartbroken and we thought, what's the use? It'll only give them something else to cry over.'

The passport, Marguerite could see, was a large green one with a gold harp and gold lettering on the cover.

'Passport photographs are usually awful things,' said Lily, 'but that one's a good likeness of Catherine.'

'Oh, it's lovely,' exclaimed Marguerite.

'The same passport did both of you,' Lily explained. 'See under children. You'll find your birth cert in there with Catherine's too.'

As Marguerite read the entries in the birth certificates, she said, 'Father unknown.'

'We thought that was strange,' said Lily. 'Sure we all knew it was Shaunie.'

'Well, it's not really,' Marguerite told them. 'Mrs. Gaynor said the mothers in the home wouldn't tell them who the fathers were. I suppose they just didn't want anyone to know. In fact, she said some of their regular customers didn't even know themselves.'

Ed nodded. 'Yeah, I suppose it makes sense.'

'Well, I tell you what,' said Lily. 'You take this box up to the bedroom and go through Catherine's things at your leisure. We still have some of her notes to read.'

It was several days before Ed and Lily felt they knew Marguerite well enough to ask her about her childhood.

'I had no childhood,' she told them. 'Well, I suppose it was all right until the twins arrived. Then they treated me like an outcast. I suppose I should have guessed. I mean, I knew there was something. But it never occurred to me that I was adopted.'

'Still,' said Lily, 'you must have got a terrible shock when you heard that the man you thought was your father had been shot. We read about it in the paper.'

Marguerite shook her head. 'No. I wasn't a bit shocked. In fact, I was glad he was dead.' Seeing the surprised look on their faces, she added, 'You don't understand, do you? He was a very violent man, especially when he was tanked up. I ran away you know. Three times. And last time I stayed away.'

'You poor thing,' said Lily.

'Then, this woman, Mrs. Gaynor, comes along and tells me I shouldn't have been in the Diego family in the first place; that it had been mistake. And if that wasn't bad enough, she admitted that she had given me away on purpose.' Marguerite broke down and began to cry. 'When I was a child, I thought things couldn't get worse. But, suddenly, this happens and I feel as if the whole world is caving in on me.'

'Did they find out who killed him?' asked Ed.

When Marguerite shook her head, Lily asked, 'Or who the nun was?'

Marguerite shook her head again and lapsed into silence.

'We've written to Susan to tell her the good news,' said Lily. 'She's Catherine's younger sister.'

'Yeah, I know. Catherine told me about her – in her notes.'

'She'll be over the moon to hear you're alive and well. We're over the moon too. It's a miracle. But now you must look to the future. You have a whole new life ahead of you now.'

'And you're welcome to stay here as long as you like,' said Ed.

But if Ed and Lily were hoping that Marguerite could put her past life behind her so easily, they were mistaken. Soon they began to regret that they had asked her about her childhood and the death of Don Diego. Almost as if they had awakened some terrible fears that had lain dormant in the dark recesses of her mind, she would wake up crying in the middle of the night. She would be in a cold sweat and, like a child who was afraid of the dark, would not go asleep again without the light on. Even in the daytime, she seemed to suffer dramatic mood swings. Sometimes she would be smiling and happy, walking through the garden like a carefree child picking flowers. Then, quite unexpectedly, she would become very withdrawn and they would find her rocking in the swing-chair on the back porch, singing quietly to herself…

Oh dear what can the matter be?
Dear, dear, what can the matter be?
Oh dear what can the matter be?

Johnny's so long at the fair...

And then, with the innocence of a child, she would say, 'I don't understand it.'

'Understand what?' Ed would ask her gently.

'Shaunie. He loved my mother, didn't he?' When they nodded, she would add, 'Why then did he stay away? I just don't understand it.'

At other times, she would ask, 'Do you think he's still alive?' And when they asked who? She would reply, 'Shaunie. My father.'

These, of course, were questions that neither Ed nor Lily could answer and, in an effort to cheer her up, they told her that perhaps one day she could go to Ireland and find out for herself.

'How could I?' she replied. 'I've no money, no passport?'

'You're Irish, aren't you?' said Ed. 'You saw your birth cert in the box?'

'Yeah, "Father unknown".'

'That doesn't matter,' Lily said. 'It's still a birth cert. As long as you have that you can get a passport.'

'And your name's already on your mother's passport,' Ed pointed out. 'So it shouldn't be a problem.'

'Money wouldn't be a problem either,' Lily added. 'You could always pay us back.'

'That's right,' said Ed, nodding to show that he had discussed the matter with Lily and approved.

'You're very good. But I don't know...'

Shortly after that Marguerite went into New York to visit the Irish Consulate. An official there confirmed that she was entitled to an Irish passport and during the return journey the words of another little song started to go through her mind. The Monkey Song, Catherine called it and, as the bus crossed under the Hudson River on its way back into New Jersey, she began singing it to herself...

'I wish I lived in monkey land
The land where I was born
A monkey kissed me on the cheek
And said goodbye to all...'

FOURTEEN

When Detective Menton returned to his desk after a lengthy lunch, he found several messages waiting for him. Most of them were from officers in other precincts whom he had contacted in relation to various inquiries he was making. Two of them, however, were from an officer by the name of Broski in a precinct uptown that he had not been ringing.

'Broski, Broski,' he said to himself. 'Nope, can't say I know him.' The times on the two calls indicated that they had been the last to come in and for a while he wondered which calls he would return first. 'Broski,' he said to himself again, and curiosity finally getting the better of him, he decided to return the last two calls first.

'I saw your circular,' Broski told him. 'The one about the nun.'

'Sister Mary?'

'Yeah, Sister Mary.'

'Why, have you found her?'

'No, but I might be able to help you. I'm not sure.'

As the officer spoke, Menton took out the file and looked through the information he had got from Detective Florentine.

'It's a few weeks ago now,' Broski went on. 'But I remember this nun. She came into the station. She was kinda elderly, and in the middle of all the hubbub she reaches up on her tippy-toes and says something like, "It's Sister Mary." "Sorry, Sister," I said, "I can't hear you with all this noise." You know what it's like? Sometimes this place is like Grand Central.'

'Yeah, tell me about it.'

121

'Anyway, she says again, "It's Sister Mary." So I says, "Okay, Sister, hold on a minute and I'll get someone to talk to you." Between junkies and drunks and God knows what, I didn't have time to talk to her myself, you understand. So I turned to one of the female officers and said, "Could you have a word with Sister Mary and see what her problem is." But when the officer went out to talk to her, she was gone. I thought for a minute we had locked her up by mistake.' Broski gave a belly laugh, adding, 'I'm only kidding, but you know how it is?'

'Yeah, I know how it is.'

'Anyway, when I saw your circular I got to thinking. Maybe this old dame wasn't saying *she* was Sister Mary. Maybe she was trying to tell us something *about* Sister Mary!'

'Could be. Do you know where she might have come from, this nun?'

'I think I might. There's a church not far from here where the nuns run a soup kitchen. It's a kinda rough area, you understand? Tell your friend Florentine if he comes to see me, I'll look after him.'

'Right, I will. And thanks.'

'You're welcome. I'll get a patrol car to take him. Tell him if he takes his own car in there, he'll be walking back to Staten Island!' Broski gave another belly laugh and hung up.

Menton immediately rang Florentine's number and left a message for him.

When Florentine returned to the station, he found two messages waiting for him. As well as the one from Menton, there was one from John Gaynor.

'Sully,' he said, after returning Menton's call, 'the guys over in Manhattan think they might have a lead on Sister Mary. I'll go over and see what they've got. You ring Gaynor and find out what he wants.'

Broski was as good as his word and when Florentine arrived at the station, he put a patrol car at his disposal. A short time later, the car pulled up at a small church. Looking up, Florentine saw that the church was sandwiched between a run-down apartment block and a derelict warehouse. At the side gate a number of down-and-outs had gathered, waiting for a handout, and as he made his way through them one shouted, 'Hey, man, don't you be giving the good Sisters no hassle, you hear?'

'Okay, cool it,' said the driver of the patrol car through the open window. 'No problem, man, no problem.'

There was no one in the church, so Florentine made his way down the side passage until he came to an adjoining building, and seeing the convent sign beside the door, rang the bell. The nun who answered nodded shyly when he showed her his badge and invited him in. As he was led along the corridors, he heard a flurry of habits here, a whisper there, and a few moments later found himself in the presence of an elderly nun.

'I'm Mother Celine,' she said. 'Have you found her? I mean, Sister Mary. We've been so worried about her.'

'I'm afraid not. In fact, we were hoping you might be able to tell us where she is.'

'But we don't know! We thought you might be able to help us find her.'

Florentine accepted her invitation to sit down. 'Maybe we should start at the beginning. A nun called to the station and said something about Sister Mary.'

'That was me. I called to tell them she was missing. But they were very busy.'

'When exactly was that?'

When Mother Celine consulted her diary to confirm the date, Florentine noted that it was only a few days after Don Diego had been shot.

'Do you mind having a look at these?' he said, spreading a number of photographs on the table. They included photographs of Mrs. Diego, her daughters Marguerite and Vitoria, and Mrs. Gaynor, but he didn't tell her who they were.

'That's her,' she said, pointing to one of the photographs. 'That's Sister Mary. Why, what's happened to her?'

'Nothing. As far as we know she's alive and well. We just want to talk to her. We think she could be an important witness in a case we're investigating.'

'She came here when she was still in her teens,' Mother Celine recalled. 'She was hungry and had nowhere to stay. After a while she began to help us feed the other unfortunates who come to us and then, eventually, she joined us.'

'Did she leave anything behind when she took —' Florentine was going to say, 'took off?' but thought better of it and added, 'when she left?'

'She only had the clothes she was wearing and, of course, the clothes she came in. She took those with her and any other little personal things she might have had.'

'And her crucifix? I see you all wear a silver crucifix.'

'She would have been wearing that too.'

Florentine produced the crucifix that had been found in the room where Don Diego had been shot. 'Do you think that might be it?'

Mother Celine took the crucifix in her hand, saying, 'It could very well be. As you can see, it's the same as ours. But I didn't know she had lost it.'

'Perhaps she doesn't either,' said Florentine, putting the crucifix back in his pocket.

As Mother Celine showed him out, she added, 'You will let us know, won't you?'

'Ma'am?'

'If you find her. We've all been terribly worried about her.'

'If we find her,' said Florentine. 'The problem is I don't think she wants us to find her.'

John Gaynor put on his old raincoat, patted the pockets to make sure he had his cigarettes and lighter, and made his way to the subway that would take him to Battery Park. As a myriad of images, real and reflected, flashed past the windows of the carriage, he thought to himself that his wife had taken the same journey on the last day of her life, and he couldn't help wondering what had been going through her mind.

He was still wondering the same thing when he arrived at Battery Park. Easing himself on to a bench, he watched as sightseers queued for the Statue of Liberty ferry. Now and then a couple of enterprising musicians would strike up in the hope of getting a few bucks, but he didn't hear the music. He was still thinking of his wife and how, when all around her people had probably been laughing and enjoying the sights, she had gone to her watery grave.

'You know,' he said, when Detective Sullivan joined him, 'We were married almost forty years.'

'That's a long time,' Sullivan agreed.

Mr. Gaynor nodded. 'A lifetime.' When Detective Sullivan had returned his call, he could have told him to come out to the house, that he had something for him. Instead, he said he would meet him at Battery Park. Why he had done so, he didn't really know. Perhaps he needed an excuse to go to Battery Park. Perhaps he needed to sit there and look out towards the Statue of Liberty and imagine his wife's last hours…

'I told you she was dying of cancer.'

'Yeah, I was sorry to hear it.'

'I think she would like to have gone back to Ireland. Spend her last days there. But, it wasn't to be.'

'You said you had something for me.'

Mr. Gaynor reached into his raincoat pocket. 'I found this among her things. She must have missed it.'

'What is it?'

'It's one of Catherine's letters. Remember? The girl I told you about; she died on the way here from Ireland. I thought Nancy had given them all to Marguerite, but she must have missed this one. It's from the people Catherine was coming to stay with.'

Sullivan looked at the address. 'New Jersey.'

'Yeah.'

'We're anxious to talk to Marguerite, but we don't know where she is. In fact, we don't know much about her at all.'

'You probably know more about her than I do.'

'But your wife must have told you a lot about her. You reckon maybe she's gone over to New Jersey to look for these people?'

'I don't know.' Mr. Gaynor lit a cigarette and, as he inhaled, he went through the ritual of coughing until his body was convulsed. When he was able to talk again, he added, 'Those letters were written a long time ago. But maybe they're still living there. Might be worth checking it out.'

When Florentine and Sullivan met again on Staten Island, it seemed that things were beginning to come together at last. However, they thought their inquiries had come to an end when, later that day, they located Ed and Lily's house in New Jersey and asked Ed if Marguerite Diego had come to see them.

'As a matter of fact she did,' he replied. 'Why? What did you want with her?'

'We're investigating the shooting of Don Diego – her father,' replied Florentine. 'We think she can help us with our inquiries.'

'Well, you're too late,' Ed told them. 'She's gone.'

'Gone? Gone where?'

Ed didn't answer right away. Instead, he reluctantly told them to come in.

'Where has she gone?' Florentine asked again.

'When Marguerite came to us,' Ed replied, 'she was a very disturbed young woman.'

'She had a very unhappy childhood with the Diegos,' said Lily.

'And she shouldn't have been with them at all,' said Ed. 'She should have been here with us.'

'And she would have been,' Lily added, 'if it hadn't been for that horrible woman – what was it she said her name was, Ed?'

'Gaynor.'

Florentine nodded. 'We know. We've been talking to her husband.'

'Well, it's not her husband you should be talking to,' said Lily. 'It's her you should be having a word with. Imagine, giving an innocent child like that to the wrong people. It's criminal. That's what it is.'

Ed nodded. 'She should be prosecuted.'

'Mrs. Gaynor's dead,' Florentine informed them. 'Did Marguerite not tell you?'

Lily shook her head in surprise. 'No.'

'Maybe Marguerite didn't know she was dead,' Ed suggested.

'Oh she knew all right,' said Florentine. 'She was with her when it happened.'

'When what happened?' asked Ed.

'They were on the Statue of Liberty ferry. A couple of weeks later Mrs. Gaynor was fished out of the water. Her husband thinks she jumped. Apparently she had cancer.'

Lily blessed herself. 'God have mercy on her. Marguerite never mentioned it.

'No. And she didn't mention it to anyone else as far as we can ascertain,' Florentine said. 'Not even when she was getting off the ferry. Never said she had been with her.'

Ed asked the two detectives if they would like a drink, but they declined. 'Well,' he said, 'it's not surprising she didn't tell anyone, considering all she had on her mind. I mean, the man she thought was her father had just been shot dead. Then this woman comes along and tells her he wasn't really her father, that she was adopted. And to crown it all, that it was a mistake – that she shouldn't have been with the Diego family in the first place. Sure, she must have been demented.'

Sullivan who, by prior arrangement, had let his partner do most of the talking, waited for Ed to fix a drink for himself and his wife, before asking, 'What part of Ireland are you from?'

'Tipperary,' said Ed. 'And you? Didn't you say your name was Sullivan?'

'That's right. My family came from Cork originally, but I was born in Dublin.' Sullivan said no more until Ed sat down again, then judging the moment to be right, continued, 'So tell me, where's Marguerite now? Where has she gone?'

'She wanted to start a new life,' Ed explained. 'Or rather the life she should have started here with us when she was a baby.'

'We were glad,' said Lily. 'The Diegos must have given her a terrible time.'

'What did she tell you about the shooting of Don Diego?' asked Florentine.

'Nothing – just that he had been shot.'

'Did you not ask her about it?'

Lily shook her head. 'As Ed said, she was quite disturbed by it all. So much had happened. She could hardly sleep at night thinking about it.'

'We could hear her crying,' Ed recalled. 'It was very sad.'

'But we were happy to have her here,' said Lily. 'We have eight children you know. Well, they're not children now. They're all grown up.'

'Penny – she's the youngest – she's gone now too,' Ed said. 'She calls in to see us now and then. But the house is very empty without her. So, as Lily says, we were delighted to have Marguerite.'

'Her real name is Katie,' Lily explained. 'So, when she realised she was never meant to be Marguerite, she decided to put it all behind her.'

'That's all very fine,' Florentine interjected. 'But legally she's still Marguerite.'

'That's not what it says on her passport,' Ed countered.

'Passport?' asked Florentine. 'What passport?'

'Her Irish passport,' Lily told him.

'But how can she get an Irish passport if she's not Irish?' asked Sullivan. 'I mean, she must be an American citizen now.'

'But she is Irish,' said Lily. 'She was born in Dublin and she has her birth certificate to prove it.'

'And where is she now?' asked Florentine.

'In Ireland, of course,' said Lily.

'And why did she decide to go there?' asked Sullivan.

Ed drained his glass. 'She's gone to try and find her real father.'

'And maybe to try and find her real self,' Lily added.

Part 2

Ireland – United States

Autumn 1988 – Spring 1989

FIFTEEN

There were only two topics of conversation in Ireland that Saturday: the weather and the 1988 all-Ireland hurling final between Tipperary and Galway. Or so it seemed to Marguerite. Mrs. Gaynor's reference to O. Henry had made her curious and on the flight from New York to Dublin she had been reading some of his short stories, including 'The Gift of the Magi'.

Later a stewardess leaned over and offered her an Irish newspaper and by the time the Boeing 737 was homing in over Howth Head to make its approach to Dublin Airport, she had read the newspaper from cover to cover. According to Lily and Ed it rained a lot in Ireland and that was why the fields were so green. However, the weather forecast in the paper said Sunday was going to be dry and mild with a moderate south west wind. It was a forecast the sports commentators were hoping was accurate as they said it would make conditions just right for the big game.

Marguerite wondered how the game was played. All she knew about it was what her birth mother had written on the RMS *Atlantia*. It was ironic, she thought, that the voyage on which she had been taken over as a baby would have taken the best part of a week, while she was now returning to Dublin in a matter of hours. If Catherine had travelled by plane instead of by ship, she might still be alive and the whole sorry affair that had followed would have been avoided. But were there transatlantic flights in those days? If so, maybe they were too expensive. Maybe travel by ship was cheaper. Maybe…

Leaving all the 'maybes' aside, Marguerite thought again about the hurling final. She wondered if Shaunie would be at it, and she was sure he would – if he was still alive. After all, Catherine had written of his love for the game. In fact, it was when he was at a hurling match that she had first met him. Togged in his hurling gear, he was a fine cut of a man, she said. And on the way up to their whitethorn of the dancing, he practised his game by tossing a small stone into the air and sending it crashing up into the mountain. He hoped one day to play for his county, and she wondered if he ever did.

As the huge plane banked and the crew lined it up for the runway, she could see Dublin port on the left, then the suburbs and she smiled as she told herself she must go and see Nelson's Pillar from which her mother and her friend Bridie had viewed the city. However, there was only one thought on her mind as the plane landed and taxied to a stop. It was a thought that had interrupted her reading and occupied her mind for much of the flight: what would Susan and her husband be like, and what kind of reception would they give her?

When she had collected her luggage and cleared customs, her worries, if that's what they were, soon evaporated. In the arrivals hall a very warm welcome awaited her from people who had long believed she was dead and were delighted to find she was very much alive.

'Katie? Marguerite? We weren't sure what we should call you?' Susan confessed.

However, their visitor put them at ease with a smile, saying, 'Marguerite will do for now.'

Susan was younger than Marguerite expected. But then, Catherine had written of the age-gap between herself and her sister. What was it she called her? An afterthought!

As they talked, Marguerite found herself doing a bit of mental arithmetic. If she was thirty-one and Susan was twelve at the time she was born, that meant her new-found aunt was still in her early forties. Somehow she also imagined that Susan would be tall and thin with long brown shoulder-length hair like her sister, Catherine. Instead she was quite plump, something her loose jacket and skirt could not hide. Her hair tended to be more fair than brown and was cut in a short, boyish style with a fringe that parted to each side at the eyebrows.

As for Susan's husband, James, he looked distinctly uncomfortable in a blue, striped suit, and it didn't seem to go very well with his brown cloth cap. It was the first time Marguerite saw anyone wearing a cap, but she would find that many men in rural Ireland wore them and, in James's case, she soon discovered why. On being introduced, he raised his cap and she could see that his black hair was thinning all over. So much so that it revealed the whiteness of his scalp and she reckoned he wore the cap to cover his embarrassment.

While James might not have been very observant, his wife was. She thought her new-found niece was, well, sort of… the first word that came into her mind was, plain. But then she said to herself, no, not plain, conservative. Perhaps she too expected Marguerite to look the way Catherine looked when she last saw her. But then, she reminded herself, that was more than thirty years ago.

As they made their way to the car park, Susan thought that maybe it was the flat-heeled shoes Marguerite was wearing that made her look so conservative. Or was it the lack of make-up? That and the hair. Short hair like her own but, as her mother used to say, there was no shape or make to it. Perhaps a visit to the hairdressers and a makeover, or even a visit to Dublin for a new outfit might be in order.

Almost as if she had read Susan's last thought, Marguerite said, 'Will we be going through Dublin?'

'We don't have to,' James told her. 'But we can, if you would like to have a look at it.'

'Is there anything in particular you would like to see?' asked Susan.

'I'd love to see Nelson's Pillar.'

James turned and smiled. 'I'm afraid you're too late. The IRA blew the Pillar up years ago.'

'Ed and Lily told me about the IRA. But they said the trouble was in the north of Ireland.'

'So it is.' James turned his attention to the road ahead of him. 'But I suppose they didn't like the thought of a British admiral lording it over Dublin from the top of the Pillar.'

'Pity,' said Marguerite. 'Catherine said she viewed the city from the top of it. I'd like to have done the same.'

When they arrived in the city centre Susan told her they were in O'Connell Street.

'And over there, on the right,' said James. 'That's the GPO. Nelson's Pillar was just opposite it.'

At O'Connell Bridge, Marguerite remarked on the number of people who were wearing colourful clothes. Some carried banners and they seemed in festival mood, cheering and shouting as they strolled along.

'It's the all-Ireland hurling final,' James told her. 'But you wouldn't have heard about that in America.'

'I read about it in the paper on the way over,' Marguerite hastened to let him know. 'Tipperary and Galway it said.'

James smiled. 'That's right. Blue and gold – they're the Tipperary supporters. Maroon and white, Galway.'

'Are you going to it?' asked Marguerite.

James shook his head. 'Not a hope. The tickets were sold out ages ago.'

'But we'll be watching it on television,' said Susan. 'You'll find it quite different from the games you have in America, but we can explain it to you.'

Marguerite smiled. 'I'd like that.' As they drove on through the city, she added, 'I was hoping to call on Catherine's friend, Bridie.'

'Who?' asked Susan.

'Bridie Flynn. But then you wouldn't have heard of her. You see, Catherine wrote it all down for me. She said she met Bridie in the home for unmarried mothers. Before leaving they exchanged addresses and promised to keep in touch. But, of course, it wasn't to be. I just thought it would be nice to look her up.'

'It's amazing, isn't it?' said Susan. 'She was my own sister and I knew nothing about it. Then, I suppose, I was too young.'

'Maybe we can call and see her another day,' James suggested. 'We wouldn't have time today.'

'If you like,' Susan said, 'we can come back up to Dublin for a day and you can go to see her then. And you can have a look at the shops – maybe even get yourself a new outfit.'

'Yeah, I'd like that. What would you suggest?'

'Something Irish to take back. A tweed jacket or an Aran jumper.'

'Is tweed in fashion at the moment?'

Susan smiled. 'Irish tweed's always in fashion.

'Anyway,' James said, 'you'll need something like that to keep you warm. The weather's very mild at the moment, but you'll find it gets chilly from here on in.'

They were silent for a little while as Marguerite looked out and tried to take it all in.

'You'll have to meet Eileen,' Susan told her. 'She and Catherine were great friends.'

'I take it that's the same Eileen who made the wedding dress for her?'

'That's right, she did. She's our next-door neighbour. Catherine and herself grew up together.'

'Catherine mentioned her all right. I'd love to meet her.'

Leaving Dublin behind them, they headed south, and when they met cars with blue and gold flags fluttering from their windows, James said, 'They're all on their way to the final.'

'Do you think Tipperary will win?' Marguerite asked.

James raised his eyes in a smile that showed he wasn't sure. 'I hope so. It's seventeen years since we won an all-Ireland.'

'Are Galway good?'

'They beat Kilkenny in the final last year and Kilkenny are good, so I'd say it'll be a tough game.'

'And are Cork good?'

James smiled and conceded, 'They can be good too. Why? How come you're so interested in hurling?'

'Shaunie – Catherine said he was my real father – he played hurling in Cork. In fact, she said his ambition was to play for his county one day. Do you think he ever did?'

'He could have. Sure I'll look it up for you.'

As they journeyed south, Marguerite marvelled at the narrowness of the roads, the height of the hedges and, not for the first time, at the fact that everything was so green. Then, as they neared Tipperary they met more and more cars sporting blue and gold flags. The occupants, she could see, were in a state of high excitement and James told her, 'It's just as well you came today. The roads will be choc-a-bloc tomorrow.'

Marguerite was delighted to learn that Susan still lived in the family home – the cottage where Catherine grew up – and she couldn't wait to see it. In the meantime, the journey itself was a wonderful experience as she saw some of the places and things Catherine had mentioned so lovingly, including the Rock of Cashel, Tipperary town, and the Galty Mountains.

'We'll take you to the Glen of Aherlow for a day,' Susan said. 'You'll love it.'

When they arrived at the cottage, Marguerite was charmed to meet her two new cousins – Susan's teenage sons, Kevin and Mark. However, the boys were shy and, after exchanging a few pleasantries with her, they made an excuse to go out.

'They want to see their friends before they return to boarding school,' Susan explained. 'You see, there's no secondary school in this area, so it was boarding school or nothing. James is taking them back there tomorrow after the match.'

Somehow Marguerite had imagined that Catherine had been brought up in a cottage with a thatched roof. In fact, it was slated, but she wasn't disappointed. Even though she had never been in it before, she loved every nook and cranny of it, for she felt as if it was part of her and of her past. And when she watched the all-Ireland hurling final on television the following day, she somehow felt closer to Shaunie than she had ever felt before.

The weather forecast turned out to be spot on for it was a dry, sunny day. Tipperary were confident and chose to play against the breeze. However, Marguerite soon discovered that hurling was a very fast game and at times she had difficulty following the ball. It was also a very physical game and, as the players stretched themselves to their limits and clashed with a resounding crack of their ash-wood hurls, she could well imagine why Catherine had described Shaunie as a fine cut of a man.

Whenever Tipperary scored, they all cheered, and none more so than Marguerite, but Galway scored a late goal and won the championship for the second year in a row.

James and Susan were greatly disappointed. So were the boys, but when the time came for them to go back to boarding school, they waved the blue and gold colours of their county out the windows of the car as it took off down the road. Those, returning from the match were doing the same, and to Marguerite it seemed to be an act of both defiance and pride.

Shortly after James returned, Catherine's friend Eileen called to see Marguerite and they all sat around the fire for a chat. Marguerite wanted to hear all about her birth mother and the others wanted to know all about her. She told them about her meetings with Mrs. Gaynor and about the mix-up, and showed them some of the notes Catherine had written for her. As they thumbed through the notepads, the others reminisced about Catherine and it was only when Marguerite indicated that she was tired after the long journey that they adjourned for the night.

Over the next few days, Marguerite spent much of her time poring over old photographs and wandering through the yard and the fields beyond where Catherine had played as a child. Sometimes Susan would go down the fields with her and, as they walked, they talked. Things were never the same after Catherine's death, Susan told her. A great sadness had descended on the family and while, after a time, she and her brothers were able to put it behind them, their parents seemed unable to do so.

'They never told us the real reason Catherine had gone to America, but after they died we found letters Ed and Lily had written to them and that was how we found out. I suppose they couldn't understand how things could have gone so badly wrong. Why Catherine couldn't have told them. It probably preyed on their minds and, in the end I think they lost the will to live.'

Susan pulled a seed head from the long grass and scattered the seeds to the wind, adding, 'Eventually the lads went to England in search of work and I married James.'

In an effort to lighten the conversation, Marguerite changed the subject.

'Catherine was saying that when she was younger, she had an awful time with a black-and-white rooster.'

'Oh, indeed she had. But then, she used to tease him. And my father was as bad. He encouraged her.'

When they returned to the house, Susan put on the kettle for a cup of tea. 'We had that old cock a long time and he became very aggressive.'

'I suppose he thought he was cock-of-the-walk?'

Susan smiled. 'I suppose you could say that. On one occasion my father helped Catherine dress the old cock up in red flannel. It was just as if a strange cock with a big red comb had come into the yard. The other cocks attacked him and that made him worse than ever. After that, I think he had it in for her. Even when she wanted to go to the toilet, she had to try and sneak over to it without being seen. The toilet was out in the yard at that time, you understand, and the old cock would be waiting outside the door for her. Sometimes she was trapped in there for ages. But she had to go to school, so eventually she would make a run for it and the cock after her.'

Susan laughed as she poured the tea, saying, 'I suppose it was all good fun. But the cock often reefed her legs, not to mention her stockings.'

'I take it then you had no running water in those days?'

'No such luxury. We had to fetch it in buckets.'

'You mean, from a well?'

'Ah no – from the pump up the road.'

'You're kidding!'

'No, that's the truth. It was hard work. I remember my mother hanging buckets of water on the handlebars of the bicycle and walking home with them.'

Later, as her visitor talked about life in New York and all the luxuries people had over there, Susan was glad that the cottage had long since been provided with running water and other mod cons. At the same time, what she really wanted to talk about was Marguerite's childhood, not her own, and about the shooting of her adoptive father, Don Diego. However, Lily had written from New Jersey advising her not to ask about these things.

'When we asked her, she became quite upset,' Lily told her. 'So, my

138

advice is to say as little as possible about it.'

Hoping that Marguerite might volunteer some information about the affair, Susan told her that news of her homecoming had been carried in the local newspaper, the *Tipperary Star*, and showed her the cutting.

Marguerite smiled as she read the heading, saying, '*The Prodigal Daughter* – that's a good one.' Looking down the report, she also saw that it spoke of an unfortunate mix-up at birth and said Catherine's relatives were elated with the news that her daughter was still alive. 'I don't suppose it made the dailies?'

Susan shook her head. 'I don't think so. At least, not that I heard.'

'I wonder how they found out about it?'

'I'm afraid we're to blame. When Lily wrote and told us about it, we were so delighted we just had to tell somebody. I hope you don't mind?'

Marguerite shook her head. 'No. Of course not.'

'What did your parents – I mean, your adoptive parents – say about it?'

'I didn't know about it myself until after Don Diego was shot. Mrs. Gaynor told me at the funeral.'

There was an awkward silence, and realising that Marguerite didn't intend to say anything more about Don Diego, Susan changed the subject. 'How about going up to Dublin? We can try and track down that woman Catherine met in the home. What did you say her name was?'

'Bridie – Bridie Flynn. But you know, I've been thinking about that, and I'm not so sure it's a good idea.'

'Why not?'

'Well, how can I? I mean, if she heard at the time that Catherine and her baby had died on the way over, I can't just arrive on her doorstep and say, "Hi, I'm Catherine's daughter." I would have to explain that there was a mix-up and that it was her baby that died. I wouldn't like to do that to her.'

'I suppose not. But then, she may not know that anyone died on the ship. She may not have heard about it.'

'That's true, of course. And I *would* like to see her.' Marguerite paused. 'Do you think we would have time to go shopping as well?'

'I don't see why not – if we leave early enough.'

'All right then, let's do it. When will we go?'

'Tomorrow if you like. After we look Bridie up we could go to Switzers. I believe it is a lovely shop.'

'It's in Dublin – right?'

Susan nodded. 'It's in Grafton Street. There are some lovely stores there. That's where all the Americans shop. You'll love it.'

'You make it sound like Fifth Avenue.'

'Fifth Avenue? I've never seen Fifth Avenue. In fact, I don't see Dublin very often, so I'm going to enjoy it every bit as much as you.'

'Do they sell those lovely tweeds you were talking about?'

'Of course they do. Tweeds hand-made in Donegal. Aran jumpers and matching berets – everything you can imagine.'

'That's wonderful. I want to look my best when I go to Cork.'

Susan gave her a sympathetic look. 'So you've still got your mind set on finding Shaunie?'

Marguerite smiled. 'Of course. He *is* my father, isn't he?'

SIXTEEN

Susan nosed her car along the quays beside the River Liffey, pointed out the Four Courts to Marguerite and cautiously took a left turn into O'Connell Street. She would have preferred it if James had been able to drive them to Dublin, but he was working. As an employee of the electricity board he had the use of a van, so at least she had the car. She had consulted a street map of Dublin the night before and had a good idea of the route she needed to take. Or at least, she thought she had. As she turned into the side streets of the north inner city, she found it all very confusing. Each street looked much like the other and after one particular wrong turn she found herself looking into the yard of a block of flats. Clothes were flapping on the lines and through the open window of the car she could hear women shouting across to one another from their balconies. Embarrassed by having lost her way in such a spectacular fashion in front of Marguerite, she beat a hasty retreat but after getting directions from yet another passer-by, eventually found the street where, according to Catherine's notes, Bridie Flynn lived.

The number they were looking for was in a terrace of yellow-brick houses, some of which had been painted various shades of red or brown. To Marguerite, who had never before seen the brick of a house painted red, or, indeed, any other colour, it seemed that the occupants kept their homes neat and tidy, but were oblivious to the need for a common colour scheme.

Leaving Susan in the car, Marguerite consulted her notes again to make sure she was at the right address and walked up to the door. All the while she was wondering if Bridie would look much different from the way Catherine had described her. She paused, looked back at Susan for moral support, then tapped almost apologetically with the brass knocker.

It was still quite early in the day and the elderly woman who answered had her hair in curlers. 'Bridie Flynn?' she replied. 'No, the Flynns' house was up there, Number 44. But sure they haven't lived here for ages, love.'

Seeing the disappointment on the stranger's face, the woman added, 'You're an American, aren't you? And did you come all the way from America to see Bridie Flynn?'

'Well, I was coming to Ireland anyway, and I thought I would look her up. She was a friend of my mother's. I don't suppose you know where she's living now?'

By this time the woman's next door neighbour had come out to mop her door-step and find out what was going on. 'Bridie Flynn?' she said, drawing deeply on a cigarette that had somehow hung on to its ash. 'As far as I know she moved out to Finglas.'

'You wouldn't happen to have her address by any chance?'

'Ah no. Sure Finglas is a big place.'

'But if you ask them up at Number 44,' the first woman said, 'they should be able to give it to you.'

The woman was right. The Flynns had left their new address with the people at Number 44 and so, a short time later, Susan and Marguerite drove back out of the city, armed not only with the new address, but with copious directions on how to find Finglas. Find it they did, but locating Bridie's house proved much more difficult. The long roads of terraced houses had a sameness about them that was even more confusing than the streets of the inner city, and had it not been for the help given to them by a young boy on a piebald pony, they would almost certainly have abandoned their quest.

'What are you smiling at?' Susan asked as they followed the young bareback rider into an estate.

Marguerite shook her head. 'I don't mean to be offensive, but they'll never believe this back in the States.'

Susan smiled. 'And what do you think James is going to say when he

142

hears about it? I mean, if I tell him we got lost in Dublin and had to be rescued by the Lone Ranger on a piebald pony, he'll say we're not fit to be allowed out on our own.'

They both had a good laugh at the very idea of what was happening, but when the young rider pulled up his mount on the pavement to point to a particular house, they really appreciated what he had done for them. So they thanked him profusely and waved to him as he galloped off across a barren field, which seemed to be the edge of the estate and the city.

While Susan waited in the car, Marguerite braced herself for the meeting she had so long looked forward to, for her sense of anticipation was laced with a strong feeling of apprehension. What if Bridie didn't want to talk to her? What if she didn't even want to see her? After all, she wouldn't want her husband to know that she had given birth to a child before she was married.

'Yes?'

The woman who answered the glass-panelled door was small and dumpy. She had jet black hair cut short all the way round, so that it curled up at the edges, and she wore a very short black skirt. However, her efforts to look young were betrayed by the bulge around her midriff and the grey parting in her hair. Both told their own story, and Marguerite reckoned she was in her late forties or early fifties.

'Can I help you?'

'Yeah, I hope so. I'm looking for Bridie Flynn. I was told she might live here?'

The woman looked up at her, surprised to hear a stranger use her maiden name. 'I'm Bridie Flynn. Or at least I used to be, before I got married. Why? Who wants to know?'

Marguerite could feel her eyes begin to moisten. 'I'm Marguerite,' she replied. 'Catherine's daughter.'

The woman looked at her and, seeing that she didn't understand, Marguerite added, 'She told me you and she were great friends.' She lowered voice. 'You know – in the home where I was born.'

'Oh Mother of God.' Bridie cast her eyes up to the heavens and hurriedly blessed herself. Then she gave a give a quick look up and down the street before pulling Marguerite inside. There she seated her visitor at the kitchen table, lit a cigarette and wrapped her cardigan tightly around herself in an effort to regain her composure.

'Catherine,' she said at last, exhaling a plume of blue smoke. 'Of course I remember her. How could I forget? She was the best friend I had. She promised to write to me, you know – when she got to America – but she never did.'

'That's because she never got there.'

'Never got there? How do you mean?'

'I'm afraid she died on the way over.'

'Oh no!' Bridie turned away to hide her tears. 'I never knew. I often wondered why she didn't write to me, but it never occurred to me that she was dead. Oh that's terrible. Do you know what happened to her?'

'Not really. Some sort of virus I believe.'

'And you're her daughter? Well, look at you.' Bridie was trying to pull herself together again. 'I mean the size of you! Janey mack, the last time I saw you, you were only a baby.'

'And you had a baby too.'

'That's right. Brigid Mary. She would be your age now. Stand up and let me have a look at you. Yes, she would be just your age. Same blue eyes and all.'

Bridie began to cry again and Marguerite embraced her and they hugged one another and they both cried.

When they had finished, Bridie looked up, saying, 'I often wondered what she would be like when she grew up and now I know. Well, maybe not as tall. I mean, look at the height of me. But then, he was tall…'

Marguerite looked around to make sure no else was listening and ventured, 'Was her father your, ah… present husband?'

'Him? Huh, you must be bleedin' joking.' Bridie went over to the worktop, filled the kettle and took out a loaf of bread. 'And you needn't worry about my husband coming in and finding you here. He's gone and he won't be back.'

Just then the back door of the kitchen burst open and two young boys crowded around her.' Hey, Gran,' one of them cried, 'can we have something to eat too?'

'Would you feck off out of here the pair of you. Can't you see I have a visitor?'

The boys grabbed a slice of bread each and were gone before she could stop them. 'And if you do that again,' she shouted after them, 'I'll bleedin' well kill you.' She closed the door and poured two cups of tea. 'Sorry about that. But they're driving me bonkers. It's all their father's fault. He was never here when he was needed – you know what I mean, like?'

'Have their parents separated?'

'Separated?' Bride lit another cigarette. 'You could say that.'

'Another woman?'

'Not at all. Sure, all he was interested in was drink.'

'No hope of a reconciliation then?'

'A reconciliation?' Bridie laughed. 'You know, it's funny you should say that, but the guard who brought him back the last time…?'

'Guard?'

'A guard – a policeman. That's what we call them here. But then you wouldn't know that, would you, you coming from America? Anyway, the last time my daughter threw him out he got drunk again, so he goes to the garda station – the police station – and gets one of them to come back here with him – hoping that she'll take him back on their say so, if you wouldn't mind. "Would you not try one more reconciliation, ma'am?" says the guard. All official like, you know? "Reconciliation?" says I. "Listen guard. Do you see all them children there? Everyone one of them is a reconciliation – and there are going to be no more reconciliatons in this house."'

'He's gone for good then?'

'Yeah – I wish!'

'And your own husband?'

'Ah he's gone years ago.'

Marguerite smiled. She could see now what Catherine and Mrs. Gaynor meant when they said Bridie was a hard case. It was also obvious that Bridie knew nothing of the mix-up that had occurred, and for that she was grateful.

Bridie refilled the cups. 'I'm sorry I can't offer you coffee, but we don't drink it.'

'That's all right. I drink tea back home too.'

'I suppose you're wondering why I gave my baby away?'

'Not really. Well, I suppose I am, but it's none of my business. I take it there was no way you could have kept her.'

'Ah no love – not in them days. Times were hard and I couldn't have brought another baby into the house. There were too many mouths to feed as it was.'

Marguerite nodded.

'But the truth is my father would have killed me if he had known I was pregnant. Janey mack, when I think of it. He was always belting me for staying out late. Said I was going to get myself into trouble. I loved going to dances, you see, and I had loads of fellas. Ah Jaysus, no, there was no way I could have told him. And my mother didn't really have any say in the matter. He was the boss. So I hid the pregnancy as long as I could and then I went to the home. Of course, they thought I was going to England to work.'

Bridie paused to light another cigarette, a wistful look in her eye. 'I wish I could have gone to England, or, better still, America, like Catherine did. You have no idea how much we envied her – the girls in the home. Imagine, being able to go to America and take your baby with you! It broke our hearts having to give our babies away, but what else could we do? Yeah, Catherine was the lucky one.'

Marguerite smiled. Lucky? Bridie didn't know the half of it.

'But here I am, going on about myself. How can I help you?'

'Catherine told me a lot about you and about the home. She wrote it all down for me on the way over to America. That's how I managed to track you down. But I wanted to learn more about it – and about her.'

'Ah, she was lovely. Not like some of the ones they got in there.'

'But what was it like in the home? I just find it difficult to imagine.'

'Well, it was run by the nuns. They always wore a white apron over their blue dress when they were on nursing duty, and they had this...'

146

Bridie put her hands up to the sides of her head to illustrate what she was saying… 'this big white head-dress with floppy ears. Butterfly's wings, we called them. They were always flopping around and it was very awkward if you were sitting beside them on a bus. But when they were on nursing duty, they would pin the ears up out of the way. Mother Benignius was the head nun. She always wore blue. Then there was Sister Aloysius.'

'That name rings a bell. Catherine mentioned her in her notes. She said they had a nickname for her, but she didn't say what it was.'

Bridie smiled. 'I'm not surprised. I suppose she didn't know what age you would be when you read whatever she wrote.'

'So… what was it they called this nun?'

'Well, to tell you the truth, we had nicknames for all of them. Mother Benignius was called Big Knickers.'

Marguerite smiled. 'And Sister Aloysius?'

'We called her Creepin' Jaysus – not to her face mind you! But she was known as nothing else but Creepin' Jaysus?'

'How come?'

'Because she was always creeping around the place in the dead of night. You know, spying on us, trying to catch us out.'

'Doing what?'

'Smoking mainly. You see, it wasn't allowed. So after we had a quiet pull we would put the fag ends into an empty jar of Ponds cream. But sometimes, when we woke, we would find that the lid had been screwed off and we knew she had been nosing around. I suppose it was her way of telling us that she knew what we had been doing. But mind you, she was good in other ways. Especially to Catherine. I think she felt sorry for her.'

'And what happened to Father Michael?'

Bridie blew a long plume of smoke into the air. 'So she told you about him too?'

It was Mrs. Gaynor who had told her, but Marguerite just said, 'Did he really fall from grace?'

'Well, that's one way of putting it. Poor Father Michael. Imagine, putting him into that place!'

Marguerite smiled and nodded.

'You see, Father Michael was a very young priest and we all thought he was gorgeous. I can still see him now. He had black wavy hair and a thin pale face. And his hands were long and slender. Yes, he was gorgeous all right, sexy in a sort of innocent way. You know what I mean, like? And some of the girls were always flirting with him.'

'Even though he was a priest?'

'Listen love, as far they were concerned, he was a man and they let him know it. Then, Mary O'Reilly put a bet on with her friends. She bet them that she could seduce him, and one day she did. The two of them were hard at it on the kitchen table when who walks in but Mother Benignius. The first we heard of it was when she ran screaming down the corridor. Somebody said she must have seen a mouse, but we all knew it would take more than a mouse to frighten her. Sister Aloysius hoisted her habit and went running after her like the clappers to see what was wrong. It was a while before we heard what had happened, but eventually it came out.'

'And what became of him?'

'Oh he was transferred. Never heard of him again. It was the kitchen table that became the problem.'

Marguerite smiled. 'In what way?'

'Well, they said that when Mother Benignius opened the door of the kitchen, she saw Mary O'Reilly lying on her back on the table, the big one we did our baking on. Her skirt was up around her head and his trousers were down around his knees and well, she didn't need anyone to draw a picture to tell her what they were doing. He was replaced by an elderly priest, Father Phelim was his name. Of course, some of the girls skitted him, you know, saying he probably didn't even remember what he had it for, that sort of thing. They were very coarse. But Father Phelim was very good and I always remember his first sermon. Of course, we were all waiting for him to make some reference to young Father Michael, but all he said was, "Nobody is more aware of sin than the clergy, and nobody is more aware of their own sin than the clergy." Imagine!'

'What did Mary O'Reilly and her friends say to that?'

148

'Nothing. They were gobsmacked. I mean, it was the last thing they expected him to say. But then, it's true, isn't it? Priests hear about sin every day in confession. And somehow you think they don't have any sin themselves, but Father Phelim told them straight out.'

'And what was the problem with the table?'

'Ah the table,' Bridie chuckled. 'Well, Mary O'Reilly was banned from working in the kitchen and some of the others were ordered to scrub the table, which they did. They scrubbed and scrubbed until the boards were white and you could see the brown knots standing out like the warts on the back of a child's hand. But no amount of scrubbing could wash away what had happened there. The girls who worked in the kitchen were always thinking about it, and I suppose it was to tease the nuns as much as anything else, but whether it was rolling pastry or whisking cream, they did it with such enthusiasm that they seemed to reach a passionate climax. You know, like? Sister Aloysius wasn't amused and she must have reported it to Mother Benignius, for the next thing we knew the table was covered with oilcloth. It was white oilcloth with blue squares and it was decorated with prints of jugs and fruit in a kind of faded red. But they soon found that the oilcloth couldn't cover the sin that had been committed there either. Some of the girls were always skitting and tittering about it.'

'So what did they do?'

'In the end they sold it and bought a new one from Clerys. It had a laminated surface and was easier to keep clean.'

'So you all had to work in the home?'

'Yes, we took our turns at cooking, cleaning, that sort of thing. The nurses looked after the babies and we would feed them and hold them for a while before they went to sleep. And then one day the nuns would take them and give them away to somebody else.'

'Sounds very cruel.'

Bridie wiped a tear from her eye with her knuckle. 'It was, but we had no option.'

'And were you introduced to the adoptive parents before the babies were handed over to them?'

Bridie shook her head. 'We never saw them. We could only guess what they were like from the clothes they sent in. You see, when the day came, we were given clothes to dress the babies. If the clothes were nice and fancy, we liked to think they were going to a good home. That maybe the father was some well-to-do person who lived out in the suburbs, you know, someone with plenty of money but no lead in his pencil. That's where we always liked to think they were going, but you couldn't help wondering about it and how they would end up.'

'And what did the nuns say to you – did they just take the babies from you, or how was it done?'

'Oh, Mother Benignius had a way. I suppose she thought she was breaking it to us gently. She would send for us and she had the same old story for everybody… "Come in and sit down." Mimicking the head nun, Bridie went on, "I have great news for you, Brigid. We have found the most wonderful parents for little Brigid Mary. You should be *so* happy and thank God for sending them here. They have no children of their own and they're *so* looking forward to having a baby daughter. They'll shower *so* much love on her. She's going to be *so* lucky. I hope you're going to be *so* happy for her. It's not every day we come across such a lovely couple. They've *so* much love to give. And they're *very* comfortable." '

The irony of this wasn't lost on Marguerite, but it was something she couldn't discuss with Bridie, not without letting her know all that had happened. So, she changed the subject. 'Catherine said the two of you used to sing a little lullaby called "The Monkey Song" to get the babies to go to sleep. Do you remember it?'

'Of course I do. It was just a bit of nonsense.'

Marguerite smiled. 'Yeah. She said it was a bit silly but I think it's cute. She wrote down the words for me, but I never heard it sung, you know, the way it was sung to the children. Would you mind?'

'What? Sing it? Sure I would sound silly singing it to an adult.'

'Please.'

'All right. Here goes…

'*I will-a-lish I lill-a-lived in mull-a-lunkey la-la-land*

150

The la-la-land where I-la-li was boll-a-lorn
A mull-a-lunkey kill-a-lissed me oll-a-lon the chill-a-leek
And will-a-laved good bal-a-lye to all-a-all...'

Marguerite smiled then spoke the words the way Catherine had translated them.

'That's it,' said Bridie. 'But don't ask me what it means.'

'And what did you do in the evenings?' Marguerite asked. 'I mean, when the babies were asleep?'

'We just went up to the common room for a smoke and a chat. Sometimes we would play records and dance with one another.'

'What sort of records?'

'Elvis mostly. He was big star at that time. *Shake, Rattle and Roll, My Blue Suede Shoes* and, of course, *Heartbreak Hotel*. We were always playing that, because that's where we were – heartbreak hotel. Some of us were heartbroken over a fella, some for our families. Not me, mind you. But with the thought of having to give away our babies, we were all heartbroken. As Elvis said, we were down at the end of Lonely Street and, when we had handed our babies over, it couldn't get any lonelier.'

Marguerite smiled sympathetically. 'It must have been heart-breaking all right.' She got up to go. 'You've been very good. I really do appreciate it.'

'Will you not stay and have another cup of tea?'

'No, but thanks a lot. My friend Susan, she's waiting in the car.'

'Oh no! I didn't realise that or I would have asked her in.'

'She's fine. We're going shopping now. All I have is what I came in.' Marguerite smiled. 'I just wanted to find out everything I could about Catherine and what it was like in the home. By the way, could you tell me how to get to it? I'd like to see it.'

'Ah, I'm sorry love, but they knocked it down years ago. No harm either.'

They embraced one another again, and as they parted, Bridie said, 'I don't suppose Brigid Mary will ever call to see me.' She sniffed and wiped away a tear. 'But at least I know what she might look like now.'

Marguerite nodded and hurried back to the car. Tears were welling up in her eyes too and she didn't look back.

SEVENTEEN

Lieutenant Jacobs waved to Detective Florentine to take a seat, indicating that he would talk to him just as soon as he got off the phone.

'There *is* an extradition treaty?' he was saying to the person at the other end of the line. 'A lot of legal problems. But it was ratified again last year?' He paused, a look of exasperation on his face. 'We can't extradite her? Why not?'

Slamming down the phone, he turned to Florentine. 'How the hell did you let that dame slip through your fingers? Did you not notify the airlines?'

'Of course I did. I asked them to keep an eye out for Marguerite Diego. How was I to know she would be able to get a passport in another name?'

Jacobs lit a cigarette and offered Florentine one, but he declined.

'So who is this dame? Is she Marguerite? Is she Katie? Or is she Sister Mary?

'She's all of them.'

'How can she be all of them?'

'Well, we know she's Marguerite and Sister Mary, but she also claims she's Katie.

'And you're sure she's the nun we're looking for?'

'Of course I'm sure. When I showed the photographs to the Reverend Mother she picked Marguerite out right away. She had no doubt it was her.'

'What about the boy who saw her on the ferry? And that officer – the one who came forward to say he spoke to a nun when they were disembarking at Battery Park? And the neighbours who saw her on the day of the murder? Have you showed them the pictures yet?'

'Not yet, but we're working on it.'

'If it *is* her, who is she now? I mean, is she travelling as Sister Mary or Katie?'

'We checked with the Irish consulate. The passport was issued in Katie's name.'

'And you're certain she's gone to Ireland?'

'Certain. She took an Aer Lingus flight to Dublin. Lily still has relatives in Tipperary and apparently she's gone to look them up. I've notified the Irish police.'

Jacobs let his cigarette burn away between his nicotine-stained fingers as he held his hand to his head and studied the latest DD5 report submitted by Florentine. 'If they find her, you want to go to Ireland to interview her?'

'Yeah, she's a vital witness. She knows who killed Diego.'

'What makes you think she ain't coming back?'

'Because she's been avoiding us from day one.'

'You'll obviously need her back here at some stage to give evidence. What happens if she refuses to return?'

'That's the problem.' Florentine shrugged. 'Unless we could extradite her.'

'Not a hope. I was talking to the DA's office when you came in. We do have an extradition treaty with Ireland, but we can only extradite someone from there if we're going to charge them. She's a witness so you can forget extradition. You'll just have to try and get her to come back of her own free will.'

'Maybe we could get her for passport violation?' said Florentine.

'Yeah, and that brings us back to my original question. Who is she? If, as you say, she's all three, how are going to prove a passport violation?'

Lieutenant Jacobs was still reading down through Florentine's report. 'Why do you think she's avoiding us? I mean, if she witnessed the murder of her father—'

'Her adoptive father.'

'All right, all right, her adoptive father. If she saw who bumped him off, why in hell didn't she come forward and tell us who it was?'

'Maybe it was someone she knew.'

'Like who?'

Florentine shook his head. 'I don't know. At first we thought it was the work of some bum using a low calibre junk gun. Then it occurred to us that it might be a woman – you know how they like small calibre pistols.'

'Did it never occur to you that it might have been her mother – all right, her adoptive mother – Diego's wife? After all, she must have had it in for the son-of-a-bitch, the way he carried on.'

'Yeah, that occurred to us all right. But it turns out she has an alibi.'

'Well, there's something in this case that doesn't damned well gel. I don't know what it is. But there's something.' Jacobs lit another cigarette. 'Is Mrs. Diego still up-state or is she back?'

'She's due back shortly.'

'Right then. I think it's time you brought her in. And don't be tippy-toeing around her this time. Her husband is dead and it doesn't matter to us what kind of bastard he was. It was murder and we have to find out who did it.'

'Will do.'

'And while you're at it, try and find out more about this dame Marguerite, or whatever the hell her name is. Talk to her teachers, her priests. I want to know what she ate for breakfast! Understand?'

'I understand.' Florentine rose to go.

'And do you really think the Commissioner will allow the two of you to go to Ireland? I mean, why would you want Sully to go with you?'

'Because he's Irish. I thought that might open a lot of doors for us. You know how the Irish stick together.'

Jacobs smiled. 'Yeah, like the Italians! Now get outa here. I'll push your request up the line – with a recommendation – but I don't fancy your chances.'

'Thanks Lieutenant.' Florentine heaved a sigh of relief and closed the door of the office behind him.

When the priest opened the door, he was surprised to see a young detective from the NYPD flashing a badge in front of him.

'Detective Sullivan,' his visitor told him. 'Can I have a word?'

'Depends on what you want to have a word about.'

The priest was an elderly man with thinning grey-hair. Judging by his curt reply, he was used to having his own way and didn't suffer fools gladly. However, Sullivan stood his ground until he was told, somewhat grudgingly, to come in.

When the two of them were seated, the priest said, 'Now then, what was it you wanted to talk to me about?'

'I'm investigating the shooting of Don Diego.'

'A terrible business… a terrible business.'

'You knew the family?'

'Of course.'

'And Marguerite. What can you tell me about her?'

'What do you want to know?'

'Did you know she was adopted?'

'Why, what's that got to do with it?'

'By all accounts Don Diego was a very violent man.'

The priest began to strum with his fingers on his left knee, and Sullivan reckoned he was anticipating what was to come.

'Did Marguerite, or for that matter, Mrs. Diego, ever come to you because of his violence towards them?'

'Maybe.'

Sullivan leaned forward. 'Father, let's get something straight. This is a police investigation, not a parish quiz. Now did they or didn't they?'

'So what if they did?'

'Can you tell me what they said?'

The priest folded his hands across his chest and tapped one thumb against the other. 'Now look, young man. What transpires between a priest and his parishioners is confidential. Just as confidential as if it were said in the Confessional. Do you understand?'

'Marguerite ran away from home three times, the last time for good,' Sullivan continued. 'Now, what I'm asking you is this. Do you know if it was because she was being ill-treated?'

'I'm sorry, but I can't give you that information.'

'Did she come here looking for help? Surely you can tell me that.'

The priest got up to indicate that the interview was at an end.

As he was shown to the door, Sullivan turned. 'Just one more question. If Marguerite had come here asking for help, would you have got her help, or is that covered by the secrecy of the Confessional too?'

The priest feigned a smile, saying, 'Good-bye, officer,' and closed the door.

The teachers Sullivan tracked down weren't much more helpful. All agreed that Marguerite had been a difficult pupil. Sometimes, they said, she was withdrawn; other times, wild, even destructive. 'It was almost as if she was lashing out at the world,' said one of them. 'Then retreating back into herself. She was a strange child. Very strange.'

At the same time, all of the teachers were adamant that Marguerite had never complained to them about her father. In fact, they had rarely, if ever, heard her speak about him. On reflection, though, they reckoned there might have been some problem at home. 'I mean,' said one, 'why else should she run off like that?'

When Sullivan returned to the office, Florentine was poring over a map of Ireland and his passport was lying on the desk beside it.

Picking up the passport, Sullivan said, 'I take it you've got the okay from the Commissioner then?'

'Yeah. And you?'

'No word yet.'

'Anyway, how did you get on today?'

'I managed to track down some of Marguerite's teachers. I also spoke to the priest.'

'So, what do you reckon?'

'I reckon Don Diego was abusing his adopted daughter.'

'Enough to make her want to kill him?'

'Maybe. Or maybe enough to make someone else want to do it.'

'The mother?'

'Could be.'

'Is she back yet?'

'Yeah. She came back yesterday.'

'Okay. Let's bring her in.'

Mrs. Diego, they found, had been on a shopping spree. She was very fashionably dressed and seemed to be enjoying the freedom of not having a drunken ex somewhere in her background.

'I told you all I know,' she insisted.

'You didn't tell us Marguerite was adopted,' said Florentine.

'What's that got to do with it?'

'Maybe nothing,' said Sullivan, 'but then again, maybe it's got a lot to do with it.'

'Why did Marguerite run away from home?' Florentine asked.

Mrs. Diego shrugged. 'How do I know? She was a very difficult child. Gave me nothing but trouble.'

'Tell us again about your husband,' said Florentine.

'I've already told you. We had good times and we had bad times.'

'But when he turned to drink, they were bad times,' Sullivan said. 'Right?'

'Right.'

'And when he was drunk he abused you?' said Florentine, taking up the questioning again and pressing home the point.

Mrs. Diego nodded and wiped a tear from her eye with her handkerchief.

'And he abused the children?' Florentine went on.

'What do you mean, abused?'

'Did he whop them? Or was it something worse?'

'You mean, sexually abuse them? My God, no! Why are you saying these things?'

'Why then did Marguerite run away?'

'I don't know. I told you. She was a very difficult child. I couldn't control her.'

'Did you know she became a nun?' asked Sullivan.

'A nun? Marguerite? You must be kidding.'

'It seems you don't know your daughter very well,' Florentine added.

'She wasn't my daughter, as you pointed out. Dear knows where she came from.'

'Did you look for her,' asked Sullivan, 'when she ran away?'

'Of course I did; we both did.' Mrs. Diego wiped her eyes with her handkerchief again. Then she looked up saying, 'You're not suggesting that she's this Sister Mary you've been looking for?'

'That's exactly who she is,' Florentine said. 'And she witnessed the killing.'

'She walked in on it,' Sullivan added. 'But for some reason she doesn't seem to want to tell us about it.'

'Why do you think that is, Mrs. Diego?' asked Florentine.

'I don't know.'

'Was it because she knew the killer?' asked Sullivan.

'Someone who had a grudge against Don Diego?' Florentine suggested. 'Maybe someone who had suffered at his hands.'

Sullivan leaned forward so that he was looking down at her. 'Tell me, Mrs. Diego, did your husband own a gun?'

'Not that I know of. At least, not in recent times. Why?'

'And what about you? Do you own a gun?'

'Of course not.' Mrs. Diego raised her head, incredulity on her face. 'You're not suggesting that I killed Don? I mean… he used to beat me all right, but I wouldn't kill him.' She lowered her head and dabbed her eyes again, adding, 'Although, God knows, sometimes I felt like it.'

'That's right,' said Florentine. 'You felt like it. The only problem was you hadn't the guts to do it. But the feeling stayed with you, didn't it Mrs. Diego? And it's been eating away at you all these years, hasn't it?'

'No.'

'The son-of-a-bitch,' Sullivan said, pressing the point home. 'Treating you and your children like that. So you finally decided it was time to make him pay for it.'

'No.'

'Only things went wrong,' said Florentine. 'Marguerite walked in, in the middle of it.'

'No, that's not true. I didn't do it.'

'And you tried to kill her as well,' Sullivan said. 'But she got away.'

'No.'

'That's why she's avoiding us,' said Florentine. 'She's still loyal to the woman she thought was her mother.'

'Even though you despise her,' said Sullivan.

'No, no no! I didn't kill him – and I don't know who did. I told you before – I was with my partner. I wasn't anywhere near Staten Island that day.'

At this stage, Mrs. Diego broke down in tears, and Florentine concluded the interview by switching off the recorder.

When she had gone, they put on their coats and adjourned to the Ferryman's.

'Well, what do you reckon?' asked Sullivan.

'I don't know, Sully. And that's the God's honest truth.'

'As you said yourself, there's only one person who knows what happened – and that's Marguerite.'

Florentine downed a shot of Scotch and ordered another round. 'I know – and I just hope we can get her back.'

They touched glasses again, finished their drink and headed home, Florentine to explain to his long-suffering wife Marie that he was going to have to go to Ireland, Sullivan to tell his father he had applied to go too. And while Marie bemoaned the news, Dan was delighted. So delighted in fact, that he sat up late into the night with his son, drinking beer and talking about it.

'So, Florentine's going to Ireland?' he said.

'Yeah. Do you think the Commissioner will let me go with him?'

'To be perfectly honest, Thaddeus, I don't think he would send the two of you. '

'You reckon not?'

'But then…' His father was smiling broadly now. 'St. Patrick's Day is a wonderful thing. You make a lot of friends when you're drowning the shamrock.'

'Dad – you wouldn't!'

'I would, if I thought it would help. And in this case I think it might. You see, Thaddeus, there's only one way the NYPD are going to get to talk to this young lady. That's if the Irish police let them. And I think the son of an Irish policeman will have a better chance than anyone else.'

Dan offered his son another beer, but he declined, pointing out that he was driving.

As they parted, Dan added, 'Tell Florentine that when he's going to Ireland, he'll have to leave his piece behind. You too. The guards will be glad to see you, but they won't allow you to carry a gun.'

EIGHTEEN

An early morning mist had brought a touch of autumn – or, as Marguerite called it, the fall – to the Tipperary countryside, but it soon lifted to reveal a glen whose beauty had inspired many a generation to sing its praises. Above its quilted slopes, the hills and peaks of the Galty Mountains played hide and seek with the sun as the shadow of one cloud after another rolled across them.

'It's just as Catherine described it,' she said, 'only it's much bigger than I thought it would be.'

James and Susan, who were standing on the road beside her, remained silent so as to let her admire the great patchwork of green fields that stretched away before them.

The weather had become slightly cooler, just as James had said it would, and Marguerite was glad of the new coat of Donegal tweed she had bought in Dublin. However, the weather was the last thing on her mind. She was now in the Glen of Aherlow, the glen her mother had told her so much about, and she was happy to stand and look and breathe it all in.

'Catherine said Shaunie used to practice his hurling by hitting small stones up into the mountain,' she said.

'Ah, the *poc fada*,' said James. 'The long puck.' Seeing that she didn't understand, he explained, 'You could say he was playing mountain hurling. Cúchulainn, the great warrior of Ulster played it when he was young. They still play it up north in the Cooley Mountains and on some of our country roads.'

'Really? And is that Gaelic you're speaking?'

'That's right – Gaelic, or as we call it, Irish.'

'Catherine used some Gaelic words in her notes. And there's a Gaelic inscription on my locket. I know what some of it means, but not all of it. You must translate it for me when we go back to the cottage.'

The truth was James had very little Irish, but he replied, 'Of course I will – if I can!'

'You know, Marguerite,' said Susan as they returned to the car. 'You look fantastic in those tweeds.'

'You reckon?'

'You sure do,' James said. 'Especially with that woollen beret. You look like Maureen O'Hara in *The Quiet Man*.'

'Now, how would Marguerite know what Maureen O'Hara looked like?' said Susan. 'That film was probably made before she was born.'

'No, it's all right, I've seen it,' said Marguerite. And as she sat into the car she smiled to herself, chuffed by the thought that she had been compared to someone so beautiful as Maureen O'Hara.

James and Susan were devoting the weekend to showing Marguerite around, and as they motored through the foothills of the Galtys they were again tempted to ask her about the death of Don Diego. However, they refrained from doing so. She seemed so happy just to be there, and full of curiosity, like a child seeing everything for the first time. So they did their best to answer her many questions about the Irish people and their customs.

Countless trees with bright red berries dotted the hedgerows, and when she asked them what they were, James told her, 'That's the mountain ash or rowan trees as some people call them.'

'So those are the rowan berries,' she said. 'They really do set the countryside on fire, just as Catherine said.'

James smiled. 'I suppose they do. The birds love them, and some people make wine with them. The same with the elder berries. Or is elder wine made from the flower, Susan?'

Susan shook her head, saying she didn't know.

'Catherine also mentioned a holy well and a pattern day when people say prayers at it,' Marguerite recalled.

Susan nodded. 'There are a number of holy wells in this part of the country. And they still have pattern days at some of them. Isn't that right, James?'

'That's right. They're named after saints who built churches here in the seventh century.'

'I don't suppose you could take me to one?'

Susan smiled. 'Of course we can – if you don't mind getting your shoes dirty!'

After driving for several miles along narrow twisting roads, James pulled up at an iron gate and they walked across a meadow to where the well was located. The ground was soft and Marguerite was glad she had taken Susan's advice to wear flat shoes. As she knelt down to cup her hand and take a sip of water, she noticed that cloths, rosary beads and various other things had been hung on a nearby tree.

'A lot of people come here in the hope of getting a cure,' James told her.

'You can tell it's a holy place, can't you?' she whispered. 'You can feel it.'

Seeing her bless herself, James and Susan did the same and said a short prayer to themselves. When they had finished, they could see she was still praying, her hands clasped, her head bowed so that her lips touched the tip of her fingers, and they wondered what she was praying for.

James, who was still holding his cap to his chest, having bared his head in a gesture of reverence, glanced at his wife and he knew she was thinking the same thing as he was. Marguerite, they reckoned, was still deeply troubled by what Mrs. Gaynor had done to her, and by the shooting of her adoptive father.

'You can still see the remains of an ancient church at one of the wells,' said James as they continued their drive. 'But it's too far in off the road to get to it. The stones are carved with crosses and there's a *cillín* there too.'

'A *cillín*? What's that?'

'It's a place where people buried children who hadn't been baptised,' Susan explained. 'Usually children whose mothers weren't married.'

'I believe they weren't allowed to bury them in consecrated ground,' James added.

'Strange, isn't it?' said Marguerite. 'How a Christian country can treat its children.'

'How do you mean?' asked Susan.

'Mrs. Gaynor told me that in the days when I was born, girls who got pregnant outside marriage brought great shame on their families. That's why they had their babies in mother and baby homes and then gave them away.'

Susan smiled sympathetically. 'Maybe so. But Catherine loved you too much. She wasn't prepared to give you away.'

'No, but most of the women in the home where she was were. So were the nuns. And so was Mrs. Gaynor. She went to America for the sole purpose of giving a baby away – and she did it, even though she knew it was the wrong one.'

Seeing that she was on the brink of tears, Susan put an arm around her. 'Don't upset yourself. That's all behind you now.'

However, Marguerite turned her head away, saying, 'I wish it was.'

'Here's a pub,' James announced. 'How about a cup of coffee – or maybe something stronger?'

A few days later, Marguerite announced that she was going to go to Mitchelstown in County Cork. Just as Catherine had longed to see the other side of the Galty Mountains, so did she. She wanted to see where Catherine had gone to work and, above all, she wanted to find out if Shaunie still lived there.

'I'll use public transport this time,' she said. 'You've both done enough.'

Susan laughed. 'Public transport? You're not in America now, girl. If you don't have a car in this part of the country, then it's shank's mare.'

'You mean I would have to walk?'

'Of course not,' said James. 'I told you, I've the van. Susan can take you.'

'And you don't mind coming with me, Susan?'

'I wouldn't miss it for the world.'

'But are you sure you know the way?'

Susan smiled. 'It's not as if we're going to Dublin!'

'Thanks. I don't know what I'd do without you – both of you.'

'You're welcome,' said James.

164

'And I'll ask Eileen,' Susan added. 'Maybe she can come with us.'

'Oh, that would be wonderful. Eileen told me she visited Catherine when she was working in Cork.'

'That's right, so she would know where the house is.'

'And perhaps she could show us the village of Skeheena-something-or-other. Catherine mentioned it in her letters.'

'Skeheenarinky,' said James. 'Sure you'll pass through it.'

Susan had been hoping for an early start, but when Eileen called next morning, she was still waiting for Marguerite to return from Mass.

'You wouldn't believe it,' she said, 'but she goes to Mass every morning.'

Eileen tapped the ash from her cigarette into an ashtray and asked, incredulously, 'Every morning?'

'Every morning. She's a very strange young woman. She wants to know about everything, but she's told us very little about herself, or what happened – you know, about the shooting.'

'Would you not ask her?'

'Aunt Lily told us not to. Said she gets very upset when she thinks about it.'

When they did get under way, Susan let Marguerite sit in the front so that she could have a better view of the countryside. Eileen didn't mind sitting in the back, but when she lit a cigarette it became obvious that her visitor didn't like cigarette smoke, so she had to suffer what, to her, was the pain of not smoking for what seemed a very long time.

It was a pain that was eased only on their arrival at the sign for the village of Skeheenarinky. When Marguerite and Susan went to have a closer look at the sign, Eileen stood back a bit and enjoyed her long-delayed smoke.

'Catherine said it means the little whitethorn bush of the dancing,' said Marguerite.

Susan shook her head. 'I never knew that.'

'That's right,' Eileen said. 'The whitethorn, or as we call it the hawthorn. I heard her talking about it. She loved to know the meaning of place names.'

As they continued their journey, Marguerite watched the Galty Mountains turn around so that when they arrived in Mitchelstown, she was looking at them from the other side. They stopped for a snack in Mitchelstown, then headed out into the north Cork countryside. By this time, Marguerite was in a high state of anticipation. Susan, however, didn't fancy the idea of knocking on the door of a remote farmhouse and asking for Shaunie. She didn't even know if he was still alive. When she said so, Eileen suggested that they should go to Major de Brún's house first. Whoever was living there now might be able to tell them about Shaunie.

When they arrived at the old rectory, they found that the front porch looked as if it hadn't been used for a long time, so they decided to try the back door. As they waited for someone to answer their knock, Marguerite spotted an old blue car in an open shed. Hens were roosting on its dust-covered roof and its tyres were flat. Could it be the major's Rover, she wondered, the one Shaunie had used to bring her mother back from Cobh?

She was tempted to go over and have a closer look at it, but before she could do so the door opened and a nurse appeared. They explained as best they could the purpose of their visit and a short time later they were ushered into the presence of Major de Brún.

The major was old and confined to a wheelchair. The gloved hand of his artificial left arm rested on a rug that was draped over his knees, and his head was slumped forward as if he no longer had the strength to lift it. Nevertheless, he managed to look up when they came in and they could see that age had taken its toll on a face already scarred by war. Fixing his monocle with his good hand, he screwed up his face and looked at them in a way that made them feel as if they had come from Mars, and for a moment they thought he might not remember. But he did.

'Shaunie?' he said at last. 'Yes, I remember Shaunie. Best driver I ever had.'

'This is his daughter, Marguerite,' Susan said.

'Daughter? Daughter? I never knew he had a daughter.'

'My mother, Catherine, she worked for you,' said Marguerite. 'Before she went to America.'

Major de Brún seemed confused and Eileen asked him, 'Is Shaunie still alive?'

'Alive? Of course he is. Mind you, he's not in the best of health.'

'Can you show us his house?' asked Susan.

166

'Well, I can't, but…' The major gestured to the nurse, saying, 'You show them.'

As they drew up at the house that had been pointed out to them, a fair-haired young man emerged from the farmyard gate. He wore dungarees and Wellingtons that were smeared with liquid cow manure.

Marguerite got out and he came over to talk to her.

'Is this Shaunie's house?' she asked him, just to make sure.

''Tis,' he said. 'But they seldom use the front door. Try the back.'

Marguerite noted that he was tall and good-looking, features she had admired in photographs of Shaunie, and she wondered if, perhaps, he was related to him.

'And you'd better drive around,' he added. 'I haven't hosed down the yard yet.'

'Thanks.'

He smiled, saying, 'You're welcome,' and as he went about his business, Marguerite reproached herself, telling herself that she was letting her imagination run away with her.

The yard, they found, was spattered with the liquid manure of cattle, but the only sign of life was a grey horse whose head was protruding over the half door of its stable. Susan and Eileen opted to stay in the car, and it was with some trepidation that they watched Marguerite's tweedy figure marching over to the back door of the house.

Marguerite, however, had no such reservations. She had waited for this moment for a long time, and while the other two thought she was walking over to the house of a stranger, she was confident in the knowledge that she was about to meet her real father. She did wonder what she would say to him, and what he would say to her. It was a scenario she had gone over in her mind many, many times. But in the end she found she needn't have worried.

The man who answered the door wasn't the handsome young hurler that Catherine had told her about. His face was gaunt and his clothes hung loosely on a body that was obviously thin and frail, but she knew immediately who he was.

'Shaunie?' she said.

167

'Katie!'

No more words passed between them; they just looked at one another for a moment, but it was a look that spanned a lifetime. Then they embraced and cried on one another's shoulder.

'Come in,' he told her. 'Come in.'

Taking her by the arm, he guided her into a room where he sat her down in a chair opposite his at an open fire. 'I knew it had to be you,' he said. Then he lifted up a folded newspaper from the floor beside him and Marguerite could see where he had put a pen mark around the article headed, *The Prodigal Daughter*. 'Poor Catherine. I didn't know she was dead. I didn't even know she had gone to America until I read it in the paper.' He began to cry, and when he had recovered, he added, 'But at least *you're* alive. 'Catherine's daughter – and mine. I still can't believe it – after all this time.'

Marguerite reached out and put her hand on his arm, saying. 'I knew it was you the minute I saw you. Catherine told me so much about you.'

Shaunie looked up, startled, and she could see that her clumsy use of words had led him to think for a moment that Catherine might not have died on the liner either, so she added hastily, 'She wrote it all down for me – shortly before she died.'

Shaunie held his head in his hand and cried again. 'I tried to get in touch with her you know, but I couldn't find her. I thought maybe she had gone to Dublin.'

'She did. She went to a home for unmarried mothers, and when I was born she left for America, taking me with her. But as the paper says she died before the ship reached there.' Tears were streaming down Marguerite's cheeks now, and the words that followed seem to flow just as freely. 'Then there was a mix-up and I was given up for adoption instead of another baby. Her name was Brigid Mary. She was born in the home too, but she died. I was given away instead of her, to a family called Diego. And so, I became Marguerite Diego. Until recently, that is. Then I discovered I was really Catherine's daughter.'

'But the paper says your name's Katie.'

'That's what Catherine called me.' She stopped to wipe away the tears. 'But I still call myself Marguerite. I suppose it all sounds very complicated.'

As Shaunie tried to take it all in, Marguerite cupped his hand in hers as lovingly as she dared, for she could feel it was only skin and bone, and told him, 'She loved you an awful lot you know. She said so.'

'And I loved her. I never stopped loving her.'

'What happened then? Why didn't you marry her?'

Shaunie shook his head as if to say the memory of what had happened was too painful to recall.

At the same time, a woman in a long dark dress emerged from the shadows and put her hand on his shoulder. 'It's time to go now,' she said. 'Shaunie's not well. The doctor says he has to take it easy – and I think he's had enough excitement for one day.'

'This is Maudie, my sister.'

Marguerite nodded and got up to go.

'You'll come and see me again soon?' he added.

Marguerite leaned down and embraced him where he sat, saying, 'Of course I will.'

Maudie made another move to indicate that the visit was at an end, showed her to the door and, without a word, closed it after her.

As Marguerite walked to the car, she realised that it had to be illness, not age that had left Shaunie so emaciated. If Catherine was 18 when she died, she would be 49 now. Shaunie would have been around the same age, which meant he couldn't be much more than fifty. The tears were still welling up in her eyes as she sat back into the car and she sniffled into her hankie to hold them back.

'Did you see him?' Susan ventured to ask.

She nodded.

'And did he know you?' asked Eileen.

She nodded again. 'I'll tell you about it later.' As they drove away from the house, she added, 'I'd love to see the lake before we go back, if that's possible.'

'The lake?' asked Susan.

Marguerite sniffled into her hankie once again. 'Catherine said she and Shaunie used to spend time up at a lake not far from where he lived. One with a whitethorn tree.'

169

'I know it,' said Eileen. 'Catherine took me up to see it. But it's a bit of a climb. And I'm not sure if I can find the laneway. Are you *sure* you want to see it?'

'Yeah, I really would love to see it – if you don't mind.'

It was by trial and error that Eileen guided Susan to the right laneway and when she did, Susan said, 'You two go ahead.' Settling her ample form back into the driver's seat, she added, 'Hill climbing's not for me. I'll wait here in the car.'

Hill climbing wasn't for Eileen either. She had been a chain smoker when Catherine had taken her up to see the lake and she was still a chain smoker more than thirty years later. It wasn't long before she was puffed out and it was only by taking numerous rests that she was able to climb the steep track that led to the lake where Catherine and Shaunie had spent so many of their evenings together.

Marguerite, however, was reliving all the things Catherine had told her about. When they reached the rock at the top of the track, she leaned back against it and listened to the gurgling of a stream in a ravine so deep it couldn't be seen. There was no sign of the goldfinches Catherine had written about, so she picked a few seeds of thistledown and sent them floating across the hillside. And finally, when they reached the boulder at the side of the lake, she ran her hand over it, almost as if she was soaking up the love that had once been made there.

While Marguerite examined the rock and the whitethorn tree that grew by the side of it, Eileen sat on a smaller rock nearby and watched. She was still breathless from the climb and, when she had got her breath back, she lit a cigarette. As she drew deeply on it, she wondered at what she considered to be the antics of an impressionable young American woman whose head was filled with silly notions of romance. It was a romance, she knew, that had once blossomed there but had withered like the blossoms on the thorn and in her view was best forgotten.

However, Marguerite wanted to savour some of the things that her mother had written about. She reached up and plucked a handful of reddening haws from an overhanging branch and held them to her breast as if they contained a precious memory. Then, still clutching the haws, she walked around the rock until she came back to the tree, just as she imagined her mother and her lover had done. There she left the haws on the boulder and, to Eileen's surprise, reached up and tied a blue ribbon to the lowest branch, all the while singing quietly to herself...

'Oh dear, what can the matter be?
Dear, dear, what can the matter be?
Oh dear what can the matter be?
Johnny's so long at the fair?'

'What's with the ribbon?' asked Eileen.

'It was on my music box. My mother gave it to me when I was a baby. That's what it played – Johnny's so long at the fair.'

On the way back down, Marguerite asked Eileen to tell her more about the time she came to see Catherine.

'What more can I tell you?' Eileen replied. 'She met me in Mitchelstown and brought me out to the rectory to show me where she worked.'

'Don't tell me you walked?' said Susan.

'Of course not. Her Uncle John lived not far from the rectory and he gave us a lift. Then she took me up to the lake for a picnic. She never stopped talking about Shaunie, but I didn't meet him. Sorry.'

Marguerite lapsed into silence and it seemed to Eileen that she was desperate to know what had happened all those years ago.

Susan was relieved to see them returning as she was beginning to worry that they might have lost their way. She had turned the car in readiness for the return journey, but it wasn't until they were well on their way that she ventured to ask Marguerite again to tell them about her meeting with Shaunie.

As Marguerite did so, she thought of Shaunie's emaciated condition; his frail body and his bony hand which she had taken in hers for that very precious moment of their first meeting.

'He asked me to come and see him again soon,' she told them, 'and I will.'

NINETEEN

Very little happens in rural Ireland that the local people don't know about, and the appearance of a strange young woman at Mass every morning soon set tongues wagging. The fact that she was wearing a tweed coat and an Aran beret made them suspect that she was a Yank. Then they saw Susan dropping her off outside the church and they knew immediately that she was the young woman the newspaper had been writing about.

The Prodigal Daughter, the paper had called her. It was a phrase that conjured up all sorts of possibilities for idle gossip and, if the truth be told, there was many a one who went to Mass each morning just to see her and for no other reason. On the way out of the church, some of the older women would even dally as they blessed themselves at the stone font and bid the stranger 'Good morning', just to hear her American accent and confirm that she was who they thought she was.

There was also little the local gardaí didn't know about the local people, and when an inspector rang from headquarters in Dublin to inquire if a young American woman had come to visit in the area, they were able to confirm it without even checking. The inspector was making his inquiry on behalf of the police in New York and when he passed the information on to them, they were impressed.

'The Irish police seem to have a good intelligence system,' remarked Lieutenant Jacobs. 'They've just been on to say they've located her. How's that for service?'

Florentine and Sullivan agreed that it was pretty good.

'Well, maybe you'll take a leaf out of their book and learn something when you're over there. Dublin may not be the Big Apple, but it appears to me they can move their ass when they have to.'

'I didn't think the Commissioner would allow the both of us to go,' Florentine said.

'Neither did I.' Jacobs glanced at Sullivan. 'But then…maybe somebody up there has a soft spot for the Irish.' He opened a folder and shoved an envelope across the table towards them. 'There's your airline tickets.' As they tucked them into the inside pockets of their jackets, he added, 'Maybe the Commissioner wants to make a good impression on the Irish police.'

'Oh yeah?' said Florentine. 'How come?'

'Well, over the years some of their members have been murdered by the IRA and a lot of the funding for the IRA campaign comes from Irish exiles here. To make matters worse, the Emerald Society police band played at an IRA function a couple of years ago.' Jacobs took some newspaper cuttings from the folder. 'Here, read these.'

Glancing at the reports, the two could see that politicians on both sides of the Atlantic had been loud in their condemnation of NORAID's support for the IRA. Other cuttings said that in spite of objections by the Irish police, the New York police band had taken part in a memorial ceremony in Donegal for IRA hunger strikers.

'But that was in 1984,' Sullivan said.

'I know, I know, but it has left a bit of a sour taste. And then there's all this trouble with NORAID… so do what you can to smooth things over. Okay?'

The others nodded.

'And this dame, Marguerite, or Katie, or whatever you call her. Treat her softly. You know? No heavy stuff. Just ask her nicely – who did she see wasting Diego? And see if she would be prepared to come back and testify.'

The two of them got up to go.

'And one more thing,' Jacobs said. 'Have you checked in your weapons?'

'We're going to do that now,' Florentine assured him.

'Right then. And take my advice. If you don't want a sore head, go easy on the black stuff. The Irish guys are used to it – we're not.'

Sullivan smiled, but said nothing. Whatever about Florentine, he was looking forward to having a few pints of Guinness with his Irish counterparts.

It didn't escaped the notice of some of those attending Mass in the small church in Tipperary that the Yank, as she was now known, was lighting candles for a special intention. What that special intention was they did not know, nor to be fair to them, did they consider it to be any of their business.

Susan, however, considered that Marguerite's well-being was her business and she was concerned about her change of mood. No longer did she explore her mother's birthplace with the curiosity and joy of a child; instead she spent her days moping around the house, eating little and saying less.

'It's Shaunie, isn't it?' said Susan at last.

Marguerite nodded. 'I'm afraid I might not see him alive again. It's just a feeling I have.'

'You don't think he has cancer, do you?'

'I don't know. But you don't need to be a doctor to know he's wasting away.'

'Well, he asked you to go back and see him soon. Just let me know when you want to go and I'll take you.'

Marguerite smiled and hugged her, saying, 'Thanks, Susan. I really do appreciate it.'

Perhaps it was a woman's intuition, or just a daughter's natural concern for her father. Susan couldn't say, but Marguerite's worries were well-founded. When they drove down to Shaunie's house again, a servant girl informed her that he had been taken to hospital.

They set off immediately for the hospital, but Marguerite's concern seemed to know no bounds. What if visiting was restricted to Shaunie's known relatives? she asked Susan. What if his sister had told the staff she wasn't to be allowed in? What if he died before they arrived? To her surprise, she found that he had left word with the nurses that, if she called, she was to be brought in to see him.

Shaunie's sister Maudie, who had been sitting by his bedside, left when Marguerite walked in, telling one of the nurses she would be in the waiting room if anyone was looking for her.

Pleased with the opportunity to be alone with him for a few minutes, Marguerite slipped into the chair Maudie had vacated and took his bony hand in hers.

'Nurse,' said Shaunie, and she could see he had hardly the strength to raise his voice. 'I want a few minutes in private.'

Seeing him gesture towards the curtains, the nurse pulled them around the bed and found something else to do.

'Now,' he said. 'You wanted to know why I didn't marry your mother. Why I left her standing at the altar.'

'I didn't say that.'

'No, but that's what happened. I'm sure she told you it was all arranged and, then, on the day, I didn't turn up.'

Marguerite lowered her eyes, not wishing to be judgemental before hearing what he had to say.

'You may find what I'm going to tell you hard to believe. I mean, they may do things differently in America, but this is Ireland. And some strange things happen here, especially when there's land involved.' He coughed to clear his throat and she fluffed up the pillow to make him more comfortable. 'My father had died and, being the eldest son, the farm was left to me. It's a fairly big farm – nearly two hundred acres. Not all good land, you understand, but it's one of the best farms around here. Anyway, when my father died, the farm came down to me, and I suppose the others – Maudie and my three brothers – didn't relish the idea of me getting married and bringing another woman into the house.' He managed a wry smile. 'You know yourself, it never works, having two women under the same roof. In any event, it wouldn't have been their home any more. It would have been my house – and Catherine's. He sighed deeply as if what had occurred was almost too painful to recall. 'You would need to have known my brothers to understand what happened.'

'I think I have a good idea what they were like. Catherine told me about them. She said they were a bit wild.'

175

'A bit is right. You see, my father got some lung disease when he was working in the mines in America, and he wasn't able to control them. As a result, they were very boisterous. They never took anything seriously, especially Francie. Always larking about. You know what I mean?'

When she nodded, he went on, 'They must have got it into their heads that if Catherine came into the house, Maudie would have to get out. I don't think they were worried about themselves. They knew they would have to go off somewhere and get a job anyway. And so, when the day arrived for the wedding, they came up with the hare-brained idea of locking me in.'

Marguerite stared at him, a look of incredulity on her face. 'They locked you in?'

'I know it's difficult to believe, but that's what they did. I don't know which of them came up with the idea. Maybe it was Francie. He was a dreadful head-case when he was young, but to tell you the truth Mick and Pat weren't much better. Anyway, they locked me in a shed. When Maudie asked them where I was, they told her I had changed my mind about getting married and had gone away until things cooled down.'

'But did you not shout to someone to let you out?'

'Of course I did, I shouted until I was hoarse, but it was no good. As I say, it's a big farm, and they took good care to make sure I was in a place where nobody could hear me. When I demanded to get out, they just laughed and said, "All in good time, Shaunie. All in good time." All I could think of was Catherine. What she would think of me, and the embarrassment of it all. I could just see her standing at the church with her father and no sign of me. I could have died with the shame of it all. And these blabbering *amadáns* – these brothers of mine – laughing at the good of it all and thinking it was a great joke.'

'How long did they keep you there?'

'Long enough to make sure I couldn't get married, and then some.'

The nurse looked in around the curtains to make sure Shaunie was all right and, when the curtains fell into place again, he went on, 'When I did get out I went to her Uncle John's house where she had been staying. His wife, Mags, answered the door. She said Catherine had gone and that she didn't want to have anything more to do with me. I assumed she had gone back to her home in Tipperary, so I went there in the hope of finding her. But her mother said she wasn't there and if she was I was the last person she would want to speak to. She slammed the door in my face, and at that moment it seemed to me that my whole world had come to an end. I had been shut out from the only thing in the world that mattered to me. Still, I couldn't accept that Catherine never wanted to see me again. I couldn't believe that, not after all we meant to each other. So I came home and wrote a letter to her. But her mother wouldn't accept it. She tore it up and flung it back at me. So I wrote another letter and posted it. I thought her mother would hardly throw it back at the postman and that if Catherine was there she might even pick it up herself. But it was no use. I don't know how many letters I wrote, it made no difference. I got no reply.'

Seeing that tears were welling up in his eyes, Marguerite gently squeezed his hand, saying, 'It's all right. You don't have to tell me any more if you don't want to.'

'But I do want to. You see I knew Catherine was pregnant, and by not turning up for the wedding I had left her in a dreadful predicament. At the same time, I couldn't tell her parents she was pregnant. I mean, it was a terrible thing for a girl to get pregnant in those days if she wasn't married.'

'I know. I heard about it.'

'It was bad enough to be left at the altar – everybody would know about it – but to be pregnant as well. At first I thought Catherine was in the house and that her mother was just refusing to let me talk to her, but as the days passed and I received no reply to my letters, I realised that she had probably gone. But where? My guess was Dublin. But where in Dublin? If the priest knew, he wasn't telling me. He was so angry with me for not turning up. He just waved me away and told me not to come back. So I went to Dublin and walked the streets looking for her.' He paused as he thought about it. 'I can still remember seeing a young girl – she looked the image of Catherine from the back – tall, long brown hair curled in at the bottom, and I ran up to her, calling "Catherine, Catherine," only to discover that it was somebody else.'

He closed his eyes to stop himself crying. 'I never did find her. I was heartbroken.'

'Did you marry anyone else?'

'No. I became a typical Irish bachelor. My brothers went their separate ways – I wouldn't have them in the house after that. And Maudie looked after me. She didn't get married either.'

He let his head loll back on the pillow, and Marguerite could feel his body relax, almost as if a great weight had been lifted from his mind.

Just then the nurse returned with a small tray of medicines and after checking his pulse, said, 'I think it might be better if you let him rest for a little while. Maybe you could wait with his sister. I'll get somebody to bring you a cup of tea.' She smiled, adding, 'But, you sound American. Would you like coffee instead?'

Marguerite smiled. 'Thank you. That would be nice.'

As she walked down the corridor to the waiting room, the nurse came running after her. 'Excuse me,' she said, 'You're Katie, aren't you?'

'Well, yes.'

The nurse handed her an envelope, explaining, 'Shaunie asked me to give this to you. He was very anxious that you should get it.'

Marguerite thanked her and glanced at the envelope. The flap was open and inside she could see another envelope. It was folded over and was flat and faded with age. When she took it out she could see it had been torn in two and realised it must be the letter he had given to Catherine's mother all those years ago, the one she had torn up and thrown back at him. Putting it into her coat pocket, she told herself she would read it later. She was anxious to talk to Maudie, but when she walked into the waiting room Maudie got up, saying sarcastically, 'I'm going back to my brother now – if you don't mind.'

'The nurse wants us to wait here,' said Marguerite. 'They're giving him his medicines.'

Reluctantly, Maudie sat down again and found a spot on the wall to look at.

There was silence for a moment.

'He told me what happened,' Marguerite went on. 'You know, why he didn't turn up for his wedding with Catherine.'

'It was just a boyish prank,' Maudie retorted, and looked away again as if to say it was none of her business anyway.

'It was a dreadful thing to do to a young girl on her wedding day,' Marguerite countered.

Maudie made no reply.

'I suppose you all thought she wasn't good enough, being a servant girl.'

Maudie still didn't reply.

'And you didn't want her coming into the house as his wife. You knew that if she did, you would be out. You also knew that if she had any children, they would inherit the farm. So your brothers decided to lock him up until he came to his senses.'

Maudie shifted uncomfortably. 'I had nothing to do with that.'

'Maybe not. But there was something you and your brothers didn't know. Catherine was pregnant – pregnant with Shaunie's child – and locking him up couldn't prevent that child being born. It couldn't prevent me being born.'

There was another uncomfortable silence, and Marguerite added, 'Well I'm here now and there's nothing you or your brothers can do to change that.'

'I suppose you're going to tell me next that you're entitled to the farm. Well, let me tell you here and now, you're not going to get it.'

'I don't want your god-damned farm. All I want is to be recognised as Shaunie's daughter.'

'And how do you propose to do that?'

'I'll asked him to make a formal declaration —'

'Shaunie's a sick man. A very sick man. He's in no mind to be making any declarations.' Looking away again, Maudie added, 'Anyway, how does he know who you are? His name isn't on your birth certificate, is it? Otherwise, you wouldn't be looking for a declaration.'

When Marguerite didn't reply, she continued, 'No, I thought not. So what does it say? "Father unknown?" I'll bet that's what it says. And I heard you myself, when you called at the house. First you said you were Catherine's Katie. Then you said you were given away as Brigid Mary somebody-or-other. Then you became Marguerite somebody-or-other. And now you want to be Shaunie's Katie. Well, I can tell you for nothing, girl: if you think you're going to get his name on your birth certificate and your grubby little hands on his farm, you've another think coming. He has willed the farm to me and I'm going to make sure he doesn't change his mind just to please some little adventurer like you.'

'But I told you,' Marguerite protested. 'I don't want the farm. All I want is to be recognised as his daughter.'

'Well then, you'll just have to prove it, won't you?'

Before either of them could say anything more, one of the nurses came in to tell them they had better come quickly.

Shaunie was still warm, but when Marguerite held his hand in hers again it was lifeless, and she wept bitterly for the man she had known for such a cruelly short time. Maudie, however, held her composure and ignored the tears that were being shed by the stranger on the other side of the bed. As far as she was concerned, Marguerite had no right to cry, no right to say she was Shaunie's daughter, no right to the farm.

Marguerite wiped away her tears and looked down at the frail body for what she knew would be the last time. And she thought of those days long ago when he had been young and strong, the days when he hurled his way up into the mountain with Catherine, the days when they chased one another around the whitethorn, the days when they made love. But then, she thought, Maudie wouldn't want to know anything about that.

Bending down, she kissed him on the brow and walked back out to the car park where Susan was waiting for her.

TWENTY

The lower half of Susan's body was hanging out of the ceiling, her feet barely touching the top rung of a stepladder.

Marguerite raised her voice to ask, 'What are you doing up there?'

'Hold the ladder,' Susan called down.

Marguerite could see that her aunt's bulky frame was blocking the rather small trap door. 'You'll never get up through that,' she called up.

'That's what I told her,' came James's voice from the attic.

Susan eased her feet down on to the ladder and, looking down through the only chink of light that was left, a small chink at one corner of the trap door, said, 'Don't mind him. I'm just looking around from where I am.'

'Looking for what?'

'Letters?'

'What letters?'

'My mother's. The only letters I ever remember her getting were from Aunt Lily, but if Shaunie sent some to her, they might be here too.'

'If she didn't tear them up,' said Marguerite, mindful of the reception Shaunie said he had got.

'Maybe she did, but I thought it might be worth having a look.'

Using a lamp from one of her son's bicycles to give her light, Susan was looking around the attic to see if she could spot a cardboard box in which she had stored her mother's things. 'Over there James,' she said. 'I think it might be over there.'

'There's so much junk up here,' James was complaining. 'You wouldn't know where to begin.'

Susan sneezed and James said, 'You'd better go on down before the dust sets you off. I'll see what I can find.'

'The dust's beginning to get to me all right.' Susan handed the lamp to her husband and called down, 'Are you holding the ladder?' Marguerite assured her she was and, not without difficulty, she extracted herself from the narrow opening.

The two of them returned to the kitchen and Marguerite sat down at the table where she had been reading the letter the nurse gave her at the hospital. It was the first letter Shaunie wrote to Catherine, the one her mother tore up and refused to accept.

Susan filled the kettle. 'Fancy a coffee?'

'Thanks, I'd love one.' Marguerite pushed the torn pieces of the letter together with the palms of her hands and let her eyes drift over the faded writing once more.

My dearest Catherine, she read, but it was the anguished voice of Shaunie she heard. *My love. My dearest, dearest love, what can I say? How can I explain? I am heartbroken by what has happened and yet, it was none of my doing. I would never willing leave you standing at the altar. Please believe me. The very thought of it makes me want to die. It was those gobshite brothers of mine. You wouldn't believe it, but they locked me in! They actually locked me in a shed so that I couldn't go to the church. They thought it was a great joke. I yelled. I cried, but it was no use. They wouldn't let me out. And the thought of you waiting there, thinking I had let you down. I was so sick at heart I wanted to die. But here I am talking about me when it was you who had to bear the brunt of it. How you must have felt, standing there at the church alone, waiting for me when I should have been waiting for you. Your disappointment, your embarrassment, your heartbreak, I can only imagine how awful it must have been. And what must you have thought of me? I hoped our love was so strong you wouldn't believe I had turned my back on you. But what else were you to think? And what were your family to think? What were the guests to think? What else, than that I had turned my back on you, deserted you on the most important day of your life. But you must know I would never do that. I would never leave you standing at the altar, at least not willingly. Not ever and certainly not when you are carrying our child. I love you too much to do that. Your situation, I know, is something you can never tell your parents and I'm deeply conscious of the fact that it must have magnified your concern a thousand times as you waited there at the altar and I failed to appear. It is also a situation I do not wish you to face on your own. I called to your house as soon as I could, but your mother closed the door in my face. If she had put a knife through my heart she could not have hurt me more. And yet I could understand it. She said you weren't there and that you never wanted to see me again. That I could understand too but I could not accept it. Our love has been so deep, so utterly complete I could not accept that you never wanted to see me again. We've been so close we've been one, inseparable in our lives and in our love. I cannot envisage a future without you, a life apart, nor can I accept that we will ever stop loving one another. Oh my darling, I'm rambling now. I don't know what to say, except that I love you with all my heart and I always will. Please come back to me. Please understand. Please… I deserted you, or so it seemed, but I am back, I am here. Please don't desert me in the belief that I deserted you. If you get this letter you will surely understand. It was none of my doing. Please believe me and let us start again. Let us set another date for our wedding. And believe me, nothing will stop me this time. This cry my darling is from the bottom of my heart. I love you dearly and always will. Please come back. Please tell me where you are and I will go and bring you back. Just the way I went to Cobh and brought you back. Please answer me. From your ever loving and devoted Shaunie. xxxxx.*

Marguerite sniffed and wiped a tear from her eye with the back of her hand.

Susan placed a mug of coffee beside the letter and, with another mug of coffee for herself, sat around the corner of the table from where Marguerite was sitting. 'It was a terrible thing to do to them?' she said.

Marguerite sniffed again and asked, 'What's a gobshite?'

'It's what we call someone who does stupid things.'

'Like Francie?'

'Exactly. Him and his two brothers.'

'What on earth were they thinking of?'

'Themselves, I imagine.'

Marguerite nodded. 'Shaunie said they didn't want another woman coming into the house.'

Susan gave a sardonic smile. 'I'd say there was more to it than that.'

'How do you mean?'

'Well, here in Ireland the family farm is the family farm. They don't like to see it passing into the hands of strangers.'

'So if you don't marry, it stays in the family.'

'Right.'

They sipped their coffee and Susan said, 'I suppose you'd like to go to the funeral?'

'Of course. Wild horses wouldn't keep me away.'

'And what about the removal?'

'I'm going to go to that too.'

'That means we'll have to stay there overnight.'

'Is that a problem?'

Susan shook her head. 'Not at all. We thought you would want to go all right.' As her husband came into the kitchen with the folded ladder, she added 'James has been making inquiries with some of the people he works with, and apparently there's a nice little hotel in the town where we could stay. It's call The Cumán Inn.'

James put the ladder back in a closet beside the cooker.

'The Come On Inn. That's cute.'

'Not the Come on Inn,' he told her. 'The Cumán Inn. Cumán's the Irish word for hurley.'

'Oh, I see.'

Susan smiled. 'I suppose it's meant to be double meaning. But I think you'll find that as far as the hurling fans are concerned, it only means one thing, – it's a hurling pub.'

'You mean a public house? I thought you said it was a hotel?'

'So it is.' James dusted down his overalls with his hands and seated himself at the other end of the table. 'But all hotels here have a pub as well.'

Susan got up and took the empty mugs over to the sink 'I don't suppose you want coffee James?'

'Well, if the two of you are drinking it. But put plenty of milk in it.'

'We never drank coffee before you came,' Susan confessed. 'Aunt Lily told us they're always drinking it in America so we got some in. I should have asked you if it's the kind you like.'

Marguerite smiled. 'It's fine. Thank you. You're very good.'

'Anyway,' said James, 'you don't have to worry about the Cumán Inn. It may not be up to the standard you have in New York, but I'm told it's comfortable. And sure you'll only be staying the one night.'

'Do you think they'll have room?'

Having put on the kettle, Susan sat down at the table again. 'These places always have room, unless there's a GAA function on or a steam engine rally, or something like that.'

'Okay then,' Marguerite said, 'let's ring them and book it.' She carefully inserted the letter and its torn envelope into the one that Shaunie had addressed to her and put it away. Then she placed her hand on Susan's, saying, 'You've both been a great help to me. I don't know how I'm ever going to repay you.'

'Don't be silly,' Susan said. 'It's the least we can do, and we're happy to do it.'

'You're a member of the family now,' James added. 'And families have to stick together.'

Marguerite lowered her head. 'Now you make me feel guilty.'

'Guilty?' he said. 'Why should you feel guilty?'

'What happened wasn't your fault,' Susan assured her.

'I know, but that's not what I mean. You see there were certain things that happened before I left America. Terrible things. Things I haven't even told Lily and Ed about.'

Susan smiled sympathetically. 'Sure they can't be all that bad. And you can tell us. Whatever it is, it won't go any further.'

Marguerite braced herself. 'Okay. But I think we'd better have another mug of coffee – a strong one this time. You too James – and hold on to your hat!'

As the enormity of what Marguerite now confided in them sank in, it seemed to Susan and James that time was standing still. They listened in stunned silence, mesmerised by her account of the abuse she had suffered at the hands of Don Diego and the final attack that led to his death.

'Well the dirty oul' bastard,' James exclaimed. 'He deserved everything he got.'

Susan was gobsmacked. She couldn't believe her ears. Her mouth hung open and for what seemed an eternity, she was unable to speak. Then, realising that Marguerite was crying, she wrenched herself out of her shocked silence and took her hands firmly in hers saying, 'You poor thing. We didn't know.'

'How could you know?' Marguerite sobbed. 'How could anyone know?'

'But somebody must have known what was going on,' Susan said.

'Oh they knew all right. Nora knew, but she turned a blind eye. Pretended it wasn't happening.'

'Your own mother?' asked Susan incredulously. 'I mean your adoptive mother? How could she?'

'That's what I asked myself – many times. She just pushed me away and told me not to be silly.'

'Did you not tell anyone else?' asked James.

'Of course I did. I told the priest, but he just told me to say a few Hail Marys. It was as if he thought it was my fault.'

'And he didn't do anything about it?' asked Susan.

'No – nobody did. My teachers knew about it. I didn't tell them, mind you, but they knew all right. They must have known. They must have seen how unhappy I was. I think they just didn't want to get involved. That's why I kept running away. I needed someone to help me, someone to say, "I know what's going on," but no one did. No one, that is, except the nuns. They didn't know what I had been through, but they knew I needed help and they took me in. They were very kind to me.'

'And you're saying you became a nun yourself?' said James.

Marguerite nodded. 'I took the name Sister Mary.'

Susan gave her a sympathetic smile. 'I wondered why you were going to Mass so often! And this nurse, what did you say her name was?'

'Gaynor.'

'She's got a lot to answer for.'

'Where is she now?' asked James.

'Dead.' Marguerite told them about her last meeting with Mrs. Gaynor on the Statue of Liberty ferry and how it ended adding, 'It was all her fault. I suppose I should have forgiven her, but I couldn't. Not after all that had happened.'

'And you haven't told Lily and Ed about this?' asked Susan.

'Some of it. Not all of it. I just couldn't.'

'Well, I think you should tell them.'

Marguerite nodded. 'I will.'

'I can't believe it,' Susan added. 'What you've gone through, I mean. It's hard to believe that anyone would do such awful things to a young girl.'

'I know,' Marguerite said, 'but it did happen, and I just can't get it out of my mind. I can't help thinking about it.'

'Well you're in Ireland now,' James assured her, 'and you're with your family. Try not to worry too much about it. We'll look after you.'

TWENTY-ONE

It was a mild evening, but those who waited for the coffin to arrive at the church couldn't help noticing that autumn had begun to creep in upon them. Many had known Shaunie either as a farmer, a hurler or simply as a friend and neighbour. As always on these occasions, they stood in small groups a short distance from where the hearse would stop and the family would gather around the coffin. They spoke in low, respectful tones, lamenting Shaunie's demise, recalling his qualities and lauding his achievements on the playing field. They also remembered the time he was to have got married but for some strange reason didn't turn up at the church. However that was something none of them spoke of as they would never speak ill of the dead.

Marguerite and Susan had arrived early and were sitting half way down the church, near enough to see the coffin when it was laid before the altar, yet far enough away from the front to be inconspicuous. Acting on Susan's advice, Marguerite had purchased darker clothes more befitting the occasion and also wore a dark headscarf.

Everyone fell silent when the coffin was carried in. The bearers, Marguerite assumed, included Shaunie's brothers, but she had no way of knowing which one was which. When the coffin was laid on its trestles, someone placed the flag of his local hurling team and a hurley on top of it. The priest spoke warmly of him, saying how much he would be missed by his family and friends and, when the short ceremony ended, he told the congregation that mass would be celebrated at eleven next morning, after which the funeral would take place at the nearby cemetery.

Shaunie's relatives were seated in the front pew next to the coffin and when the priest had shaken hands with them, there was a pause while the congregation waited to see who would make the first move. Then everyone seemed to move at once, forming a queue in the central aisle so that they could file past the family and offer their condolences. Marguerite immediately got up and joined them.

Surprised, Susan followed her. 'What do you think you're doing?' she whispered. 'If you try to shake hands with them, you'll make a scene.'

'I have no intention of shaking hands with them,' Marguerite whispered back. 'I just want to pay my respects to Shaunie.'

'Oh!' Susan lowered her head, sorry she had asked.

Nothing more was said as they shuffled their way down the aisle. One by one the people at the front of the queue approached the coffin and turned right to where Maudie and her brothers were sitting. Quickly they shook hands with each in turn, mumbled a few words of condolence and moved on. Some would be back in the morning for the funeral while others would be relieved that they had done their duty and wouldn't have to go to the funeral. In any event, they knew the family would be pleased they came.

Susan and Marguerite edged closer to the front of the queue, all too aware that the family would not be pleased to see them. Marguerite moved ahead and when she reached the coffin, she stopped. Susan came to a halt behind her and the people behind her stopped too, respectfully waiting their turn. Marguerite knelt and blessed herself, then rising to her feet, bent down and kissed the coffin. For a split second she glanced to her right. Her eyes met the scowling faces of Maudie and her brothers. Quickly she turned to her left and moved away. Susan blessed herself and followed.

Having done what she came to do, Marguerite was now anxious to get out of the church but again their progress was agonisingly slow as queues from the side aisles merged and choked the doorway. When, eventually, they did get out they found it was raining. It wasn't heavy rain, more of a light drizzle, but it couldn't hide the tears that ran down Marguerite's cheeks.

'I want to go now,' she told Susan and, turning her back on the other mourners, she hurried out to the street where a shiny black limousine was parked alongside the pavement. Between her tears and the rain she could hardly see where she was going, and on rounding one of the large granite gate pillars she collided with a fair-haired young man who was just arriving.

'Sorry,' she mumbled.

'No problem,' he said, and was about to let her past when he added, 'Didn't we meet before – at Shaunie's? You asked me if it was his house.'

Marguerite nodded, and he asked, 'Are you all right?'

'How could she be all right, after what she's been through?' Susan retorted. Then, afraid Marguerite might think this was a reference to what she had told James and herself in confidence, she added, 'I mean, after the way you lot have treated her.'

'How do you mean, my lot? I'm not related to Shaunie. I just lease his land for grazing.'

'Oh,' Susan said. 'Sorry. I thought...'

The young man smiled. 'I know what you thought. It was only natural.' He pulled his collar up around his neck to keep off the rain. 'Look, I found a parking place across the street. Someone was leaving just as I arrived. Why don't you sit in out of the rain – unless, of course, your own car's nearby.'

'No, we left the car at the hotel.' Susan told him. She looked into Marguerite's tearful face. 'We'll be soaked if we don't get out of this. Maybe we should sit in for a minute, at least until the rain eases.'

Marguerite sniffed. 'All right. If you say so.'

'She does and so do I.' The young man ushered them across the street. There he helped them into the back seat of his car, closed the door behind them and sat in behind the wheel.

'Funny weather,' he said. 'Sunny one minute, raining the next.' When there was no reply, he proffered his hand to Marguerite across the back of his seat, saying, 'I'm Martin – Martin O'Driscoll.'

'Marguerite.'

'Shaunie's daughter?'

Marguerite began to sob, adding, 'Sorry Mr. O'Driscoll.'

'No need to be sorry. And you can drop the Mister O'Driscoll bit. Just call me Martin.'

Marguerite nodded. 'Okay. It's just that, this is the first time anyone else has called me Shaunie's daughter. How did you know?'

'I didn't, but my mother did. When she saw the report in the paper about the Prodigal Daughter, she told us she knew Catherine. She said Shaunie and Catherine were going to get married, but for some strange reason didn't. Then, when I told her about you calling to see Shaunie, and your American accent, she guessed you were his daughter – right?'

'Yes. And this is Susan – my aunt.'

He shook hands with Susan and settled back into his seat. The drizzle was beginning to gather on the windscreen, so he put on the wipers for a moment to clear it and watched the people filing out of the church. 'I take it you've met Shaunie's brothers?'

'No,' Marguerite replied. 'And I don't think they would want to meet me.'

'Maudie's given you the cold shoulder then?'

'I guess you could say that.'

'That's them standing at the car, shaking hands.'

Susan wound down the side window and Marguerite leaned over her in time to see Maudie slipping into the black limousine out of the rain, leaving her brothers to shake hands with a few people at the gate.

'Which one's Francie?' Marguerite asked.

'The one in the fawn coat.'

Francie, they could see, was bareheaded and not at all dressed for a funeral. As well as the fawn coat, he wore a blue shirt and red tie. He had fair wavy hair going grey, and each time he shook hands with someone, he had what they thought was a very peculiar habit. As he leaned forward to hear the words of condolence, he wrinkled his forehead in a deeply furrowed frown. Then, as he straightened, up the wrinkles disappeared and he smiled as if his sorrow was momentarily gone.

'Who's that with him?' Susan asked. 'The woman in the floral dress?'

'Ah, that's Trixie. That's his dolly bird.'

191

'You mean his wife?' asked Marguerite.

'I doubt it. You see, Francie lives in England. Nobody knows what he does, but he seems to live the life. Doesn't take anything seriously, including his women. Trixie is his latest.'

Marguerite and Susan leaned closer to the open window. Trixie had a hand on her head to protect her blonde hair from the rain and, even from across the street they could hear her high heels clicking on the concrete as she quickly followed Maudie into the limousine.

'And that's Mick, with the hat,' Martin continued. 'He's a cattle dealer. Lives in Tipperary.'

Mick, they could see, wasn't dressed for a funeral either. He was short and stout and wore a soft brown hat that was pushed on to his head in a way that suggested he seldom took it off. It contrasted with his dark blue three-piece suit, but matched his brown shoes. His stomach stretched his waistcoat to the limit and he stood with his thumbs hooked on its tiny pockets, a stance that emphasised his corpulent form.

'And the small woman with them?' asked Marguerite.

'That's Lizzie, Mick's wife.'

Lizzie, they could see, wore a black coat and black headscarf. The scarf was tied beneath an undershot chin, and when a man brought over a big black umbrella to shelter them from the rain, she took off the scarf to reveal a head of grey hair tied back in a bun.

Marguerite couldn't help thinking that Lizzie and Trixie couldn't be more different, either in appearance or dress, but she refrained from saying so as she didn't want to sound uncharitable. Instead she said, 'I thought Shaunie had another brother – Pat?'

'That's right,' said Martin, 'but he's in Australia.'

The man with the umbrella ushered the family towards the limousine. Lizzie went in first and, having accepted a few more handshakes, the brothers followed. As the limousine pulled away Marguerite sat back into her seat and Susan wound up the window.

'Can I drop you somewhere?' Martin asked them.

'We're staying at The Cumán Inn,' Susan replied. 'If you're going that way…'

'No problem. What do you think of it – The Cumán Inn, I mean?'

'It seems very nice,' Susan told him. 'We checked in shortly before we came to the removal.'

'Then you'll join me for dinner.' They protested, but he told them, 'Of course you will. Sure my sister Mary runs the inn – you probably met her when you checked in.'

'We thought she was the receptionist,' Susan said. 'We didn't know she was the owner?'

'She's not. My mother is, but she's getting on in years and after my father died she sort of took a back seat. Mary runs the hotel part of it. I look after the pub and the farm.' As he turned the corner of the street where the hotel was located, he added, 'It's only a small farm. I think my father just bought it for the sake of having a few acres. That's why I lease Shaunie's land. I need it for grazing.'

'Was your father a hurler?' Marguerite asked.

'He was of course.'

'Is that why he called it The Cumán Inn?'

'What else?'

'And what about you? Are you a hurler?'

Martin looked back at them in the mirror and smiled. 'In this part of the country, all the lads play hurling and the girls play camogie.' A short distance farther on, he pulled in at the hotel and opened the car door for them, and even though they had already checked in, he told them, 'Welcome to The Cumán Inn.'

Maudie was furious. They had just returned from the removal and were sitting in the parlour of the farmhouse. As with most farmhouses in Ireland, it was a parlour that was never used, except for special occasions such as weddings and funerals. Now that Shaunie had died, Maudie had opened it up in preparation for the people who would call next day following the burial. Having accepted an offer from some neighbours to make sandwiches and bake cakes, she had removed the dust covers from the armchairs and settee and brought in extra chairs, as well as some small tables. She had dusted the large mantelpiece and the sideboard, and now as she took off her black hat and put it on the sideboard, she fumed about what had happened in the church.

'Did you see her? The cheek of her! Kissing Shaunie's coffin – and in full view of the whole congregation. What are the neighbours going to think?'

'Who cares what they think?' said Trixie.

Francie had settled into in one of the armchairs and Trixie was sitting cross-legged on the soft arm beside him admiring the red paint on her fingernails.

Lizzie ignored her, saying, 'She probably just did it to embarrass us. It's a wonder she didn't come over and try and shake us by the hand.'

Mick had taken off his hat to reveal a scalp that was almost bald and white. 'If she had come near *me* she would have got her answer.'

'It was the same when she came to see Shaunie,' Maudie continued. 'Marched up to the door, bold as brass.'

Francie lowered his head and frowned. 'Why didn't you run her?'

'If I had answered the door I would have. Unfortunately, Shaunie opened it. He wasn't a well man and, of course, he fell for it.'

'There's no proof that she's Shaunie's daughter, is there?' asked Mick.

'Of course not, but as I say, Shaunie fell for it hook, line and sinker. Greeted her with open arms.'

'So there's no way she can get her hands on the farm?' said Francie.

'Not if I can help it,' Maudie asserted. 'Shaunie willed it to me and I've no intention of letting any stranger get her dirty little hands on it.'

Trixie put an arm around Francie's shoulders saying, 'I thought you would have inherited some of it, Duckie.'

'Well, he hasn't,' snapped Maudie. 'Now, if you don't mind, I want to talk to my brothers alone. Lizzie, you don't mind, do you?' She nodded towards Trixie as if to say, 'Would you get this trollop out of here?'

Taking the hint, Lizzie got up. 'A cup of tea everybody? Come on Trixie, give me a hand.'

Francie took his hand from Trixie's knee. 'And I wouldn't mind a sandwich.'

When they left, Mick said, 'So, tell me Maudie, what exactly did this woman say?'

Maudie related word for word what had been said at Marguerite's meeting with Shaunie at the house and then with herself at the hospital. When she finished, Francie puckered his brow in a puzzled frown and said, 'But the paper said Catherine and her baby died on the way over to America.'

'That's right?' Mick said. 'So who is this woman?'

'That's the point,' Maudie replied. 'Who is she? She has used several names. I heard her. She admitted as much to Shaunie. Now she calls herself Marguerite. Claims Catherine is her mother and that she wrote it all down for her.'

Francie puckered his forehead again. 'Wrote what down?'

'Everything – you know, about Shaunie and herself. The question is, who did Catherine give it to if, in fact, she did write something down? I mean, her daughter was only a baby when she died. It could have fallen into anyone's hands.'

'Does she know we locked Shaunie in the day he was supposed to get married?' Francie asked.

'Of course she does. Shaunie told her himself in the hospital. I told you, she knows everything.'

'But that was just a joke,' Francie protested.

'Well, joke or not,' said Maudie, 'it has come back to haunt us.'

Mick scratched his balding head. 'So what exactly does she want?'

'I told you. She wants us to accept that she's Shaunie's daughter.'

'Sure if we do that we might as well give her the farm.'

'She can't inherit the farm,' said Francie, 'even if she *is* Shaunie's daughter. She's illegitmate.'

'She says she doesn't want the farm,' said Maudie. 'She says all she wants is to be recognised as Shaunie's daughter.'

'That's what she says now,' said Mick. 'But if we recognise her it might be another story.'

'So, what are we going to do?' asked Francie.

'*You* are going to do nothing,' Maudie replied. 'It's my farm now and I'll handle it in my own way.'

'Well,' said Mick, 'be careful. I think you're right. It sounds like a scam to me.'

'What if she turns up at the funeral tomorrow?' asked Francie.

'If she does,' Maudie said, 'we'll make it clear to her in no uncertain terms that she's not welcome!'

'Where is she staying?' asked Mick.

'I don't really know,' Maudie replied. 'Up in Tipperary with Catherine's people, I suppose.'

Mick nodded. 'Well, if she is, I'll talk to some people when I go back and see if I can find out anything more about her.'

Standing at the back of the church, Marguerite held Susan tightly by the arm and cried quietly as Shaunie's coffin, still draped in the flag of his local hurling team, was hoisted on to the shoulders of several men, including two of the brothers who had destroyed his life. She was still crying as she followed the coffin into the nearby cemetery, but she stayed well back from the graveside, knowing as she did that she wasn't welcome.

It was another wet day, but even so, the men who had gathered around the grave removed their caps and all fell silent as they listened to the priest's oration. His words were dispersed by the head stones and, try as she would, Marguerite couldn't make them out. Her tears were mixing with the rain now but she could still feel the salt on her lips and she had a distinct feeling of *déjà vu*. Once again she was watching her father's funeral. Once again she was forced to stay back. Watch it from afar. Unwanted by her family. Unwelcome at the grave.

It was almost as if a recording of her life had somehow been wound back and was being replayed in slow motion. However, there was one big difference. This time it wasn't Don Diego but her real father, her beloved Shaunie, who was being laid to rest. The problem was, the only person who had accepted that she was Shaunie's daughter was Shaunie himself, and now he was gone.

TWENTY-TWO

Americans visitors discover, to their surprise, that Dublin's Phoenix Park is more than twice the size of New York's Central Park. The main feature is the official residence of the President, a palatial white building from which various Viceroys once oversaw British rule in Ireland. Nearby is the residence of the United States Ambassador and, slightly closer to the city, a collection of grey stone buildings which are the headquarters of An Garda Síochána, the Irish police.

On the eve of the arrival of the two American officers, the detective inspector assigned to act as their liaison officer was called in by a member of senior management to receive his instructions. As far as the gardaí were concerned the incident with the New York police band had been consigned to the past, and the inspector's instructions were short and to the point. 'Look after them,' he was told gruffly, and while this might have seemed a rather curt way of putting it, the inspector knew from experience that he was being directed to extend to them all the courtesy and co-operation that members of the gardaí got when they went to New York, especially on St. Patrick's Day.

As a result, the inspector went across the parade ground to make arrangements for the Americans to stay in the Officers' Club. In contrast to the grey stone of the main complex, the Officers' Club is built of faded yellow and red brick and stands slightly apart from the other buildings. Behind its colonnaded entrance is an elegant staircase and the inspector knew that this, together with some fine pieces of antique furniture, would remind the New Yorkers of Ireland's colonial past. At the same time, its proximity to the headquarters complex would make it an ideal place for them to stay while they pursued their inquiries into Don Diego's death.

A big bluff man with thinning fair hair, the inspector had a Gaelic surname that Florentine found impossible to pronounce, let alone remember. It was a name that Sullivan even had difficulty getting his tongue around, so the inspector told them to forget it. 'Just call me Joe,' he said with a smile that showed he was amused at their predicament. And so they did.

'They tell me you father was a guard,' said Joe as he drove them in from the airport.

Sullivan nodded. 'That's right. Dan. His father was a guard before him. They came from Cork.'

'What part of Cork?' When told, Joe began to wonder aloud about which branch of the O'Sullivan family they had come from. So much so that it seemed to Florentine there must be a lot of O'Sullivans in County Cork and that their host knew them all.

When the O'Sullivan family tree had been dissected to the stage where it could be dissected no more, and without any firm conclusion being reached, Florentine said, 'This woman we want to talk to. The address we were given is in Tipperary. Is that far from Dublin?'

'Not far. A couple of hours should take us there.'

'Can we talk to her?' asked Florentine. 'Or do we have to do it through you?'

Joe smiled. 'Well, strictly speaking, you have to leave it to me. But we'll see how it goes. You can brief me this afternoon and I'll take you down to Tipperary tomorrow.'

After checking his visitors in at the Officers' Club, Joe took them on a quick tour of headquarters, a tour that ended up in the office of his superintendent where, it had been arranged, the briefing would be held. Florentine gave them a quick run down on the shooting of Don Diego and outlined the reasons why they were so anxious to talk to his adoptive daughter, Marguerite.

'So you're satisfied she's the nun?' asked the superintendent.

'That's right,' Sullivan said. 'We've reason to believe she's now travelling on an Irish passport using what she claims is her real name.'

The superintendent nodded. 'I must get our people to check that out.'

'Well, if you could ease up on that aspect of the case for the moment,' said Florentine, 'we could check it when she goes back.'

'And let's face it,' added Sullivan, 'your people would be asking us to run a check on it anyway.'

'I know you're anxious to get her back,' said the superintendent, 'but you know you won't be able to make her go back and give evidence if she doesn't want to.'

'We know that,' said Florentine. 'But we reckon she saw the killer. If we could just talk to her – find out who it was – we could take it from there.'

Florentine produced a list of the questions which they wished to put to her and, after reading them, the superintendent gave them to Joe, saying, 'All right. But Joe, you'll do the questioning – and make sure you keep me informed. If there's dual citizenship here, it could turn out to be tricky.'

The briefing over, Joe took his visitors for a sightseeing tour of Dublin before inviting them to join him in his favourite pub for what he called 'a quick one'. This turned out to be a glass of whiskey, after which he told them they would have a pint of stout. However, Florentine soon discovered what Sullivan had long known, thanks to his celebration of St. Patrick's Day: there was no such thing as a single pint. The pints came in multiples of three, often, it seemed to Florentine, without even being ordered. Over the first few pints they gave Joe a more detailed briefing on their investigation of the Diego shooting but somehow, as the evening progressed, the Diego case was forgotten. Instead, the three of them began to tell one another of other murder investigations in which they had taken part, emphasising the twists and turns that had made the outcomes stranger than fiction.

How long they stayed in the pub, no one could recall, for when it became obvious that the visitors were lagging behind with their pints, Joe reverted to whiskey which, he told them, came from the Gaelic *uisce beatha*, meaning water of life. The result was that when they set off for Tipperary next morning, Florentine and Sullivan were suffering badly from the sore heads that Lieutenant Jacobs had warned them about.

For his part, Joe appeared to have no ill effects, and as he drove down through the countryside, he gave a running commentary on the geography, history and current crime rating of each county. The Americans listened, nodded and held their hands to their heads. They were grateful that they didn't have to respond to what was being said and even more grateful when Joe stopped at a roadside pub to get them what he called 'a cure'.

By the time the Rock of Cashel came into view, the visitors were feeling a bit better.

Mindful of the other piece of advice Lt. Jacobs had given them, Florentine inquired, 'I hear some of your members have been murdered by the IRA?'

'That's true. Since the Troubles began about eleven of our members have been killed, four or five of them I'd say by the IRA.'

'Is there much support for them in this part of Ireland?' Sullivan asked.

'They couldn't operate without support. Now take Tipperary. It has always had a strong republican tradition. The first shots in the War of Independence were fired here. But then that was done by members of the Old IRA.'

'You mean there's a difference?' asked Florentine.

'There's a difference all right. But it's too complicated to explain. Why don't we talk about something simpler – like the death of Don Diego?'

In spite of their sore heads, the visitors had to smile. Joe, they had discovered, had a peculiar sense of humour. They were also glad that the row over NORAID and the Emerald Pipe Band hadn't been mentioned and that they were being given all the co-operation they needed.

The divisional chief had been informed of the fact that the New York cops would be visiting his area, and he in turn had informed the local guards. Nevertheless, Joe made a point of calling in to the station to tell them he had arrived. Apart from anything else, he knew the local officers would want to be able to say they had met the Americans. He also knew that once that courtesy had been extended to them, there was nothing they wouldn't do for the visitors, and for a start they were provided with a guide, a guard by the name of PJ.

Easing his considerable bulk into the car seemed to exhaust PJ and the

Americans wondered if his ruddy complexion was the result of the fresh country air or a little too much of what Joe called *uisce beatha*. As they drove along the narrow winding roads they also wondered, more than once, if PJ knew where he was going or was taking them on a wild goose chase. 'Only a mile or so now,' he would assure them, but somehow they got the feeling that Irish miles, like Irish pints, didn't come singly. Sensing their impatience, Joe pointed out that the winding roads always made the journey seem longer. 'And you mustn't forget,' he added with a wide smile, 'Irish miles are longer than English miles, or American miles for that matter.'

It was the middle of the afternoon when they finally arrived at the cottage where Marguerite was said to be staying. The others remained in the car while Joe identified himself to the woman who answered the door and informed her of the purpose of their visit.

'You mean they've come all the way from America to talk to her?' asked Susan.

'They want to talk to her about the shooting of her father,' Joe explained.

'Her adoptive father you mean. She's been reunited with her natural father, you know. He was still living down in Cork.'

Joe nodded.

'She met him just before he died. He was only buried recently, so it's not really a good time to be talking to her. Anyway, she's not here.'

'Where is she?'

'She's gone into town to see her solicitor. You know, to try and sort out all this business about her natural father.'

'When will she be back?'

'I don't really know.' Susan looked towards the road and, seeing no sign of her, added, 'Why don't you come back tomorrow? I'll tell her you called and she can get herself ready.'

'All right. First thing in the morning then. And you'll make sure she's here?'

'Of course she'll be here. Sure why wouldn't she be?'

'Why indeed?' said Joe to himself as he returned to the car to inform the Americans.

'Damn it!' exclaimed Florentine, banging his thigh with his fist. 'That dame is never in when we call.'

'How do you mean?' asked Joe.

'We asked her not to leave New York or change her address without informing us,' Sullivan explained. 'But when we went to the deli where she worked, she had left.'

'Then we discovered she had gone to stay with relatives in New Jersey,' said Florentine, 'but when we called there, she had gone.'

'It was the same with the convent,' Sullivan continued. 'When we called the nuns told us she had left there too.'

'Well, you don't have to worry,' Joe assured them. 'She'll be here in the morning – you'll see.'

At the mention of the word convent, PJ had pricked up his ears. Unlike Joe, he hadn't been briefed on what was going on, but decided to offer his opinion anyway. 'Sure Ireland is only a small place. I mean, even if she did take off, where would she go?'

This wasn't much comfort to the two visitors, but they decided to take Joe's advice and booked into the local hotel for the night. Back home they would have mounted a stakeout on the house, but Joe said there was no need. For some reason he seemed to believe what the woman had told him and that their witness would be there in the morning.

Marguerite had been overjoyed to find her natural father and greatly saddened by his death. Even before she met him, she felt an affinity with him, a bond that never existed with Don Diego. Diego she despised; Shaunie she adored and when she met him, when he embraced her and accepted her as his own, it was heaven, the sum total of all her dreams. The sum total, she knew, of all Catherine's dreams.

But now Shaunie was dead and his family was refusing to recognise her as his daughter. And somehow that recognition, that acceptance, was the most important thing in the world to her. Why it should be so, she did not know. But it was, and she was determined to get it before she returned to America.

The solicitor she went to see was a man by the name of Murphy, a legendary figure in the town and, indeed, far beyond. A short, stout man with very little hair, he smoked a curly pipe that always seemed in need of being lit. There was also a twinkle in his eye that reflected the fact that he enjoyed the cut and thrust of a court battle over things that others might have thought weren't worth fighting over. According to Susan, who had recommended him, he was renowned for the fact that he would make the most complex legal arguments in what appeared to be the simplest of cases. Whether it was to argue the rights of a stray cow over the rights of a motorist, the right of a woman to cross a field to draw water from a well, or the right of a dangerous dog to have its day in court, he was the man to do it.

His office was in an unpretentious terraced house that looked like all the other houses, except for the fact that it bore the name Murphy, Murphy and Murphy, Solicitors on a shiny brass plate beside the door. Which member of the firm he was, Marguerite didn't know, but he received her very graciously. At their first meeting he had told her he needed time to study her documents and now he asked her to tell him again exactly what had happened and what she wanted. Having succeeded in lighting his pipe, he listened as she again explained her predicament. Now and then he jotted down notes on a large writing pad but apart from asking for clarification of some things, he said very little until she had finished.

'So all you want is for the family to recognise you as Shaunie's daughter,' he said at last. 'And how will you prove it?'

'You have Mrs. Gaynor's account – it's all there.'

Mr. Murphy took several handwritten pages out of a folder and the pipe out of his mouth, and as he looked over the pages he said, 'I have examined Mrs. Gaynor's account very carefully. It doesn't prove that you are who she says you are. However, it does raise a problem.'

'Yeah – and what's that?'

'Well, leaving aside the identity of the child for a moment, she says she gave a baby to the Diegos for adoption, but my office has been in touch with the authorities in New York and they can find no record of the Diegos ever having adopted a child.'

'How can that be?'

Mr. Murphy shrugged. 'At this stage we can only guess. In the 1950s and 60s the nuns in mother and baby homes sent hundreds if not thousands of children to America for adoption. There was a big waiting list and when wealthy Americans were involved, I gather the nuns sometimes cut corners.'

'You mean, for money?'

'Of course. Some of these people were willing to pay and the nuns needed the money to run their convents.'

'According to the letters I found in Don's old desk he was sending money back to Mrs. Gaynor in Dublin... Our little transaction, she called it.'

'There you are then.'

'You mean they sold us?'

'I suppose you could say that. And for some reason it appears to me the Diegos didn't formally adopt the baby they got.' Mr. Murphy paused. 'But even if it turns out that they did – and that baby turns out to be you, or should I say, Catherine's baby – you still weren't adopted, at least not legally, if Nurse Gaynor gave you to them in place of someone else.'

'And is that a problem?'

'Well, under the law here an adopted person cannot claim to inherit anything from their biological parents. So if you were adopted, Shaunie's family would have nothing to fear. They could recognise you as Shaunie's daughter knowing you couldn't lay claim to the farm. But if you were not adopted – as appears to be the case – recognising you as Shaunie's daughter could open the way for you to challenge Shaunie's will – provided, of course, you can prove who you say you are.'

'But I'm not interested in inheriting anything – all I want is for them to recognise me as Shaunie's daughter.'

'And how do you propose to do that?'

'The notes my mother – that's my birth mother – wrote for me on the liner when we were going to New York. She states quite clearly that Shaunie was my father. Then there's my birth certificate.'

Mr. Murphy left his pipe down in a glass ashtray. 'I have read her notes very carefully. And they are all very interesting, but they still don't prove that you are who you say you are.'

Marguerite dipped into her handbag. 'I also have this letter which Shaunie gave to me shortly before he died. He wrote it to Catherine – my mother – but she never got it. In it he says he knows she is pregnant, and he accepts that he is the father.'

Mr. Murphy adjusted his glasses and examined the letter in great detail. 'The problem is,' he said at last, 'there's nothing to say that you are the issue of their relationship.'

'Except what it says on this envelope. The letter Shaunie wrote to my mother was in it. It says, *To my darling daughter Katie, from Shaunie.* Here, see for yourself.'

As she passed the envelope to him, she thought she detected a twinkle in his eye. 'Very good,' he said. 'But how do we prove it was meant for you and not for somebody else?'

'Well, the nurse at the hospital will tell you. She said Shaunie asked her to give it to me.'

'Ah, that's different. It gives us the link we need.' Mr. Murphy put his pipe in his mouth and attempted to light it again. 'It shows that Shaunie accepted you as his daughter, and that's important. But mind you, it still doesn't prove that you are who you say you are. However, if you took a blood test and it proved positive, we could ask the court for a Decaration of Paternity.'

'I don't mind taking a blood test, but I don't have time to go to court. I have to return to America.'

'So what do you propose we should do?'

'Go see them I suppose.'

'And how will you allay any fears they might have that you could be after the farm?'

'I don't care a damn about the farm. I'll sign a form renouncing any claim to it, or whatever is necessary. All I want is to be recognised as Shaunie's daughter.'

'And what do you think Shaunie's sister – what did you say her name was?'

'Maudie.'

'That's right, Maudie. What do you think would be her reaction to such a proposal? Do you think she would agree?'

'I don't know. I suppose she might, if I renounced any claim to the farm.'

'What size of a farm is it?'

'Shaunie said it was nearly two hundred acres, as far as I remember.'

'Two hundred acres. That's quite a big farm. It must be worth a lot of money.'

'I told you I'm not interested in it.'

'Still.' Mr. Murphy left his pipe down again and looked her straight in the eye. 'It must have cost you a fair bit to come here and locate Shaunie.'

'I had to borrow.'

'A considerable sum, I would imagine?'

'Well, it was considerable to me.'

'There you are then. I'll check out the current value of land and we'll see where we go from there.'

'But I told you, I don't want the farm. I don't want any part of it. All I want is recognition.'

Mr. Murphy sat back in his leather chair and she could see that he had got his pipe going again. 'That's very commendable,' he said, exhaling a plume of blue smoke, 'But let me explain the situation. In the realm of Irish law, a renunciation is a contract. For a renunciation to be enforceable, to be a valid act, like every other contract there must be a consideration – something passing from one person to another in consideration of what the other person is doing. In this case, you would be renouncing your claim to the farm in return for recognition. For her part, Maudie would be giving you what we would call a letter of comfort, recognising you as Shaunie's daughter in consideration of what you are doing. But there is no reason why there shouldn't also be a financial consideration. You follow what I'm saying?'

'I think so.'

'Mind you, should Maudie agree to recognise you as Shaunie's daughter, it wouldn't make you Shaunie's daughter. It wouldn't establish the truth of

206

what she says, you understand? That would be a matter for the courts. All she would be saying is that she accepts that you are Shaunie's daughter.'

'But that's all I want.'

'Right then. I'll find out who Maudie's solicitor is and draw up the papers. Usually these things take a long time, but I'll impress upon him the fact that you are anxious to return to America and that should hurry things up. What if I suggested a meeting down at Maudie's place next week? How would that suit you?'

Marguerite smiled. 'That would suit me very well.'

TWENTY-THREE

Detective Florentine took the silver crucifix from his pocket and dangled it from his hand, saying, 'Do you recognise this, Marguerite?'

'I told you, I'm not Marguerite. I'm Katie.'

Joe had brought the two Americans back to Susan's cottage where, to their surprise, they had found Marguerite waiting for them. Then, in the privacy of the small sitting room, they had begun to question her.

'Listen,' said Joe, leaning across the small mahogany coffee table, 'these guys know that you came here in search of your family roots. Ed and Lily have told them all about that. But they're investigating the shooting of Don Diego, and whether you like it or not you were brought up as his adopted daughter, right?'

Marguerite nodded.

'Good. Now without prejudice to which name you wish to use, they have to talk to you about your life in America as Marguerite, or as they have reason to believe, Sister Mary. You understand that?'

'Yes. But there is something you all must understand first?'

'What's that?'

'I have found my real family now – here and in Cork.' She sniffed as tears came into her eyes. 'If I agree to answer your questions, I want an assurance from you that whatever transpires between us won't be made public – not while I am still here. It wouldn't be fair to them.'

'Well, we certainly won't be going public with it,' said Florentine.

'Otherwise, I won't answer your questions and I won't return to New York.'

208

'You do intend to return to New York then?' asked Florentine.

'Of course I do, but only on that one condition.'

'Well, as I say, the newspapers won't hear about our interview from me or my buddy here.'

'Or me,' Joe assured her.

'All right then. What do you want to ask me?'

'Well, strictly speaking,' said Joe, 'I have to ask you the questions but, if you have no objection, it would be easier if they could put some questions too.'

Marguerite sniffed to clear the tears that had gathered in her nose. 'I don't mind who asks them.'

'Good,' said Joe. 'Now, to begin with, do you accept that you are Marguerite Diego, daughter of Don Diego?'

'Adopted daughter – or at least I thought I was adopted. But I wasn't. In fact I should never have been there in the first place.'

'Ok, whatever. But you're also Sister Mary. Isn't that right?'

Marguerite nodded.

'So you recognise this?' said Florentine, dangling the crucifix in front of her again.

'Yes.'

'Here, take it, look at it carefully and make sure.'

'I don't need to take it. It's mine. Why, where did you find it?'

Florentine paused to give Joe time to write down the answers. Sullivan, he could see, was taking notes as well.

'It was found at the scene of the shooting of Don Diego,' he continued, 'which makes us believe you were there when it happened.'

Marguerite bowed her head and made no response.

Joe looked up from his notepad. 'Well? Were you there?'

'Yes.'

'Who did you see?' asked Florentine. 'Who else was in the house that day when you called?'

'No one else.'

'What do you mean, no one else?'

'There was no one else there. Only him and me.'

Florentine was about to question her further, when Joe said, 'Sully, maybe you would stay here with Marguerite for a minute. Toni and I have to consult outside.'

'What's going on?' demanded Florentine when Joe closed the door behind them.

Joe put his hand to his lips, saying, 'Let's go out to the yard. We can talk there.'

'Is everything all right?' asked Susan from the kitchen as they passed.

'Everything's fine,' Joe assured her. 'Just taking a break.'

'The kettle's on,' she told him. 'Let me know if you'd like a cup of tea. Or coffee for your friends.'

'Thanks. That's very kind of you.'

'Okay, what's the beef?' demanded Florentine, when they were out of earshot of the house.

'Well, it appears to me that this woman – Marguerite, or Katie or whoever she is – may be about to make a self-incriminating statement.'

'I thought she was just going to say she walked in and found Don Diego dead.'

'That may well be, but if, on the other hand, she's going to incriminate herself, she has to be cautioned. The question is, which caution do we administer to her – yours or ours?'

Florentine squeezed his jaw with his right hand as he looked at the ground. 'Damned if I know.'

'Nor I. I think I'll get on to headquarters and get them to check with the DPP's Office.'

'The DPP? Who's he?'

'The Director of Public Prosecutions. He would probably be the equivalent of your District Attorney.'

It seemed to Florentine to be a long time before Garda Headquarters rang back with instructions from the DPP's office, but in fact it was less than half an hour. 'Well,' he asked, as he followed Joe out to the yard again, 'what did he say?'

'The super wasn't talking to the DPP himself. It was one of his legal officers.' Joe stopped and looked at his notes. 'He says that under the Offences Against the Person Act of 1861 an Irish citizen can be charged and tried here in Ireland for murder or manslaughter committed anywhere in the world. Therefore, I should bear in mind that if this woman is an Irish citizen, and she makes a confession, she could be tried here under Irish law, even though the offence occurred in the US. But if she is going to return voluntarily to the US, you should be conscious of the fact that you might be using the statement made here in your presence, in an American court of law.'

'So?'

'So he suggests we should both caution her. He mentioned something about the Miranda case.'

Florentine smiled. 'He knows his American law. *Miranda* v. *Arizona*, Supreme Court, 1961. It ruled that we have to inform suspects of their rights – you know the drill... You have the right to remain silent. Anything you do say may be used against you in a court of law. You have the right to have an attorney present...'

'A bit like our caution. You are not obliged to say anything, but anything you do say will be taken down and may be used in evidence...'

'But the US Supreme Court was talking about suspects, not witnesses,' Florentine added.

'Maybe so,' said Joe, 'but it seems to me that the situation in this case is about to change, and the advice is that we should both caution her.'

'Okay then, let's do it.'

When Marguerite had been advised of her rights, she was also informed that she was entitled to have a solicitor present, but she declined.

'Are you sure?' Joe asked her. 'Susan told me you were in the town yesterday seeing one about some family matters. Would you not like him to be present?'

'No. I don't want him involved in this.'

'Okay, it's your choice. Now, you were about to tell us what happened in the house the day Don Diego was shot.'

211

'I would like to start at the beginning, if it's all right with you?'

'Of course. Tell us in your own words what happened.'

Marguerite sank back into the corner of the settee and pulled her legs up under her. 'Well, it all started when I was a child. Everything was fine until the twins arrived. After that my mother – or the woman I thought was my mother – seemed to lose interest in me. All she was interested in was the twins. They got all the love, all the attention. I got nothing but the cold shoulder. I was an outcast in my own home, or what I thought was my own home. I couldn't understand it. I was heartbroken. Then Don began to comfort me. He would cuddle me and tell me how much he loved me. But it wasn't love he had in mind. Before long he began to touch me – you know – he would touch me and fondle me in a way I knew he shouldn't be doing.'

She began to cry and Sullivan took a hankie from his breast pocket and gave it to her.

'Take your time,' said Joe and, as she dried her tears, he jotted down the last part of what she had been saying.

She sniffed and nodded. 'Next thing I knew the bastard was raping me.'

'What age were you when he started to rape you?' asked Florentine.

'About eight.'

'And how often did that happen?'

'Once a week. Sometimes more.'

When she started crying again, Joe said, 'It's okay, it's okay.'

'No one would believe me,' she added, 'not even Nora and she was supposed to be my mother. Or the priest. They didn't do anything to help me. I ran away three times, you know. Twice they brought me back. The third time I made sure they wouldn't find me.'

'Maybe you'd like another break,' Joe suggested. 'Time to think about it.'

Marguerite nodded and dabbed the tears with the hankie. She was grateful for the break, but she really didn't need time to think about the last time she ran away. Don had gone on another of his binges and she knew he would be coming in to her that night. All sweet talk, then another clumsy, painful rape. But she was older then and made up her mind that there would be no more of it. So she went to a drawer where he kept his pistol.

As she thought about it now, Marguerite could see the inscription on the pistol, for it was etched on her mind just as clearly as it was on the side of the gun. *For Services Rendered.* Don said it had been given to him by a couple who were grateful for finding them a particularly nice piece of property. Nora must have suspected the real reason he had got it – probably a gift from some dame who was past her best, grateful for sexual favours, and with more money than sense. But if she did, she turned a blind eye to it. Just as she turned a blind eye to what he was doing to their adoptive daughter.

Being young and innocent Marguerite, recalled, she thought the pistol, with its mother-of-pearl handgrip, was a lovely little gun. She often watched Don firing it in the woods behind the house. When she admired it, he allowed her to fire it but while holding her from behind in a way he shouldn't be holding her. She didn't admire it after that, but watched from a safe distance as he went through the ritual of putting in a magazine and pulling the slide back to cock it.

It wasn't until several years later – years of countless rapes and torment – that she took the pistol from the drawer. She put a magazine into it and cocked it, just as she had seen him do, and when he came into her room that night she told him she would blow his fucking head off if he touched her again. He left the room, though very reluctantly, and she was unable to sleep, knowing full well that he would be back for the gun – and for her. So she stuffed a few belongings into a small suitcase and climbed out the window, taking the gun with her.

Seeing that she had composed herself, Joe continued, 'You were saying the third time you ran away you made sure they wouldn't find you.'

When she nodded, Florentine asked, 'Was that when you joined the nuns?'

'Yeah. I was living rough. Then one day I went to the convent for food. After a while I began to help the nuns and then, eventually, I joined them.'

'And that was when you became Sister Mary?'

She nodded and Florentine waited until Joe and Sullivan had finished writing.

However, Joe was anxious to keep control of the interview, so he resumed the questioning. 'Now, tell us about the day Don Diego was shot. How did you come to be in the house?'

'Well, during the years I spent in the convent, I prayed a lot. I was traumatised by what had been done to me. I mean, I thought this man was my father. I prayed to God to forgive him, and I prayed to God to help me forgive him. But I couldn't. Not for a long time. Then, with God's help, I found an inner strength that somehow enabled me to come to terms with it. Eventually, after much prayer and contemplation, I mustered the courage to go back to Staten Island. In the Lord's Prayer we ask God to forgive us our trespasses as we forgive those who trespass against us. So I decided to find him and try and effect a reconciliation.'

She paused and didn't continue until Joe and Sullivan looked up to signal that they had stopped writing.

'But, it didn't work out that way. The son-of-a-bitch had been drinking and when I went in he started all over again. First he wanted money. Then it was something else. He put his arms around me and began telling me the same things he used to tell me when I was a child. "Don't be afraid, I'm not going to hurt you." All that shit. And that's precisely what he was planning to do. I struggled of course, but it was no use. He dragged me into the bedroom, threw me on the bed and began to...'

When she didn't complete the sentence, Joe asked, 'Began to what?'

'Sorry. I'm trying to tell you the best I can. He ripped my clothes off and began to rape me. I pleaded with him to stop, but it was no use. The more I struggled, the more violent he got. I remember him hitting me across the face with the back of his hand. And all the time he was saying horrible things. "It's the first time I've had sex with a bride of Christ." Things like that. And then I felt my hand touching something on the bedside locker. I realised it was his gun and, in desperation I hit him with it, but he just said, "Fuck you" and tried to wrestle it from my hand.'

She paused again and took a deep breath before continuing. 'That was when I heard the gun going off. When I pushed him off me onto the floor, I could see powder burns on his shirt, but the strange thing was, when I

214

opened the shirt I couldn't see where he had been shot. So I felt his pulse, but he was dead.'

'What did you do then?' asked Joe.

'Somehow, I felt that nobody would believe me. I mean, who would believe that my own father would do such a thing? And to a nun? So I ran out.'

'And what happened to the gun?' Florentine asked. 'We didn't find it in the room.'

'I think I panicked. I suppose I didn't want anyone to know what had happened. I was so ashamed. So I took it with me.'

'And what did you do with it?' asked Sullivan.

'I threw it away.'

'Where?'

'I don't know. I mean, I can't remember. I was in a terrible state.'

'Where did you go?' Florentine asked.

'I spent the night in the woods. They reminded me of the woods where I'd played as a child, but somehow I didn't seem to know them. I was in such a state of shock. At the same time, I thought I heard a whip-poor-will.'

Joe looked up. 'A what?'

'A whip-poor-will,' she replied. 'It's a bird. I remember listening for them in the woods when I was a child. Did you never hear one?'

'No. I never did.'

'Sometimes,' she went on, and it seemed to Joe that she was now drifting back into her childhood, 'sometimes if you're lucky you can hear a whip-poor-will.'

'If you're lucky!' said Joe to himself. 'God help us.'

Marguerite listened impassively as Joe read the statement over to her and then she signed it. He also signed it and asked the two American detectives to do likewise.

'What happens now?' she asked when they got up to go.

'That's not for us to say,' said Joe.

'Well, I'm going to Cork next week to complete some family business. Then I'm returning to New York.'

'In that case,' Joe added, 'I imagine it'll be up to the people in New York to decide what to do.'

'When exactly are you going back?' asked Florentine.

Marguerite shrugged and shook her head. 'I don't know yet.'

'More tea or coffee anybody?' asked Susan, opening the door slightly to look in.

'Come in,' said Joe. 'No, we're fine. Marguerite was just telling us she plans to return to New York soon. Will you make sure we're informed of the date? You can contact me at this number in Dublin.'

Susan took his card and promised she would. But she was clearly worried. 'Is everything all right?' she asked anxiously.

'Everything's fine,' Joe assured her. 'Marguerite's been very helpful.'

As they drove back to Dublin, Sullivan remarked, 'That guy Diego was some bastard.'

'Yeah,' said Florentine, 'It must have been a living hell for her when she was a child.'

'You don't think it'll go to court then?' Joe asked.

Sullivan shook his head. 'I wouldn't think so. He's raping her. She resists. In the ensuing struggle he tries to take the gun from her and ends up with lead in his gut. Self-defence. I don't think there's a jury in the world that would convict her.'

On their return to Dublin, Joe sent Marguerite's statement to the DPP, while Florentine faxed it to Lieutenant Jacobs who, he knew, would consult the DA's office. And so, feeling very pleased with themselves, they adjourned to the nearest pub to celebrate.

Perhaps it was because they had already suffered a severe hangover or because they were on a high, having obtained the confession from Marguerite, but neither Florentine nor Sullivan had a bad hangover the next morning. A hangover yes, but one that was tolerable. And, when Florentine took a telephone call from Lieutenant Jacobs that afternoon, he was still on a high. However, it was a high that was to be short-lived.

'Well?' said Joe, when the two of them joined him in the canteen.

'What did your people say? I bet they were pretty pleased.'

Florentine shook his head. 'They don't buy it.'

'Buy what?'

'Marguerite's story,' Sullivan said. 'They don't buy it.'

'You mean they don't believe it was self-defence?'

Florentine shook his head. 'No way. They say there are too many holes in her story. They want us to talk to her again.'

TWENTY-FOUR

As Joe drove his two American guests back to Tipperary, they saw the Rock of Cashel rising up out of the countryside ahead of them once more. But, majestic though the ancient fortress was, none of them commented upon it this time. The conversation was solely about Marguerite and the second interview they were about to do with her.

'I thought you'd wait until she went back to the States,' said Joe.

'We thought of that,' Florentine replied. 'But then it occurred to us that she might get some smart-assed lawyer over there who would advise her to keep her trap shut. For some reason or other, she says she doesn't want a lawyer at the moment and, if she's prepared to talk without one, then this seems the best time to do it.'

'Are you not afraid that if you press her too hard, she won't want to go back?'

'That's a chance we'll have to take. But she did say she doesn't want to embarrass the people she claims are her natural family – at least, not while she's here. So that should work in our favour.'

As they continued their journey, Florentine turned around to Sullivan, who was in the back seat. 'Sully,' he said, 'remember when Joe and I were out in the yard talking about reading her, her rights? I know it was probably only small talk, but how did the two of you get on?'

Sullivan leaned forward so that they could hear him better. 'As a matter of fact, we got on fairly well. She guessed I was Irish and when she asked me where I was from, that seemed to strike a chord. She said her real father was from Cork too, and that she had met him a couple of times before he died. That seemed to mean a lot to her.'

'Well done,' said Florentine. 'That should make it easier for us.'

'How do you mean?' asked Joe.

'Come on now,' said Florentine. 'You know the good cop, bad cop routine.'

'Maybe so, but I don't want any heavy stuff.'

'Of course not. You and Sully do the interviewing. I'll stay out of it. Maybe throw in a question or two, but leave it to you.'

When they arrived at the cottage, Susan showed them into the sitting room where Marguerite was waiting, then made a diplomatic withdrawal.

'Why do you want to talk to me again?' Marguerite asked. 'I thought I told you everything you wanted to know.'

'Well,' said Joe, 'it's not as simple as that. You see, an investigation is like a coin. There are always two sides to it. On one side there are the facts as we find them and what people tell us. On the reverse side there are other possibilities that we have to explore. We are not doubting you, you understand, but we have to talk about these other possibilities, satisfy ourselves that we are not overlooking anything; you know, that we have arrived at the truth.'

'But I've told you the truth.'

'I know, but still, there are one or two things that don't add up.'

Florentine got up and paced the room impatiently.

'Now Marguerite,' Joe continued, 'what we want to know is this – '

'I've had enough of this pussy-footing around,' Florentine fumed.

The other two watched as Florentine went over and fixed his eyes on Marguerite.

'Now look here,' he demanded, and he banged the coffee table with his fist. 'What we want to know is very simple. You say you killed Don Diego in self-defence. But there are certain things in your statement that make us wonder if you went to Staten Island that day with the express purpose of bumping him off.'

'What? Why should I do a thing like that?'

'Revenge, of course. Revenge for all the horrible things he did to you as a child. What else?'

'I had no thoughts of revenge. I prayed to God to forgive him. It was a reconciliation I wanted, not revenge.'

'I put it to you,' said Florentine, banging the table again, 'that you prayed to God to forgive him, but you couldn't forgive him yourself. You said so.'

'Yes, but – no, not the way you mean it.'

'You couldn't bring yourself to forgive him, and while you prayed, it festered in your mind like a boil that had to be lanced. Isn't that right?'

'No.'

'So you got yourself a little pistol and you went to Staten Island to give him what he deserved. Isn't that what really happened?'

'No, no, that's not how it happened at all. It was his own gun. It was on the locker beside the bed.'

'According to Mrs. Diego he didn't have a gun – hadn't had one for a long time.'

'How would she know? She wasn't living with him any more.'

'Be that as it may, I suggest you bought yourself a pistol and went over there for one purpose and one purpose only: to kill him for what he had done to you. The first shot didn't kill him, so you fired again to finish him off. And you were glad the bastard was dead. Isn't that right? You were glad.'

Marguerite looked at Joe and Sullivan, her eyes like those of a frightened animal. 'Why is he saying these things? Make him stop! Make him stop!'

Hearing the commotion, Susan knocked on the door, inquiring if everything was all right.

Joe went over and, peeping out, told her, 'Sorry. These Americans are very loud. I'll ask them to keep it down. Any chance of a cuppa?'

Florentine was still on his feet, hands on his hips, demonstrating his impatience.

'Okay Toni,' said Joe. 'That's enough. We'll take it from here.'

'I'm not going to answer any more questions,' said Marguerite. 'Not from him.'

'That's all right,' Joe assured her. 'Toni, I think you should wait outside.'

Florentine shrugged. 'It's your call.'

When he had gone, Sullivan said, 'Sorry about that. But we get some tough customers in New York. I suppose, after a while you forget that everybody's not like them.'

Susan knocked on the door and brought in a tray with tea, coffee and biscuits and when she had left, Marguerite asked, 'Does that guy really think I killed Don Diego deliberately?'

'Well,' said Sullivan, 'there are one or two things that need explaining. Maybe you could clarify them for us.'

'Okay. But give me a minute.'

'Take your time,' said Joe. 'Finish your coffee.'

As Marguerite sipped her coffee, she thought about what Florentine had said. She had taken the gun with her all right – Don Diego's gun. But she couldn't tell them that. And she couldn't tell them why – they would never believe it. Knowing how much Don Diego loved the gun, she had decided to give it back to him. If he had said he was sorry for what he had done to her, she would have said she was sorry for taking the gun. It would have been a gesture of goodwill, a Christian gesture, and maybe they could even have put it all behind them. But then she recalled how apprehensive she had been about going to see him and how the gun had given her a feeling of security. Did that mean that in some way the shooting was premeditated? No, she told herself, Florentine was wrong. It wasn't premeditated.

Confused, she muttered, 'No, it was self-defence.'

'I know,' said Joe, 'but as I say there are one or two things you might clarify for us.'

'Like what?'

'You say Diego raped you,' Sullivan said. 'But we found no sign of rape. For example, we would have expected to have found semen stains on the bed or on his clothing, but there were none.'

'I didn't say he raped me. I said he tried to rape me.'

'But his trousers were up around his waist and his belt hadn't been undone. Even his zipper was closed.'

Marguerite shrugged. 'So what? I guess he hadn't reached that stage when the gun went off.'

'We know it must be very difficult for you,' said Joe, 'but we have to get the answers to these things, and you are doing very well.'

'Another thing,' Sullivan continued. 'You keep saying the gun went off during the struggle. But as Detective Florentine says, the autopsy shows he was shot twice. How do you explain that?'

'Well, it did go off during the struggle. But it didn't kill him. He was still looking down at me, swearing at me, and I felt his hand move. He was still clutching my hand, which was around the gun. I was afraid he was going to turn it on me. So I pressed the trigger, and he slumped down on top of me.'

'But the gun wouldn't have fired unless you had taken off the safety catch?' Sullivan pointed out.

'I don't know anything about that. Maybe the catch was accidentally switched off, or on, or whatever you do with it, when he was trying to wrestle it from me. I don't know.'

'But even with the safety catch off,' Sullivan continued, 'it wouldn't have fired unless it had been cocked – and to do that the slide has to be pulled back to strip a round off the magazine and put it into the chamber.'

Marguerite's thoughts went back to the night she had threatened to shoot Don Diego. She had put in a full magazine, pulled back the slide and cocked it. But she hadn't un-cocked it or taken out the magazine. She didn't know how. And so it must have remained loaded and cocked all those years it had lain in her suitcase. Years when she had nightmares about Don Diego coming into her room again. Years when nightmare blurred reality and she feared she might need the gun again. But she just shrugged and said, 'I don't know. Maybe it was cocked when I picked it up.'

Sullivan nodded. 'All right. Now, you said that after the shooting you took the gun with you and threw it away. Where exactly did you throw it?'

'I can't remember. A lake. Or a pond. I don't know.'

'But that's another thing that makes us think you're not telling the truth,' said Sullivan. 'You didn't tell us in our last interview that you threw it into a pond. And you must agree. Taking it with you was a very strange thing to do in the first place.'

'I told you why.'

'But you say you shot him in self-defence. Why then should you take the gun with you and dump it? It doesn't make sense.'

'Nothing made sense that day. Nothing in my whole life has made sense. Until I came here and found my real father. And now he's gone too.'

'But why should you think no one would believe Diego tried to rape you?' asked Sullivan.

'I don't know. Maybe it was because no one ever believed me before.'

When Joe finished writing, he said, 'Okay. Maybe it's time we had a break.'

For the next fifteen minutes or so, the three detectives walked up and down the yard discussing the interview, while in the kitchen Marguerite helped Susan wash up, looking out while she was doing so and wondering what they were saying.

Florentine lit a cigarette and puffed away as he listened to what Sullivan and Joe had to say. Having remained outside the door of the sitting room, he had heard most of what Marguerite said but he wanted to know what the others thought of it.

'She seems to have an answer for everything,' said Sullivan.

Joe nodded. 'She sounds very convincing all right.'

'Maybe too convincing,' said Florentine.

'How do you mean?' asked Joe.

'Well, she says she was confused, that she doesn't know why she took the gun with her when she left the scene. But I think she knew well what she was doing. She threw it into a lake to make sure we bloody well wouldn't find it. She didn't want us to find her prints on it. Didn't want us to trace it back to her. That doesn't look like self-defence to me.'

Sullivan nodded. 'And now she admits she fired a second time, but only because she was afraid Diego would turn the gun on her. It's almost as if she's making it up as she goes along. What do you think, Joe?'

'I don't suppose it matters what I think. But I can't imagine an Irish nun doing something like that on purpose.'

'We still have to talk to her about Mrs. Gaynor,' Florentine reminded them. 'Our people have their own ideas about that too.'

When the three of them walked into the sitting room, Marguerite repeated that she would answer no further questions from Florentine. However, she didn't object when he retreated only as far as the table at the window where he seated himself and waited to hear what else she had to say.

'Now,' said Sullivan, easing her back into the interview as gently as he could. 'Tell us about Mrs. Gaynor. She was the Irish nurse who travelled with Catherine and the two babies to New York. Is that right?'

After glancing at Florentine, Marguerite nodded, 'That's right. Catherine had her own baby. That was me. The other baby's name was Brigid Mary. She was going over for adoption by the Diegos, but she died and Mrs. Gaynor gave me to the Diegos instead.'

'How did you feel when Mrs. Gaynor told you that?' asked Sullivan.

'How do you think I felt? I was devastated. I had gone through the most horrific childhood, and then I discovered I wasn't supposed to have been there in the first place.'

'Mr. Gaynor told us she was meeting you on the ferry. Is that when she told you what she had done?'

When Marguerite nodded, Florentine jumped to his feet and, looking into her eyes told her, 'By this time, you had killed Don Diego. A horrific childhood that had ended in murder. And you realised it would never have happened if it hadn't been for Mrs. Gaynor, isn't that right?'

'Well, yes. I mean, none of it wouldn't have happened if Mrs. Gaynor hadn't done what she did. But Don's death wasn't murder. I told you that.'

'You couldn't forgive Don Diego for what he had done. And you couldn't forgive Mrs. Gaynor for what she had done. Isn't that the truth of it?'

'Yes, but no… you're trying to confuse me.'

'And just as you took revenge on Don Diego for what he had done, you took revenge on Mrs. Gaynor, didn't you?'

'No. Of course I didn't.'

'This woman comes along and tells you she's sorry, that the mess you're in is all her fault. You must have felt like strangling her. But that would have been too obvious. So what do you do? You play her along until you meet her on the Statue of Liberty ferry. Then, when nobody is looking, you throw her over the side.'

'That's not true. That's not the way it happened at all. And anyway, you just can't throw someone over the side of the ferry; there are safety rails.'

'A good heave then,' said Florentine. 'Up and over. Isn't that the way it was done?'

'No. It's not.' Marguerite looked at the other two again, saying, 'I've told you already, I'm not going to answer any more of his questions. And I'm not going to answer any questions while he's in the room.'

'Toni,' said Joe, 'Do you mind?

'All right, all right, I'm going.'

When Florentine closed the door behind him Sullivan said, 'Sorry, Marguerite. I thought he had agreed not to ask you any more questions.'

'So tell me,' said Joe, 'what did happen on the ferry?'

'We got off at the Statue of Liberty. She had given me a bundle of my mother's letters, and notes my mother had written for me on the way over on the liner. While we were waiting for the next ferry, I read some of them, and then we boarded again for Battery Park. That's when she dropped the bombshell. She told me that she had given me to the Diegos instead of Brigid Mary, even though she knew I was Katie. I couldn't believe it. And then she asked me to forgive her.'

There was silence as Marguerite waited to continue, a silence broken only by the sound of writing.

'However, I couldn't forgive her. Not then and there. She had ruined my life.'

Marguerite put her hands to each side of her nose and sniffed to hold back the tears. 'I'm sorry now. Maybe if I had forgiven her, she would still be alive.'

'It's all right,' said Joe. 'Take it easy. You're doing fine.'

As Marguerite reflected on the sequence of events now, she told herself that Florentine was right. When Mrs. Gaynor had told her what had happened she *had* been very angry with her. Very very angry. To add insult to injury, Mrs. Gaynor had even suggested that an inheritance might make it all right, and that she herself might share in it. Share in an inheritance after the terrible thing she had done to her! She remembered bursting into tears as she buried her head in her hands. She remembered hearing someone shouting, 'Man overboard'. But nobody had seen Mrs.Gaynor going overboard. Florentine would just have to take her word for it that she hadn't pushed her.

'You were saying that maybe if you had forgiven Mrs. Gaynor, she might still be alive,' said Joe. 'What did you mean by that?'

'Well, she jumped, didn't she? I can still see her black coat floating in the water. And her little pill box hat. It was black too.'

Joe stopped writing and looked up. 'So you deny that you pushed her, or as Detective Florentine has suggested, that you gave her a heave over the side?'

'Of course I do.'

'Why then did you leave the ferry without telling them who she was?' Sullivan asked.

'I don't know. I suppose I didn't want to become involved – you know, after what had happened to Don Diego. But I'm sorry now. My whole life has been a failure. Even my life as a nun. I couldn't forgive – and that's what Christianity is all about, isn't it? Forgiving.'

Joe nodded. 'I know. Sometimes it's not easy.'

When the formalities were completed, they thanked Susan for her hospitality and headed back to Dublin.

'Well?' said Joe, 'what do you think?'

'Me?' Florentine flicked a cigarette butt out of the passenger door window and wound it back up again. 'I think she's guilty as hell. But it's going to be very difficult to prove.'

'And you, Sully, what do you think?'

Sullivan stretched himself out on the back seat and rested his head at the corner window. 'I don't know. Somehow I can't help feeling sorry for her after all she's been through.'

'Me too,' said Joe.

'It's all very circumstantial,' Sullivan added. 'But I think the DA might let it go to a jury – you know, let them decide if she's telling the truth.'

'And I can just see the headlines,' said Florentine. 'It won't be Marguerite or Katie they'll be talking about. It'll be Sister Mary and they'll be asking the same question as we are – saint or serial killer?'

TWENTY-FIVE

It was now well known in the area where James and Susan lived that gardaí were watching the American woman. In response to a request from Florentine, the garda authorities had agreed to put Marguerite under twenty-four-hour surveillance. This took the form of a uniformed garda from the local station sitting in his car outside the cottage, following her wherever she went. It wasn't very discreet, but then, it wasn't meant to be. Joe and his American friends wanted Marguerite to know that she was being watched, so that she wouldn't attempt to leave the country without telling them.

Like all good stories, the one that began to circulate in the locality was far removed from the truth. The word being whispered around was that the Yank's father had been murdered by the Mafia in a gangland shooting in New York and that she had witnessed the shooting. She was now under garda protection, for, according to the story, a Mafia hit man had been sent over to silence her.

In spite of the garda surveillance and the gossip, Marguerite continued to attend Mass in the local church each morning and, whatever the priest had heard about her, he was pleased to see her there. For as the stories about her grew, so also did the congregation. When she lit her candles for a good intention, there were those who nudged each other and nodded knowingly, while outside the church, small groups gathered to see her depart, followed by her garda escort. At the same time, those who watched took good care to do so from a safe distance. If there was a Mafia hit man in town, they didn't want to be in the line of fire!

Having booked into the local hotel, Joe and the two Americans were soon doing their share of the surveillance work and when, a few days later, Susan's car set off in the direction of Cork, they followed. While Marguerite had signalled her intention of visiting the family of her real father in Cork before returning to New York, the two NYPD men were afraid she might do her disappearing act again – a fear they had voiced when they had learned there was an airport near Cork city.

However, they needn't have worried. Marguerite was indeed on her way to see Maudie and, not far behind the unmarked garda car was the car of her solicitor. Like everyone else in the town, Mr. Murphy had heard the rumours about Marguerite and the Mafia. She confirmed that her father had indeed been shot dead in New York but didn't elaborate. He offered to help her any way he could, but when she declined the offer he didn't feel it appropriate to inquire further about it. She made it clear that all she wanted him to do was to sort out her family affairs in Cork.

Mr. Murphy had been attending courts long enough to know an unmarked garda car when he saw one. For a start, all the cars used by the force had Dublin registration numbers because they were purchased by headquarters in Dublin. And if that wasn't a dead give-away in a rural area, the occupants often looked too big and burly for their cars. As a result they could usually be identified by most members of the public for what they were. And so, while the three detectives followed Susan and Marguerite down into County Cork, Mr. Murphy sucked on his curly pipe and followed the detectives. As far as he was concerned, they were protecting an essential witness from the Mafia and, when they parked a short distance from the farmhouse with the clear intention of waiting for his client, he didn't query their presence. Susan also stayed in her car, declining Marguerite's invitation to go in with her.

It was only a short time since Maudie had opened up the parlour to serve tea and sandwiches to her neighbours following Shaunie's funeral. By the time the visitors arrived, she had once more removed the dust covers from the armchairs and settee and raised the blinds to allow in a little more light. Yet, the removal of the dust covers couldn't remove the mustiness, and it was obvious to her visitors that it was a room that was seldom if ever used.

Whatever about Mr. Murphy, Marguerite got the distinct feeling that she was in a room in which time had stood still. The furniture belonged to another era, as did the pictures on the walls. Colourless and in heavy wooden frames, the pictures were of stags and long-haired cattle in remote mountain settings. Someone long ago, she thought, must have considered them appropriate for a farmhouse and she wondered if that someone might have been Shaunie's father or grandfather. She looked around to see if there were any photographs of them on the walls or on the sideboard, but there weren't. She suppressed an urged to sniff at the musty odour in the room and when the talks got under way, she didn't object when Mr. Murphy asked if he could smoke his pipe.

Maudie and her solicitor sat on the settee, Marguerite and Mr. Murphy in the armchairs. The introductions were cool and minimal, nods taking the place of handshakes. Marguerite didn't quite catch the surname of Maudie's solicitor at first. Sweeney or MacSweeney, she wasn't sure. In fact, it turned out to be Sweeney. Not that it mattered. He didn't address her anyway. He was, she observed, a big man, bald with horn-rimmed glasses. He wore a pinstriped suit and she reckoned that, like Mr. Murphy, he made a comfortable living from the law.

From the small talk exchanged between the two men before they got down to the business in hand, she gathered that they had met before and wondered if they had been adversaries in court. For they maintained a certain courtesy to one another and even addressed one another by their surnames.

'Mr. Sweeney and I have exchanged certain documents in this case,' said Mr. Murphy, 'and he confirms, Maudie, that you are the one and only named beneficiary in Shaunie's will.'

Maudie raised her chin slightly and looked away as if she had just won the first point. 'That's correct,' she replied rather loftily. 'The one and only. And why shouldn't I be? Didn't I look after this house all my life? And Shaunie until his dying day?'

'I'm not disputing that. I'm just outlining the facts as I understand them.' Mr. Murphy paused. 'So there are no other claimants to the property?'

'None, except this…' Maudie glared at Marguerite as she searched for the appropriate word.

'Adventurer?' said Marguerite coolly. 'That was what you called me last time we met.'

'Adventurer. And that's just what you are. An adventurer. Coming here to try and lay claim to the farm.'

'I told you – I don't want the farm. All I want is to be recognised as Shaunie's daughter.'

'Huh!' Maudie gestured towards the documents which her solicitor had put on the table. 'And if you don't want the farm, what's all this talk about a financial consideration? If it's not the farm you're after, it's money.'

Marguerite was about to reply, when Mr. Murphy restrained her by putting his hand on her arm.

'Marguerite has made it abundantly clear,' he assured Maudie, 'that she doesn't want the farm. But let's face it. If this matter goes to court and if the court confirms that she *is* Shaunie's daughter, then there is, in my opinion every likelihood that as his sole heir, she could be awarded the farm.'

'However,' cautioned Mr. Sweeney, 'there is one important hurdle that your client must cross first. She has not taken a blood test, so we don't really know whether she could be Shaunie's daughter or not.'

'That's true,' Mr. Murphy countered, 'but if the matter goes to court, she is quite prepared to take a blood test. However, I suggest that a court case for what we require – a statement of recognition – is not necessary. There is quite an amount of evidence to show that she *is* Shaunie's daughter: Catherine's letters, his letter to her and his note to Marguerite. It's quite clear from them that Catherine was pregnant by Shaunie, and that Shaunie accepted that Marguerite was the issue of their union.'

'Union!' Maudie snorted. 'What union? They weren't married.'

'They would have been,' declared Marguerite, 'if you and your brothers hadn't done what they did.'

'I had nothing to do with that. I told you before.'

'Maybe not, but it was the actions of your family that prevented Shaunie and my mother getting married. As a result of what they did, she had to leave her family and go to America. But she died before she got there and I ended up with the most godawful childhood you could ever imagine. So don't talk to me about marriage.'

There was an awkward silence, a silence that was broken only when Mr. Murphy attempted to re-light his pipe. Coughing as he did so, he dropped the charred remains of the match into an ashtray, saying, 'She's right. Absolutely right. And my instructions are that if this matter is not resolved before she goes back to America, I will initiate court proceedings (a) to establish that she is Shaunie's daughter and (b) to establish her rights in the matter.'

Maudie was about to say something, but Mr. Sweeney spoke first. 'You mentioned a financial consideration. May I ask what sum you had in mind?'

Mr. Murphy lifted one of his documents. 'Well now,' he said, 'that's a difficult one.' He scanned the document as if he had forgotten its contents, while the truth was he had written them himself. 'Do you agree that the farm consists of roughly two hundred acres?'

Maudie shook her head. 'A hundred and seventy-five.'

'And how much would you say it was worth? Two hundred thousand pounds?'

'Huh!' Maudie turned away as if to say he was out of his mind. 'You must think it's all prime grazing land. A lot of it is hill and bog – scrubland that wouldn't feed a snipe.'

Mr. Murphy smiled. 'All right then, would you say it's worth a hundred and fifty thousand pounds?'

'Not with the price of land these days,' Maudie retorted.

'Okay then. Let's say a hundred thousand? And that's not including stock or machinery.'

When this estimate went without comment, Mr. Murhy continued, 'Now, I only ask so that I can put the matter in context. I have advised my client that in renouncing any claim to the farm, she is entitled to a financial consideration, and compared to the value of the farm it is a relatively small amount.'

'How much?' asked Mr. Sweeney.

'Well, she has incurred the not inconsiderable expense of coming from America, plus her expenses while she is here, and then there's the cost of legal advice, which will be ongoing until the matter is resolved. I have advised her that twenty thousand should cover it.'

Maudie gasped. 'Twenty thousand pounds? You must be joking. Where would I get that kind of money? All the money is tied up in the farm.'

'You're asking a lot,' said Mr. Sweeney.

'Not as much as we'll be asking if you force us to go to court.'

Mr. Sweeney was tapping his fingers on his knees now as he pondered the situation and wondered what to do. Then he gathered up his papers and got to his feet. 'I'd like to consult with my client, if you don't mind.'

'Of course,' said Mr. Murphy. 'Take your time.'

When they had retired to another room Mr. Sweeney said, 'Well, Maudie what do you think?'

'What do I think? I think it's outrageous. That's what I think.'

'Well, if you want to contest the matter in court, I'll fight it all the way – you know that.'

'Do you think we would win?'

Mr. Sweeney pursed his lips. 'Mmm... we might. Depends on the blood test. Then again, we might not. It's very difficult to predict.'

'And what happens if I lose?'

'Well, if the court holds that she *is* Shaunie's daughter, she could contest the will and, in that event there is the possibility that you could lose the farm.'

Maudie looked at him in alarm. 'But she's illegitimate!'

Mr. Sweeney shook his head. 'The law's been changed. There's no such thing as being illegitimate – not any more.' Seeing that this information had added to Maudie's alarm, he added hastily, 'But, of course, I'm sure the court would make a generous provision for you. After all, as you said yourself, you have looked after the house and Shaunie all these years. You'd be entitled to something.'

Maudie paced the floor as she weighed up the pros and cons. 'The truth is,' she said at last, 'I don't want to go to court. I don't want the whole country knowing about this – you know, that Shaunie had a child, and him not married.'

Mr. Sweeney nodded. 'I can understand that but family law cases are heard in private.'

'Still…' Maudie went over to the window and peered out between the net curtains. 'Excuse me for a moment. There's someone at the gate.'

While the negotiations had been going on in the house, Joe and the two Americans had got out of the car to stretch their legs and were leaning over the gate waiting for Marguerite to come back out.

'Who are you?' asked Maudie. 'And what do you want?'

'Garda Síochána,' said Joe, showing her his warrant card.

'What are you doing here?'

'We're trying to sort out this business of Marguerite's father.'

'I didn't think that would be any concern of yours.'

'It might surprise you what concerns us.'

'Has she made a statement?'

'As a matter of fact she has,' said Joe, wondering how she knew. 'Is she still inside?'

Maudie nodded and returned to the house.

'Who is it?' asked Mr. Sweeney, who had been peering out between the curtains.

'It's the guards. It seems she's gone to them and made a statement.'

'I don't see how it's any business of theirs.'

'Maybe not, but they're out there.' Maudie thought about her predicament for a moment and it was clear she was agitated by the presence of the gardaí. 'What do you think I should do? Should I sign?'

Mr. Sweeney took off his glasses and cleaned the lenses with his handkerchief. 'No Maudie. I don't think you should be panicked into doing something you might regret.'

'What then?'

'I suggest we play for time. Stall this woman. Tell her we want a blood test. After all, we don't really know who she is. The whole thing could be a scam.'

When they returned, Mr. Murphy asked, 'Well, have you made a decision?'

'As my client has already told you,' Mr. Sweeney replied, 'she just doesn't have that kind of money.'

Mr. Murphy put his pipe down on top of his papers. 'And as I've already told you, it's my belief that my client would get a more appropriate consideration – if not the whole farm – if she went to court. She has, after all, suffered greatly as a result of what was done to her mother. She has also incurred substantial expense in coming here to trace her natural father. Twenty thousand pounds, I think, would be fair recompense but, living as I do in a rural area, I accept what your client says, that much of her capital is tied up in the farm. Perhaps a sum of, say, fifteen thousand would be a more equitable figure.'

Mr. Sweeney looked at Maudie, saying, 'Fifteen?'

When Maudie closed her eyes and shook her head, Mr. Sweeney said, 'Perhaps it's time I consulted with my client again. If you'll excuse us…'

Back in the privacy of the other room, Maudie peeped between the curtains. 'The gardaí are still there,' she said. 'Do you think she told them about my brothers – you know, that they locked Shaunie in?'

Mr. Sweeney shrugged. 'What if they did? It's a long time ago now.'

Maudie hesitated. She didn't want to give Marguerite anything. At the same time, she didn't want to lose the farm. And now the guards were at the gate. She didn't realise that when Joe had said they were anxious to sort out this business of Marguerite's father, and that she had made a statement, he was referring to her adoptive father. She thought he was referring to Shaunie. Thus, it seemed, the odds were stacked against her. 'Fifteen thousand is a lot of money,' she said. 'But it would be better than losing the whole farm. Maybe I should sign.'

'Again Maudie, I would advise caution. This woman seems in a hurry to get her hands on this money and get back to America. However, we're in no hurry. Let's call her bluff – ask her to take a blood test.'

'Does that mean I'll have to give blood?'

'Give me a moment. Do you mind if I use your phone?'

Maudie waited anxiously while Mr. Sweeney consulted with someone about various maintenance cases and the blood samples that had to be given to establish whether or not certain people could be the father.

'You know Maudie,' he said when he had left down the phone, 'I think this woman – whoever she is – may have left it too late. Blood testing is a very complicated business, but from what I've just been told, her blood would have to be compared with the blood of her biological parents, not yours.'

'But Shaunie and Catherine are both dead.'

'Exactly.'

Maudie looked at him and slowly her eyes lit up as the import of what he was saying sank in. For the first time since this matter had arisen she could now see a chink of light at the end of the tunnel.

When they returned to the parlour, Maudie resumed her seat on the settee and sat with her hands clasped in her lap as her solicitor put his papers back on the table.

'Well?' said Mr. Murphy at last. 'Have you come to a decision?'

Mr. Sweeney cleared his throat. 'The fact is – and I think you have already alluded to it Mr. Murphy – the fact is that although Shaunie accepted your client as his daughter, it doesn't mean she is his daughter.'

Mr. Murphy nodded. 'And if your client accepts that she is Shaunie's daughter it doesn't mean that she is. It just gives my client the recognition she desires.'

'I understand that,' said Mr. Sweeney. 'However, you have indicated that she has no objection to taking a blood test. Perhaps you could arrange for her to do so.'

'Blood testing takes time and she has to return to America in a few days.'

'Nevertheless,' said Mr. Sweeney, 'we are not prepared to discuss the matter further until we see the results of a blood test.'

'Very well,' said Mr. Murphy gathering up his papers. 'If that's your decision?'

'It is.'

TWENTY-SIX

When her visitors had gone, Maudie felt greatly relieved. However, she was acutely aware that the threat to the farm and her continued existence there had not gone. She didn't believe that the American woman was entitled to anything, even if she was Shaunie's daughter. After all, Shaunie and Catherine weren't even married, so if they had a daughter, she was, in her eyes, illegitimate and had no rights. Nevertheless, she told herself, if push came to shove she would pay the money and get rid of her.

For her part, Marguerite was very disappointed. She now realised that she would have to leave Ireland without the recognition from Shaunie's family that she so ardently desired. However, as they discussed the matter out at the car, Mr. Murphy seemed to think they had done quite well. Maudie, he pointed out, had left the door open for further discussions. He thought it wasn't unreasonable that she should ask for a blood test and suggested that it would save a lot of time if Marguerite gave a blood sample before returning to America.

'Once I get the results of the blood test,' he told her, 'I'll set the wheels in motion and don't worry, you'll get the recognition you deserve.'

Acting on an impulse, Marguerite stepped forward and gave him a hug saying, 'Thank you Mr. Murphy. Thank you very much.'

'For what?' He disentangled himself from her embrace with a slight touch of embarrassment and chuckled, 'Sure I haven't done anything yet.'

'You've accepted me for who I am,' she told him. 'And that's very important to me.'

Still feeling somewhat embarrassed, Mr. Murphy sat into the car and headed back to Tipperary.

Marguerite turned to Susan. 'You know I'm worn out with all this business. Why don't we stay the night in the Cumán Inn? It isn't expensive and I'll tell you all about our meeting with Maudie over dinner.'

Susan smiled. 'Hang the expense. I've been sitting long enough in the car for one day. I'm dying to hear what happened in there – and I wouldn't mind having a glass of wine!'

As they drove into town, Susan wondered if, in spite of what Mr. Murphy had said about progress having been made, Marguerite would ever get recognition from Shaunie's family. She also wondered if the real reason she wanted to stay at the Inn was to see Martin O'Driscoll, or was that just wishful thinking on her part?

Whatever the reason Marguerite wanted to stay, her police escort had to stay too, and when she booked into the Cumán Inn they booked in too. However, when they sat down to dinner they had to be content to watch Marguerite through the glass panelling that separated the public dining room from a smaller private room that Martin and his sister Mary used on occasion to entertain special guests. They also watched the glasses of wine come and go and while they would like to have been a fly on the wall of the other room, they much preferred their pints of Guinness.

Over dinner, Marguerite recounted the gist of what had been said during the meeting with Maudie, although she omitted any reference to the financial consideration that had been mentioned as she thought that would sound as if all she was interested in was money.

'Maudie's a tough old cookie,' Martin remarked. 'And when it comes to land the Irish – well, they get very defensive about it.'

Marguerite gave a wry smile. 'Yeah, tell me about it! But I meant every word. I'm not interested in the god-dammed farm. All I want is for them to accept me for who I am – Shaunie's daughter.'

'If you don't mind me saying so,' Mary confided, 'I never thought Maudie would even talk to you about it. I mean, all this business about Shaunie and the wedding has been a closed book. Ah, here's my mother.

She'll tell you. They never talked about it, never explained what happened.'

As Mrs. O'Driscoll shuffled up to them with the aid of a walking stick, Marguerite and Susan noted that advancing age had made her seriously overweight and that in turn seemed to have caused her problems with her legs and feet. In her free hand she carried a tin box that she placed on the table before sitting down beside them with the great effort that her weight required. Many years before, the box had probably contained chocolates or biscuits, but now as she lifted the lid, they could see it was full of old black and white photographs.

Picking one of the photographs out of those nearest the top, Mrs. ODriscoll passed it over to Marguerite, saying, 'I thought you might like to see that one.'

As Marguerite studied it, Mrs. O'Driscoll added, 'That's Shaunie and Catherine.'

Marguerite's eyes were sparkling now with delight. 'I know,' she said, and unclasping the chain on her neck, she compared the photograph with those in her locket.

'That was at a GAA function,' Mrs. O'Driscoll went on. 'That's me in my younger days, and that's Paddy, my husband.'

As Marguerite continued to study the photograph, Mrs. O'Driscoll told her, 'That was the last time they ever came to the club. Whatever happened between him and Catherine we never found out. Shaunie never spoke about it. Just kept to himself – him and Maudie up at the big house. He stopped farming and leased the land. Paddy had it for a while, and now Martin.'

Marguerite handed back the photograph, but Mrs. O'Driscoll said, 'No, no. You can keep it.'

'Really? Are you sure?' Marguerite put the chain back on her neck. 'The photos in the locket are tiny. Thank you so much. I'll treasure this one.'

'As I say, that was the last time the two of them were at the club. When the wedding didn't take place, Catherine went back home to Tipperary – or so we thought at the time. We didn't know she was pregnant. None of us did. Shaunie never socialised with his friends again. Never came back to the club, or the pub for that matter. Never told anybody why he left her standing at the altar.'

Mrs. O'Driscoll closed the box 'It never occurred to us that the brothers might have had anything to do with it. But then Francie…' She shook her head. 'He's always had a screw loose.'

Seeing that Marguerite's eyes were glistening with tears now, Mrs. O'Driscoll added, 'Anyway, I hope you get what you came for. You deserve that much.'

As they watched her amble away, Susan remarked, 'What a lovely woman.'

'That's Mam for you,' Mary said. 'We didn't know she was going to do that.'

Martin turned to Marguerite. 'I suppose you'll be going back to America now?'

'Well, I was going to go back next week, but they want me to take a blood test and I don't know how long that's going to take.'

'So we might see you again before you go?'

Marguerite smiled. 'Maybe. It depends on how long I have to wait to get the result.'

Before they retired for the night, the others lifted their glasses and toasted Marguerite, wishing her good luck and hoping that everything would work out well for her.

A few days later, Marguerite had one further meeting with Mr. Murphy.

'It appears,' he told her through a lungful of pipe smoke, 'that we require your blood sample to be compared with the blood of your biological parents.'

'Oh.' Marguerite sat back in her chair to consider the implications of what he had just said. 'Does that mean Maudie has pulled a fast one on us?'

'She may think so, but we're not snookered yet.'

'But how can we get a blood test if there's no one to test it with? I mean, Shaunie's dead. Catherine too – a long time ago.'

Mr. Murphy left down his pipe and took up one of the documents from his desk. 'Well, Shaunie may be dead, but his hospital records should still be available. I understand from what you told me that he had been ill for a long time. That being the case, the hospital should have all the details of his blood we need. They may even have samples.'

'But will they hand them over?'

'They will if the court orders them to do so.' Mr. Murphy smiled. 'Don't worry. As we say here in Ireland, there's more than one way to skin a cat.'

Marguerite didn't quite know what that meant but she knew by the twinkle in Mr. Murphy's eyes that he was beginning to enjoy the challenge presented by her case. What was it Susan had said? If it was a question of a right-of-way or the right of a cow to cross the road, he was the man to deal with it. Now it was a question of another right and as she left his office she felt much happier about things.

'So,' said Susan when she returned. 'What are you going to do?'

'Well, I was going to book my flight, but I would like to get this thing about the blood test sorted out first.'

Susan nodded. 'I can understand that.'

'But I don't want to impose on you. I mean, I've been here a good while already.'

'You know,' said Susan, 'I'd like to see you taking the blood test too. That would put Maudie in her place. And sure you can stay as long as you like, you know that.'

Marguerite had now begun to keep a diary and one day as she re-read her entries, Susan asked, 'Can I get you anything?' Marguerite smiled and told her, 'No thanks. I have everything I need for the moment.' Susan meant coffee of course, but Marguerite was pre-occupied with what she had just been reading and told herself it was true. She had found Shaunie, her real father, and he had accepted her as his daughter. That had been a momentous occasion for her, and one she would always treasure. Brief as the meetings with him had been, the conversations had been warm and loving. He had welcomed her home, a tearful welcome that reflected the heartbreak he had felt for his beloved Catherine. But before she could really get to know him he had passed away and Maudie had taken over. With Shaunie gone, acceptance by his family had been very important to her. But there had been no such welcome from Maudie or her brothers.

Maudie, she recalled, had said some awful things about her, things she might some day regret. So had Detective Florentine but she wasn't afraid of him. He had no proof that she had set out to kill Don Diego, no proof that she had killed Mrs. Gaynor, no proof in fact that things hadn't happened the way she said they had happened.

Having interviewed Marguerite at length there was nothing more Florentine and Sullivan could do, so they were told to return to New York. But if they were hopeful that their interviews had provided the additional proof they needed to press charges against her, they were in for a disappointment.

Lieutenant Jacobs leafed through the papers on his desk and shook his head. The file detailing the evidence that had been gathered in the course of their investigation, including their report of the interviews with Marguerite, had been forwarded to the DA and it was clear he wasn't happy with it.

Florentine and Sullivan waited patiently to hear what the DA had to say.

Jacobs raised his head and looked at them. 'He doesn't think you've enough evidence.'

'In which case?' asked Florentine.

'In either of them. In Diego's case he states the obvious. Without the gun we can't determine if it was his or if she purchased it and took it with her. If she took it with her, it would go a long way towards proving premeditation. But as it is, it's your word against hers.'

'So, no sign of it yet?'

'No. But the divers are doing their best. If they knew which pond it was in it would be a great help.'

'And what about Mrs. Gaynor?' asked Sullivan.

'Same thing.'

'Fuck it,' Florentine protested. 'I know it's circumstantial in Mrs. Gaynor's case. But considering it in the broad context of the overall investigation, I think a jury would come to the conclusion that Marguerite chucked her overboard.'

'The DA doesn't agree. He thinks the defence would apply for separate trials and, short of someone coming along and saying they saw her throw Mrs. Gaynor overboard, it's your word against hers.'

The two waited as the lieutenant continued to leaf through the DA's report. 'But apart from all that, he asks a very pertinent question – one I've asked you myself and still haven't got an answer. This dame Marguerite. We don't seem to know who the hell she really is. I mean, was she Brigid Mary or Katie when she was given up for adoption?'

'When we were in Ireland,' Sullivan said, 'she maintained she was Katie – still does.'

'And we didn't think her claim was relevant to our investigation,' said Florentine. 'She had the motive in both cases, regardless of who she originally was.'

'Revenge for what Don Diego had done to her,' Sullivan added. 'Revenge for what she believed Mrs. Gaynor had done to her.'

'You say Maudie's people have asked her to take a blood test,' said Jacobs. 'When she comes back – if she comes back – we'll want to know the result. In view of the claims she's making, the DA thinks it's important we should know who she really is. Tie up any loose ends. If we do manage to mount a prosecution, he doesn't want the defence springing any surprises on us.'

'If it's negative, I doubt if she'll tell us,' said Sullivan. 'She's adamant she's Katie.'

'Well, you'd better ask her.' Jacobs closed the DA's report. 'And if she doesn't tell you, ask your friend Joe. Maybe he can find out.'

Florentine nodded. 'Will do.'

'Good. The DA reckons you've still a long way to go on this one.' He slid the report across the table. 'Here, read it for yourselves.'

As inquiries into the death of Don Diego had progressed, blanks in the rows of photographs on the investigation display board had been filled in and pictures discarded as people had been identified or ruled out. Eventually, as Detective Florentine and his team had narrowed their focus, the board itself had been pushed aside and left in a corner of his office.

It had been a long time since Florentine had studied the photographs, but now he looked long and hard at them again and wondered anew. Don Diego, his wife Nora, Marguerite, the twins Felipe and Vitoria, Mrs.

Gaynor and the most recent one, a photograph of Sister Mary, provided by the convent. Taking the last photograph, he rearranged the row so that Sister Mary was beside Marguerite. Then he rearranged them again so that he could fit two blanks in between Marguerite and Sister Mary. On one blank he wrote the name Katie, on the other, Brigid Mary, and after each he put a large question mark.

Until the report had come back from the DA, he had been happy in the knowledge that he had filled in all the blanks, answered all the questions. Now he wasn't at all sure he knew anything and he had more questions than ever. Two children had come from the mother and baby home in Ireland, one destined for New Jersey, one for Long Island. But only one had survived the voyage. Which one? Which one had gone on to Long Island to join the Diego family? Was it Katie or Brigid Mary? And which one had gone back to Tipperary?

He took out the silver crucifix that had been the first real clue to the killer of Don Diego, and pinned it to the display board so that it dangled between the two blanks and between the photographs of Marguerite and Sister Mary. Then he returned to his desk and stared again at his handiwork.

It all went back to that day in the graveyard when Don Diego was being buried, he told himself. And to think that Sully and himself had been standing at the gate only a few yards away. If only they had heard what Mrs. Gaynor had said. But they hadn't and now they only had Marguerite's word for it. He lit a cigarette, leaned back in his chair and wondered about all the times the two had met. For a woman who was dying of cancer, Mrs. Gaynor had taken her time about telling Marguerite what had happened. First there was the encounter in the graveyard, then the conversation over coffee, then the meeting in Pete's and, finally, the trip on the Statue of Liberty ferry. Had Mrs. Gaynor been letting the story unfold bit by bit out of consideration for Marguerite, or had she been planning a scheme in which she would pretend the mix-up had occurred? A scheme that would enable them both to capitalise on Marguerite's misfortune.

The door opened and Sullivan came in. When he saw that the display board had been pulled out of the corner, he asked, 'Well, what do you reckon?'

Florentine drew his right hand down over his face. When his eyes opened again he replied, 'I reckon we're up shit creek without a paddle.'

'How do you mean?'

'This blood test.'

'What about it?'

'Think Sully. This dame claims she's Katie, but what if she turns out to be Brigid Mary?'

'I don't see that it makes any difference.'

'It makes no difference to our case, I agree. But if the test shows she's Brigid Mary, how would that look if the papers got hold of it. The two of us standing at the gate while she tried to convince Maudie she was Katie.'

Sullivan shook his head. 'I think she really does believe she's Katie.'

'But if she's not,' Florentine continued, 'it doesn't matter what she believes. The papers would say we stood by while she tried to con Maudie into giving her money. It would leave us with egg on our face – not to mention the Commissioner. We'd be the laughing stock of the NYPD.'

'But we didn't know what she was doing in the house,' Sullivan pointed out, 'at least not then.'

'I know, but hindsight's a great thing. You know the way these press guys twist everything. They'd call it a scam and they'd dump it on us.'

'So what do we do now?'

Florentine got up to go. 'I don't know about you, but I'm bushed. I'm going home.'

'You're not coming to the Ferryman's then?'

'Nope. Marie says if I don't spend more time at home, the kids won't know me and she won't want to know me.'

'It's as bad as that?'

'Not really. But you know what I mean. We were away a long time.' Florentine paused on the way out. 'I suppose you're meeting the old man?'

'Yeah. He's already in the Ferryman's.'

TWENTY-SEVEN

The Prodigal Daughter, as the *Tipperary Star* had called her, was no longer a matter of interest to gardaí. They took the view that when the American detectives had gone, saying they would interview her again on her return to New York, Marguerite had ceased to be an Irish problem. For a while she also ceased to be a subject of gossip. Those who had watched the Yank with such interest soon found somebody else to talk about. However, there is a saying in rural Ireland that what goes around comes around, and it wasn't long before another piece of gossip began to circulate about the Yank, one that was much more interesting than the first as it contained more than a whiff of scandal.

What exactly the story was, Maudie didn't know. All Mick had said was that it was something to do with what he disdainfully called 'this American woman' and they needed to have a family conference. He could have told them on the phone but he said he wanted them to hear it from the horse's mouth, whatever that meant. Try as she might, Maudie couldn't imagine what it was, but Mick seemed to think it was important enough to bring Francie back from England. The more she thought about it, the more she feared she had been taken for a fool, and the matter greatly exercised her mind as she motored towards Mick's place in Tipperary.

Sensing from Maudie's silence that she was preoccupied with her thoughts, Martin O'Driscoll glanced in the mirror now and then to make sure she was all right. It was seldom she took the Wolseley out, and when she did she always called on him to do the driving. Last time it was out he had hosed it down and returned it to its cocoon of protective sheets in one of the sheds. He would do the same again and there it would remain until he got the next call. It was all part and parcel of the arrangement whereby he leased her land on the understanding that he would keep an eye on things and give her a hand whenever it was needed.

As Martin looked back at Maudie again, he smiled. She had this lovely Wolseley 16/60. Seldom used and good as new, it was a rich deep green in colour and had the comfort and luxury of a design that the motor industry and its younger customers now considered old-fashioned. Big steering wheel, walnut panels on the dashboard and on the inside of the doors, red leather upholstery, red carpeting. A car fit for a queen, some might say, and yet she couldn't drive. The only other luxury she indulged herself in was her horse. Apart from a few hens, ducks and geese which she allowed to roam the fields around the house, the grey gelding was the only animal she kept. Misty she called him. A lovely hunter, and yet she didn't hunt. Martin smiled again. A car she didn't drive and a horse she didn't ride!

Until a few years ago, he recalled, Maudie had enjoyed horse riding. Because of that and the fact that she had lost some of her poultry to foxes, she had given the local fox hunt access to her land. She didn't ride with the hunt herself now but occasionally rode down as far as the village pub to meet them and share in their traditional libation before returning home. When age militated against that, she refused offers from various members of the hunt who wanted to buy Misty. She liked to see him grazing in the meadow in front of the house and, when he was stabled, she fed and groomed him with loving care. She had him re-shod every six weeks and in winter put a weatherproof rug on him to keep him warm.

Martin smiled to himself again. His only involvement with the horse was to telephone a farrier who worked in a stud in the area to get him to come and do the shoeing. The blacksmith, Maudie called him. 'Will you ring the blacksmith Martin?' She was well able to ring herself but for some reason she always asked him to do it. He had offered on numerous occasions to clean out the stable for her but she liked to do it herself. Said it gave her something to do. For the same reason, he imagined, she collected hens' eggs from the hedgerows and ducks' eggs from the meadows and sold them to locals who preferred free-range eggs to the ones they could buy in the shops. Strange woman. Grumpy, some people said. But he got on well with her.

These things were still going through Martin's mind when Maudie said, 'Turn right here.' He did so and a short distance farther on had to pull in close to the ditch to let a cattle truck past. He guessed they weren't far from Mick's house now and he was right. At the end of the road they drove into Mick's yard. The concrete was splashed here and there with liquid cattle dung and Martin apologised, saying, 'Your wheels are going to be a bit of a mess, but I'll hose them down when we get back.'

'That's okay, Martin, I know you will.' Maudie was getting out of the back and before she closed the door she added, 'Why don't you go down to the lower yard and have a look at the cattle. I won't be long, or least I hope I won't.'

Mick, who was standing at the door of his house, his thumbs hooked in the pockets of his waistcoat, was smiling broadly. 'Watch you don't step in that Maudie. One of them broke loose when they were being loaded. Skidded and skittered all over the place. The lorry's just left so we haven't had a chance to hose the place down.'

'Don't worry, I'm used to it.'

Having watched Maudie pick her way around the splashes of manure, Martin reversed the car on to the clearest part of the yard he could find and wandered down to the lower yard. There he examined the cattle in the sheds before returning to the car in time to see Francie and Trixie arrive.

Francie's drive, unlike Martin's, had not been a quiet one. Trixie had insisted on talking. 'Where's Tipperary?' she wanted to know. Francie did his best to tell her, but it was clear she had no idea where she was or where it was. 'When are we going to get there, Duckie?' she asked more than once, and when Francie told her it was a long way she began to sing, 'It's a long way to Tipperary…' Francie told her to shut up, but of course, she didn't and by the time they arrived at Mick's house, his patience had worn thin.

'Shit!' Trixie had been looking in the mirror to make sure her hair and make-up were in order and didn't notice that the yard was covered in large splatters of liquid cow manure. When she did, it was too late. 'Shit!,'she said again. On getting out of the car, she had stepped into the middle of a large splatter. She made an impossible manoeuvre to try and get out of it and in doing so went over on the side of her shoe, breaking her high heel in the process. Leaving the shoe in the middle of the manure she hopped on the other one, crying, 'Help me Duckie. Look what I've stepped in!'

Still annoyed by her incessant chatter, Francie caught her by the arm. At the same time she bent back down and retrieved the shoe, before he unceremoniously propelled her towards the door where Mick and his wife were waiting for them.

'Well, doesn't that beat all Lizzie,' said Mick. 'Gold-coloured shoes. And heels as high as a heifer's leg. Well I'll be damned.'

'Damn you and your cows!' exclaimed Trixie. 'All they do is shite. It's all over the fucking place.'

'What do you expect,' said Mick as Francie helped her hop in through the door. 'And I'll have you know they're not cows, they're bullocks.'

Trixie took off the other shoe and left both shoes just inside the door. 'Cows, bullocks, what's the difference?'

'Oh there's a big difference,' Mick told her.

'If it wasn't for cows we wouldn't have milk,' said Lizzie dryly.

Holding Trixie as if she had been mortally wounded, Francie eased her down onto a chair in the kitchen.

'Milk?' she asked. 'What do you mean?'

'You know, the stuff that goes into your tea,' said Mick. 'Where do you think it comes from – a supermarket?' Clearly annoyed now, Mick added, 'And if it wasn't for bullocks we wouldn't have beef. But I don't suppose you'd know what a bullock is either.'

Curious, but not wanting the others to know that she didn't know, Trixie whispered to Francie, 'What's a bullock?'

'It's a bull that's been castrated,' he whispered back.

'Castrated?'

'That's right. It's had its things cut off, you know.'

'You mean its balls?'

'Exactly, it's had its balls cut off.'

Trixie leaned closer and whispered in his ear, 'Well listen to me, Duckie. If you don't get me out of this shit-hole and soon, I'm going to cut yours off.'

Francie raised his head and puckered his brow but didn't reply. It was only now that he realised there was a garda sitting at the table.

'There's a shoemaker in the town,' the guard told Trixie. 'He'll fix that heel for you while you wait.'

Trixie wasn't impressed by the suggestion, but Lizzie said, 'That's right, he's very good. But if you don't wash that dung off before it hardens, you'll never get it off. Come on, there's a tap in the back garden.'

Seeing that Francie was wondering who the hell the guard was and what he was doing there, Mick said, 'This is PJ.'

PJ was sitting back sipping a glass of whiskey, his greatcoat wide open revealing the great expanse of his stomach, his cap lying upside down on the table.

Mick gave a glass of whiskey to Francie, poured one for himself and refilled PJ's glass.

'Ah, you can't beat a drop of Paddy,' said PJ. 'Do you know it used to be called Paddy Flaherty whiskey?'

'Is that a fact?' said Mick.

'It is. You see, Paddy Flaherty was a salesman for the company in the early days and he became so famous for standing rounds of his favourite whiskey that they named it after him. Here.' PJ reached for the bottle. 'You can still see his name on the label.'

Fearing that PJ would keep the bottle, Mick took it back, saying, 'Where? Well, doesn't that beat all?'

'I hope you didn't bring us all this way to talk about whiskey?' Maudie had emerged from a back room and the coldness of her voice seemed to have a sobering effect on all concerned.

'Ah Maudie', said Mick, 'This is PJ. PJ – Maudie.'

Ignoring the introduction, and ignoring PJ, Maudie continued to talk to Mick, saying, 'Is he here on an official visit?'

Francie retreated to an old armchair in the corner, where he leaned his head forward, puckered his brow and listened in silence to the frosty exchange.

'Well…' Mick put the offending bottle back on the sideboard. 'He is and he isn't.'

'What do you mean, he is and he isn't? Either he is or he's not.'

'You might say he's here on a friendly visit and I suggest it's in your interest to sit down and hear what he has to say. In fact it's in all our interests.'

Maudie sat down just as Lizzie and Trixie returned. Trixie sat on the arm of the chair beside Francie and began twirling his hair with her fingers in an effort to make up with him, while Lizzie went to the sink and filled the kettle. Mick ventured to fill PJ's glass again, and said, 'Now PJ, tell them what you told me.'

'Well,' said PJ. He rolled the glass of whiskey between his thumb and fingers before lifting to his lips and savouring its contents. 'It's like this. I was in Ger O'Donovan's having a drink after I finished work when I met Mick.'

'Huh!' grunted Maudie.

'We hadn't met before,' said Mick. 'I had just done a deal for some cattle and was having a quiet drink when Ger leaned over and whispered something to PJ about the Yank.'

'He wanted to know if there was any more word about the American woman,' said PJ. 'Naturally I couldn't tell him, even if there was.'

Maudie raised a sceptical eye but made no comment.

'Then,' said Mick, 'Ger asked him if it was true that she was wanted over in the US of A for murder.'

Maudie and Francie raised their heads and looked at them in astonishment.

PJ put his empty glass down on the table and waited for Mick to fill it. 'Of course I told Ger I couldn't disclose that sort of information, even if it was true.'

'So I introduced myself,' said Mick, 'and PJ told me the whole story.'

'Only because of who he was,' PJ stressed. 'Otherwise my lips would have been sealed.'

'And is it true?' asked Maudie, addressing PJ for the first time. 'Is it true that she's wanted for murder?'

'I'm afraid it is ma'am. Not one murder, but two.'

'My God!' Maudie exclaimed.

'But you said she was on the run from the Mafia after seeing her father murdered?' said Francie.

'That's what I was told,' Mick said. 'After Shaunie's funeral I was asking around to see if I could find out anything about her and that's the story I heard – that she was on the run from the Mafia.'

'She's on the run all right,' PJ said, 'but not from the Mafia. As far as I can gather she murdered her father herself, then threw some woman off the ferry when she threatened to expose her.'

'Jesus!' exclaimed Francie. 'If that doesn't beat all!'

'You know Mick,' said Maudie, 'when you told me that story about her being on the run from the Mafia I smelled a rat.'

Francie leaned forward and puckered his brow again. 'Did you not smell a rat when you saw the gardaí with her?'

Maudie shook her head, a look of desperation on her face. 'Sure I thought she had made a complaint to them. That's why I asked them if she had made a statement. When they said she had, I thought it was a statement about her claim that she was Shaunie's daughter. But, it must have been about whatever happened in America.'

'I think she led you up the garden path,' said Mick.

'How much did you pay her?' asked Trixie. It was the first time she had spoken since the word murder had been mentioned and when Maudie just scowled at her she shrugged and added, 'Just curious.'

Mick coughed to let PJ know they were now entering upon family matters and extended the bottle towards him, saying 'Here, you'll have another before you go.' Then, shaking the bottle to show it was empty, he added, 'Ah, it seems we've had the best of it.'

Taking the hint, PJ got to his feet. 'No thanks. I've had enough. Have to be careful when I'm driving you know. Can't be setting a bad example.'

In normal circumstances, the irony of that would surely have brought a caustic comment from Maudie, but as PJ put on his cap and left, she was sitting like a statue, stunned into silence by what he had told them.

When Mick returned after seeing PJ off, he said, 'It's a fair question Maudie. I know you said you would handle it in your own way, but I think we're entitled to know: did you pay her to get rid of her?'

Maudie squirmed in her chair, clearly uncomfortable with the thought of having to admit that she had even entertained the woman's demands.

Francie raised his eyebrows so that his brow puckered again. 'Come on, Maudie. You'd better tell us.'

The whistle on the kettle sounded its shrill note signalling that the water was boiling and, seeing it as a fortunate intervention in what had now become a somewhat tense situation, Lizzie said, 'Come on Trixie. We'd better wash our hands in hot water. You wouldn't know what we picked up.'

Reluctantly Trixie followed Lizzie up the stairs towards the bathroom. Half way up she paused and looked back down in the hope of hearing what Maudie had to say. However, Maudie said nothing. She just sat at the kitchen table, her hands folded in front of her, staring at the grain of the wood.

Mick reached under the sideboard behind him and took out an unopened bottle of Paddy. He also took out another glass, placed it in front of Maudie and half-filled it, saying, 'Better drink that.' Then, as if to brace themselves for what they were about to hear, he refilled the glasses for Francie and himself.

Maudie downed the whiskey and screwed up her face to show she wasn't used to it. 'Well…' She cleared her throat. 'Her solicitor was there. He said that if I signed a form saying I recognised her as Shaunie's daughter she would renounce any claim to the farm. But he said she was also entitled to something in return.'

'How much?' Mick asked.

Maudie looked towards the stairs to make sure Trixie wasn't listening. 'They wanted fifteen thousand.'

'Well holy God!' Mick put the empty glass down on the table so hard it was only the thick rim on the bottom that kept it from breaking.

'Fifteen thousand?' repeated Francie in disbelief, and for once it seemed he had good reason to pucker his brow.

'Her solicitor said if I didn't accept the agreement she would go to court and might even get the whole farm.'

Mick refilled their glasses, but Maudie pushed hers aside.

'And did you?' he asked. 'Did you pay her fifteen grand?'

Maudie shuffled and straightened her back in a gesture meant to convey a feeling of indignation. 'Of course not. I, we… Mr. Sweeney and I told her we wouldn't discuss the matter further until she took a blood test.'

'Well thank God for that!' exclaimed Mick.

Maudie shook her head. 'The little schemer. I should have known.'

'You did well Maudie,' Francie said. 'I mean, fifteen grand's a lot of money.'

Mick nodded. 'But the important thing is you didn't sign the form, did you? You didn't recognise her as Shaunie's daughter.'

Maudie shook her head. 'No, but I was tempted to do it. It all happened so quickly. I just wanted to get rid of her. I was under the impression she had lodged her claim with the guards – you, know, her claim to be Shaunie's daughter. I'm just glad Mr. Sweeney stopped me. He said it could be a scam.'

'He obviously didn't know she was wanted for murder,' said Francie.

Mick shook his head. 'Obviously not.'

'But there's something else,' said Maudie. 'Mr. Sweeney said he thought she wouldn't be able to have her blood tested, even if she agreed to it, now that Shaunie's dead. But her solicitor has told him he's going to try and get access to Shaunie's medical records.'

Mick leaned back in his chair and, hooking his thumbs in his waistcoat pockets, added, 'That might be just another ploy to get you to give her the money.'

Francie frowned. 'What do you think we should do then?'

'I think,' Mick said, 'the sooner Maudie talks to Mr. Sweeney the better. Tell him about this murder business. He can check it out and see if it's true.'

Francie went over and put his arm around Maudie's shoulder. 'Don't worry,' he told her. 'She'll never get away with it. Mr. Sweeney will know what to do.'

'Ok. I'll go in and see him; tell him what PJ has said.' Maudie looked up at the landing. 'Lizzie! I'm off now.'

Lizzie appeared at the top of the stairs and, however she had managed it, the others were grateful that she had kept Trixie upstairs and out of the way.

TWENTY-EIGHT

Lieutenant Jacobs was sitting at his desk examining a small silvery pistol which he was holding in the palm of his left hand.

'Where did you find it?' he asked.

'The divers found it not far from the lake shore,' Florentine informed him.

'Ballistics have confirmed it was the gun used to kill Diego,' added Sullivan.

'*For Services Rendered*,' mused Jacobs, seeing the inscription on the flat surface below the slide. 'I wonder what that means?'

'Presentation of some sort, I guess,' Florentine said.

Jacobs nodded and, rubbing the mother-of-pearl handgrip with the nicotine-stained finger and thumb of his right hand, asked, 'What have you been able to find out about it?'

'Made in the 1920s,' Florentine told him. 'Serial number still on it. Date and place of manufacture. But I doubt if that'll be of much help to us. Must have passed through a lot of hands since then. Question is where did Marguerite first lay her hands on it – in Don Diego's bedroom, as she claims, or somewhere else?'

Jacobs put the pistol on the desk and lit a cigarette. 'I'll get some of the other guys to start work on it. See what more they can find out. Now, any word from your friend Joe about when she might be coming back?'

Florentine shook his head. 'Not yet.'

'Well, when she does, bring her in. It's time we had another chat with her.'

When Marguerite heard the flap of the letterbox on Susan's front door, she was hoping it might be a letter from Mr. Murphy with the results of the blood test. It was from Mr. Murphy alright, but not about the blood test. She had told Susan and James about the events leading to the deaths of Don Diego and Mrs. Gaynor but she hadn't told Mr. Murphy. Now he wanted to know why and it was with a feeling of trepidation that she went into town to see him.

'It's a pity I had to hear of this from Mr. Sweeney,' he said. 'It puts us at a great disadvantage.'

He then proceeded to read out the letter from Mr. Sweeney outlining the allegations Maudie's brothers had made.

'I'm sorry,' she replied. 'I should have told you, but somehow, it didn't seem to matter. I mean, the New York cops were just here to interview me. What happened to Don Diego was self-defence. The bastard was trying to rape me. And Mrs. Gaynor. Well, she jumped. There was nothing I could do about it. One minute she was there, the next she was in the water. I didn't even see it happening...'

The memories of these events brought tears to Marguerite's eyes and as she fumbled for a handkerchief, Mr. Murphy cleared his throat and tapped the bowl of his pipe on the edge of the heavy glass ashtray on his desk. The tapping routine was to knock out some of the ash but on this occasion was probably done to mask a certain embarrassment at seeing one of his clients burst into tears.

'You're quite right,' he said when Marguerite had sufficiently recovered. 'You should have told me. But in view of the fact that you are still here I assume the NYPD saw no reason to issue any charges against you.'

Marguerite shook her head. 'Of course not. Why should they? I haven't done anything. It's what other people did to me. That's why I came here in the first place.'

Mr. Murphy took up his pipe again and endeavoured to relight the remaining tobacco. 'I suppose, in view of what you have told me, it would be a waste of time to write to the police in New York and ask them to vouch for you?'

'Huh!' Marguerite gave an ironic smile. 'You must be kidding.'

Mr. Murphy nodded. 'I know, I know. When an investigation is ongoing they're not going to rule anybody in or out. However, had you told me about these matters I would have been able to refute the allegations on your behalf, maybe even saved you the trouble of having to do so yourself.'

Marguerite nodded.

'I take it then you are prepared to go back to Cork?'

'Of course.'

'Good.' Mr. Murphy took up his pipe again. 'It will demonstrate (a) that you are free, in other words that you are not in custody. And (b) it will enable you to confront your accusers and establish your *bona fides* in the matter.' He leafed through some of his papers before continuing. 'Now, I've arranged with Mr. Sweeney for you to meet Maudie and her brothers on Friday, if that is suitable to you.' When she nodded again, he went on, 'I will accompany you, of course, and if, as you say, Susan and James are aware of these matters it might be a good idea if they came too. They could testify to the fact that you told them of the manner in which Don Diego and Mrs. Gaynor met their deaths. In other words, that you felt you had nothing to hide.'

Back at the house, Marguerite asked Susan, 'Do you have a dictionary?'

Susan smiled, 'Well, to tell you the truth James and I don't have much use for a dictionary. But I'll have a root among the boys' books. I'm sure they have one.'

The dictionary Susan produced was quite small. It was wrapped in brown paper that was somewhat tattered and ink-stained, but it gave Marguerite the definition she required.

'*Bona fides*,' she read. ' Good faith.'

Susan, who was getting tea ready for herself and coffee for Marguerite, joked, 'Sure I could have told you that.'

Marguerite smiled and closed the dictionary. 'So Mr. Murphy says I'll be showing my good faith in the matter. Well, I hope he's right. What was it Shaunie called his brothers?'

Susan smiled and putting a cup of coffee in front of Marguerite said,

'Gobshites. And you won't find that in the dictionary.'

Marguerite leafed through the dictionary again. 'Oh but it is here,' she exclaimed. 'It says, *Slang, chiefly Irish, stupid, foolish or incompetent person.*'

'Well, if Shaunie said they were gobshites, that's what they are. But you want to be careful when you meet them. They may have done something foolish, but it doesn't mean they're stupid.'

The Irish had a funny way with words, Marguerite thought. Mr. Murphy used Latin words and phrases as if English was his first language and Latin his second. James used some words like *poc fada* which he said were Irish, the country's first language. Yet he spoke English all the time, although it must be his second. All very confusing. At the same time, Susan's warning about Shaunie's brothers was very clear. The fact that they were foolish didn't mean they were stupid and it was with considerable foreboding that she reflected on Susan's words as they made their way down to County Cork.

James was driving, Susan was in the passenger seat and Marguerite was in the back. Mr. Murphy's car was ahead of them and Marguerite wondered what he was thinking. She turned and looked out the back window. No police tail this time! She breathed a sigh of relief and as she lapsed back into her reverie, Susan said, 'Don't worry. Everything will be all right.'

James adjusted his cap and, keeping his eyes firmly on the road ahead, added, 'Of course it will. I know it won't be easy, but if you can just tell them what you told us, everything will be fine.'

Marguerite nodded, but knew that telling strangers things, intimate things, embarrassing things, was easier said than done. She wondered if she would see Martin at Maudie's place. If not she would go and see him at the Cumán Inn afterwards. Him and his sister. And his mother, of course. She was a lovely woman, a person who had known and socialised with Catherine and Shaunie, a direct link with them, a friendly link, which was so important at a time when Maudie and her brothers were in denial about Catherine.

When they pulled up outside the house, Marguerite looked around to see if Martin was there, but there was no sign of him. Mr. Murphy knocked on the front door and it was Mr. Sweeney, not Maudie who opened it. When he had ushered them into the hallway, he opened the door to the sitting room and there they found themselves in the presence of Maudie, Mick, Lizzie and Francie. No sign of Trixie, Marguerite noted, the one Martin called Francie's fancy woman.

The furniture was so arranged that the two parties would be facing one another and as they took their seats, nothing was said. The only gesture to good manners was made by James when he removed his cap, and that was something he always did whenever he entered a house, even his own.

The atmosphere was chilly and for a moment they looked at one another but said nothing. Then Maudie broke the silence. Shifting a little uncomfortably, she glared at Marguerite, saying, 'I don't know how you have the cheek to come here, after what you've done.'

'Me?' Marguerite was about to respond when Mr. Murphy cleared his throat and said, 'I think it would be better for all concerned if we tried to conduct this meeting in a civilised manner…'

'Huh,' grunted Maudie. 'Civilised is right!'

Ignoring her, Mr. Murphy looked at Mr. Sweeney and said, 'Perhaps if what has to be said is said through us…?'

Mr. Sweeney nodded. 'I agree.'

'Now,' Mr. Murphy continued, 'Marguerite has come back to explain her position and, hopefully, convince you that she really is Katie.'

Maudie uttered a sarcastic laugh. 'Katie! She's no more Katie than I am.'

'The last time she came down here,' said Mick, 'she did more claiming than explaining. She forgot to tell Maudie she was on the run. Wanted in the US – for murder no less.'

Francie puckered his brow and added, 'Two murders.'

Mr. Murphy made downward motions with his outstretched hands to try and calm the situation. 'If Marguerite was wanted for murder in the US, how in God's name do you think she would be free to be here today? Now she's come to address these allegations so the least you can do is listen.'

'I agree,' said Mr. Sweeney. 'The sole purpose of this meeting is to hear what your client has to say about these allegations.'

Mr. Murphy, who was in the process of taking out and filling his pipe, added, 'Allegations, I might add, that have been levelled by your clients.'

Mr. Sweeney ignored this remark and, addressing Marguerite said, 'Go ahead then, we're listening.'

At the same time, Maudie folded her hands on her knees, threw her head back and grunted as if to say to Marguerite, 'Well what have you got to say for yourself?'

Marguerite cleared her throat, and Susan, who was sitting beside her, put her hand on her forearm to give her support.

'It's difficult to know where to begin.'

Mr. Murphy was lighting his pipe now and he stopped for a moment to say, 'Just start at the beginning. Tell them what you told me.'

'And us,' said James. 'She told us all about it.'

'Well,' said Marguerite, 'I guess it all began the day I met Mrs. Gaynor – she was the nurse who was with Catherine on the ship to America…'

Marguerite went on to relate what Mrs. Gaynor had told her about the two babies. 'Each time we met, she told me a bit more. And then, during our last meeting – it was on the Statue of Liberty ferry – she made a horrible confession. She told me the baby she was bringing out for adoption had died – probably from the same thing that killed Catherine – and she was left with Catherine's baby. Apparently Catherine had told her all about Lily and Ed, and as they had eight children and the Diegos had none, she decided to give the baby to the Diegos. I was absolutely devastated. It meant she had given me to the Diegos when she should have given me to Lily and Ed.'

Marguerite put her hand to her nose to suppress a sniffle. 'I just couldn't believe that anyone would do such a thing.' She paused again. 'What happened after that is a blur. I had suffered so much at the hands of Don Diego, and when she asked me to forgive her, somehow I just couldn't. The enormity of what she had said was so great. The next thing I knew she had thrown herself overboard. I guess she just decided to end it all.'

'Naturally,' said Mr. Murphy, 'the police wanted to question Marguerite about it, she being a witness to what happened. But it would appear to me, and to any objective observer, that what we are talking about here is suicide, not murder.'

Maudie rested her elbow on the arm of the settee and began tapping her lips with her forefinger, still not convinced and waiting to hear more.

'Now Marguerite.' Mr. Murphy laid down his pipe as if what was to come was a much more serious matter altogether. 'You said you had suffered at the hands of Don Diegos. Tell them about that and about his death.'

Marguerite took out a handkerchief and put it to her nose and sniffed and, seeing that she was under considerable stress, Mr. Murphy said, 'I know it's difficult, but do your best. It's important.'

'I was very young when it started,' Marguerite began. 'Five I think, or maybe six. Don Diego was very nice to me. Gave me sweets and toys. Then he began to fondle me. I didn't know there was anything wrong with it at the time, but one thing led to another, and by the time I was eight he began to rape me.'

'My God,' exclaimed Maudie.'

'Once a week, twice a week.' Marguerite went on. 'Whenever he was drunk or just felt like it. I would hide if I was in the house on my own, or lie awake crying, waiting, knowing what was to come. But my tears meant nothing to him. He hurt me, but he didn't care. He just went ahead, promising me things, then threatening me if I told. It was horrible. I prayed, I pleaded, but it was no use.'

'My God!' Maudie exclaimed again.

'I ran away twice,' Marguerite continued, but they caught me and brought me back. Nobody would listen to me, not even the woman who was supposed to be my mother. Nobody would help me. So, eventually, when I could take it no longer, I ran away again. This time I was older and I was determined I wasn't going back. But it's difficult being a vagrant in New York. The back streets are not a nice place when you are young and on your own. I was hungry. I had nowhere to sleep. Nowhere safe, that is. So I went to the nuns. They have a hall beside their convent where they help people in need. You know, soup and sandwiches, that kind of thing.

They took me in and gave me work, helping in the kitchen, sweeping up, dusting, and a place to sleep. They were very good to me and eventually I – ah…' Marguerite looked down and fingered the silver ring on her right hand. 'I decided to join them. That's when I became Sister Mary.'

'Are you saying you're a nun?' asked Maudie.

Marguerite dabbed her eyes with her handkerchief and nodded.

Susan patted her on the arm, saying, 'You're doing great. Tell them what happened next.'

Marguerite sniffed. 'When we weren't looking after the down-and-outs, we prayed a lot. We prayed for the world, we prayed for peace, we prayed for those stricken by poverty and ill health. I also prayed that God would forgive Don Diego for what he had done to me. And I prayed that God would forgive my so-called mother for not helping me.' She cleared her throat. 'I suppose time heals, and as a nun I felt I could not completely devote myself to God if I continued to harbour thoughts of hate. So one day I decided to go and see Don Diego. Face him down, and if he was sorry for what he had done, try and do what Jesus has taught us to do – forgive.'

Marguerite stopped and sniffed again. Then, as if mustering the courage to continue, she straightened herself up, tilted her head back slightly and told them, 'But the bastard grabbed me. He threw me down on the bed and began raping me again.'

'Mother of God,' gasped Mick.

'And you a nun!' said Maudie.

Francie's eyes opened wide and he puckered his brow in the process.

'I was wearing my nun's clothes, but it didn't matter. Nothing mattered to him but the lust he still had in his heart. "First time I've had sex with a Bride of Christ," he told me. 'I struggled, but he was a big man. Very heavy. I couldn't break free…'

Marguerite paused and Maudie and her brothers waited, stunned into silence by what they were hearing.

Marguerite was now about to tell them about the gun, but couldn't tell them she had taken it with her for the same reason that she couldn't tell the police: it would look as if she had set out to kill Don Diego. So she told them what she had told the police; what she had told James and Susan and Mr. Murphy – that it was Don Diego's gun and that she had grabbed it from the bedside table.

'When he tried to take it from me,' she continued, 'it went off. But it was a very small pistol and, as I say, he was very big. He just he kept on doing what he was doing, so I pulled the trigger again…'

Maudie and her brothers were still looking at her, their mouths open as they tried to comprehend what they were hearing.

'Well holy God,' exclaimed Mick, finding his voice at last. 'If that doesn't beat all.'

Susan put her arm around her saying, 'You've done well.'

Marguerite sniffed back her tears, adding. 'That was it. It finally stopped him. He was dead.'

'And if that's not self-defence,' said Mr. Murphy, 'I don't know what is. Hardly a case of murder, wouldn't you say Mr. Sweeney?'

Mr. Sweeney drew his hand back across his bald head to wipe the beads of sweat that had begun to appear. 'That certainly puts a new complexion on the matter.'

Marguerite could no longer contain her pent-up emotions. Bursting into tears, she ran to the door in an attempt to leave the room. However, she was blinded by her tears, confused by the emotions that had welled up inside her, and she couldn't find the handle. As she groped for it Maudie hurried over to her and, putting a consoling arm around her, took her out into the kitchen.

'Marguerite,' she whispered, 'I'm so sorry. I never knew.'

'How could you?' Marguerite cried. 'How could anybody know? How could anybody care?'

'Well, I care,' Maudie assured her.

Susan came into the kitchen now to see if Marguerite was all right and was just in time to hear Maudie tell her, 'Don't worry. I'll look after you now. And I hope you can forgive us for what we have done.'

Marguerite, who was still sobbing, nodded.

'When does she go back?' Maudie asked, looking at Susan.

'I'm not sure. I don't think she's booked her flight yet.'

Maudie pulled up a chair and sat down facing Marguerite. 'I tell you what you do so. Why don't you come down for a day before you go. Susan and yourself. A woman's day, and we'll have a good talk. Sort things out – things that should have been sorted out a long time ago.'

Marguerite looked up, saying, 'Thanks. I'd like that.'

'Okay then. How about this day week. Would that suit?'

Marguerite nodded. 'If it's okay with Susan?'

'Sounds good to me,' Susan said.

'Right then. I'll show you around. There's not much to see, mind you, apart from Misty – he's my horse. But we can sit down and have a good heart-to-heart. Visit Shaunie's grave if you like…'

Marguerite nodded. 'Yeah. I'd like that.'

'And what about your brothers?' asked Susan. 'They said some very nasty things to her in there.'

Maudie put her hand on Marguerite's arm. 'When you're ready, we'll go back in. Hear what they have to say now that they know what really happened.'

Marguerite was reluctant to return to the sitting room. Maudie's brothers had been very insulting to her, accusing her of not one murder but two. However, she had come back to settle the matter and she knew she must finish it.

When they came back in, Mr. Murphy said, 'Well,' Mr. Sweeney, 'I assume we can now sign off on this aspect of the matter.'

'Sign,' said Mick. 'Sign what?'

Mr. Murphy sighed. 'I am not asking you to sign anything. By coming here and addressing your allegations, I suggest my client has made it clear that there is no truth in them. What I am asking you is, do you accept that?'

'Aye, I suppose I do,' Mick replied. 'I only knew what I was told.'

Turning to Mr. Sweeney, Mr. Murphy went on, 'Suppose is not good enough. Your clients accepted rumour as fact. Now they've had a first-hand account of what happened. Do they or don't you accept my client's word for it.'

'I do,' said Maudie. 'And so do they.'

The others nodded, and Mr. Murphy added, 'A word of apology wouldn't be out of place.'

'Perhaps you would allow me to do it,' said Maudie. 'On behalf of all of us, for this mistake, and for others. We're sorry.'

Mick grunted in agreement and Francie nodded.

'A lot of things have happened that shouldn't have happened.' Maudie added. 'I've invited Marguerite to come down and see me again before she leaves. We can talk more about things then and perhaps we can put them right.'

TWENTY-NINE

Mr. Murphy informed Marguerite that he and Mr. Sweeney were now exchanging letters of a different kind. No rancour this time, but documents confirming the arrangement between her and Maudie.

'It's hard to believe,' said Marguerite. 'Maudie has agreed to recognise me as Shaunie's daughter. I can't believe it.'

'Well, she would need to have a heart of stone not to do so,' said James.

'I was in tears myself,' said Susan. 'I know it was very difficult for you going over it all. But they had to know.'

'And I hope she's giving you a few bob as well,' said James. 'After all the trouble her and the brothers have put you to.'

'Not to mention the heartache,' Susan added.

'Mr. Murphy says it's all in the contract. So at least I'll be able to pay you back for all you've done for me.'

'Pay us back?' exclaimed James. 'There'll be no paying back.'

Marguerite smiled. 'Well, we'll see about that.'

'I take it you've told Martin you've patched things up with Maudie?' asked Susan.

'Of course. Sure you know I've written to him.'

'Just asking! And I suppose you'll be meeting him when you go down to see her again?'

'Susan. I told you. We're just good friends. And that's all it can be.'

Susan gave a questioning smile, adding, 'Yeah, yeah, I believe you.'

'Susan,' Marguerite added. 'You're an incurable romantic.'

Hearing the whinnying of a horse, and the sound of a hoof against a door, Maudie said. 'That's Misty.' She led Marguerite and Susan across to the stable where her horse was poking his head out over the half door. 'Good boy,' she whispered, stroking his nose. 'Good boy.'

'I used to ride him,' she said. 'But he's getting on now.' She paused, adding, 'So am I, I suppose.'

When they returned to the house, Maudie asked Marguerite, 'Have you been to Cork yet – I mean the city?'

Marguerite shook her head. 'No. Only as far as here.'

'Well, now that you've come this far…'

'It's a bit late in the day to be going into Cork,' Susan told her. 'I'm afraid we'll have to be getting back.'

'Thank you for having us down Maudie,' said Marguerite. 'It's been a great day. And I'm so glad we have sorted things out.'

'It's no more than you deserve,' Maudie assured her. 'I'm just sorry for some of the things that I, well, my brothers and I said to you. They must have been very hurtful.'

'You've more than made up for it,' Marguerite replied. 'I really appreciate it.'

They got up to go when they heard a car driving into the yard.

'Ah,' said Maudie, 'that'll be Martin.'

Marguerite's eye lit up. 'Martin?'

'You know him?' asked Maudie.

'Yeah. We stayed at the Cumán Inn last time I was here.'

'Come out then and say hello.'

'Marguerite!' Martin exclaimed as he got out of the car. 'I think you must be getting to like Cork.'

'I think she *is* a Cork woman,' said Maudie. 'But you know she's never been to the capital.'

'You mean Dublin?' asked Susan.

'No,' Maudie scoffed. 'The real capital – Cork city. '

They laughed and Maudie added. 'I was just saying to Susan she should take Marguerite for a run to see it.'

'But we must be getting back,' said Susan. 'Maybe another time.'

'There's no time like the present,' Maudie insisted. 'Martin, why don't you run her in – show here around?'

Martin smiled. 'I'd love to. But I'm afraid my car's not in the best of shape – it is due to go in for a service.'

'Well then, take the Wolseley.'

'Are you sure?' asked Marguerite.

'Of course I am. Isn't it sitting there doing nothing?'

'Okay,' Martin said. 'That's fine by me. But as Susan says, it's late in the day. There wouldn't be much time for sightseeing before it gets dark.'

Maudie turned to Marguerite. 'Why don't you stay at the inn tonight and go to Cork tomorrow? I'll look after the bill.'

'There'll be no bill,' said Martin.

'But how will I get back to Susan's house?'

Maudie smiled and put her arm around Marguerite's shoulders. 'Didn't I say Martin could have the Wolseley. He'll take you back. Won't you Martin?'

Martin smiled. 'Of course I will.'

They were about to go when Maudie said, 'Just one more thing,' and went back into the house.

When she re-emerged she took Marguerite aside and pressed an envelope into her hand, saying, 'I nearly forgot. This is for you.'

Seeing the puzzled look on Marguerite's face, she added, 'Go on. Open it.'

The envelope wasn't sealed and Marguerite found, to her amazement, that it contained a cheque for 7,500 pounds.

'But...' she began. 'I haven't...'

'Take it as an advance,' said Maudie. 'A gesture of goodwill. I'll give you the other half when you come down to sign the papers. In the meantime you have to live and you must be strapped for cash, coming from America and all. We owe you that much.'

'Well, if you insist.'

'I do,' said Maudie. 'Now off you go.'

Susan dropped Marguerite off at the Inn and then headed back home to Tipperary. She was very happy, not only with Maudie's gesture but with the thought of Martin taking Marguerite on a sight-seeing tour of Cork. She smiled to herself. Perhaps she was an incurable romantic. But it seemed to her that the relationship between Marguerite and Martin was coming along very nicely. And, she said to herself, who knows what will happen when the two of them get together on their own?

It was something Marguerite herself wondered about as she set off with Martin in the green Wolseley the following morning. She was still intent on adhering to her vows, but in her thoughts she did admit to straying from them somewhat on the journey to Cork. Martin turned out to be a very pleasant companion and she wondered if, on occasion, he was reciprocating her innermost thoughts.

Martin took her on a tour of Cork city and then headed east.

Along the way, Marguerite squinted up at one of the signs asking, 'What does it mean, Cob H?'

Martin smiled. 'It's not Cob H, it's Cobh. That's the Irish for Cove. The Cove of Cork. That's where we're going.'

When Martin parked the car, they wandered over to the seafront and sat on a wooden bench looking out at the islands. There was a chill wind coming from the sea, a wind the islands couldn't block, and they wrapped their coats around themselves to keep warm.

Behind and above them the soft notes of carillon bells rang out across the terraced houses overlooking the sea.

'Hail Queen of Heaven,' said Marguerite.

Martin turned to her, surprised that his visitor would recognise the hymn.

Marguerite smiled. '*Mother of Christ, Star of the Sea, Pray for the Wanderer, Pray for me.*'

'I didn't think you'd know things like that,' said Martin.

'There are a lot of things about me you don't know.' Marguerite turned and looked back up to where the sound of the bells was coming from.

'Saint Colman's Cathedral,' Martin informed her. 'It's famous for its carillon bells.'

Marguerite smiled. 'My mother told me about them. She wrote it all down for me on the way to America. She said she heard the bells when she was waiting to go to the shipping office. I wonder if they were playing the same hymn?'

'Could have been.'

'She said she was sitting on a bench. I reckon it could even have been this one.'

Martin pointed to a low building on the seafront. 'That's where she would have checked in. A tender would have taken her out to the ship.'

'But she didn't go that time,' Marguerite hastened to add. 'Shaunie came and took her back. Told her they were going to get married. But, of course, they didn't, and the next time she was here, she had me, a baby born out of wedlock, and there was no turning back.'

'The bells of Saint Colman's have said farewell to thousands of emigrants. Probably did so for the *Titanic* too – this was her last port of call, you know.'

Marguerite shook her head. 'I didn't know that. But it was a band that was playing as the *Atlantia* set sail. It was the one that took Catherine to America. She said it was very sad. Everyone was waving goodbye and the band was playing 'The Holy Ground'.

'*And still I live in hope to see the Holy Ground once more…*In those days few of them did. Some of them did well in America, of course, and came back. But most of them never saw the Holy Ground again.'

'What does the next line mean? *Fine girl you are.*'

'I don't know. Just a thumping chorus, I suppose. Everybody sings that bit as loudly as they can.'

'Catherine said she didn't feel a fine girl. She felt she had let her family down. But the truth was it was Shaunie's family who let her down. She thought it was Shaunie, but it wasn't. It was those brothers of his.'

Martin had seen Marguerite crying when she came out of Maudie's house but decided not to ask her about it until he felt the time was right. 'I take it the brothers were giving you a hard time?'

'Yeah. Mick and Francie thought they had the dirt on me. They

269

reckoned they could stymie my discussions with Maudie – you know, stop her from recognising me as Shaunie's daughter.'

'Ha ha! They're afraid you might be able to get your hands on the farm.'

'I've told them. I don't want the damned farm.'

'So what kind of dirt could they possibly have on you?'

Marguerite sighed. 'Oh, it's a long story.'

'How about a cup of coffee?' Martin suggested. 'It'll warm you up.'

'Catherine said she and Shaunie went to a small diner somewhere around here.'

'Probably one of those cafés across the street. Come on. We can talk there.'

When the waitress heard Marguerite's American accent, she said, 'We don't get many visitors at this time of year. Too cold.'

'Yeah, I know what you mean.' Marguerite smiled and turning to Martin said, 'You must have thought I was stupid asking you where Cob-h was when I saw the sign.'

'Not at all. Sure how were you to know it's pronounced Cove.'

'And that's another thing. Catherine told me about a village called Skeheena- something.'

Martin smiled. 'Probably Skeheenarinky.'

'That's it. She said it means the little whitethorn bush of the dancing.'

'Could be. It's another name for hawthorn.'

'And did people really believe the fairies danced around those bushes by the light of the moon?'

'Of course they did. Some people still call them fairy thorns.'

'And is it true the farmers won't cut them down?'

'Absolutely. You can see them out in the middle of the fields. There's still a lot of superstition about them.'

'And the one up at the lake. Is that a fairy thorn?'

'The lake?'

'The one above Maudie's place. There's a big boulder near the shore and a whitethorn tree wedged in beside it.'

'Ah yes, I know what you're talking about now. Sure that *must* be a fairy

270

thorn. Didn't it stop the boulder from rolling into the lake?'

Marguerite smiled. 'Catherine said Shaunie chased her around the boulder until he caught her, and then he kissed her under the whitethorn.'

'They must have been very happy. I wonder what happened that they didn't get married?'

'I'll tell you what happened. And then I'll tell you what happened to Catherine and to me.'

The waitress came over to see if they wanted anything else, and when she had gone, Marguerite added, 'I think I need more privacy for what I'm about to tell you. Let's go for a walk.'

Outside, they pulled their coat collars tightly around themselves and walked up the street. Marguerite put her arm through his and told him. 'It's not a very pleasant story, but I think you deserve to know. I only hope that when I'm finished, you'll still be talking to me.'

Starting with Shaunie's story of what happened to him on the day he was to marry Catherine, Marguerite told Martin how Catherine had no option but to go to America with her baby and of the fateful events, as related by Mrs. Gaynor, that occurred on the way over. When it came to the death of Don Diego, however, she spoke in the broadest of terms, omitting the intimate details and saying only that he attacked her when he was drunk.

By this time they had seated themselves on another bench on the seafront. Now and then Martin shook his head and mumbled to himself as if to say he couldn't believe what she was saying. To her surprise, it wasn't the shooting of Don Diego that drew his first comment. It was the fact that she was a nun.

'But you're not wearing…'

'Nun's clothing?' Marguerite gave a wry smile. 'No. After what happened I left the convent, and after what Mrs. Gaynor told me I needed to find out who I was, so I came here to find Shaunie. But Maudie wouldn't accept me – or her brothers. They made all sorts of allegations against me. Even accused me of murder.' She paused. 'But now I've explained everything to them, I think they accept me for who I am.'

Marguerite was still linking Martin's arm. Reaching over, he took his

271

hand in hers, saying, 'Thanks for telling me.'

'You don't think any less of me then?'

Martin smiled. 'Why should I think any less of you? As a matter of fact I think you're very brave.' He paused. 'But what do I call you now? Sister Mary?'

'No. Marguerite will do.'

The carillon bells of St. Colman's rang out again. Martin looked at his watch and, getting to his feet said, 'Time we're on our way. It'll be getting dark soon.'

Marguerite identified the hymn on the carillon this time as 'Faith of Our Fathers', adding. 'Do think we could visit the cathedral – just for a minute?'

In view of what he had just heard, Martin could only say, 'Of course.' He looked up at the cathedral. 'It's a steep climb, but I'm sure we can find a way up to it by car.'

When they went into the cathedral, Marguerite slipped into one of the pews and knelt to say a prayer. Martin knelt beside her and said a prayer too – not for himself, but for her. However, what exactly each of them prayed for, they kept to themselves.

THIRTY

James had gone to work. Marguerite had slept late and the kitchen was now filling up with the smell of bacon and sausages that were sizzling in the pan.

'That sure is appetising,' she said.

'I hope you like it.' Susan replied. 'And these are fresh eggs – you won't get them any fresher.'

'I suppose you miss the boys?'

'Of course I do. But, you know, they'd eat you out of house and home – they've got so big.' Susan placed the fry in front of Marguerite. 'Now, see if you can wrap yourself around that.'

'My, I don't know if I can eat all that!'

Susan filled her cup with coffee. 'Of course you can. After what you went through with Maudie and her brothers, you need to get your strength back.'

'You were great to go with me – James too. I don't think I could have done it if the two of you hadn't been there to support me.'

'It was an awful ordeal. Awful, but you did very well.' Susan sat down at the table and put her hands around a mug of tea to warm them. 'Now, tell me all about your trip to Cobh with Martin.

Marguerite smiled. 'What is there to tell? We sat on a bench and talked. We had a cup of coffee and we talked some more. And then we went up to the cathedral and said a few prayers.'

'And what did you talk about?'

'Not the sort of things you're thinking about. We talked about Catherine and what had happened to her and I told Martin what had happened to me.'

'Everything?'

'Well, not everything, but as much as I could.'

'So what happens next?'

Mr. Murphy says there's no need to see Maudie again, that the documents can be signed and exchanged by post. But I would like to go down again before I go back.'

'You mean to see Martin.'

'Susan, you're incorrigible. I told Mr. Murphy I would go in with Maudie to Mr. Sweeney's office and sign the documents there. Seriously though, do you think you could take me once more – or am I asking too much of you?

Susan smiled. 'No problem. After all, it is your big day. Unless, of course, you want Martin to drive you!'

'Very funny.'

'Well, he does seem to have taken a shine to you.'

'He knows we can't have that kind of relationship.'

'Maybe not now. But I take it he knows you're considering your situation?'

'Of course. I felt I owed him that much.'

'Well then...?'

'Susan, Martin and I are just good friends, that's all. And that's all it can be.'

Susan got up and made Marguerite another cup of coffee, adding 'Well, if you say so...'

Marguerite's big day turned out to be a fresher day and as Susan and Marguerite set off, a gust of wind lifted withered grass and other debris and swirled them around the road.

'The *sí-gaoithe*,' Susan told her. 'That's what we call those little whirlwinds.'

'The shee-gwee? You're speaking Gaelic again, aren't you?'

Susan nodded. 'A fairy wind. It comes out of nowhere and swirls things around.'

'That's cute. Fairy thorns. Fairy wind. Quite a country!'

'Tradition has it that if they're good fairy winds they'll help the farmers gather up their hay.'

Marguerite smiled. 'Well, I hope it'll be a good fairy wind that takes us to Cork.'

The wind picked up and by the time they neared Maudie's place it was blowing hard. It bent the trees and tugged at the leaves as if to lay the branches bare. Now and then a particularly strong gust rocked the car, and Marguerite observed, 'My, that's not a fairy wind now – that's a gale.'

It began to rain and Susan put on the wipers. 'We're nearly there,' she said, peering through an oil slick on the windscreen. 'Yes, there's the turn.'

A short time later they pulled in at the front of Maudie's house.

When Susan made no move, Marguerite asked, 'Are you not coming in with me?'

Susan smiled. 'I'm not going out in that gale.' Then, as an afterthought she added, 'I'll wait until she opens the door.'

Marguerite put a scarf over her head and tied it under her chin. 'Well, here goes!'

As Maudie was expecting her, Marguerite hurried up to the front door, rather than the back, and banged on it with the knocker. There was no response and she knocked again. When there was still no response, she pulled the collar of her raincoat around her and ran around to the back.

A few minutes later, Martin appeared at the car.

Susan wound down the window and shouted, 'Is Maudie in?'

'What's that?'

'Maudie. Is she in?'

'I think so.'

'Marguerite tried the front door but there was no reply. So she's gone round to the back.'

Martin nodded. 'Maudie's probably down the yard. I'll see if I can find her. Better close the window or you'll be soaked.'

When Martin went into the yard he was surprised to see Misty galloping away towards the meadow and knew by the way his tail was curled above his back that he had bolted. At the same time he saw Marguerite dragging Maudie from the stable. He immediately ran to her assistance, asking, 'What happened?'

Breathless from the exertion she told him, 'The top part of the door was banging,' Misty was going mad. I think it must have spooked him.' She laid Maudie gently on the ground, adding, 'I could hear her crying for help. She must have bolted the bottom part of the door when she went inside, and when I opened it Misty came charging out.'

Martin secured both doors, saying, 'You're lucky he didn't run you down.'

As Marguerite cradled Maudie's head in her lap they could see she had suffered severe injuries to her head and was bleeding profusely.

'Misty,' Maudie groaned.

Martin, who was kneeling beside her now, assured her, 'Misty's all right. But he's given you a right kick on the head.'

'The top of the door,' Maudie managed to say. 'I tied it back. But the wind...'

Maudie's hair was matted with blood and her eyes were closed but she was trying to say something else.

'What is it Maudie?' Martin leaned closer to hear what she was trying to say. 'This is Martin.'

Maudie managed to put her hand on Marguerite's wrist and they heard her say, 'Thank you Marguerite.'

Untying her headscarf, Marguerite patted it gently on Maudie's injuries in a vain effort to staunch the bleeding and turning to Martin, told him, 'Get me a wet towel. And hurry. Ring the doctor!'

Martin sprinted to the gate and waved to Susan to come into the yard, then hurried into the house to ring the doctor. When he returned, Susan was kneeling beside Marguerite, giving her what assistance she could. He gave them the wet towel, asking, 'Well? How is she? The doctor's on his way.'

Marguerite was still nursing Maudie's head in her lap. She wiped the rain and the tears from her eyes with a hand that was dripping with blood and told him, 'I'm afraid it's too late. She's dead.'

The newspapers were fulsome in their praise for Marguerite and none more so than the *Tipperary Star*. Susan spread the paper on the kitchen table so that the two of them could view it together. The banner headline, they could see, quoted Maudie's dying words: 'Thank you Marguerite', while the sub-heading added, 'Prodigal daughter risks life to save local woman'.

The story was accompanied by a large black and white picture of Maudie sitting side-saddle on Misty. The caption said it was taken on the last occasion she had ridden down as far as the local pub to join the fox hunt in a stirrup cup of sherry before seeing them off.

Susan lifted the paper so that she could read the story. 'It's an interview with Martin,' she said. 'It says you were very brave, that you could have been trampled to death yourself when you opened the door to let Misty out.'

Marguerite shrugged. 'It was no big deal. I only did what anybody else would have done.'

'"The storm, however, had taken its victim,"' Susan went on as she quoted snippets of the story. '"The high wind had loosened the binder twine tying back the top half of the stable door and the banging of it must have made the normally docile horse panic. A *post mortem* examination showed that Maudie died from a kick to the head."'

Marguerite sipped her coffee. 'Does it say anything about when they might hold the inquest?'

'Not that I can see.' Susan turned to an inside page where there were more photographs of Maudie, mostly taken at local events. 'And there's a picture of Shaunie,' she added, leaving the paper back down on the table for Marguerite to see it.

'"Double blow for local family,"' said Marguerite, reading the heading of the story beside Shaunie's picture. '"Maudie's tragic demise occurred only a short time after the death of her brother, well-known farmer and former GAA star..."'

James arrived with some of the daily newspapers including back copies of the *Cork Examiner* and, not surprisingly, they too were full of praise for Marguerite.

When they had all digested the various reports and re-examined the photographs, Susan asked, 'Will you be staying for the inquest?'

'The police don't seem to think that will be necessary. They have my statement, so once the funeral is over I'll head back. I've stayed much longer than I intended.'

'You're welcome to stay as long as you like,' said James. 'We told you that.'

Marguerite got up and hugged them. 'I know. You've both been wonderful. Really wonderful. But I've booked the flight.'

Knowing that the boys would be home for Christmas and would need the bedroom, Susan didn't press her further.

'What about the results of your blood test?' She asked.

'Mr. Murphy says he'll send them on to me.'

'You came as the Prodigal Daughter,' said James, 'and just look at the papers. 'You're going back as a hero. Or should it be heroine?'

Marguerite smiled. 'Don't mind that. The important thing is I saw Shaunie before he died. And his family have recognised me as his daughter. That'll do for now.'

Maudie's funeral took place shortly after the *post mortem* examination and she was buried next to Shaunie. No one objected to Marguerite's presence this time, but if the newspapers had been fulsome in praise of her actions, Maudie's brothers were less so.

As Mick and Francie lived elsewhere, they didn't consider it appropriate to entertain mourners in Maudie's house. Nor did they feel obliged to entertain them in any of the local hostelries, especially as they had been entertained only a short time ago on the occasion of Shaunie's death. And so, while James left immediately after the funeral so that Marguerite could get ready for her flight, Maudie's brothers retreated to a pub in the town to drown their sorrows, mull over events and ponder the future. Normally, the Cumán Inn would have been their choice, but not now as they were aware of the friendship that had developed between the owners of the inn and Marguerite and didn't want to be overheard. They had, as the *Tipperary Star* reported, suffered a double blow, but now as they gathered in a quiet corner of the pub it was fear of another loss that began to dominate their thoughts.

Francie wrinkled his brow and poured a bottle of beer into his glass. 'Pity Pat couldn't come home for the funeral.'

'Australia's a long way away,' remarked Lizzie. 'Even in these days of air travel.'

'Still, it would have been nice to talk to him about things,' said Francie. 'You know, face to face. What else did he say on the phone?'

Mick took another sip of his whiskey. 'Just that he was sorry he wouldn't be able to come for the funeral.'

'I know. But did he mention the farm?'

'He asked me if Maudie had made a will.'

'And had she?'

Mick shook his head. 'Sure Shaunie's will hasn't been cleared yet.'

'But he left the farm to her, didn't he?'

'I know, but now that she's dead the whole thing may have to go to probate?'

Trixie, who was sipping a gin and tonic asked, 'What's probate?'

'Not that it's any of your business Trixie,' Mick said dryly, 'but it means it will probably have to be cleared by the courts.'

'But if Shaunie left it to her,' said Francie, 'and she wasn't married, that means we get it, doesn't it?'

Mick nodded. 'All things being equal it would be divided between you and me – and Pat. He may be in Australia, but he's still a beneficiary.'

Trixie rubbed Francie's leg with her foot and smiled. 'That means you'll be in the money, Duckie.'

Lizzie, who had sipped her mineral and listened quietly to the exchange, turned to her and told her sharply, 'Do you mind? It's our farm they're talking about – not yours!'

'Okay, okay', Trixie replied. 'Keep your hair on.'

France puckered his brow again. 'What do you mean Mick, all things being equal?'

'Well, things are not equal now, are they?'

'You mean this American woman?'

Mick nodded. 'She's still not out of the picture. The day Maudie died she was to sign the declaration renouncing any claim to the farm. But she didn't and if the blood test shows she could be Shaunie's daughter, we could be in trouble.'

'But is it true,' asked Francie, 'that she could inherit the farm even though she's illegitimate?'

Mick nodded. 'I was talking to a solicitor up in Tipperary and he confirmed what Mr. Sweeney told Maudie – it makes no difference.'

Trixie put her empty tonic bottle down. 'So where does that leave us Duckie?'

'It doesn't leave you anywhere,' said Mick caustically. 'But if this woman decides to lay claim to the farm, your Duckie here might not inherit a red cent.'

Francie's brow was still puckered from the perplexity of it all. 'But she said she didn't want the farm. She gave Maudie her word.'

'That's right,' said Mick, 'but Maudie's dead and we haven't exactly endeared ourselves to her, have we?'

'So, what are we going to do?' asked Francie. 'Give her a few bob and get rid of her?

Mick got up to go to the toilet and nodded to Francie to come with him.

As they stood at the urinal, Mick lowered his voice in case he might be overheard. 'Get rid of her for a few bob? You must be joking. Aren't we the ones who locked Shaunie in? Aren't we the ones who accused her of murder? If the blood test is positive she's hardly going to settle for a few bob.'

As they washed their hands, Mick went on, 'But you know, I was thinking. She may have convinced the American cops that she didn't kill those people in New York. But she might not be so free to come and go if it was discovered that she had killed somebody else.'

'Who?'

'It's something I discussed with Pat on the phone, and he's inclined to agree.' Mick dried his hands. 'Did you never wonder about the way Maudie died? I mean, the twine gets loose on the top half of the stable door and the bottom half is bolted.'

'But Maudie said the wind must have loosened the twine.'

'That's what she thought. But who's to say the Yank didn't do it?'

Francie puckered his brow as the import of what his brother was saying began to sink in. 'But the papers said she opened the bottom part of the door to let Misty out.'

'Aye, after Maudie had nearly been trampled to death.' Mick paused to give emphasis to his next statement. 'And the big question is, who bolted the door in the first place?'

'But why would the Yank do that?'

'Ah will you cop yourself on. Why do you think? For revenge of course.'

'You mean, for what we did to Shaunie?'

'Exactly.'

'Well holy God. I never thought of that.'

'Well think of it now.'

Francie nodded. 'But the guards seem satisfied with what she told them.'

'They are now, but then they don't know the background to it, do they?' Mick looked around to make sure there was no one in the cubicles. 'Look. Do I have to spell it out? If the guards knew that we locked Shaunie in a shed on the morning of his wedding, it would show them that this woman had a motive for killing Maudie, wouldn't it? They might take the view that she locked Maudie in the stable to get her own back – and to get her out of the way so she could inherit the farm.'

'So, do you think we should tell the guards?'

'I do, but would they listen to us?' Someone else came in and Mick lowered his voice. 'No, Mr. Sweeney put the skids under her the last time. I think it would sound better coming from him.'

When they returned to the table, Mick ordered another round. However, to Trixie's disappointment she found that the subject of the farm and who might inherit it was now closed.

THIRTY-ONE

The inspector whose Gaelic surname the men from the NYPD couldn't pronounce was now a superintendent. He was doing nothing important enough to be called up to the Commissioner's office, and he couldn't imagine why he had been summoned.

'Tell me, Joe,' said the Commissioner, 'didn't you look after those two officers from the NYPD?'

Without waiting for a reply, the Commissioner handed him a copy of the *Cork Examiner*. 'And wasn't that woman involved in some way or other?'

Joe could see that a story on the front page with a photograph of a woman had been ringed with red biro. It was headed, 'FARM OWNER DIES IN FREAK ACCIDENT.'

'Yes Sir, we met her briefly,' he said and checking the caption, added, 'That's right. Her name was Maudie.' As he glanced down through the report, the Commissioner asked him, 'And this woman, Marguerite. Wasn't she the one they came over to interview?'

'That's right. She went down to Cork with her solicitor to see Maudie. Claimed she was the long lost daughter of Maudie's brother.'

'And remind me. What exactly did they want to interview her about?'

'It's a long story, but apparently she shot her adoptive father. Said he was trying to rape her and claimed it was self-defence. But the American cops weren't convinced. They thought his death was very suspicious. They also had their suspicions about the death of a woman on the Statue of Liberty Ferry. They thought Marguerite might have pushed her overboard.'

'Well, I have a letter from Maudie's solicitor and he thinks her death was very suspicious. I want you to go down to Cork and talk to him. See what he's on about.'

Before going to see Mr. Sweeney, Joe called into the local garda station and studied the report that had been sent to the Coroner. An unfortunate accident due to the strong winds, it concluded and, having examined the stable door himself, Joe came to the same conclusion. Why, then, did her solicitor think otherwise?

Mr. Sweeney, he found, was glad to see him, but reluctant to say too much in case he might be quoted. When Joe asked him about his concerns, he put his hand to his mouth and coughed as if he was about to betray a confidence, before recounting the gist of what had been said at the first meeting between Maudie and Marguerite.

'During those negotiations,' he said, 'this woman made the point that the reason Shaunie had not married her mother was that on the morning of the wedding his brothers locked him into a shed.'

'Was that true?'

Mr. Sweeney nodded. 'Apparently. It seems they were a bit wild. However, she seemed to think Maudie was a party to it. Maudie denied it, of course, but the fact remains, this woman had convinced herself that Maudie was, in part at least, responsible for her predicament.'

'So where does that leave us?'

Mr. Sweeney took off his glasses and daubed his eyes with a white handkerchief.

'She believed the motive of the brothers in locking Shaunie in and preventing the marriage was to make sure her mother didn't inherit the farm. Now Maudie, who was going to inherit the farm, gets locked in and meets an untimely death. Does that not strike you as strange?'

Joe shrugged. 'Probably just a coincidence. Our people think Maudie would have reached out and bolted the door herself because of the storm.

Mr. Sweeney put his glasses back on and shook head. 'Her brothers don't think so.'

'Are you suggesting this woman locked Maudie in, in revenge for what they did to Shaunie?'

'It's not for me to say. I am merely relating to you what my clients have told me.'

'But Martin O'Driscoll and her aunt, what's her name? – Susan – have both made statements testifying to the fact that it was an accident. In fact they have praised Marguerite's courage in getting Maudie out. And Maudie herself thanked her with her dying breath.'

Mr. Sweeney shrugged. 'That may be, but the fact is neither Martin nor Susan – nor even Maudie for that matter – actually saw what happened. They only had this woman's word for it. And taking everything into consideration, my clients are of the opinion that Maudie's death was not accidental.'

'But surely the brothers stand to inherit the farm.'

'In the normal course of events, yes, but they make the point that with Maudie's demise the way is now open for this woman to stake her claim to it – providing, of course, she can prove who she says she is.'

'But I thought she told Maudie she wasn't interested in the farm; that all she wanted was to be recognised as Shaunie's daughter?'

'That's what she said.'

'And where is she now?'

'After Maudie's funeral she returned to America.'

'I take it she'll be back for the inquest?'

Mr. Sweeney laid his glasses on the desk. 'I'm not a betting man superintendent, but if I was I wouldn't bet on it. Would you?'

Having studied Joe's report, the Commissioner considered the allegations made by Maudie's brothers to be of such a serious nature that Joe should contact the police in New York and ask if they knew where Marguerite was.

Joe immediately rang Florentine and told him what had happened to Maudie. 'The Commissioner wants to know if Marguerite's coming back for the inquest,' he said. 'We really need to talk to her. Any idea where she might be?'

'We had to let her go,' Florentine informed him. 'Not enough evidence. But we have a tail on her. Let me check and I'll get back to you.'

Detective Sullivan was sitting on the porch talking to his father.

'Thaddeus,' said Dan, 'are you sure you won't have a beer?'

'No thanks,' he said, letting the use of the name Thaddeus pass. 'Coffee's fine. I'm driving.'

His father gave an ironic smile, and let the reference to driving pass. He opened a bottle of beer for himself and they talked for a while about a game of baseball that was about to be shown on TV. Then they raked over the visit to Ireland again. But what Dan really wanted to talk about was the return of Marguerite.

'I take it you pulled her in,' he said.

'Of course.'

'And did you get anything more out of her?'

'Not really.'

'What do you reckon then?'

'Toni thinks she's guilty on both counts. Me? I'm not so sure.'

'So where's the proof?'

'I know. The DA says it's our word against hers.'

Dan finished his bottle of beer. 'Where do you go from here then?'

'As far as Diego's death is concerned, the DA says the gun is the key to it. But it seems to have gone through a lot of hands and we're having great difficulty finding out who had it and when.'

'Nothing to support her claim that it belonged to him?'

'No. And nothing to show she took it with her when she went to see him. If we had it would go a long way to proving premeditation.'

Dan nodded and got up to go into the house. 'Are you sure you won't have a beer?'

'No. I'm good. You go ahead.'

When Dan returned his son continued, 'Even if we do pin it on her, the DA says she might get off on the sympathy factor alone.'

'Yeah, if she's a rape victim she'll get a lot of sympathy all right. And what about Mrs. Gaynor's death?'

'Without a witness it's going to be very difficult to prove.'

'What's the latest on the blood test?'

'Marguerite says she hasn't got the results yet. Apparently her solicitor is having difficulty getting the hospital to hand over samples of Shaunie's blood.'

'And is that a problem?'

'It may be a problem for her, but it's not a problem for us. In fact, we'd be happy if the hospital doesn't hand over the samples. As I told you before we don't want a blood test that shows she isn't Katie. If it turns out she's Brigid Mary we could have egg on our face.'

Dan nodded. 'It would look as if she led the two of you a merry dance, as they would say in Ireland.'

'Yeah, all the way to Cork and back.'

'How much did she get from the people in Cork?'

'She claimed she wasn't interested in inheriting the farm – that all she wanted was for the family to recognise her as Shaunie's daughter. Then she admitted that she tried to screw a few grand out of them in return. Claimed it was her lawyer's idea.'

'How much?'

'Fifteen grand.'

'Not bad.'

'But she says she only got half of it. Maudie died in some kind of accident with her horse before the deal could be signed, so she didn't get the other half.'

'And where did she get the money to go to Ireland?'

'Apparently she borrowed five grand from Lily and Ed.'

'So, she got five grand from the doting relatives of a dead woman here and seven and a half from the relatives of a dead man over there. Twelve and a half grand! Not a bad pitch – and a holiday in Ireland thrown in.'

Dan opened another bottle of beer and asked, 'Where is she now?'

'Back with Lily and Ed.'

'What makes you think she won't skip town again?'

'We couldn't hold her, but we've put a tail on her in the hope she might lead us to something.'

'What if she decides to go back to Ireland?'

'I doubt it. Not when she hears the Irish police want to talk to her about Maudie's death. Anyway, we seized her Irish passport when she came back and asked the DA's office to check on the legality of it.'

'What if she applies for another passport? I mean, if the heat's on she could go somewhere else.'

'Well, it appears she never had a passport in the name of Marguerite. However, we've taken steps to block an application, just in case.'

'What if she uses one of her other names?'

'If she proposed travelling as Sister Mary she would still have to use her adoptive name.'

'I wasn't thinking so much of Sister Mary. It was Brigid Mary I had in mind.'

'But she would need a birth certificate. Where is she going to get that?'

'Well, she managed to lay her hands on one for Katie. Who knows what other documents Mrs. Gaynor may have given her.'

'Fuck it. I never thought of that.'

Dan smiled. 'Sorry son. I didn't mean to wind you up, but you see, it may well be this woman doesn't really know herself who she is. After all, she has lived her young life as Marguerite, her adult life as Sister Mary, and her new life trying to figure out whether she's Katie or Brigid Mary. I'm no shrink, but it appears to me she could slip into, or out of, any one of those roles at a moment's notice.'

His son got up to go. He was thinking about what his father had said about Marguerite and almost absent-mindedly told him, 'I must be off.'

Dan walked him to the door. 'Are you sure you won't stay and watch the game?'

'No thanks. I'm still feeling a bit tired.'

'Okay then Thaddeus. See you at the Ferryman's on Friday?'

'Yeah. See you then. Slán.'

'Slán. And take care.'

Instead of returning to his apartment, Detective Sullivan headed for the Bayonne Bridge that would take him into New Jersey. What Florentine had said about the consequences for them both if Marguerite turned out to be Brigid Mary, had unsettled him. He had tried to put the possibility of such a scandal out of his mind, but now his father had not only renewed his worries, but added to them, and he was deeply troubled.

Could it be that Marguerite had, as his father put it, led them a merry dance? Had she played them for suckers when they were in Ireland, pretending to be Katie so that she could try and screw a few grand out of the people in Cork? And, as Florentine said, under their very noses!

It would explain a lot of things, Sullivan was thinking. Why, for example, she had steadfastly refused to have her lawyer present at the interviews. Why she didn't want the accusations being made against her getting into the public domain while she was in Ireland. She could have been afraid it would scuttle her chances of getting the fifteen grand.

She had also turned out to be a most elusive person. What if his father was right and she might be thinking of skipping again? No, it was just his father's imagination. She was probably still at Lily and Ed's house. After all, they had it staked out. However, the thought that she might have disappeared again had him on edge.

Pulling up outside the house, he located the unmarked car from which one of his colleagues was carrying out surveillance and asked him if the suspect was still inside.

'Yeah, she's still in there,' said the officer. 'She went to the supermarket with her relatives this afternoon. They purchased some groceries and came straight back.'

Sullivan knocked on the door and, reluctantly, Ed told him to come in.

'I need to talk to Marguerite,' he said.

Ed made no reply, nor did Lily who was sitting on the settee munching chocolates.

'Marguerite,' he said again. 'I must talk to her.'

A bedroom door opened and closed and assuming it was Marguerite coming down the stairs, Sullivan glanced around, saying 'Ah, Marguerite. Sorry to trouble you again.'

'It's not her,' Ed told him. 'It's Penny, our youngest daughter. She just dropped by to see how we were getting on.'

'And where's Marguerite?'

'You mean Katie,' said Ed. 'I'm afraid you're too late. She's gone.'

Sullivan's heart sank. 'Gone! Gone where?'

Lily ran her tongue around her top teeth and reached into the box for another chocolate. 'When Penny and ourselves came back from the supermarket, she was gone. She left a note saying she had imposed on us long enough and thanking us for all we had done for her.'

'She told us everything,' said Ed. 'What happened to Don Diego and Mrs. Gaynor, and how you guys followed her to Ireland. The hassle you gave her.'

Sullivan doubted very much if she had told them everything, but said, 'We were just doing our job.'

'It wasn't your job to accuse of her of something she hadn't done,' Lily said.

Sullivan was still standing as he hadn't been asked to sit down. 'Do you mind if I ask you something?'

Ed shrugged. 'I do, but I guess you'll ask it anyway.'

'The money she borrowed from you. Did she pay it back?'

'It wasn't so much that she borrowed it,' said Lily. 'We were glad to give it to her.'

'But she will pay it back some day,' Ed added. 'She said so.'

'Did she say in the note where she was going?'

Lily shook her head. 'No. But she left us this as a little memento. It's the music box I sent to her soon after she was born. It belonged to one of our boys.'

Lily pulled the string and, when the music box began to play, she sang quietly as if she was singing to a child.

'*Oh dear, what can the matter be?*
Dear, dear, what can the matter be?
Oh dear, what can the matter be…'

'All right, all right,' said Sullivan, 'I got the message.'

'Are you sure you won't have one?' asked Lily, holding out the box of chocolates.

Sullivan ignored the sarcasm in her voice, saying, 'Thank you, but I have to go now.'

Back out on the street, Sullivan berated the other officer for letting the suspect get away.

'No one told me there were *two* young dames in there,' the officer protested. 'I thought there was only one.'

'Well, while you were down at the supermarket with the others, she high-tailed it out of here.'

Typical, thought Sullivan as he returned to his own car. A change of shift. A breakdown in communications. 'Hell,' he fumed, 'the lieutenant's going to love this. And Florentine. And Joe.'

THIRTY-TWO

George Washington looked down on Marguerite, but she didn't see him. She was walking past the arch that towers above the entrance to the park at Washington Square. The statues of Washington as general and President that adorn the arch were viewed with much interest by visitors to the Village. However, she didn't notice them. Nor did she notice the row of beautiful red brick period houses opposite, for her head was buried in a book – a small book that had taken its name from the square.

On her return from Ireland she had gone to the convent to see Mother Celine. The reverend mother had always been very good to her and she felt she owed her an explanation for her sudden departure. But when the time came she found it very difficult to put it into words.

A gentle soul, Mother Celine had spent a lifetime in the service of Christ. She was good; she was pure and somehow Marguerite felt she couldn't sully her purity with talk of rape. There were other things too. Things that had happened in Ireland. Things that had stirred other emotions in her mind.

Sensing there were things she couldn't bring herself to talk about, Mother Celine, gracious as ever, didn't press her about it. Instead, she showed great understanding when Marguerite said she needed more time to think about what she was going to do. In her own quiet way, Mother Celine wasn't accepting that she had left the fold, and very kindly arranged for somewhere she could stay, somewhere private where she could have the time she needed to think things over.

As Marguerite walked past Washington Square, she thought, how odd.

But it wasn't the square that was odd. Or the arch that was modelled on the Arc de Triomphe. It was the little book called *Washington Square* that she had found in a second-hand book shop. The odd thing, she discovered, was that it was about another young woman called Catherine. Poor Catherine, the author Henry James called her. Like her own mother, poor Catherine in the book had also hoped to get married but was prevented from doing so. What a coincidence, she thought.

Henry James, the book said, had been born in Washington Place and Marguerite looked up and around, wondering where the house was. Telling herself that she must find out, not now, but another time, she put the book back into her handbag and walked on towards Christopher Street. There she turned left and crossed the junction at Hudson Street. She glanced across the river towards the high-rise buildings of New Jersey before stopping to look at the church of St. Veronica on the other side of the street.

The brick façade of the church was faded and she wondered if, perhaps, someone some day might decide to paint it. Like the brick façades of the small terraced houses in Dublin where her mother's friend, Bridie once lived. But not bright red or brown like them. A wine colour might be appropriate. Burgundy, perhaps. And the arches above the three doors, cream. Yes, that would be a nice match. She allowed herself a fleeting smile at the thought, something she didn't do much these days and, crossing the street, glanced at the sign listing the Mass times. She knew well what the times were, but it was the words 'All are welcome' that somehow gave her comfort. Then she went in through the black iron gateway and, beyond the door beneath the third arch, climbed the wooden steps that took her up into the church.

Turning to her left, Marguerite put a match to two candles at the back of the church and watched them light in a reddish glow before taking a seat in the shadow of one of the green marble columns. The pews were of oak that was smooth and warm, and she slid off and on to her knees to pray for her intentions. As with all visitors, she had found that the church had a very colourful interior. The coloured panes in the high narrow windows complemented the colours in the tall arched murals above the altar that depicted the birth, crucifixion and resurrection of Christ. Even the Stations of the Cross lent colour to the walls. But when she closed her eyes and prayed, it was in the darkness of her mind that she sought to resolve her conflicting emotions.

The voice of the priest delivering his sermon made Marguerite open her eyes. High up and to the left of the altar, she could see him trying to relate to the few who had come to Mass. Her eyes then fell on the large, life-sized representation of Christ hanging on the Cross on one of the marble columns near the altar and she blessed herself and left.

Making her way back through the side streets, Marguerite felt secure among the terraced houses whose cast iron railings seemed to maintain a privacy that belonged to another age. They were so different from the sky-scrapers of Manhattan, and she could see why they had become home to many celebrated artists and writers. Having begun as a country village, Greenwich had also been an escape for city dwellers during the yellow fever epidemic of 1822. Or so the guide books said. How ironic, she thought, for now it had become a place of escape for her.

Climbing the stone steps to one of the houses, Marguerite picked up her post and made her way to an apartment on the second floor. It was at the request of Mother Celine that the priest allowed her to stay there, albeit on a temporary basis, so that she could have the time she needed to reflect. The apartment had been purchased by the diocese so that priests in transit – or even an occasional bishop – could stay a night or two at no cost to themselves. It was self-contained and furnished comfortably, though somewhat conservatively, in a way that reflected its purpose.

As Marguerite closed the door of the apartment behind her, she saw from the stamps that the two letters she had received were from Ireland. Dropping her handbag on the settee, she opened the first and found that it was from Susan saying she hadn't found any more letters from Shaunie to Catherine, but that she would continue looking. The second was from Martin O'Driscoll, and although he didn't have much to say, the fact that he had written to her pleased her. She was also pleased to find that he had enclosed a small black-and-white photograph of Catherine and Shaunie that his mother had asked him to send.

It's a bit faded, he wrote, *but she says it's a very good likeness of your mother and she thought you would like to have it. It was taken in the GAA club, of course. Where else?*

Any chance of you coming back? How about Christmas, or the New Year? You could stay at the Inn. We would be delighted to see you and you would be our guest.

Marguerite smiled as she wondered what Martin meant by 'We' when he said they would be delighted to see her. Somehow she thought he meant he. Or maybe that's what she wanted to think. It was a thought she knew she shouldn't be thinking, so she looked again at the photograph of Catherine and Shaunie. It was a little bit faded all right, but was one she would treasure. Then, in spite of her reservations, she curled up in one of the big leather armchairs and read Martin's letter again.

'God works in mysterious ways,' said Mother Celine.

'How do you mean?' Sullivan asked her.

'We prayed that Sister Mary would return.'

'And did she?'

'No, but she sent us a cheque – a donation to help feed the needy.'

'So she didn't come back after all,' said Florentine.

'No, but she's with us in spirit and in our prayers.'

Florentine sighed. 'We just wanted to talk to her. Any idea where she is?'

When Mother Celine didn't respond, Sullivan said, 'You do realise it's an offence to withhold information that might help us in our inquiries?'

Godly and genteel as Mother Celine was, she wasn't above bending the truth when it came to protecting her flock. On a previous occasion she had told the detectives Sister Mary had just spent one night there and then left, a shrug of the shoulders indicating that she didn't know where she had gone. In doing so she hadn't been entirely truthful. By shepherding her wayward sister to a safe haven, she was hopeful that by giving her a time of contemplation she would change her mind. She regarded her denial, if it was a denial, as nothing more than a white lie, told in obedience to a higher authority. However, the police were back and if, as they were saying, it was an offence to withhold information she now feared the consequences of misleading them again. Opening a drawer in her desk, she took out a letter and told them, 'She sent me a note with the cheque. Her address is on it. Greenwich Village I think. Yes, there it is.'

Florentine looked at the letter. 'The West Village. Got it.'

A short time later, the two detectives were driving along Washington Square. At the north-west corner a group of tourists were hanging on to every word their guide was saying.

'Bet he's telling them this used to be Potter's Field,' mused Florentine.

'Potter's Field?' said Sullivan. 'Never heard of it.'

'This is where they used to give offenders the chop.'

'You mean public executions?'

'Exactly. See that big tree? That was the hanging tree. Or so they say.'

They took a left through the village whose cafés, shops and pubs offered a way of life that no other part of New York could offer.

'You know, I love this place,' Florentine said. 'It's so different.'

'Yeah, I know what you mean.' Sullivan drew his hand down across his mouth and chin. 'Don't suppose we've time for a beer?'

'Just as soon as we find this address.' They were driving down Barrow Street now and Florentine added, 'If this dame's still living here, we got to pin her down. Can't have Joe coming over for nothing.'

They located the address farther down Barrow Street. It was an old red building not far from the church of St. Veronica. They parked a short distance away and Sullivan went to a nearby deli where he got two hot dogs, to which he added liberal helpings of mustard and ketchup, and two bottles of beer to wash them down. 'Well?' he asked when he returned, 'any sign?'

Florentine shook his head. He took a large bite of his hot dog and Sullivan waited until he had reduced it to malleable proportions. 'So what do we call this dame now – Marguerite, Katie or Sister Mary?'

Florentine took a long swig of beer. 'As far as we're concerned, she's Marguerite.'

They sat in silence for a while, too busy eating to say anything more. Then Florentine scrunched up his wrapping paper, saying, 'I hate this stuff, it makes a fucking mess of the car.'

'Here, give it to me,' Sullivan said. 'I'll get rid of it.'

However, Florentine had now leaned forward to peer through the windscreen. 'Talk of the devil,' he exclaimed. 'That's her.'

They watched as Marguerite came down he steps and walked briskly along the street.

'Okay, Sully,' said Florentine, 'off you go, and whatever you do, don't lose her.'

It seemed to Joe that his friends in the NYPD would never ring. He hadn't been to New York before but a colleague who had been there told him what to expect. He also discovered that his passport was out of date, but after making a phone call to the Department of Foreign Affairs he was quickly provided with a new one. The US Embassy also fast-tracked a visa for him, and he was ready to go by the time the phone call came.

While Sullivan continued the stakeout at Marguerite's apartment, Florentine collected Joe at the airport and after helping him check into his hotel, drove him straight to Greenwich Village. 'Time for sight-seeing later,' Joe told himself and, while he looked up in awe at the skyscrapers of Manhattan, his mind was on the business at hand – a briefing for the two officers, then his interview with Marguerite.

There was a look of shock and disbelief on Marguerite's face when she opened the door of her apartment and saw the three of them standing there.

Florentine smiled. 'Hi Marguerite. Long time no see!'

'What do you want?'

'Joe here has come all the way from Ireland. He wants to talk to you.'

'What about?'

'About your friend Maudie.'

'Hardly a friend. She's dead. But I suppose you know that?'

'As it so happens, we do.'

Florentine was beginning to lose patience. 'Are you going to let us in? Or would you would rather talk to us down town.'

Reluctantly, Marguerite stepped aside and showed them into the sitting-room. There she seated herself in one of the big leather armchairs, drew her feet up underneath her, and waited for them to be seated, but they remained standing.

'You remember Joe, don't you?' Florentine walked around the room, admiring its plush furnishings and thinking it was a far cry from the sparsely furnished rooms at the convent. 'He's a superintendent now. Gone up in the world since we last met, but then, I guess, so have you.'

When Marguerite ignored him, he came over and, placing both hands on the arms of her chair, looked her straight in the eye. 'What made you think you would get away with it? Huh? I mean, do it once and you might. Do it a second time, and you're pushing your luck. But a third time. No way! We know you did it, and we're going to nail you for it.'

Marguerite pulled back from him. 'I don't know what you're talking about.'

'Look, Marguerite,' Joe said, 'this is a very grave matter.'

'And it's time you gave us some answers,' Florentine declared. 'We're talking about a homicide for God's sake.'

'Homicide?' Marguerite looked up, startled. 'What homicide?'

'Maudie's. Who else?'

'But Maudie's death was an accident!'

'You say accident. We say homicide.'

'Murder,' said Joe. "That's what we call it back in Ireland. Murder.'

'I didn't murder Maudie,' Marguerite declared. 'I told you, it was an accident.'

Florentine turned away, but in a manner that suggested he wouldn't leave it long, and Joe took over.

'Now, Marguerite,' he said, 'I think it would be in your own interests to come clean with us. You wanted the farm, and when you didn't get it you decided Maudie wasn't going to get it either.'

'So you took the law into your own hands,' added Florentine.

'That's not true. All I wanted was for Maudie and her brothers to accept that I was Shaunie's daughter. I told them, I didn't want the farm. So Mr. Murphy suggested I go to Cork and answer all those terrible allegations they were making about me. Tell them my side of things.'

'So you convinced them you were genuine?' said Joe.

'I think so, yes. I wanted to confront them and tell them the allegations weren't true.'

'But you went back to see Maudie on her own. Why did you do that?'

'She was prepared to accept me and asked me to go and see her before I returned to New York. She wanted to apologise for the awful things her brothers had said about me.'

Joe moved aside and Florentine leaned close so that he was looking her straight in the eye again. 'You mean you wanted to see the look on her face when you told her you were going to take the farm from her?'

'No. I told her I didn't want the farm. How many times do I have to tell you?'

Florentine leaned even closer so that they were eyeball to eyeball. 'You wanted to see the look on her face when you told her you were going to throw her out?'

'No. It wasn't like that.'

Florentine backed off and Joe took over again. He was looking into her eyes now and was getting serious in a way she had never seen before. 'When you knocked on the front door and there was no reply, you went around the back.'

'Yes.'

'You spotted Maudie going into the stable.'

'No.'

'And at that precise moment you saw the opportunity for revenge.'

'No!'

'Her brothers had locked Shaunie in, so you decided to lock her in.'

'No!'

'You untied the cord on the top part of the door and slammed the bottom part shut. Isn't that what happened? Revenge for what had they had done to Shaunie. Revenge for all the things that had happened to you.'

'No, no. How could you say such a thing?'

Joe was still leaning over her, pressing home his argument. 'You knew that with Maudie out of the way, it would be easier for you to inherit the farm. Isn't that right?'

'No, it isn't right. I had nothing to do with Maudie's death. It was an accident.'

Ignoring her reply, Joe continued, 'It wasn't the wind that untied that door. It was you, wasn't it?'

'No, it was the wind.'

'The wind doesn't untie knots, Marguerite. It was you. We know it was you.'

Before she could answer, Florentine stepped in again. 'And it wasn't the first time you took the law into your own hands, was it? As Don Diego's adopted daughter, you took revenge on him because he had abused you.'

'That's not true. It was self-defence.'

'Then you took revenge on Mrs. Gaynor because you believed she had swapped you at birth and left you with an abusive father.'

'No. She jumped. I had nothing to do with it.'

'And finally, you took your revenge on Maudie because of all that had happened, and because you wanted the farm.'

'That's not true.'

Sullivan, who had remained silent stepped in. 'If that's not true, then what is? That you were just pretending to be Katie?'

'Stop. You're twisting things.'

'Mrs. Gaynor put it into your scheming little head that she might have made a mistake. She told you Katie's people were rich farmers and that if you pretended to be her, you might have an inheritance waiting for you in Ireland. Mrs. Gaynor was terminally ill and wanted to die back in Ireland. But you wanted it all for yourself, so you chucked her overboard.'

'That's ridiculous.' She looked pleadingly at Joe, but he didn't respond. 'Anyway, you can't have it both ways.'

Sullivan was staring into her eyes now. 'So which way was it? You tell us.'

'There's nothing more to tell. Everything happened the way I said it did.'

'Well we don't believe you,' Sullivan went on. 'You saw the opportunity to get rich quick. So you got rid of Mrs. Gaynor. Then you decided to get rid of Maudie.'

'You wanted it all for yourself,' said Joe, 'so you locked her in, just the way her brothers locked Shaunie in. But they let Shaunie out. You left Maudie to die.'

Marguerite got up and stamped her foot on the floor. 'No, no, no. I've told you a hundred times. That's not what happened.' She went over to the door and opened it. 'Now get out. I won't answer any more questions unless my lawyer is present.'

'We may need a blood test,' said Florentine as they filed out.

'Go whistle for it!'

'We can get a court order.'

'Yeah, do that.'

'One more thing,' said Joe. 'If you do come to Ireland to claim the farm, I'll be waiting for you.'

'Don't hold your breath.'

'I'll want to talk to you again.'

'And what makes you think I'll want to talk to you?' Marguerite cocked her head and smirked. 'I thought you were a nice guy – but you're just as bad as those other two jerks.'

With that, she slammed the door shut behind them.

When they returned to Manhattan, Florentine and Sullivan took their visitor to a bar to talk matters over.

'What will it be, Joe?' Sullivan asked.

'I don't suppose there's any point in asking for a pint?'

Florentine smiled. 'You're in the Big Apple now – you'll have a shot.'

Sullivan ordered three shots of bourbon.

'If you do get her to give a blood sample,' said Joe, 'whose blood are you going to match it with?'

'Good question,' Sullivan replied. 'At first we thought Lily might do it seeing as she's a blood relative, but Ed and herself are satisfied she's Katie. In fact they're very happy about it. They won't even contemplate the possibility that she might not be.'

'Could you not apply for a court order?'

Florentine shook his head. 'No point.'

'How come?'

'Well, this blood testing seems to be a lot more complicated than we thought. According to the guys in forensics, it's the blood of the parents and child that have to be tested.'

Joe nodded. 'Pity Shaunie didn't hang on a bit longer.'

'You would think a test of the brothers' blood would give us the answer?' said Sullivan. 'I mean, it must be the same as Shaunie's.'

'I don't know,' said Joe. 'Even if it is, I doubt if they would co-operate either. They wouldn't want to take the chance – in case she *is* Shaunie's daughter.'

'In the meantime,' said Florentine, 'we may be able to get her for a passport violation.'

Joe raised his glass. 'I'll drink to that.'

They touched glasses, then Florentine and Sullivan took Joe on a tour of the bars of Manhattan.

THIRTY-THREE

For a long time after the detectives left, Marguerite sat in the armchair, her feet tucked in beside her, her face buried in her hand. The rough manner in which they had treated her and the allegations they had made against her, had left her in a state of shock. Her brain was numb and she was unable to move, unable to think. How long she sat there she did not know. Time had no meaning. Nor had the jumble of thoughts that came and went through the darkness of her mind. It was only time, however, that could thaw the numbness of her brain and eventually she managed to raise her head. She tried to focus, to calm herself, compose herself, to think clearly. They had said terrible things to her, awful things, and she wondered what to do, how to respond.

As on other occasions, it was the dark recesses of a church that offered her a place of refuge, a place to pray and a place to think. Pulling on her coat, she made her way back to St. Veronica's. Sliding in beside one of the smooth granite pillars, she sat in its shadow and once again wondered what to do. She began to tremble and pulled her coat around her although she wasn't cold. After a while she dropped forward to her knees and clasped her hands to pray. Before doing so she looked up at the life-sized image of Christ before the altar, then closed her eyes and prayed for guidance.

Before leaving, she lit a candle for a special intention. Not one of the intentions she had prayed for before, but a new one. For she now knew what she was going to do; how she was going to respond. Normally she would have lit the candle first and then prayed. This time it was the other way round, but it didn't matter. Nothing seemed to matter – except that special intention.

A few days later the priest from St. Veronica's called to tell Marguerite he would be needing the apartment for a visiting bishop, so she packed her things into her small leather suitcase and got a bus over to New Jersey. Lily and Ed were delighted to see her and invited her to stay with them for Christmas. Penny, they said, was coming too and it would be a nice family get-together.

Shortly before Christmas, Marguerite received a letter that had been redirected from the apartment in the Village. It was from Mr. Murphy and it gave her the best possible Christmas present she could have wished for.

You will be happy to hear, he wrote, that your blood test has proved positive. According to the results, the blood groups of Shaunie and yourself have a common antigen. This means that paternity is not excluded, or to put it another way, that he could have been your father. It does not prove that he was your father, just that he could have been. However, it is very important, for if Shaunie's blood did not have an antigen possessed by you, we would not, in the absence of your mother's group, have been able to draw any conclusion.

It must be a source of great satisfaction to you that Shaunie and Maudie were both prepared to accept you as his daughter. It's just a pity they died before they could officially do so, and it is unlikely, even with this positive test, that their brothers will. That being said, there is another way in which you can obtain the recognition you desire.

Now that we have a positive blood test, and a substantial amount of documentation to support your claim, you could apply for a Declaration of Paternity. Such a claim would be unusual in that you are now an adult, but on the basis of what I know of your case, I would be confident that you would be granted such a declaration and then it would it official, i.e. that you are Shaunie's daughter. Again, let me congratulate you on the result of your blood test and assure you that I will be happy to take your instructions in this matter. Yours etc...

Seeing the tears that had welled up in Marguerite's eyes, Lily asked, 'Bad news?'

'On the contrary,' she replied, handing her the letter. 'It's great news.'

As the others edge closer to Lily to look at the letter, she put on her glasses and read it aloud. 'A Declaration of Paternity,' she added. 'That would be wonderful. Congratulations.'

Ed and Penny who were a bit more mobile than Lily, got up and threw their arms around Marguerite, and congratulated her too.

Marguerite sat down, daubed her tears and read the letter to herself again.

'Well I haven't got the declaration yet,' she said, 'but he seems confident that I would get it. And he hasn't used a word of Latin.'

'How do you mean?' asked Ed.

'Just that Mr. Murphy sometimes uses words of Latin. Susan and I had to look up the dictionary to find the meaning of some of them.'

'Why would he use words of Latin?' asked Lily.

'You work in a lawyer's office, Penny,' said Ed. 'What do you think.'

Penny shrugged, 'Beats me but they all do.'

'It's probably traditional in Ireland,' said Lily. 'Like the way they wear wigs and gowns.'

Marguerite was incredulous. 'Wigs and gowns? You must be kidding!'

Lily smiled. 'No, I'm serious. They wear wigs and gowns in court – black gowns.'

'I think,' said Ed, 'it goes back to the time in England when one of their kings or queens died and the legal profession wore black as a sign of mourning.'

'And the wigs?' asked Penny.

'They're white,' Ed added. 'Or off-white. The judges wear them too. Why, I don't know.'

'The courthouses are old too,' Lily said. 'Some of them are a hundred years old or more, and they usually have stone steps leading up to them and huge stone pillars at the entrance.'

Marguerite smiled. 'Sounds Grecian to me.'

'Far from it,' Ed said. 'They're very Irish – or maybe even British, they're so old.'

So heartened was Marguerite by Mr. Murphy's letter that in spite of her interrogation by the detectives, she enjoyed Christmas. She and Penny did much of the baking and other preparations for the Christmas dinner. They also served the dinner so that Lily and Ed could take it easy. Ed, however, insisted on doing the carving.

During the course of the dinner, the conversation ranged over inconsequential things such as Christmas shopping. Ed asked Penny how her work was going, but if he was hoping she would tell them about some of the cases she had typed up, he was due for a disappointment.

'Dad,' she said. 'You know I can't talk about things like that.'

Ed just smiled and nodded. Of course he knew, so Lily asked Marguerite to tell them more about Susan and James and their two boys.

It wasn't until they had adjourned to the sitting room and exchanged presents that Ed ventured to raise more serious matters with Marguerite. He had poured a drink for all of them except Lily, who had opened a box of chocolates.

'Susan told us about Maudie,' he said. 'That was a very brave thing you did.'

Marguerite shrugged. 'It was nothing.'

'That's not what the papers said,' Lily countered. 'Susan sent us over the cuttings.'

'I've just been reading them,' added Penny. 'You were great. They should have given you a medal.'

Marguerite gave a wry smile. 'Unfortunately her brothers don't see it that way,'

'So you didn't get on too well with them,' said Ed.

'I guess you could say that. Did Susan not tell you?'

'She did,' Lily said, 'but there's only so much you can say in a letter.'

Lily offered the others a chocolate but they declined, and she took one for herself.

'Maudie accepted me before she passed away,' Marguerite continued, 'but her brothers never did – not really. They're afraid I might try to inherit the farm.'

'You should inherit it,' Lily asserted. 'You're Shaunie's daughter, aren't you? – the blood test proves it.'

'I would go for it if I was you,' said Penny.

Ed agreed. 'So would I. Put some manners on those guys.'

'They said some awful things about me alright,' Marguerite said. 'I told them I didn't want the farm, but that wasn't good enough for them. They've tried to blacken my name, discredit me in every way they could. You wouldn't believe the things they said about me.'

'Like what?' asked Lily.

'Well, first they said I was wanted here for the murder of Don Diego and Mrs. Gaynor.'

'My God!' Ed went over to the cabinet and poured a highball for Marguerite, then one for himself.

Penny who was drinking a gin and tonic almost choked and had to cough to try and recover.

Lily's mouth was already open as she was about to put another chocolate in it, and it stayed open, the hand holding the chocolate suspended a short distance away.

'Now they've accused me of murdering Maudie,'

'Murdering Maudie?' Lily put the chocolate back in the box. 'That's ridiculous.'

'Sure you could have been trampled to death yourself,' said Ed.

'But how could they think such a thing?' asked Penny.

'They're saying I locked her in – in revenge for what they did to Shaunie.'

'Well in that case,' said Lily, 'I would make sure they didn't get one acre of that farm.'

'Me too,' said Penny.

'So, why don't you go for it?' urged Ed.

'If it's money you're worried about,' Lily assured her, 'we can stake you for another flight to Ireland.'

'I'm afraid there would be more than that involved.'

'You mean, legal fees?' asked Ed.

'Exactly.'

'Then talk to Mr Murphy,' said Lily. 'Ask him what it would cost.'

'And you'd better not leave it too long,' Penny warned. 'Sometimes there's a time limit on these things.'

Marguerite smiled. 'Okay, I'll think about it.'

In fact, Marguerite had been thinking about it ever since the visit from the detectives, and when the New Year celebrations were over and Penny had left, she sat down and wrote to Mr. Murphy. Having told him how pleased she was to hear about the blood test, she informed him of the new allegation that had been made against her.

Such a scurrilous accusation, she wrote, *could have been made by no one else but Maudie's brothers and for no other purpose than to discredit me, thus removing any possibility that I might inherit the farm. Their sole objective since the time they were young was to ensure that the farm stayed in what they saw as their family. It was their motivation in locking Shaunie in the shed on the day of his wedding. It was their motivation in raising the allegations that were made against me here in the US. And because of those allegations they found it convenient to suggest that I might have been responsible for Maudie's death. Even when I went to Cork and confronted them they didn't really accept that the allegations were untrue. Nor did they accept that I was Shaunie's daughter, simply because they didn't want to accept it. For some reason best known to themselves they didn't accept my word that I didn't want the farm. I gave my word to Maudie that I didn't want it. Maudie accepted it; they didn't. Had they done so I would not be taking the action I am now proposing to take.*

Because of their malevolence in this matter and after much consideration, I am now asking you to lodge a claim on my behalf, asking the courts to recognise me as Shaunie's daughter and as such, entitled to inherit the farm. I hasten to add that it was never my intention to take this course of action, but it is now a matter of principle. Maudie's brothers have driven me to it.

In asking you to take instructions in this respect, I am concerned to know what fees might be involved. You seem confident that I would win my case, but because of my circumstances I would need to know that I could afford it.

When Mr. Murphy replied, he said he was shocked to learn of the allegation that the detectives had made against her.

Had they any evidence to support the allegation they surely would have put it to you. Clearly they have not. Therefore, I would advise you not to speak to them again unless you are accompanied by a lawyer.

He then went on to deal with some of the matters she had raised in her letter.

With regard to the Declaration of Paternity, there are certain forms to be filled in, and I will then apply to have your application listed.

With regard to your instructions to proceed with a claim to inherit the farm, if and when the Declaration of Paternity is granted, we will have to prove that Shaunie failed in his moral duty to make proper provision for you. That may seem harsh to you but we will, in effect, be challenging his will. I must advise you that we may not get everything we ask for. However, it is my opinion that we will get some of it.

The hearing in each case should not take more than a day or two and will be heard in camera, i.e. in private, so you need have no fears that any of allegations made will be aired in public.

Normally, the wheels of justice turn slowly in Ireland, but we should get an early enough hearing for the first application and there is a six-month time limit for the second, so you should make arrangements to return to Ireland as you will be required to be present for both. Yours etc.

When Marguerite had read the letter to Lily and Ed, she asked, 'Well, what do you think?'

'I think you should go for it,' said Lily.

' So do I, said Ed.

'It's the cost that's worrying me,' Marguerite confessed. 'Mr. Murphy didn't really say what it would cost.'

'If the hearings only take a day or two,' Ed reasoned, 'it can't be that expensive. And wouldn't the seven and a half grand Maudie gave you go a long way towards it."

Marguerite nodded. 'I suppose it would, but I was planning to repay you the five grand you lent me out of that, or what I spent of it. Apart from the air fares I didn't spend much of it.'

'Well then hold on to it' said Lily.

'That should leave you the guts of ten grand,' Ed added. 'Surely that would cover it.'

'And there's no hurry paying us back,' Lily assured her.

Marguerite hesitated. They had been very good to her and she didn't want them to think she was taking advantage of them.

'Anyway,' Ed added, ' Mr. Murphy thinks you'll win. So you'll be well able to pay for it.'

Marguerite smiled. 'Thanks. You're very good. But I will pay you back. I promise.'

Unknown to Lily and Ed, there was something else troubling Marguerite. As a nun, she had taken a vow of poverty. That was why she had put Maudie's money aside. Now she was proposing to claim the farm. That would be an inheritance and likewise contrary to her vow of poverty. However, as she wrestled with her conscience, she consoled herself with the thought that it was, as she had told Mr. Murphy, a matter of principle. She would decide later, if and when she got the farm, what she would do with it.

Of more immediate concern was the fact that she didn't have a passport. The police had taken the one she had used for her last visit to Ireland. How, she wondered, was she going to get another one. There was no way the police would agree to give the passport back. That meant she would have to apply for a new one using another name. But whose? She didn't know where Nora Diego now lived and even if she did, she knew Nora wouldn't assist her in any way. That left her with only one option.

She rooted out the papers Mrs. Gaynor had given her, among them the travel documents that had been issued for Brigid Mary. She had only given them a cursory glance at the time and was pleased to see that her recollection was correct. They included the baby passport issued to Brigid Mary by the Department of External Affairs in Dublin, her visa and a copy of her birth certificate. She didn't like the thought of taking on the name of Brigid Mary, but desperate situations required desperate measures, and she was now desperate.

THIRTY-FOUR

Dan O'Sullivan had predicted that Marguerite might apply for a passport in the name of Brigid Mary but, fortunately for her, his son had not taken any action to block it and she managed to get it in time to return to Ireland for the paternity hearing.

Spring, she found, had brought a splash of colour to the Irish countryside. Daffodils were nodding in a breeze that still carried the chilly breath of winter, but the hedgerows were greening and the small birds were singing.

In contrast, the courthouse turned out to be old and uninviting.

At first Marguerite thought, she would be going to Dublin for the hearing, but Mr. Murphy told her that because Shaunie had been living in Co. Cork, it would have to be held in the local District Court.

Then I thought it would be in Mitchelstown, she would tell Lily and Ed, *but for some reason it was held in Fermoy, a small town on the banks of the River Blackwater. You said most of the courthouses in Ireland were very old. Well, this one was no exception, Someone told me it was built in 1805, about the same time as the White House. Imagine!*

When they arrived, Marguerite, accompanied by James and Susan, consulted quietly with Mr. Murphy on one side of the entrance. On the other side, Mick and Francie consulted with Mr. Sweeney.

Lizzie was there too, Marguerite wrote, *but as it was a family court, she was not allowed in. Nor, unfortunately, were James and Susan. Even Mick and Francie had to wait until the judge agreed that they could attend.*

I guess I was a bit apprehensive before going in, but Mr. Murphy told me that because it was a family court, it would be very informal. Apparently wigs and gowns are dispensed with at such courts so as to make them less intimidating when children are involved, although here I was, an adult!

Marguerite went on to say she wished Martin could have been there but added, *Maybe it's just as well as there are certain things I wouldn't want him to hear. In any event, he wouldn't have been allowed in and I wouldn't want him hanging around the courthouse all day when he has the cattle to look after.*

Joe, the Irish cop I told you about, was waiting outside, no doubt expecting to be called as a witness. As I went in he smirked at me in a way that said, 'it's all going to come out now' and when the case opened, I feared that he was right and that all the dirt would be dished up at me again.

The two sides sat as far away from one another as they could as if to emphasise their differences, yet the high-ceilinged room was full of echoes and they knew they were near enough to be heard unless they spoke in whispers.

I glanced over and I could see Mick and Francie were smiling too, Marguerite continued. *With Joe as their star witness I reckoned they were confident they could discredit me with their allegations, and when Mr. Sweeney got to his feet to address the judge I thought my case was going to be over before it could even begin.*

'There are certain matters I wish to raise,' he said, and turning to me in what I thought was a very pointed manner, added, 'matters which bear directly on the credibility of the applicant and on her bona fides *in seeking this declaration.'*

However, Mr. Murphy objected. He said that because of the rancorous attitude that had been adopted by Mick and Francie, certain allegations had been made against me that were totally unfounded and not pertinent to the case.

Fortunately, the judge agreed. He told Mr. Sweeney he would only allow matters of an evidential nature to be introduced and if his clients attempted to rely on rumour or innuendo or allegations not supported by evidence, it could greatly harm their case. As a result, Joe was not called to give evidence about the allegations they had levelled against me and for that I was very thankful.

When it came to proving that I was Shaunie's daughter, Marguerite continued, *I thought Mr. Murphy argued my case very well. As you know, the blood test showed that Shaunie could have been my father, and building on that he listed all the other things in my favour, including Mrs. Gaynor's belief that she had given me away by mistake, Catherine's letters and Shaunie's acceptance of me as his daughter shortly before he died.*

However, Mr.Sweeney said there was one crucial flaw in my claim – that Mrs. Gaynor had said she believed she had given the wrong baby to the Diegos, not that she had actually done so. 'For all we know,' he declared with a wave of his hand towards me, 'the woman who stands before the court claiming to be Shaunie's daughter, is Brigid Mary.' Then, to add insult to injury he told the judge the blood test merely showed that Shaunie – together with any one of thousands of other men –could have been my father. As for Shaunie's acceptance of me as his daughter, he claimed that Shaunie was a sick man, that he was delusional and didn't know what he was doing.

I found these statements very hurtful. Calling me a phoney was one thing, but accusing a dead man – a man who couldn't defend himself – of being delusional was hitting below the belt. In fact, I found Shaunie to be very lucid. He knew exactly what he was saying and he had no difficulty in recalling what had happened to him and Catherine.

At the end of the day, however, it made no difference. After listening to all the arguments for and against, the judge ruled that on the balance of probabilities I was Shaunie's daughter – his words, not mine! Apparently that is all that is required in this kind of application, and he granted me the Declaration of Paternity.'

As the judge left the bench Mick and Francie made their way out, scowling and muttering about the outcome. Marguerite, on the other hand, was elated. She hugged James and Susan. She hugged Mr. Murphy and then she found someone else to hug. To her delight she found Martin waiting for her.

'I can't believe it she cried, throwing her arms around his neck, 'The judge said it – I *am* Shaunie's daughter.'

Martin was smiling and as she released him he whispered, 'Congratulations. I'm really pleased for you.'

'Thanks,' she replied. 'But what are you doing here? I didn't expect to see you.'

'I just came to see how you were getting on. I didn't know the case would be over so soon.'

Mr. Murphy, who was standing nearby lighting his pipe, said, 'It's not over yet. We've a long way to go, and maybe the hardest bit has yet to come.'

'I don't care,' Marguerite exclaimed. 'I don't care.'

'Why don't you stop off at the Cumán Inn,' Martin suggested. 'It's on the way. My mother will be dying to hear all about it. You can tell her yourself.'

Marguerite gave a questioning look at Susan, who said, 'Ok, but we can't stop for long.'

'Maybe long enough for a little tincture to celebrate?' Martin added.

Susan glanced at James. 'Oh, I don't know about that. We have to be getting back to Tipperary. But we will stop off for a minute. Thanks.'

'Ok then, that's settled. Marguerite, you can come with me if you like.'

She smiled. 'It's not Marguerite. From now on you can call me Katie.' Turning to the others she added, 'You all can. It's official! I'm Katie.'

To Mr. Murphy's obvious embarrassment, she hugged him again, saying, 'Thank you,' but he just chuckled and with a wave of his hand, ambled to his car.

'Well Katie,' said Martin as they left Fermoy. 'You must be very pleased.'

'Very.' She wiped a tear from her eye. 'I thought the day would never come. First the cops. Then Maudie's brothers. They said some awful things about me. God-damned awful.'

'Well, it's done The court says you're Shaunie's daughter and that's it.'

'I really meant it you know, when I said all I wanted was recognition, but Mick just wouldn't accept my word for it. He wouldn' accept me for who I was. Him and Francie. Shaunie was right – they're a pair of gobshites.'

Martin smiled. 'That's not a word you'll hear in America! They're thick. And they're greedy. All they want is to hold on to the family farm.'

'Well I'm family now,' Katie asserted. 'I'm Shaunie's daughter, his next-of-kin. We'll see how they like that when I come back to court looking for the farm.'

She lay back and closed her eyes and after a while began to sing quietly to herself.

'What's that?' Martin asked.

'Just a little thing my mother used to sing to me when I was a baby. It's called the Monkey Song.'

'How does it go?'

She looked across at him, saying, 'You wouldn't understand it. It's just a piece of nonsense – a lullabye.'

Martin smiled, 'Try me.'

'Okay – if you insist...' Closing her eyes again, she sang it in the same lilting way Catherine had sung it in the mother and baby home.'

'What does it mean?' he asked.

'I told you, you wouldn't understand it. It means...

'*I wish I lived in monkey land*
The land where I was born
I monkey kissed me on the cheek
And waved good bye to all...'

'Well, you can say goodbye to them all now,' said Martin. 'And I know you're not saying this is monkey land, but when you get the farm I hope you'll come and live here.'

Closing her hand on his, which was on the gear lever, she replied, 'We'll see.'

Susan didn't tell Katie why she couldn't stop long at the Cumán Inn as she wanted it to be a surprise. In anticipation of a successful outcome to her application, she had made a provisional booking in a restaurant in Tipperary town. There they celebrated her success over dinner. And it was a family affair in the true sense of the word, for Katie was now officially a member of the family. They also opened a bottle of champagne, raised their glasses and wished for the same success when she claimed the farm.

THIRTY-FIVE

Because of the time limit involved, and the need to have consultations with her legal representatives, Katie stayed on. Over the next couple of months she had several meetings with Mr. Murphy, and also met the barrister who was to present her case in court. In between meetings she waited patiently for news of the hearing, and it seemed to her that the wheels of justice were indeed turning slowly.

However, the wheels were in fact turning quite quickly. Mr. Murphy had done his homework, and she felt a great sense of relief when, not long after their last meeting, he contacted her to tell her that the date for the hearing had been set.

This time, she learned, her case was being held in Cork city and loyal as ever, James and Susan drove her there. The countryside was in full bloom. Along the hedgerows the whitethorn bushes were laden with blossoms and the long grass was beginning to shine in the sun of summer. Katie remarked that she had never seen the hedges so white or the grass so green, but it was only a passing thought as her mind was on the case that awaited her.

Unlike the courthouse in Fermoy, she found that the one in Cork was a huge building. It had many stone steps leading up to it, and the entrance was surrounded by massive stone pillars. To her surprise, she also discovered that it was in a street with an American name -Washington Street.

For longer than anyone could remember the giant pillars had imposed a sense of foreboding on those who had climbed the steps, and demanded a stony silence as they went into the courthouse to await their fate.

The same sense of foreboding was felt by many of those who were now engaged in huddled conversation with bewigged counsel in the great hall beyond the entrance. However, Katie was reassured by her barrister. As they climbed the stairs to the room where her claim was to be heard, he said he still believed she had a good case.

My claim is being held in private, she told Lily and Ed, *but it's a much more formal affair than the last one. The judge wears a wig and gown. So do the barristers, and they're the ones who do the talking, not the solicitors. Mick and Francie are there as 'interested parties'. However, they 're only interested in getting the farm for themselves.*

Writing at the end of the first day, she continued, *My lawyer argued that Shaunie's brothers had, in effect, kidnapped him to make sure he couldn't get married. As a result, I had suffered untold misery and abuse and ended up destitute on the streets of New York. When Shaunie learned that I was alive, he had accepted me for who I was but had failed in his moral duty to make proper provision for me. Now as his daughter – certified as such by my Declaration of Paternity – it was I who should inherit the farm, not the brothers.*

Their lawyer contended that Shaunie saw it as his moral duty to provide for the woman who had looked after him all his life. Maudie had done all the cooking and all the housework and cared for him until his dying day. It was only natural, therefore, that he should leave everything to her.

Difficult as it is for me to write it, their lawyer also said it was inconceivable that Shaunie would change his will at the last moment for a complete stranger who had turned up on his doorstep claiming to be his long lost daughter. And now that Maudie was dead, the brothers should inherit the farm, not me.

The arguments took many twists and turns, and to tell the truth I sometimes found it difficult to follow them as they were of a very legal nature. The judge listened carefully to everything that was said and asked many questions. I listened carefully to everythng he said, trying to figure out if he was leaning towards my side or theirs, and I was dying to hear his decision. However, he said he would consider the issues overnight and give his decision tomorrow. Fingers crossed!

Katie put the letter aside, telling herself she would finish it when she heard the result.

When the hearing resumed the following morning, the judge had further discussions with the two barristers, then annouced that he would give his decision at two o'clock.

I thought two o'clock would never come, Katie wrote. *We all took our places in the courtroom some time before that, and when the judge came in to give his decision you could have heard a pin drop.*

I can't remember everything he said, nor could I understand it all. But he rubbished the brothers' claim that what they had done was a boyish prank. As a result of their actions, he said, Catherine had been deprived of her husband and I had been deprived of my father. In consequence, I had also suffered socially, sexually and financially.

When I heard that, I was overcome with emotion and had to fight hard to hold back the tears. This judge of a higher court was also believing my story. Accepting what had happened to Catherine. Accepting what had happened to me. Reprimanding the brothers for what they had done and reminding them of the consequences.

I was overjoyed, and I felt sure I was going to be awarded the farm. Then the judge veered off in a different direction. He started talking about the law of succession under which the farm would pass to the brothers on Maudie's death. I was confused. Now I thought, they're going to be awarded the farm. However, I needn't have worried, for the judge delivered what Mr. Murphy called the judgment of Solomon.

He ruled that the brothers should get a portion of the farm – mainly the good grazing land – to be disposed of as they wished, together with a sum of money which he calculated would have been due to Maudie for helping Shaunie run the farm and look after him all those years. I didn't think they deserved anything, but I suppose Maudie did. And then came the good bit. All other monies and investments, he ruled, should come to me, including – wait for it! – the house and the remainder of the farm, including the hills at the back and the lake.

I couldn't believe my ears. I just burst into tears and even though I couldn't see the judge, I was aware of him waiting for me to stop. He didn't hurry me or ask me to be quiet. He was very patient and considerate, and when

I had wiped away my tears and pulled myself together, he asked, 'Who has the keys to the house?'

The other lawyer consulted Mr. Sweeney. He consulted Mick who said, 'I have.'

'Very well,' said the judge, ' you can hand them over to Katie.' He then smiled at me, and said, 'I'm sure you'll want to do some spring cleaning before you move in.'

I nodded but I couldn't answer him, I was so overcome. What happened then seems like a blur. I remember the judge gathering up his papers and leaving the bench, and Mr. Murphy and the barrister turning to congratulate me. But even then I couldn't take it all in. I couldn't believe it. I had won. For a moment it was bedlam. We were all shaking hands with one another, and in the middle of it all, I remember looking across at Mick's side. Needless to say, there were no handshakes there.

When we got out to the front steps, they were still standing there talking to Mr. Sweeney, so I went over to Mick and said, 'I told you I didn't want the farm, but you wouldn't believe me. Well now you can have it.' Mick stood back, his hands on the sides of his big stomach, wondering if things were going to fall his way after all. Francie puckered his brow in the same stupid way he always does when he doesn't understand something. Lizzie didn't understand either, but she was the first to speak. 'You mean...?' she said.

'I mean,' I said, 'if you want the house and the rest of the land, you can buy it. I'm going to put it up for sale.'

I know it wasn't very Christian of me, Katie added, *but I couldn't help it. After all they had done to me, the truth was it was a very sweet moment.*

It had been another long wait for James and Susan, but they embraced her warmly saying it was worth every minute of it. Then, as they milled around wondering what to do next, Katie said, 'I told Martin I would call in on the way back and let him know the result. Maybe this time we can have that – what was it he called it?'

James rubbed his hands together and smiled, saying, 'A tincture?'

'Exactly, A tincture.'

'Sounds good to me,' said Susan.

'Dinner too,' Katie added. 'and this time it's on me. Thanks to the judge,

I can afford it! And thanks to you too, Mr. Murphy.'

In her letter to Lily and Ed, Susan recalled, *Mr. Murphy was enjoying the moment every bit as much as we were and accepted Katie's invitation to join us in the Cumán Inn. We all booked in for the night, and what a night we had. I doubt if Katie knew what a tincture was – in Irish terms! She had a sip, but didn't really drink. As for the rest of us, one tincture followed another. Martin joined us and it wasn't long before we all entered into the spirit of things. Mr. Murphy is a man of few words, but he enjoys a drop of whiskey, and as the night went on and we had a sing-song, we persuaded him to sing. After much modest prevarication, he announced that he would sing 'Slievenamon'. Then he looked at Katie, toasted her and to applause that nearly raised the roof, said no, he would sing 'The Maid of Slievenamon'. That, as you may know is another name for the same song and the way he said it, it was full of meaning not only for Katie, but for us all.*

What a wonderful night we had. Katie was Katie and she was home at last.

Up at the lake, the blossoms were still clinging to the whitethorn tree, but only just. Katie reached up and pulled down a branch, and when she released it a shower of pink and white petals fell on her like confetti at a wedding.

Martin smiled and dusted them off. Then, leaning against the rock, he asked her, 'Are you really going to sell the house?'

'I don't know. I haven't decided yet. There are a lot of things I have to sort out with Mr. Murphy first.

Martin picked up a small stone and threw it far out into the lake. 'Well, if you are going to sell it, I would like to buy it. And I could do with the rest of the land.'

Katie smiled. 'You won't need to buy it. I would like you to look after it for me until I come back.'

'So you *are* coming back?'

'Of course!'

Martin put his hands on her shoulders and leaned forward to kiss her, but she pulled back slightly.

'Sorry,' he said, 'I forgot. You're still Sister Mary. You haven't renounced your vows, have you?' When she shook her head, he added, 'Well, if you do, I'll be waiting for you.'

Katie smiled and kissed him lightly on the cheek. 'Thank you,' she whispered.

Martin picked up another stone and skimmed it across the water. 'So,' he said, straightening up, 'What are your plans now?'

'Well, as I say, there are a lot of legal costs and things to be sorted out, so I'll have to call and see Mr. Murphy. And before I leave Dublin I would like to see Bridie again.'

'Bridie?'

'The woman I told you about. She was the mother of the other baby.'

'Why do you want to see her?'

'Well, let's put it this way. If I wasn't Katie, she would be my mother!'

Martin nodded. 'But you *are* Katie.'

'Of course I am.' She paused. 'Still, I'd like to see her before I leave. Come on.'

Linking him, they walked to where small birds were sporting themselves among the thistles. There they stopped for a moment to look across the vast expanse of the valley. Then, arm in arm, they walked back down the lane.